FEEDING THE LEOPARD

L. T. KAY

MJB

Published by [MJB]
ISBN [978-0-6482772-0-0]

Typesetting services by BOOKOW.COM

To Maggie

With my love and thanks for the support and encouragement that enabled me to write this book

ACKNOWLEDGMENTS

I am indebted to all those who helped me in writing this book. These include my beta readers.

Maureen made many useful comments which were most helpful in the editing process. Holly and Fay pointed out factual errors and made suggestions that improved the story. Melody and Russell carried out a final line edit, picking up several small omissions and typos.

I especially want to thank Maggie, my editor-in-chief, who read and re-read the manuscript several times, pointing out many errors affecting the narrative's flow.

Any remaining typos or grammatical mistakes are those I have made when correcting earlier errors brought to my attention. For me, eliminating errors is a rich source for creating new ones.

Finally, I wish to thank you, the reader, for taking the time to read my book. If you notice any further typos or errors of fact, no matter how small, please let me know, so I can improve the reading experience for those that follow.

L. T. Kay

Author website https://ltkay.com

Nothing is as difficult, or as easy, as one might first imagine.

L. T. Kay

Prologue

Zimbabwe 1979 – 2014

Part One—The People of Zimbabwe

Politics can be a dirty and dangerous game. It's a game that's played partly in the full glare of the public spotlight, and partly in the shadows. Played deep in the shadows, it can turn deadly.

The Lancaster House Agreement in London, in December 1979, led to a general election in Zimbabwe in February 1980. That election saw Robert Mugabe voted in as Prime Minister of the country. From the time of the Lancaster House Agreement, Zimbabwean politics has moved deeper and deeper into the shadows. It is ironic that those shadows lengthened as the ethnic differences in the country diminished.

At two percent of the population, the whites in Zimbabwe are a tiny minority and present no political threat. But they have been a convenient scapegoat for all the government's failures and problems.

The two major tribal groups in Zimbabwe are the Shona at eighty-two percent of the population and the Ndebele at fourteen percent. Tribal differences are at the root of much of Zimbabwe's troubles, but clans within the Shona tribe add a further level of complexity.

The eastern Shona comprise five major clans: the Karanga, Korekore, Manyika, Ndau and Zezuru. Together, they form the largest ethnic group in the country. In the country's west the main ethnic groups are the Ndebele, and the western Shona which consists solely of the Bakalanga clan in the south-west.

Mugabe's Zezuru clan, at twenty-five percent of the population, has held a disproportionately high number of senior posts in the cabinet, army, police and other government departments. The Karanga clan of the Masvingo Province is the largest, making up thirty-five percent of the population. They provided most of the fighters and military leaders in the Bush War. They felt they were not aptly rewarded for their contribution, and that their leaders were sidelined.

There have been a lot of suspicious deaths of senior black political leaders. Many were at the highest levels of Zimbabwe politics and the military. There have also been other deaths and suspicious accidents that resulted in serious injury.

Who then might be responsible? Many people attributed these deaths to Mugabe or his close supporters, but there's little clear evidence supporting these claims. The deaths could be down to senior figures in ZANU-PF—*the Zimbabwe African National Union-Patriotic Front*—or the security forces, working to secure their own positions by protecting Mugabe's presidency. They could also include both genuine accidents and foul play. Mugabe benefited from many of the deaths, and that added fuel to the rumours. Several of his opponents attributed the deaths directly to him, but how many he ordered, condoned or knew about, remains an open question.

In the many accusations, it's hard to distinguish fact from fancy, and we may never know the truth.

Part Two—Mugabe Regime Campaigns

Gukurahundi Campaign—Late 1982 to Late 1987: Gukurahundi is a Shona word meaning 'The early rain which washes away the chaff before the spring rains.'

After independence and black rule in 1980, several criminal incidents in Matabeleland involved dissidents who were former members of ZIPRA—*the Zimbabwe People's Revolutionary Army*, the military wing of Joshua Nkomo's ZAPU—*the Zimbabwe African People's Union.*

In late 1982, under the guise of dealing with the dissidents, Mugabe sent the North Korean trained Fifth Brigade into Matabeleland on a genocidal campaign against the Ndebele people. The Fifth Brigade reported to the Prime Minister's office—Mugabe's office. Their distinguishing feature, their red berets, struck terror into the hearts of the civilian population. Not part of the Zimbabwe National Army, even their equipment and communications were not compatible. Under the command of Colonel Perence Shiri, the Fifth Brigade launched a violent spree of terror, intimidation, torture and murder, which continued for five years until late 1987. Estimates of the number of civilians killed vary, but a common figure is around twenty thousand. A similar number reputedly suffered torture and serious injuries.

Fast-Track Land Reform Program (FTLRP)—Commenced February 2000: Under this campaign the pro-Mugabe War Veterans' Association forced white farmers off the land without compensation. Where the war veterans met resistance, they sometimes killed the white farmers and their black farm workers. The invasions even included farms bought with the regime's approval, often leaving hundreds of thousands of black farm workers homeless and unemployed. Many of the farms ended up with Mugabe, his family and cronies. After the farm invasions, lots of farms fell into disuse and farm machinery and equipment deteriorated and rusted in the fields. The farms based on export crops of tobacco, tea and coffee were worst affected. This led to a dire foreign currency shortage which affected the import of a variety of essential items.

In the first decade of the twenty-first century, food production almost halved, and the manufacturing and the banking sectors collapsed. At independence in 1980, the Zimbabwe dollar was more valuable than the US dollar. The inflation rate picked up in the nineties and ran out of control from 2001, rising to over sixty-six thousand percent in 2007. In July 2008 it exceeded two hundred and thirty-one million percent, and by mid-November it reached almost eighty billion percent. When a one-hundred-trillion-dollar note circulated, the government abandoned the currency. From 2009 the US dollar, the Euro and the South African Rand were in use in Zimbabwe, with the US dollar being the most accepted.

In November 2016, the Zimbabwe government introduced bond notes to combat the critical cash shortage and resultant deflation. People feared this would lead to the return of hyperinflation.

Murambatsvina Campaign—Commenced May 2005: Murambatsvina in the Shona language means 'drive out the rubbish'. Mugabe ordered this infamous campaign in May 2005. The authorities ejected hundreds of thousands of urban poor from their homes in Harare, bulldozing their houses and possessions, often at a moment's notice. With no alternative accommodation on offer, an estimated ninety percent of those displaced in 2005 had not found suitable permanent housing by November 2013. Mugabe claimed the campaign would clean up the slums and help fight crime. Others saw it as a move against the supporters of the opposition MDC—*the Movement for Democratic Change*—and its members from the Karanga clan. It is estimated that over seven hundred thousand people lost their homes or livelihood. The Mugabe regime foreshadowed a repeat of the campaign.

Part Three—Suspicious Deaths

Black politics in Zimbabwe has always been a risky business. Before black rule, aspiring African nationalists risked bans and imprisonment, but since black rule, things have become even more deadly.

Prior to black rule, significant deaths included Herbert Chitepo's assassination in March 1975 and Josiah Tongogara's motor accident on Boxing Day 1979. Both were potential rivals to the leadership of Robert Mugabe, who many blamed for their demises.

During the Gukurahundi period, two senior opposition party members died. Jini Ntuta, ZAPU's Secretary for Defence, was shot and killed in November 1984 after a rumoured exchange of harsh words with Mugabe in parliament. Lieutenant General Lookout Masuku, ZIPRA's Bush War commander, died of disputed causes in April 1986 after a period in prison for allegedly plotting a coup against Mugabe.

Between then and June 2013, at least ten high profile political or military figures died in circumstances regarded by many as suspicious. They reputedly criticised Mugabe or incurred the displeasure of the governing party's leadership.

Solomon Mujuru, also known as Rex Nhongo, died under suspicious circumstances. Mujuru, one of the most feared men in Zimbabwe, supposedly died from smoke inhalation in a fire at his farm in Beatrice in August 2011. Many people believed he was murdered. Two farm employees testified they heard gunshots up to two hours before the fire. Curiously, his cell phone and grocery shopping were still in his car. His family asked for his exhumation and a second independent post-mortem by a South African pathologist, but the authorities denied the request. The widespread and persistent rumours surrounding his death required his wife, Joice, to intervene and appeal to his supporters for calm.

In December 2014, Mugabe dismissed Joice Mujuru from her position, after ten years as vice-president of Zimbabwe, and expelled her from ZANU-PF for allegedly plotting against him. Her main accuser, Mugabe's wife Grace, was rumoured to have political ambitions of her own. Many people linked Solomon Mujuru's death and Joice Mujuru's dismissal as a coordinated plan to get rid of potential rivals.

CHAPTER 1

December 1983

IAN Sanders learnt early, when life was perfect, change could only be for the worse. He ended junior school on a high, coming first in his class exams. Now he looked forward to senior school. When he grew up, he planned to be a hunter and write stories about his adventures. How lucky that he lived in such a wonderful country with its wildlife, the bush and the Victoria Falls. Yes, life was great, and to cap it all, it was his favourite time of the year, the wet season.

It rained all night, and the ground was damp. Thick, heavy clouds hung overhead, blotting out the sun. The air smelled fresh and full of oxygen. Twelve-year-old Ian loved these summer mornings that threatened rain. The weather was warm but not oppressive. The heavy clouds would temper the heat of the day. He was sure it would rain again in the mid to late afternoon. Ian liked to imagine the thunderous drumming of the rain on the corrugated iron roof of their house up on the farm. The louder, the better he liked it. He often walked in the downpour to feel the warm rain on his skin. If his clothes got soaked, it didn't matter. They would soon dry out in this weather. The first rains signalled Christmas and the long, end-of-year school holidays, yet more reason to make it Ian's favourite time of the year.

Ian gulped down a breakfast of tea, cereal, fried eggs and bacon, and now he was full of beans and raring to go. Today, he was going with his parents, Greg and Norma, to their farm on the Victoria Falls road, about an hour's drive from Bulawayo. This didn't happen too often these days because of the fuel shortages that plagued Zimbabwe. In the last couple of years of the Bush War, Greg had moved the family into town for security reasons. He would leave their house in Hillside early every Monday morning and ride out to the farm on his motorcycle. Norma knew to expect him home at six o'clock on Friday evening. Ian kept her company during the week, but she worried about Greg being all alone on the farm. 'I'm not alone,' he would say. 'I have my workers to keep me company.'

It was a Sunday, but Greg needed to attend to urgent repairs to fences on the farm. It was three months since Norma and Ian were last there, but today they'd drive out in the old Toyota *bakkie*. Norma packed a picnic lunch and off they went.

A few churchgoers walked along the almost deserted city streets. They drove passed Northlea High School on the right and big single-storey houses on large blocks of land on the left, and soon the open road lay ahead.

Ian loved the car trips and enjoyed watching the grass and trees on the side of the road race past in a blur. Although he looked forward to visiting the farm, he always wished they could drive on farther to the Hwange National Park or the Victoria Falls.

All too soon, they turned off the main road onto the dirt road with its corrugations. Greg slowed the Toyota. 'That's funny. It looks like our cows are on the road.' He hooted, and the cattle turned and set off back to the farm gate.

Ian jumped out of the bakkie and chased the cows, shouting to make them go faster.

'The gate's open,' said Norma.

'That's strange,' said Greg, 'I've never known the boys to be careless.'

The boys Greg referred to were the seven good, long-serving, black workers who helped tend the cattle and do the heavy work. Their families lived with them on the farm, and the women cared for the maize crop and lucerne field. The men, women and children made up a vibrant little community in their village at one end of the property.

When Greg arrived, one or two workers would always come to greet him. The old cook would boil water for tea. Today, there was no sign of anyone. It was silent, apart from the chirping of the birds. 'I'm going to the village,' said Greg. 'Maybe they had a party last night and drank too much *Chibuku*.'

'I'll come,' said Ian.

'You two do that, and I'll make tea.'

Greg and Ian set off for the village on foot, a walk of half a kilometre. The cattle seemed skittish. 'It's quiet,' said Greg. 'The women and children are always around even if the men have gone to the beer hall. And even if you can't see them, you can hear them laughing and shouting to each other.'

Ian found the whole situation a little creepy, and he could feel the hairs on the back of his neck rising. 'There, Dad, look there in the *mealies*; someone moved.'

Greg stared at the area where Ian pointed. Cautiously, he stepped into the mealie field, and suddenly, a black face with the whites of wide eyes appeared before him. The man looked terrified. 'Andrew, what are you doing here? Where is everyone?'

The man trembled and struggled to speak. 'They have gone *Baas*.'

'Gone! Gone where?'

'The soldiers took them, Sah.'

'What soldiers?'

'The ones with the red hats took them, Baas.'

'You mean the red berets?'

'Yes, Baas.'

'When did they take them?'

'They took them last night, Baas, when it was getting dark.'

Greg knew it was the *Gukurahundi*—the notorious Fifth Brigade that reported to the Prime Minister's office. 'Why the hell would they come here? What about the women and children?'

'They are all gone, Baas. But Jacob and his wife are in their hut.'

Jacob, the boss boy, managed the farm when Greg wasn't there. Greg ran to the hut and called out through the open doorway. There was no reply. He peered into the dark room. A bundle of cloth lay on the floor. Greg gasped when he realised it was Jacob's wife, Mary. A deep gash across her head showed the white bone of the skull. Greg's eyes adjusted to the dark, and he saw Jacob sitting on a stool against the far wall. He looked to be in shock with his eyes wide open. 'Jacob, are you OK?' There was no response. Greg crossed the floor to him but stepped back. A gaping wound ran across Jacob's throat. Greg turned and caught Ian staring open-mouthed at the bodies. It was not a sight for a twelve-year-old boy.

Jacob and Mary treated Ian as one of their own. Ian loved them. They taught him Ndebele and gave him food when he visited the village. At the farm, Ian followed Jacob everywhere. Sometimes he played with Jacob's son and two daughters and the other village children.

Andrew emerged from the mealie field and waited outside the hut for Greg. He'd hidden in the field when the truck with the soldiers arrived. Everyone knew the fearsome reputation of the Fifth Brigade. The screaming and shouting at the village terrified Andrew, and he hid all night amongst the mealies. When he heard Greg's bakkie, he feared the soldiers were returning.

Still single, Andrew was lucky. He'd not lost family in the incident. Two of Greg's men were away visiting their parents on the Christmas break. They'd have lost their wives and children. Greg's old cook and the two other farm hands were missing. He assumed the Fifth Brigade took them. Jacob and his wife were dead. They and the old cook worked for Greg's parents, and he'd known them his whole life.

Greg phoned the police, and they surprised him with their prompt arrival. Andrew and Greg gave accounts of what had taken place. The police assured Greg they'd do everything possible to find the missing people. Greg felt shattered. He knew the police wouldn't cross the Fifth Brigade, and he did not expect to see his missing people again.

His poor workers deserved better, but Greg was sure they would have already met their fate somewhere out in the bush. Why would the Fifth Brigade come here? Could it have been a loose word at the beer hall, or was it by chance? Did the Fifth Brigade need a reason?

An ambulance came to remove Jacob and Mary's bodies, and soon after it drove off, the police left. An eerie silence fell over the farm. The family packed their things and jumped in the bakkie to head for home. Greg left Andrew to tidy up and promised to return the next morning. 'I don't envy Andrew all alone out here,' said Norma.

At the farm gate, Greg stopped, and Ian got out and closed the gate and jumped back in the bakkie and slammed the door. Greg pushed down on the accelerator, trying to reach a speed high enough to reduce the bone-jarring effect of the corrugated dirt road. But now the road was wet from the rain, and he needed to be careful. Halfway to the main road, a lorry appeared in the distance. It was approaching fast. Greg moved over to the left to allow it room to pass, but as it came barrelling down the centre of the road, it was clear it wouldn't move over to its side. The lorry hurtled straight towards them.

'Look out!' Norma shouted. 'He's not pulling over.' Greg slammed on the brakes and pulled the steering wheel to the left, a little harder than he intended. The bakkie shuddered to a halt in the shallow ditch that ran alongside the road.

'You bloody idiots!' Greg shouted. As the lorry passed Greg saw the red berets of the soldiers sitting in the back of the lorry. They shouted and shook their fists as they sped past. 'It's the Fifth Brigade. Hell, I hope they're not going back to our place. If they are, Andrew better make himself scarce in a hurry.'

'They might be going to the Davidson's farm,' said Norma. 'There's nothing else down this road since the quarry closed. It's lucky they're away on holiday.'

'We're not sticking around to find out,' said Greg, as he eased the bakkie forward. But in the muddy ditch, the tyres slipped, and the vehicle slewed to one side. Greg tried again, but the tyres could find no purchase and the wheels spun.

'Be careful,' said Norma, 'the ditch gets deeper in front of us. We'll get stuck.'

'Yes, c'mon, Dad, let's go before they come back.'

'Take it easy, Son. Let me sort it out.' Greg put the bakkie in reverse and gently depressed the accelerator. The wheels spun before gripping, but slowly the bakkie inched back, slipping a little in the mud and then gripping a little. Slowly, slowly the bakkie backed out of the shallow ditch. They all breathed a sigh of relief when they were back on the corrugated dirt road.

The afternoon storm that Ian looked forward to now seemed so gloomy on the journey home. The realities of life in Zimbabwe closed in as they drove in silence back to Bulawayo.

That day, the blood and the rain washed away Ian's childhood innocence.

Greg's thoughts turned to taking the family to a safer place to live, somewhere far from the madness. He realised Zimbabwe held no long-term future for the whites.

CHAPTER 2

June 2000

A cold wind blew on the grey winter's afternoon in the farming area between Norton and Chegutu. Jan and Mila Marais relaxed in front of the fireplace in the cosy lounge of their small three-bedroom farmhouse. On a Saturday afternoon, Jan would usually be out and about on the farm, working on a piece of equipment or repairing one of the farm fences. But today, a heavy head cold kept him indoors.

These days, sixty-nine-year-old Jan needed to take more frequent breaks from the daily grind of back-breaking work on the farm. He'd lived there all his life and run the farm since his father's death almost fifty years ago. Through sweat and calloused hands, he'd made the property into a piece of paradise. He hoped, one day, his son would return from working in Joburg and take over the running of the place. The productive farm supported them and the sixty farm workers and their families. The large, old trees Jan planted all those years ago surrounded the property, giving it a picturesque quality.

Loud voices disturbed Jan's thoughts. The dogs barked. Something was wrong. Mathias, the cook, came into the room. 'Baas, men have come.' Mathias looked nervous and shuffled his feet.

Jan got up from the armchair and went onto the front veranda. A crowd of about thirty African men stood there, holding *knobkerries*, iron rods and *pangas*. A wild-looking man with missing front teeth, and wearing a bandanna, came forward. 'My name is Goddard Makoni. I'm taking this farm. You must go now!'

'What do you mean? This is my farm. Leave, or I'll call the police!' As Jan spoke those words, he noticed two policemen sitting in a Land Rover parked by the farm gate.

'The police are here to arrest you if you do not leave.' said Goddard.

Jan walked towards the police in the Land Rover, but they started the engine and drove off before he could reach them. As Jan turned to go back to the farmhouse, he saw the mob attacking Gideon, the farm foreman. 'Leave that man alone,' Jan shouted. But then a group standing nearby turned on him. He took a heavy blow to the right shoulder, and his arm went numb. A crack on his head from a wooden pick handle stunned him, and a trickle of blood ran down his face. Jan staggered but reached the front door and got inside the farmhouse. Mila stood there with a handgun, and Jan rushed to load a rifle.

Outside, the dogs yelped. It was the nightmare Jan feared ever since the start of the farm invasions. The phone line was dead. They tried to call for help on the farm radio, but no help was close at hand.

'Let's just leave' said Mila, in a shaking voice.

Banging on the front door drew Jan's attention. Rifle at the ready, Jan opened it. Goddard stood there. 'Mr Marais, you must leave this farm now! If you don't go, my men might kill you. They go mad when they smell blood. You are on our land. You must leave. I will give you ten minutes, and then you must go. After that, I'm not responsible.'

Jan and Mila rushed to fill their suitcases. Passports, birth certificates, land title deeds, money, cheque books, credit cards and clothing. There was no time to think. Did they have everything they needed? They grabbed the car keys. Another banging on the door; Goddard again. Jan noticed his eyes were red with drink, drugs or hepatitis A; maybe all three. 'You must go now. You must leave the guns. If you carry guns, my men will attack you for sure.'

Jan and Mila walked to the car through the hooting and shouting mob. He turned to call the dogs but saw their lifeless forms on the lawn. There was no sign of Gideon, Mathias and the other farm workers. As they drove away, Jan and Mila looked in the rear-view mirror and saw the mob rushing into the farmhouse. They realised they'd been lucky to get away with their lives.

* * *

The front door slammed shut behind Sam Kagonye, and the neat, little house shook with the force of the impact. He was home earlier than usual from work at the ZANU-PF (Zimbabwe African National Union-Patriotic Front) governing party offices in Harare. Sam walked to the kitchen where his wife, Esther, was preparing the evening meal. Each evening, he would walk in with a cheerful hello and give her a kiss, but today, he stood in the doorway with a worried frown.

'What's the matter,' said Esther.

'The war veterans have invaded the farm. Mr and Mrs Marais had to flee.'

'Are they OK?'

'Yes, but Gideon and Enos, are dead.'

'Oh No! Gideon's poor wife, fancy losing her husband and son on the same day.' Esther covered her mouth and nose with her hands. 'How could that happen?'

'The war veterans locked them in a hut and set it alight. It had a thatched roof. They never had a chance. All the rest of the workers ran for their lives.'

'When did it happen? Are you sure it's true?'

'Solomon, the farm mechanic, came to the office and waited downstairs for me to finish work. He told me all about it and said others were missing. Solomon ran away like the rest of them. He said the war veterans arrived at lunchtime yesterday and beat the farm workers. They also beat Mr Marais.'

When Sam's daughters came home within minutes of each other, they could sense something was wrong. The news stunned eighteen-year-old Jemma, and her eyes glistened with tears. It was nothing like the sixteen-year-old Sarah's reaction. 'They stole our land, so now we're taking it back.'

'Mr Marais didn't steal our land, Sarah. When I was a boy, most of it was still dusty bush. He worked hard to make it the beautiful farm you see today.'

'Well, it's ours now.'

'Don't forget, my girl, Gideon took my job at the farm when we left. If we were still there, it would have been us lying dead. And remember, Enos was your best friend when we lived on the farm.'

'They wouldn't have killed us. You support ZANU-PF.'

'So did Gideon.'

'So why did they kill them and evict the others?'

'Gideon was the boss boy. He must have been trying to protect the farm. They beat the farm workers because they worked for Mr Marais. They would have seen them as supporting the whites.'

'At least the blacks own the farm, now they've kicked Mr Marais out.'

'Mr Marais treated me like a son. He paid for my schooling, and he paid the *lobola* when I married your mother.' Sam's voice was getting lower and more measured. 'We have him to thank for where we are today. He was a good boss. It shouldn't be a black versus white thing.'

Sam didn't get angry often, so Sarah missed the changed tone in his voice, and she wasn't one to back down in an argument. 'But Papa, you supported majority rule. That was a black versus white thing.'

'No, majority rule was just that—majority rule. It had nothing to do with black versus white. There are good whites and bad whites and good blacks and bad blacks.'

'Papa, you sound more like the MDC (Movement for Democratic Change) opposition than ZANU-PF.'

'Enough!' Sam shouted. 'Don't dare speak to me like that. Go to your room.' Sam shook with anger. He admired Sarah's spirit, but she'd overstepped the mark.

Sam was born and grew up on the farm which lay between Norton and Hartley (Chegutu). After leaving junior school, he followed in his father's footsteps and got a job on the farm. Mr Marais, the white farm owner saw something in Sam and paid for his high school education. After his school days, Sam returned to the farm to learn about commercial farming.

Ten years on, and almost thirty years of age, Sam was now the boss boy—foreman. Although he'd done well on the farm, Sam found the lure of the city irresistible. He got a job in a textile factory in Salisbury (Harare). He was sad about leaving, and Mr Marais was sorry to see him go. Sam's young wife, Esther, taught at the local African junior school. She handed in her notice with a heavy heart. Sam and Esther packed up their belongings and left. His retired parents still lived on the farm, and Sam promised to visit often.

While Sam and Esther occupied modern staff quarters on the farm, his more traditional parents preferred to live in the old staff village, in a thatched mud hut. Visits over long weekends and Christmas showed the girls how the family once lived. They were unimpressed. Sam and the girls were free to roam the farm, thanks to Mr Marais' high regard for him. Every visit taught the girls more about farming. But it also made them appreciate the home comforts of city life. While Sam and the girls explored the farm, Esther preferred to keep Sam's parents' company, sitting and chatting in the shade of the big Jacaranda tree out front. When the girls were in their teens, Sam's parents died within a short time of each other. The visits to the farm ceased, and for Sarah, its questionable lure soon faded.

Although new to the textile industry, Sam soon advanced, moving through the ranks to the role of Payroll Manager. Each week he attended the management meetings and joined in the discussions. He didn't mind that management rejected many of his suggestions, but he worried he would go no further in the company. Sam always got on well with his white work colleagues, but he felt an invisible barrier between them. At the weekly meetings, he was a black man in a white man's world. He joined them for tea during the meetings but seldom for drinks afterwards.

Prior to black rule, many of the larger white-owned companies appointed black, non-executive directors. At home, Sam expressed his anger to Esther. 'The whites treat me with respect. They know the value of my work. The black directors treat me like a junior clerk. They have degrees but little business experience.'

Not long after he and Esther moved into the city, a work-colleague took Sam to a ZANU (Zimbabwe African National Union) meeting. He could relate to the party's goals and soon volunteered his time after hours. In due course, his efforts paid dividends. When the party came to power in 1980, Sam jumped at the offer of a role in its administration.

Sam was not a militant or extremist, but he believed in majority rule. As a Shona, it was natural he fell in with Robert Mugabe's ZANU. His sober counsel was an asset to the party, and in time, he rose through the ranks to a senior position.

* * *

The dull July morning in Melbourne brought dark news from Zimbabwe.

'Ian, have you heard? There's been another white farmer killed in a farm invasion. I think that's six now.' Greg Sanders only phoned Ian at work when he had big news.

'Anyone we knew?'

'No, it was someone near Harare. I know the name, but I never met him.'

'Well, it's lucky we got out when we did.'

'Yes, but we can't get our money out of that damned country. We sold the farm and the house, but the money is sitting there in the bank. Let's hope, in time, they'll relax the foreign exchange rules.'

'Dad, it will be too late. When Mugabe took over, the exchange rate with the US dollar was better than one to one. Now a US dollar is worth one hundred Zimbabwe dollars. It'll all be gone before long.'

'I know that.' Greg didn't need reminding that his life savings were on the endangered list.

'What news of the old farm?'

'The last I heard, Son, it was still OK. But it's only a matter of time before those murdering bastards occupy it.'

'You know, Dad, the media reports the murder of white farmers and African farm workers, but what about the murdered MDC people? They would outnumber the farm deaths by a long way.'

'Those political types can kill each other if they want, but I draw the line at the farm murders.'

'You can't separate the two. The farm invaders are also the ones who kill the opposition supporters. Both crimes are heinous. Mugabe lost popularity with the electorate; that's why he's supporting the white farm invasions.'

CHAPTER 3

May 2005

AFTER Solomon, the farm mechanic, and his family fled the farm, they were homeless. They moved to Harare and set up home in a shanty Solomon built out of scrounged pieces of wood and corrugated iron. Other similar ramshackle dwellings sprung up on the edge of the city. Most of the former farm workers were still homeless and unemployed, so it was no surprise the residents in these areas opposed the government.

Hunched over a wooden table on one side of the shelter, Solomon spent his days repairing various small items such as sewing machines and radios. Skills gained through work on the farm enabled him to turn his hand to repairing a surprising assortment of household goods.

It was a cold May morning with a chill in the breeze, and Solomon wore his jumper with holes at the elbows. He kept another old jumper for best wear. Hannah, his wife, worked as a housemaid and left home before sunrise at six o'clock each weekday morning. Solomon was already busy when the first weak rays of the sun crept through the open front door. The first job of the morning was to replace the wiring on a standard lamp. He focused on his task, oblivious to the warning shouts and the throb of the large diesel engine. There was a massive scraping sound and then a loud crack, and Solomon's heart jumped as he realised his home was moving. He ran for the door, but the roof fell and knocked him to the ground. The dust was choking, and he coughed and spluttered. Solomon couldn't see the way out and panic welled up inside him. At that moment, someone grabbed his arm and pulled him clear of the pile of tin and wood. A voice said, 'Man, don't you know it's the *Murambatsvina*? They say they are here to drive out the rubbish.'

The government claimed to be clearing the urban slums and illegal businesses that grew like a cancer in Harare. Other cities in the country feared a similar fate. The council claimed the demolition would prevent the spread of disease and curb criminal activity. But the opposition MDC said the government targeted their supporters. Occupants of the slums got little notice of imminent demolition, and many people lost all their possessions. Even houses built with council approval met the same fate.

* * *

Jemma hurried through the front door, closing it behind her.

'Mama, have you heard what's happening? They're knocking down people's houses.'

'Yes Jemma.'

'But Mama, it's winter. What will the people do?'

'Papa will be home soon. Perhaps he can tell us more.'

But Sam was not home soon. Most days he would return from work by half past six in the evening, but on this occasion, Sam arrived past nine o'clock.

'Where were you?' said Esther. 'We were getting worried.'

'Where is this country going? Things are getting worse. Solomon, the mechanic from the old farm, was waiting downstairs for me after work. He was covered in dust and bleeding from a big cut on his head, and his right leg had a bad cut.'

'Goodness! What happened?'

'After the farm invasion they were homeless. They came to Harare and built a shanty where they lived and where Solomon ran his business. Early this morning, the authorities demolished the area with almost no notice. Solomon tried to grab his tools when the bulldozers came, but the house collapsed around him. He's lucky to be alive. I took him to hospital. That's why I'm late.'

'What will he do? Where will he live now? What about his family?'

'There's only him and his wife, Hannah, but she was at work when it happened. The children left home long ago. Thousands are in Solomon's situation.'

'Why couldn't they wait until summer? Why do it when winter is starting?'

'What would Sarah say?' said Jemma.

'I shudder to think,' said Sam. 'It's just as well she's not here.' Sarah was in her second year at university in Johannesburg, and Sam knew his younger daughter had hardened her heart against all those who opposed ZANU-PF.

A loud knocking interrupted the discussion. Sam went to open the door.

'Mrs Madanhi, we were just talking about you.'

It was Hannah, old Solomon's wife. 'Mr Kagonye, I'm sorry to trouble you, but they've knocked down my house and Solomon is missing.'

'Calm yourself, Mrs Madanhi. Solomon is in hospital, but he will be fine. I took him there myself, and I'll take you there, but first, you must have something to eat and drink.'

'All our things are lost in the rubble or stolen.'

'What will you do now, Mrs Madanhi?' Esther enquired.

'Tomorrow, I will look for my sons. Maybe they can help us.'

'If you can't find them, you can stay here with us until Solomon comes out of hospital. I'm sure he won't be in too long.'

After Sam and Mrs Madanhi left for the hospital, Esther turned to Jemma. 'You asked a good question, Jemma. What will the people do? The government says it's clearing out the slums. Most of the residents are MDC supporters. That might be why they didn't wait until summer.'

* * *

'Zimbabwe is back in the news.' said Greg Sanders.

'Relax, Dad. What now?'

'First, Mugabe goes after the Matabele with that Gukurahundi nonsense. Then, he goes after the white farmers and the farm workers while his "war veterans" are killing off the MDC supporters left, right and centre. Now, he's going after the poor slum dwellers. Who will he set his sights on next?'

'Being a high-flying member of ZANU-PF is no guarantee of longevity, so things might heat up in that area.'

'That would be no surprise.'

'You know, Dad, so much happens in that country, it's exciting. I wouldn't mind seeing it for myself.'

'Don't be stupid, Son. We didn't move to Australia for you to end up going back.'

'I don't mean a permanent move, more like a sabbatical to write about my experiences over there.'

'Yeah, right, that'll be the day.'

'It's just an idea.'

'Yes, well, it's best you forget that idea.'

CHAPTER 4

March 2004 – March 2006

SARAH sat on the hard, wooden chair not wanting to hear what the policeman told her. She frowned, with her hands folded in her lap. Her right hand squeezed the fingers of her left hard and they were turning numb.

The chief inspector looked back at Sarah with steady, hard eyes. 'I'm sorry, Miss Kagonye, but you must appreciate Joburg is a big city. There are many foreign criminals here. We deal with major crimes every day, but I can't promise we'll find the culprits. We don't have the resources to chase down all of them.'

Sarah went to the Braamfontein police station to help with their enquiries. She told them everything she knew about the suspects, but the problem was she knew little. She couldn't recall the licence number of the blue Mercedes sports car. The police needed more. 'The car might be white by now, Miss Kagonye.'

As she walked back to her university residence, Sarah's mind churned with thoughts and emotions. To rely on others for justice often led to no justice at all. And even if the police found the culprits, a judge might give them a light sentence or dismiss the case on a technicality. How often she'd heard it said, judges focused on the finer points of law but not on common sense? She knew the police would do little, and once she realised that, a cold anger crept over her. It hardened her resolve, and Sarah vowed no bastard would ever best her. She'd mete out her own justice.

The next day, Sarah made enquiries about self-defence training for women. There was a big choice. After investigating a confusing number of options, she settled on *Muay Boran*, an old form of Thai kickboxing. The technique focused on body conditioning and using hands, feet, knees, elbows, shins and head butts as weapons. This combination was more lethal than fists alone where there was always the risk of injured or broken wrists. From then on, Sarah put as much effort into martial arts training, as she did in her studies. She became obsessed with it.

Two years earlier, getting a place at university thrilled Sarah. Time raced by, but now she dreaded having to face the remaining days at *Wits* (the University of the Witwatersrand).

* * *

Sarah was first in the family to enter university, and it made them proud when she gained a place at Wits in Joburg. She planned to study for a Bachelor of Arts degree in languages—French and Portuguese.

Day one is daunting for new students. For Sarah, it seemed everyone knew everyone else, but she was alone, a black Shona student from Zimbabwe. Registration day meant formalities to complete.

A young black man greeted Sarah in English and showed her which queue to join. After a long wait in the registration hall, it was her turn to go through the process. On her way out, the young man hailed Sarah in Shona. Thomas Chimedza was a final year student doing the same subjects as her. He too was a Shona from Harare, Sarah's hometown.

Sarah was lucky to get a place in Sunnyside, a residence for young women students. It was a grand old building in a garden setting on campus, close to the student facilities.

Few blacks at Wits spoke Shona, and before long Thomas introduced Sarah to most of them. Though they mixed in the same social circle, they only became close mid-way through the year. With exams approaching, they often studied together. Although two years ahead of Sarah, Thomas found helping her with her studies also helped his own. He saw truth in the old saying *teaching is the best way to learn*. One thing led to another, and soon they dreamed of a future together. The next six months flashed by, and Thomas graduated.

* * *

In her second year, Sarah focused social life around her studies. Nights out with French and Portuguese speaking friends improved her language skills. She resolved to become fluent in the languages.

Netball and hockey kept Sarah fit and in great shape.

Many other girls saw Wits as an opportunity to party and meet boys. Sarah was a light social drinker, but she did not smoke. Her confident and relaxed manner and good sense of humour made her popular with the other students. She could have fitted in with the party crowd, but she didn't accept many of the invitations.

Sarah wouldn't waste the opportunity for a good future that her father, Sam, gave her. She did not want to end up like her sister, who worked as a housemaid in Harare. Sam's steady rise through the ranks of ZANU-PF gave him the means to put Sarah through high school and university. Jemma, his older daughter, was not so lucky. She began high school before Sam's fortunes took a turn for the better. Lack of finances forced him to withdraw Jemma after only one term at high school. The decision pained Sam, but there was no alternative.

In her second year at Wits, Sarah befriended Kemi Adebayo, in the room next door. Kemi, an attractive young girl from Lagos in Nigeria, was intelligent and funny but a little naïve. Sarah found her to be a welcome break from study, and like Sarah, Kemi did not socialise too often with the other students. The two girls spent most evenings chatting and laughing over cups of coffee while winding down from a hard day at lectures or in the library.

Kemi Adebayo was slender and attractive, with a tinkling laugh. She was a girl that men noticed, and they flocked around her, but she remained aloof. Then one day, somewhere in the city, she met Godwin Okonkwo from Lagos.

Sarah sat on her bed, propped up with pillows, reading a book. Kemi burst in and jumped onto the bed. She sat cross-legged in front of Sarah, her face flushed, and her eyes twinkled.

'Oh, Sarah, you must meet him. He's so handsome, and he has a nice car and lots of money.'

'You've only just met him, Kemi. Can you trust him?'

'This one is different. He's confident and mature. He wants to take me out on Sunday and said I can bring a friend. Will you come with me?'

'Kemi, my assignment is due on Wednesday.'

'Oh please, please come with me.' Kemi put her hand on Sarah's arm. 'I'd prefer it if you came along for the day.'

'OK.' Sarah sighed. 'I suppose I could work on it all day, Monday and Tuesday.'

Kemi gave Sarah a hug.

For the rest of the week, Kemi bubbled with excitement about the Sunday outing. Sarah found it difficult to share her enthusiasm, but she didn't want her nagging doubts to dampen the occasion for Kemi. Sunday morning came at last, and at ten o'clock Godwin arrived in his powder blue Mercedes cabriolet to pick up the girls. Kemi hopped into the front passenger seat, and Sarah jumped into the back. Godwin, a wiry young man of average height, wore his hair shaved on the sides and thick on top, making him look taller. Sarah thought him flashy, and his pencil-thin moustache gave him a somewhat sly look that she found unnerving.

'Did you girls bring your cossies?' Godwin glanced over his shoulder at Sarah in the back seat of the car. 'After lunch, we can swim.'

Godwin's place turned out to be an impressive, modern, single-storey house in Midrand. Tall fir trees bordered the large front garden, and a two-and-a-half-metre high wall gave privacy to the back garden. Attached to the back of the house, a huge atrium enclosed a large swimming pool and barbecue area. The smell of the chlorinated water hung heavy in the air.

Within half an hour of their arrival at Godwin's house, his friend Ugo turned up in a red sports car. He was a big man, clean-shaven with a cropped flat-top hairstyle, and a pleasant face and manner.

Godwin took the girls on a tour of the house. The grand interior and the furniture and fittings impressed Sarah. To her it looked like a palace.

Godwin's lavish lifestyle struck her. 'What do you do for a living?'

'Buying and selling.'

'What do you buy and sell?'

'Oh, lots of different things. Have you ever been to Nigeria?'

'No, I've only been in Zimbabwe and South Africa.'

Soon they were back in the barbecue area by the pool.

'Would you girls like wine?' Godwin took out a bottle of white from the refrigerator near the pool and held it up for their inspection.

The smell of the sizzling sausages and fried onions made them all hungry. While the meat cooked, Godwin opened another bottle of white, and they were all merry and ready to eat by the time he served the food. Soon, a third bottle of white was on its way.

Godwin put on loud music with a hypnotic African beat and a modern disco touch. 'This is one of the most popular bands in Nigeria,'

After lunch, they swam in the pool. The warm water was inviting. Sarah learnt to swim at school, but Kemi only waded in the shallow end. They lay on the pool loungers after the swim, and Sarah struggled with heavy eyelids. The wine was having a soporific effect on both girls, and Sarah dozed. A touch on her upper thigh woke her. She sat up and opened her eyes. 'Ugo, what are you doing?'

'Don't you want company?'

'No, thank you, I have a boyfriend.'

'Why did you come here if you didn't want fun?' Ugo's face darkened.

Sarah looked around her. 'Where are Kemi and Godwin?'

'They're in the house. They'll be back soon.' Ugo rested his hand on Sarah's knee.

She jumped to her feet. 'Leave me alone! Stop touching me!'

'I'm wasting my time here.' Ugo picked up his things and stalked out of the atrium. Sarah heard him start his car, spinning the wheels as he sped down the driveway.

A little later Kemi and Godwin returned. When Sarah explained what happened, Kemi was aghast. Sarah saw the anger in Godwin's face. He didn't comment, but she realised he blamed her.

Back in the residence that evening, Kemi was light-hearted. 'Well, what do you think of Godwin?' she asked, as she sat down on the end of Sarah's bed.

'I didn't like his friend, Ugo. You know what they say about birds of a feather.'

Kemi blinked. 'But Godwin is nice Sarah. I'm sure he's not like that.'

Sarah frowned. 'Be careful, Kemi, you don't know him.'

The following Sunday, Sarah used her workload as an excuse to stay back in the residence, but she felt guilty for not accompanying Kemi. Sarah feared for her friend and warned her again to be careful.

For the first part of the year, Kemi spent most of her Sundays with Godwin. This gave Sarah a chance to concentrate on her studies, and Sundays became her most productive day of the week. Godwin often pestered Kemi to spend the night at his house, but she always refused. The mid-year exams loomed, and Kemi wanted to cut back on the Sunday outings. Godwin was not happy, and one Sunday Kemi returned to Sunnyside with a bruised left eye.

Sarah looked up when her friend came into her room. 'What happened to your eye?'

Kemi touched her eye gingerly. 'I slipped and banged it on the edge of the pool.'

'Don't bullshit me, Kemi. He hit you, didn't he?' Sarah stood up for a closer look.

'Oh, Sarah, he didn't mean it.' Kemi put her hand on her friend's arm. 'He said he was sorry and wouldn't do it again.'

'No, Kemi, once a man hits a woman, it doesn't stop. He's a cowardly bastard.'

'Oh please, Sarah, don't say terrible things about him.' Kemi screwed up her face and looked about to cry.

Sarah's chest tightened, and her voice was hoarse with anger. 'Have you found out where he gets all his money?'

'No, he doesn't talk about his business. He told you he buys and sells things.'

'What things, Kemi? Do you mean things like drugs?' Sarah's mouth felt dry and bitter.

'Godwin would never do that,' Kemi sobbed.

Sarah worried about Kemi and held her dear friend close. If that bastard hurts my friend again, I'll kill him. But if Kemi wouldn't listen, what could she do?

The bubbly Kemi seemed more withdrawn as the year end approached. Sarah sensed it was something to do with Godwin. Then one Sunday evening, Kemi walked into Sarah's room and sat down on the end of the bed. She looked subdued and spoke in a quiet voice. 'You were right, Sarah; he deals drugs. That's where he gets all his money. I've told him we're finished.'

'Goodness, Kemi, what did he say?'

'He said I'd regret it.'

Much to Kemi's relief, Godwin made no further contact. One evening, a few weeks later, Kemi came into Sarah's room with her eyes sparkling. 'You'll never guess what!'

'OK, I'm dying to know. Tell me.'

'I've met a nice man. His name is George.'

'Are you sure, Kemi? That's what you said about Godwin.'

'No, this one is different. He's white and rich, and he comes from a good family.'

What! 'Where did you meet him?'

'He works in the city and comes here two evenings a week to study accounting. When he qualifies, he'll join his father's firm here in Joburg.'

'You didn't say you were seeing someone. Have you been out with him?'

'We've often had coffee together in the cafeteria, and he's taken me to a nice restaurant in Sandton.'

'Where was I all this time? Why didn't you tell me?'

'You were in the library as usual. Until I was sure of him, it was pointless saying anything.'

'Isn't it too early to be sure, Kemi? It may be OK for him to date a black girl at university, but will he introduce you to his friends? Those white guys can use you and then drop you at a moment's notice.'

'He wants me to meet his parents, and we're going out for dinner again tonight. When he comes to pick me up this evening, I'll introduce you.'

When Sarah returned to the residence, Kemi had already left on her date. Later, when she returned, she was in a tearful state. 'Oh, Sarah, you wouldn't believe what happened. When George came to pick me up, and we were going to his car, Godwin arrived. He told me, right in front of George, that I should get an HIV test as he was HIV positive. Then, he told George he should also go for a test.'

'Oh, no! That bastard Godwin, he could have phoned you or spoken to you in private. He did that on purpose, I bet. Is it possible, Kemi, you might be infected?'

Kemi hung her head, her voice a whisper. 'It's possible, but not George. We haven't had sex yet.'

Kemi's test proved negative, but the doctor advised her to return after three months for a second test to make sure. George and Kemi tried to put on a brave face, but the shadow of Godwin's revelation loomed large over their relationship. By the time she received her second negative test result, it was all but over between them.

With a heavy heart, Sarah said goodbye to her friend at the end of the year. 'See you next year, Kemi. We'll have these same rooms again. Have a super vacation and try to forget about this year.' Sarah caught the train for home, the day before Kemi was due to fly back to Lagos.

Chapter 5

December 2005 – March 2006

Sarah looked forward to the Christmas vacation at the end of her second year at Wits. She'd worked hard all year and needed a break. The train trip back to Harare would be long and tedious, with a bus connection over the border at Beitbridge. And if the train in Zimbabwe wasn't running, it meant an even more exhausting bus trip. She was eager to get home and back to Thomas. Tall and handsome and from a respectable family, he was everything that a girl might want. A happy disposition gave him a boyish charm, but there was a serious side when the mood took him. Thomas planned his future well, and he hoped his job with the Ministry of Foreign Affairs would lead to a career in the country's diplomatic service.

Thomas and Sarah suited each other, and their families approved of the match. He was caring and fun, so it came as a surprise to Sarah when, in the Christmas vacation, he seemed changed. Thomas never wanted to go out. Like any other young couple, they'd always enjoyed the city's night life. Now, Thomas wanted to stay home and watch television or play cards. In the week before the start of the new term at Wits, Sarah could hold back no longer and confronted him. She stood in front of Thomas with her arms folded. 'You've met someone else. That's why you're afraid to go out with me in public.'

Thomas did not meet her eyes. 'No, I'm not seeing anyone else. There's no one else for me but you.'

'Well, you'd better explain yourself. You never take me out anymore.'

'It's hard to explain,' said Thomas, shifting in his seat.

Sarah put her hands on her hips. 'I bet it's hard to explain.'

At first, Thomas couldn't give a good reason for his changed behaviour. But Sarah wouldn't let it rest. 'OK,' said Thomas, 'but you must promise to keep it secret.'

'Yes, OK.'

'Not even our families can know.'

Thomas' job with the Ministry of Foreign Affairs was thanks to his language skills. Those same skills caught the eye of state security.

Thomas lent forward in his chair. 'You've heard of the CIO, the Central Intelligence Organisation?'

'Yes, you're not in trouble with them, are you?' The pitch of Sarah's voice rose in alarm.

'No, the CIO often works with Foreign Affairs to keep a watch on dissidents.'

'Yes, they work for the government and intimidate the opposition.'

'Don't believe all the gossip, Sarah.' Thomas lowered his voice to a hoarse whisper. 'Everyone knows the CIO works on matters of state security. But there's another unofficial group called the COU, the Covert Operations Unit. This is a top-secret group they want me to join. They say it will be a good experience and will help me go far in the diplomatic service. Also, the salary is much better, but I'd have to sign a three-year contract.'

'Will it be dangerous? What do you have to do?'

'They haven't yet told me. Maybe I'll translate messages the CIO have intercepted; stuff like that.'

'So why can't we go out in public together?'

'Ah, well, that's the problem. One condition is I'm not allowed to be in a personal relationship during my contract. They say they can't afford to train me and spend all that money if I have other commitments. If I join them, I must be one hundred percent focused on the COU. I haven't told them about us, so we must be careful.'

'That doesn't sound good. Three years is a long time.'

'Listen, Sarah, you have one more year at Wits. Then if you do an honours year, by the time you finish, I'll have just one year left on my contract. The time will fly past, you'll see.'

* * *

After the Christmas vacation Sarah returned to Wits, not at all happy about the new arrangement with Thomas. She enrolled for an honours year to help the time pass.

Back in Sunnyside, Sarah was impatient for Kemi's return. But the next day, Sarah was shocked to find another girl in Kemi's room.

'Miss Adebayo is not coming back,' the Assistant Registrar told Sarah.

'Why?'

'You must ask her parents why.'

Sarah and Kemi exchanged addresses, and Sarah sent her a Christmas card, but she'd not received one in return. She thought nothing of it as letters and cards often went astray. Sarah couldn't contact Kemi on her cell phone, so she wrote to Kemi in Lagos to find out why she was not returning to Wits. The reply she received shocked her.

Dear Miss Kagonye,

Kemi told us what a good friend you were to her at Wits.

I am sorry to have to tell you that Kemi died in Johannesburg on the day she was due to return for her end-of-year vacation.

She drowned in the swimming pool of a house in Midrand. The police suspect foul play because she had bruises on her body. We believe the former occupants vacated the house at short notice. So far, there has been no arrest.

We are all very sad about what has happened, and we hope you will stay in touch with us. She cared so much for you.

Yours sincerely,

Arthur and Edwina Adebayo

The contents of the letter hit Sarah like the blast of an icy wind. Her blood ran cold. She sat in stunned disbelief. Tears welled up in her eyes. It must have been that bastard Godwin. If only she'd accompanied Kemi more often on Sundays, this might not have happened. Sarah felt guilty about leaving Kemi to her fate with that monster. She had no proof it was Godwin, but who else could it have been?

The bright March mornings in Johannesburg now seemed so bleak. Two remaining years at Wits was a daunting prospect for Sarah. The cosy room at Sunnyside wouldn't be the same without her bubbly friend next door.

Chapter 6

March 2006 – January 2008

Thomas wouldn't talk about his new job, saying it was so secret even the CIO didn't know of it. Sarah found it dull, trying to keep their relationship to themselves. Thomas remained the same caring person he'd always been, but now he was more serious, even a little boring. Sarah put this down to him maturing, and she became used to the changed circumstances.

Over Sarah's Christmas holidays, they spent the summer evenings at his house or hers, watching television and chatting. Sometimes they played Scrabble or cards, but they no longer went into the city together. She longed for the freedom of going out in public with Thomas, and she missed their long walks together. Sarah needed to keep active, but if she went to the gym or wanted to play squash, she was on her own.

* * *

Sarah was back in Harare for the mid-year vacation in her honours year. One evening, when she and Thomas chatted, he said, 'My boss would like to meet you.'

'Have you told him about us?' asked Sarah in surprise. 'Didn't you say you mustn't be in a personal relationship for three years?'

'No, I never told him about us. He asked me if I knew anyone else at university who had studied languages and could do the work, so I mentioned you as a possibility.'

'But if I joined the COU, wouldn't they also prohibit me from having a personal relationship for three years?'

'Yes, but Sarah, imagine the money we would earn. It would set us up for the future. If I signed on for another three years, by the time you finished your three-year stint, I'd have only one more year left on my second contract. Then, we'd be out of the COU with a lot more money than most couples our age.'

'We've already agreed to give up almost three years of our life because of the COU. Do you believe it's worth giving up another three, just for the money? I don't want to be a middle-aged woman before we can get married.'

'Come on, Sarah, it would give us a good start, and we'd have plenty of time ahead of us to enjoy life.'

'There's no harm in meeting your boss, I suppose. But I don't want our life postponed yet again.'

Sarah lay awake that night thinking about what Thomas said. Was his boss serious? People often said things they didn't mean. She worried about the job opportunities after she left Wits. There was high unemployment in Zimbabwe. Even a first-class honours degree was no guarantee of a job. She knew of her father's good contacts. Maybe he might help her find work? But now the COU gave her the opportunity to find her own job. Sarah did not want her father indebted on her behalf.

Thomas' boss meant what he said, and two days later Sarah was on her way to meet him. She didn't know where Thomas worked, so it didn't surprise her that the meeting was to take place in a quiet café on the edge of the CBD. As he'd admitted to only a passing acquaintance with her, Thomas wouldn't be there.

The gloomy café was empty when Sarah arrived for her appointment, and it seemed like the ideal spot for a secretive meeting. She looked around and chose a quiet table in the corner, away from inquisitive ears. A young waiter asked her what she would like to order, but she waved him away, saying she was waiting for someone and would order when they arrived. Sarah was ten minutes early, and as she waited, she fiddled with the salt and pepper shakers. This was her first job interview. At eleven o'clock, a dapper looking man entered the café, and Sarah guessed he would be Thomas' boss.

'Hello, I'm Jedson Ziyambi, and you must be Sarah. I must congratulate you on your choice of the table. It shows forethought.'

Sarah stood and shook hands. She guessed Jedson would be in his early fifties. He was of medium height with an athletic build, and he wore his hair short and sported a neat military moustache. Shiny black leather shoes and a light blue tie set off his mid-grey, pinstripe suit and crisp white shirt. It showed him to be a man of taste and style, a snappy dresser. With his fine features, Sarah took him to be a ladies' man. Jedson sat with his right leg crossed over his left, exuding a relaxed air of confidence that soon put Sarah at ease. Although she'd only just met him, she felt comfortable in his company.

'I haven't met your father, Sarah, but I understand he is a respected member of ZANU-PF. That alone commends you for the work we do.'

'What does the work entail, Sir? To whom would I report?'

'You're very direct, Sarah. I like that, but I can't tell you the nature of the work until we are sure you're a serious candidate for a job with us. Do you support the government?'

'Our whole family supports the government, Sir. We wouldn't vote for any other party.'

'That's good. With your language skills and qualifications, you could be useful to us. After you've completed your honours year, I will contact you. What is your phone number? You have a cell phone, don't you?'

The rest of their discussion comprised small talk about politics and the state of the country. Sarah realised he was testing her on her claim she supported the government.

That evening when Sarah spoke to Thomas about her interview, he didn't want to talk about it. 'Must you take the secrecy so seriously?' She realised the decision would be down to her if Jedson offered her the job at the end of the year. Jedson had not mentioned the COU in their discussion, and nor had she. Sarah realised she would need to be careful to not reveal her relationship with Thomas.

For Sarah, the rest of the year flew by, and she worked hard for her first-class honours degree. The relationship with Thomas was going nowhere, and it was a relief when early in the New Year Jedson Ziyambi contacted her to meet once more. It was a Friday afternoon, and Sarah stopped in front of an old house on the western edge of the CBD. A guard in civilian clothes stood at a gate in the high wall that surrounded the property. He instructed Sarah to enter the building and wait in room number one. In the dreary interview room was a desk, two chairs and a door in one corner near the window. Sarah supposed the door led to an adjacent room or cupboard. The gloss, light green walls brought back memories of her old school classrooms.

A few minutes later, Jedson Ziyambi came into the room, wearing a smart charcoal, woollen suit. He motioned for Sarah to sit down, and he sat in a chair on the other side of the desk. He leant back, crossing his right leg over his left knee. His manner was pleasant, as in their first meeting, but on this occasion the interview was more formal.

Jedson passed a form across the desk. 'Please sign this confidentiality agreement, Sarah.' She signed the form and handed it back. 'It would be a criminal offence,' said Jedson, 'if you discussed our meeting or our location with any other person. That includes members of your family. Even if you're all loyal supporters of the government, that rule still applies.'

'Yes, Sir.' Sarah sat still on the wooden chair with her hands folded in her lap.

'Have you heard of the CIO, the Central Intelligence Organisation?'

'Yes, Sir.'

'What do you know about them?'

'The former white government of Rhodesia established it in 1963. They're the secret police. People say they intimidate, beat and have even killed members of the MDC opposition.'

'Sarah, it's untrue, but that's the difficulty we face. The CIO has an image problem. That hinders its freedom to carry out its work to protect us from those who would use propaganda, rumours and lies to undermine the government.' Jedson uncrossed his legs and sat forward in the chair, lowering his voice. 'The CIO is overt in the way it carries out its work for the country. But there's another organisation called the COU, the Covert Operations Unit, which, as its name suggests, carries out its work covertly. It's top secret. I manage a team within the COU, made up of a team leader, that's me, and two operatives. Thomas is one operative, and I am looking for a second to complete the team. You both studied languages at Wits, and that could be most useful for the work we do when we travel outside our borders. Do you have any questions?'

'May I ask, where would I work and what would I do?'

'This would be your base. The work is diverse, but given your language skills, I can tell you there would be translation work among other duties. We have a focus on physical fitness and health, so you would have a lot of self-defence training. You would also learn how to handle weapons, sky-dive and other new skills. Do you have a driver's licence?'

'No, I don't.'

'You need to get one. We'll send you now and then for specialised training with the military, air-force or the police. You'd also be expected to keep up your language skills and learn Ndebele. Do you speak Ndebele?'

'No, I don't.'

'A black, female James Bond is what you'd be,' said Jedson, laughing at his little joke. 'A lot of money would go into your training and health, so you would have to undertake a half-yearly health check. We must protect our investment in you. There is one other thing. You would also have to sign an agreement to avoid any personal relationships for three years. Are you in a relationship?'

'No, Sir,' Sarah lied.

'That's good, but I don't need an answer from you today. Think about it over the weekend, and phone me on Monday with your decision.'

The prospect of working with Thomas excited Sarah, and she was pleased about the fitness regime she would have to follow. Maintaining and honing her language skills was a bonus. It sounded a perfect job for her, but she didn't like the three-year ban on personal relationships. Sarah worried about the COU being a covert form of the CIO. She recognised the need for the CIO, but everyone knew of its reputation.

It disturbed Sarah that she couldn't discuss the job offer with her father, who'd always been a great sounding board. And when she spoke to Thomas about it, he seemed to have cooled to the idea.

'Are you sure you want to undertake that work, Sarah? Spying on people can sometimes make big trouble for them, and it's also dangerous for you.'

'Why shouldn't I join the COU? My father has supported ZANU from the time of the struggle against Ian Smith and the days of white rule. While he supports the government, so will I. If people don't want trouble, they shouldn't try to undermine the party. If they do, then they get what they deserve. You've been with the COU for two years already. Have you done anything you considered wrong?'

'No, I've done translation work most of the time. But there're other teams I've not met, and I'm not sure what they do. Jedson says they keep us apart so that no one's cover is blown. The training includes unarmed combat and self-defence, and weapon training with firearms and knives. It's good I can defend myself, but the focus on it makes me wonder.'

'A self-defence course is just what I want. I told you, I trained in Muay Boran while at Wits. If I don't like what they want me to do I can always leave, can't I?' The next time these words crossed Sarah's mind was in the second week in her new job.

Sarah's office was the dreary interview room where she'd seen Jedson for their second meeting. The added refrigerator and kettle did little to brighten the gloomy room, which belied the bright sunshine in the yard. A white metal canopy shielded her window from the sun and kept the office cool. In winter her office would be like an ice box, and a bar heater would be essential.

A high wall gave privacy to the property. Sarah's office window looked onto a large, bare open area of hard, sun-dried earth at the side of the building. A high storm mesh fence with a locked gate separated it from the front yard of the house. It looked like a long-disused tennis court. Poor rendering did not disguise the bricked-up window that once overlooked the front yard. The building's reflective windows made them one-way mirrors, ensuring the privacy of the occupants.

Although Thomas' office was directly across the hallway from hers, Sarah saw little of him during working hours. He always seemed to be out on a training exercise or running errands for Jedson. On most days she was alone in the office. Part-way down the passage, a closed door prevented access. Sarah never even glimpsed what lay beyond it. Thomas said he'd often heard voices and laughter coming from the back of the house. Apart from Thomas and her boss, Sarah met no one else in the building.

Jedson didn't like Sarah or Thomas going into the passage, nor did he approve of them going into each other's office. It seemed he was trying to keep them apart. Perhaps he saw a risk in two young people of the opposite sex working together. 'If we are a team, shouldn't we work together?' said Sarah. 'It's uncanny how Jedson always turns up when we cross the hallway. It seems like he has an alarm system that tells him when one of us is out of our office.'

When Sarah arrived at work each morning, the only person she saw was the guard on duty at the front gate. Jedson would come to her office whenever he needed to discuss work with her. Sarah couldn't hear anything in the hallway with her office door shut, and only the turn of the doorknob signalled Jedson's appearance. She found it an eerie environment for work.

Sarah's office was the first on the right upon entering the building. The front door was often wide open, and natural light flooded the passageway. Early one afternoon after lunch, Sarah left her door ajar, just a chink, to ease her sense of isolation. It was surprising how much brighter her office looked. She was about to sit down at her desk when a shuffling sound in the hallway attracted her attention. Sarah peeped through the crack in the doorway. Two men in the passage struggled to carry a large, long, black, zipped plastic bag. They took it to a van parked in the yard near the front door. Footsteps in the passage alerted Sarah, and she hurried to return to her seat.

When Jedson entered, he noticed the look on her face. 'Sarah, I told you to keep your door closed at all times. We don't want visitors or anyone else to see you and associate you with the COU. Not even the people working here. We can't risk your cover being blown.'

Jedson's words explained why he never introduced Sarah to anyone else in the old house that served as their workplace. If she needed to speak to him, she rang a two-digit number, or called him on his cell phone, and he'd come to her office. It all made sense now. Jedson's office was in the same building, but Sarah never visited it. In her office, the door near the window led to an ensuite bathroom, making it unnecessary for her to venture elsewhere in the house. In fact, she'd never gone down the passageway farther than her own office door.

After a long, awkward silence, Jedson said, 'We recruited him, but it turned out he was a spy. We must be careful and alert at all times.' Jedson's words shocked Sarah. Did it mean what she thought it meant?

Since that incident almost six months passed, and it faded in Sarah's mind. Thomas seemed more like his old self, full of fun and good humour once again. Though no longer the over-serious Thomas who emerged when he first joined the COU, he remained anxious about the need to conceal their relationship from Jedson. 'I don't understand what the big fuss is,' said Sarah. 'What's Jedson going to do if he finds out we're engaged? If we're both in the COU, what's the big deal about us being in a relationship? Why don't we tell him?'

'Sarah, you might be right, but I won't test him. Rules are rules and the COU is serious about them.'

'If we're out together, and he saw us, couldn't we say we bumped into each other? As work colleagues in a small team, it would be unnatural for us not to share a coffee if we met by chance when out one Saturday morning.'

'Yes, you're right, Sarah, but I don't want to give him any reason for suspicion. Anyone might see us together, and if they saw us even twice, it would look suspicious. Jedson, and those like him, have suspicious minds. They always think the worst. That's how they stay one step ahead of everyone else.'

'By thinking the worst, you mean he might think we are in a relationship. I find it difficult to think of our relationship in those terms.'

'You know what I mean. If he found out, he might put us into different teams, or fire us. Is that what you want?'

'No, but it still seems an unreasonable rule.'

'Look at it from the COU's point of view. If we were on an operation together, I'd worry more about your safety than the success of the operation. We'd be reluctant for each other to take risks.'

'But you couldn't have a relationship even before I joined the COU.'

'That's right, and they believe if an operative has loved ones at home, they wouldn't take risks while on an operation. They'd want to make sure they got home safely to their loved ones.'

'So, you're saying someone in a relationship would take fewer risks to achieve the goals of an operation?'

'Yes.'

'But we are in a relationship.'

'Yes, and I wouldn't want you or me to take unnecessary risks on an operation, but I wouldn't tell Jedson that.'

'Sometimes, I wish our contracts were finishing.'

'Yes, I do too, but until then we must carry on and keep our relationship a secret.'

CHAPTER 7

June 2008

THE voice on the other end of the phone sounded less threatening than usual. 'Good morning, Captain. How are the plans progressing?'

'Good morning, Sir. We're all prepared. Two operatives from teams A1 and one from team E2 will go on ahead to familiarise themselves with the lay of the land. Team LA4 will follow two days later.'

'Who knows the objectives of the trip?'

'Only teams A1 and E2. LA4 is unaware of the destination or purpose.'

'Good, we can't risk any of this getting out. Why are you taking LA4? Do they have the experience?'

'Exposure to a live operation is a valuable part of their training, Sir.'

'Are they ready and willing to do what it takes to achieve the goals of the mission?'

'Until we test them in a live operation, Sir, we won't know for sure.'

'We can't afford any mistakes on this operation, Captain. Things mustn't go wrong.'

'No, Sir. I take it the old man approved the operation?'

'No, he knows nothing of it, and neither do I.'

'Yes, Sir.'

'We're setting aside special funds for this operation, but it doesn't mean you can go crazy with the spending.'

'We'll watch the expenses, Sir.'

'Good.'

The phone went dead.

Captain John hung up the phone, leant back in his swivel chair and thought about the mission. The opportunity to work outside the country's borders didn't come around too often. This operation was a biggie and took precedence over everything else. If successful, it would have huge consequences and prove the COU's reputation. If it failed, there would be a price to pay. Captain John hoped he'd not be the one to pick up the tab.

The COU was John's baby. It helped build his reputation, and important people whispered about its activities. No, failure was not an option for the COU's biggest and boldest operation. There might never be a bigger one. It was top secret with only a handful of government bigwigs privy to it. At least, that's what John believed.

Things almost always fell John's way, and his star was on the rise since his stint with the Fifth Brigade in the Gukurahundi campaign. Ambitious and astute, he strove to prove his value. But he kept his head down and showed no outward sign of political ambition. Naked ambition led to the early demise of many promising political careers in Zimbabwe. Not only were political careers cut short, but often lives too. John wasn't silly. He could afford to wait. Still in his early fifties, with time on his side. John was a lone ambush predator, and his nickname, 'The Leopard', fitted him well. He'd reap the benefits, using the other members of the COU as the tools of his trade.

Teams A1 and E2 would front the operation. If that didn't work, he'd send in team LA4 to do the job, but not before the other teams returned home safe. The back-up plan, so simple, even an inexperienced team like LA4 couldn't fail. And afterwards, one way or another, they wouldn't be around to answer questions. There'd be accusations and blame but no proof. No one could be held responsible.

John took great care in organising the COU. He ran four teams; A1 and E2 each composed of three operatives. They shared an office at the back of the building. Sonny Mutezo led a third team, A3, which worked on the streets. Apart from Sonny, John did not know the members of that team. They were a gang of thugs that Sonny led and were not an official part of the COU. Each Monday evening after hours, Sonny would come into the office to pick up his pay and receive instructions from John. Jedson, Thomas and Sarah made up LA4, the fourth team. Teams A1 and E2 were John's trusted old guard. Team A1, John's original hit squad of hand-picked men, was not squeamish about following orders. Team E2 was similar but with explosive and engineering skills. Teams A3 and LA4 worked in isolation.

The numbers in the team names reflected the order in which Captain John established the teams, and the letters reflected their area of expertise. The letter A stood for assassination, E for explosives, and L for languages. In time, he would blend the teams into self-sufficient units.

John was ambitious with big plans for the COU. He saw them as a private guard, loyal to him alone. The Fifth Brigade had reported to the president, but he would have the COU.

There was always a bottle of Scotch secured under lock and key at the back of the cupboard under John's desk. Every time he flew out of the country, he would buy duty free Scotch at the airport shops. He fancied himself a connoisseur of all things Scotch and talked with authority on single malts, blends and the value of ageing. John cracked the seal of the unopened bottle, unscrewed the cap and poured a large tot into the tulip shaped, crystal nosing glass he kept on the bookcase behind his desk. He held the glass up to the light through his office window and admired the clear burnt amber colour of the Scotch. He rotated the glass at an angle, to coat the wall of the glass before placing it upright on the desk. The liquid on the wall of the glass formed legs flowing downwards, thick and spread well apart, signalling a well-aged Scotch. Printed on the label were the words, *twelve-year-old single malt*, but he still liked to carry out the ageing test on every new bottle he opened.

Captain John swivelled in his chair and opened the door of the built-in minibar in the bookcase behind his desk. He took out the ice tray and dropped two cubes into the glass. Yes, things were coming along nicely, and he planned to grow his operation in the next couple of years. Perhaps he would move his office into one of those shiny new high-rise buildings in the CBD. The old house on the edge of the city didn't fit his self-image. The operatives would have to stay at their present location. They needed the yard to park their motor vehicles and the space to carry out their training. In the CBD it would be just him, a pretty secretary and his personal bodyguards. He didn't have a secretary or personal bodyguards at present, but in a year or two...

The first sniff of the single malt invaded his nostrils with a strong tingling and burning sensation. He sniffed twice more and took a sip. It stung the tip of his tongue where it lay, and then it permeated his mouth with warmth and flavour, like water spreading through blotting paper. All his taste buds came into play—the sweetness on the tip of his tongue, the saltiness on the sides, and the dryness and bitterness at the back of his throat. It was wonderful.

Captain John loved his work. He loved the power it gave him to instil fear into people and to decide if they should live or die. For him, it was a thrill, better than sex, and the reason he fared so well in the Fifth Brigade. John's cunning and stealth earned him the nickname, The Leopard. But killing Ndebele was like canned hunting. Now, he could target anybody labelled *an enemy of the state*. Hunting them down was fun. The chase was a game.

A knock on his door brought John back to the present. 'You wanted to see me, Sir?'

'Come in, Elijah, and shut the door.'

Elijah was a tall, well-built man with a military moustache and a bearing like John's. He'd been a sergeant in the Fifth Brigade when John first met him. Elijah was more the traditional soldier and not typical of the blood-thirsty members of that unit. Loyalty, discipline and order were his guiding principles, and he did not fit well into that genocidal band of killers.

'Are you and the others prepared for the trip?'

'Yes, Sir, we're ready to go.'

'When I arrive, I don't want you three acknowledging me. As far as anyone is concerned, we've never met. Got it?'

'Yes, Sah.'

'And remember, you don't know LA4 either.'

'Well, that's true, Sah.'

'We've rehearsed the plan, so you should be familiar with your part by now. If I get the opportunity, we may run through it one more time, but you guys should know the plan backwards.'

'Don't worry, Sah, we're well prepared.'

'Good man. I'll see you in two days then. Good luck.'

'Thank you, Sah.'

Chapter 8

28th June 2008

Sarah sat next to Thomas on the mid-afternoon Johannesburg flight and let the excitement wash over her. She fastened her seat belt and looked around the cabin. She saw businessmen in dark suits, but the casual attire of many other passengers surprised her. Several of the Europeans—whites—looked like backpackers, and a few wore dread-locks, which she found amusing on a white person.

Thomas helped Sarah stow her hand luggage in the overhead locker above her head. Now, she watched each time the air hostess opened the locker to look for space for the hand luggage of latecomers. Many items of carry-on luggage seemed too large, and she hoped the extra bits and pieces squeezed in on top of her bag wouldn't crease her business suit.

Sarah flipped through the inflight magazine before stuffing it back in the pocket in front of her. She tested the fold-down table and looked through the food and drinks menu. Sarah gazed out the window and studied the figures in the terminal and the activity around the plane. A trolley piled high with luggage lay unattended on the apron below her window. She realised for the first time, how high off the ground she sat. Sarah glanced through the inflight magazine and checked her seatbelt once more. This was her first flight on a commercial jet; an international flight no less. Before this, she'd found it exciting just to visit the airport. She sensed the thrill of air travel, watching the planes land and take off. Sarah never imagined that one day she would be aboard one of those shiny machines and fortunate enough to have a window seat.

Without warning, the plane moved backwards, away from the terminal. After a further delay, the engines hummed, warming up, and then the plane trundled out to the end of the runway. The intercom crackled into life, asking for the passengers' attention. Sarah listened and watched as the hostesses smiled and demonstrated the safety features. Afterwards, she studied the safety instructions card for the fourth time since boarding.

After what seemed like another interminable delay at the start of the runway, the engines' noise increased to a scream like a swarm of enraged hornets. The pent-up power shook the plane, and then as the pilot released the brakes, the plane eased forward before gathering pace as it hurtled down the runway. To Sarah, it was like a rocket taking off for the moon. She couldn't help being nervous, with a sense of helplessness, as the plane hurtled down the runway. She'd read take off and landings were the most dangerous parts of a flight. Sarah grabbed Thomas' arm, but he pulled away. The reaction was because of their boss and team leader, Jedson Ziyambi, seated in the aisle seat next to him. Thomas was also nervous. This was also his first commercial flight, and he sweated. Possibly because the flight crew were yet to switch on the air-conditioning system. Jedson looked across at his charges and smiled. He'd been on many such flights and regarded himself a seasoned traveller, and it showed in his relaxed manner.

Sarah and Thomas had no idea as to their destination until Jedson gave them their tickets at the airport—Johannesburg, the city of gold, in South Africa. Sarah noted the return date, four days hence, and her heart tingled with excitement. A sudden thought crossed her mind. Did she pack the right clothes for the Joburg scene? But then, she worried her friends would recognise her dresses from her days at Wits.

O. R. Tambo International Airport, Johannesburg; Sarah couldn't sit still. Impatient to get her overhead luggage, she stood up, only to be re-seated by the air hostess. Thomas took his lead from Jedson and looked the picture of patience, but inside, he bubbled. With a little more warning, Sarah might have met her old friends from Wits. Could she get together with them at this late stage? How would she contact them? Many of their phone numbers were in her address book at home in Harare. At last the Fasten Seatbelt sign turned off, but the passengers stood in the aisle without moving. Why the delay? The air hostesses made the economy class passengers wait for the business class to disembark first. Jedson warned them to travel light with only hand luggage, so they would avoid the crowd of impatient travellers waiting at the baggage carousel.

In the airport building they followed the crowd, but then Jedson stopped them. 'Hold on, we go this way.' When she saw the Transit Passengers sign, Sarah's heart fell. If not Joburg, where were they headed? In the transit area, Jedson gave Sarah and Thomas their connecting tickets. Cairo and then on to Sharm el-Sheikh, that wasn't too bad. Yippee!

'Sir, what are we going to do in Sharm el-Sheikh?'

'Don't you know better than to ask me that, Sarah? We'll get our instructions once we're there. Perhaps we are to provide extra security for our president. There's a summit meeting of the African Union taking place in the next couple of days.'

Sarah found it all new and exciting, apart from the five-and-a-half-hour wait in the transit area. Air travel was not always so glamorous. Sarah and Thomas relished the inflight service, including dinner, refreshments and movies. Jedson took it in his stride. Halfway through the second movie, Sarah and Thomas fell asleep.

Early in the morning, they woke, feeling groggy and drugged. Already a queue formed outside the toilets. The shadow of the plane flitted across the sand dunes, which ran to the horizon like yellow waves on a vast ocean. They ate breakfast while they enjoyed the views over the Sahara. All too soon, the inflight entertainment switched off, and the voice on the intercom asked passengers to fasten seatbelts for landing.

Sarah scanned the airport buildings as the plane taxied up to the terminal. Yes, they were at the right place. The sign on the airport building said, Cairo International Airport. While waiting in the queue to disembark, Sarah observed the mess the passengers made of the once tidy cabin.

The packed terminal was like an ants' nest, with people scurrying in all directions. 'Even busier than Joburg!' said Sarah. The two-and-a-half-hour wait for the connecting flight passed in a flash, and they boarded their third flight, on a different plane, in just a few hours. Each new experience added to her excitement, and they hadn't yet arrived at their destination.

From the airport in Sharm el-Sheikh, it was only a ten-minute drive to the Peninsula Hotel. Sarah looked around the hotel lobby. 'What a beautiful place! I'm surprised they put us here.'

'If we're protecting the president, we need to stay close by him,' said Thomas.

'Now listen you two,' Jedson interrupted, 'less chatter. Once we've checked in, you're free for the rest of the afternoon. Meet me in the lobby bar at five o'clock sharp. We may have our instructions by then.'

Check-in, another new experience for Sarah and Thomas. 'They treat us like royalty,' she said. An attentive bell boy showed them to their rooms. Sarah was almost sorry she'd agreed to meet Thomas in the foyer in half an hour. She wanted to relax and enjoy the opulence. Although only a superior room, it was more glamorous than anything she'd ever seen. A huge king size bed did little to diminish its spaciousness. Beautiful views of the hotel's landscaped gardens completed the picture. It was almost a whole day since leaving home, and she needed a shower.

'Let's explore the hotel and grounds,' said Sarah, 'and then the town area. We can swim in that beautiful pool later this afternoon, but I must buy a swimming costume.'

Naama Bay town centre was hectic with crowds of people, and hawkers hounded the tourists to buy something. Sarah and Thomas were thankful the European visitors received most of the attention. And it was hot, with the temperature in the high thirties. Sarah bought a modest one-piece swimming costume that cost her more than she had hoped to pay. The price and the amount of fabric in the swimming costumes seemed to have an inverse relationship, so Sarah got off lightly.

'What a pity we must have separate rooms,' Sarah said.

'There's no way we could share. Jedson's room is right next door to mine. I wonder what he's doing right now. He always seems to be off on some task or private business. That's the penalty for being the team leader, I suppose.'

'Let's have lunch at one of these cafés,' said Sarah, 'and then we'll swim. Have you noticed how much rubbish is lying around in the street?'

After a burger at the Hard Rock Café, they returned to the Peninsula for their swim in the magnificent pool. They left the hot, crowded streets of Naama Bay to those unable to afford the luxuries of the Peninsula, one of the most glamorous hotels in the region. Sarah and Thomas made a handsome couple, but they couldn't risk showing any attachment to each other. She thought it a great shame, given the romantic environment.

Sarah presented a striking figure in her yellow swimsuit with scattered, black splashes. She was tall, with an athletic build and slender hands and feet. Her unblemished skin was a mid-brown, and her arching brows framed wide set, penetrating almond eyes. These, together with her high cheek bones gave her an alluring, exotic look. Full lips and even white teeth set off a sparkling smile. She kept her hair a little longer than the ubiquitous, short cropped style favoured by many African women. Her slender neck and shoulders belied the strength that lay in them. She didn't go unnoticed by the few hotel guests at the pool.

Unlike many Africans, Sarah and Thomas were competent swimmers. They'd learnt to swim while at Wits and with the COU. After an all too short but refreshing swim and showers, they were ready for the evening's activities.

Jedson sat in an armchair in the bar lounge, sipping a Scotch on the rocks. He looked relaxed and the picture of elegance in cream coloured slacks, pink shirt, lightweight beige jacket and dark tan shoes. Sarah and Thomas walked in, dressed for the evening in smart casual wear, but Thomas looked gauche compared with his more mature boss.

'We'll have dinner here at the hotel,' said Jedson. 'From now on we are on standby. The Al Forno restaurant should be good.' It boasted the best stone-oven pizza in Sharm el-Sheikh, and Sarah savoured every mouthful. She preferred it to the more exotic dishes on the menu. After pizzas and ice cream they wandered out to the Lobby Bar where they had coffee. It made a change from their usual cups of tea at home. They spent much of the evening exploring the hotel lobby and adjacent areas, and they had a drink in the Windsor Bar with its regency striped armchairs. Jedson ordered a cognac for himself and beers for Thomas and Sarah. He reminded them they were still on duty and would have to limit themselves to one drink. Through the evening, he checked his watch and cell phone, as if he expected a call. The minutes dragged by with a lot of small talk between Jedson and Thomas, and Sarah's eyes felt heavy. Relief came soon after midnight when Jedson received a phone call advising him to stand them down from duty.

'Let's meet for breakfast at seven o'clock sharp,' said Jedson. 'Good night.'

Sarah brushed her teeth and tumbled into bed, grateful after all to have her own room. After the air flights and a long day, she didn't bother with the television.

The telephone beside Sarah's bed rang. It can't be morning already.

'Good morning, this is your six o'clock wake-up call.'

'Thank you.' She closed her eyes momentarily but then thought better of it. She risked going back to sleep, and Jedson wouldn't be happy if she were late. It had been nothing but rush, rush, since they'd arrived. Sarah had no opportunity to enjoy the luxurious room. Ah well, it was not supposed to be a holiday.

Despite her lack of sleep, the shower refreshed Sarah. The exotic location and luxurious surroundings got her adrenalin working. When she arrived on time at breakfast, Thomas and Jedson already sat at their table.

'Good morning. Did you both sleep well?'

They nodded, acknowledging Sarah's greeting. Then Jedson spoke. 'The two of you are returning to Harare this afternoon. Our team is no longer needed here, and we are surplus to requirements. I must stay for meetings, but you are needed back home.'

Sarah was aghast, but she tried her best to hide her disappointment. 'Sir, can we stay one more night for a little sightseeing?'

Jedson seemed irritated by her request. 'Zimbabwe can't afford to pay for a holiday for you two. Our purpose here has passed.' Sarah said no more, and Thomas remained silent.

The return trip was not as exciting as their outbound journey. The novelty of air travel was wearing off fast though they still enjoyed the inflight service. But both Sarah and Thomas were deep in their own thoughts.

After a while, Sarah said, 'I wonder what the purpose of our trip was.'

'Whatever it was, I'm glad it's ended.'

'Why?'

Thomas spoke in a low voice. 'Come on, Sarah, you don't imagine we were there to protect the president, do you? He would have had all the protection he needed from his regular bodyguards. Our role in covert operations is for attack, not defence.'

'Do you think so?'

'What do you imagine happens to all those people named in our reports? Somebody, CIO or COU or someone else, deals with them. You've seen how much of our training is aimed at maiming or killing an imaginary foe. They'll want to test us sooner or later. You knew when you joined the COU it was a covert version of the CIO.'

'I suppose you're right. Did you notice that other group drifting around the hotel last night? They may have been from Zimbabwe. Perhaps they were part of the president's bodyguard or even another COU unit.'

'They could have been from anywhere. All the African leaders and their teams are here for the summit. We didn't hear those guys speaking, so we will never know.'

'I'm sure Jedson was interested in them.'

'Jedson told me our team number LA4 didn't stand for Los Angeles Four. He said it stood for Language and Assassination Four as that would reflect our capabilities. He also said if our language skills proved useful, he might transfer one of us to another team.'

'Oh, no! I wouldn't like that. If they tried to transfer one of us, I'd leave the COU. Do you think he might've been joking about what LA4 meant?'

'I don't know, but he seemed serious about it. Sometimes, he tells me things.'

'Jedson never seems to tell me anything. He talks to you because you're a man. Has he mentioned who runs the COU?'

'Yes, he said the boss' name is Captain John. He's also known as The Leopard. Not even Jedson knows his real name. Captain John and the other teams must use the back entrance to the office because I've never seen them.'

'Remember, I told you about the time I saw two men carrying out a body bag through the front entrance? But I only glimpsed the face of one of them.'

'Then you've seen more than I have.'

Sarah and Thomas sank back into their own thoughts, and before long were fast asleep after a hectic two days. Sharm el-Sheikh seemed like a dream. Did it happen? Were they ever there? If they'd known how short their trip would be, they might have done more exploring while they had the opportunity. Would they again get the chance for a real holiday together in such a romantic spot? Sarah's thoughts and dreams merged into one. Thomas' were a little darker. Why the trip? Why the sudden departure? They saw little of Jedson, their team leader. Did he know those other Africans sitting in the Peninsula Hotel lobby? He seemed to keep a close eye on them. Were they another COU team?

An exhausted Sarah and Thomas arrived back in Harare the next morning. The taxi dropped Sarah off first. 'See you this evening,' said Thomas. 'If you're not too tired, I'll come to your place.'

As Sarah walked through the front door, her mother rushed over and gave her a big hug. 'Have you heard the news?'

* * *

It was dusk when Sarah's mother woke her. 'If you sleep much longer, you won't be able to sleep tonight. Thomas is here. I will give him a cup of tea. Do you want one? Your father will be home soon.'

Sarah felt drugged. Sleeping in the daytime often did that. 'Thomas, you look exhausted. Didn't you get any sleep?'

'No, I've been thinking about our trip. You've heard about the Zambian president? I wonder if that's why they suddenly sent us home. Jedson seemed edgy yesterday morning. Remember, he said our purpose had passed?'

Sarah laughed. 'I'm sure we weren't part of a hit squad to assassinate the Zambian president.'

'Don't you think it strange? All that business with Jedson telling us we would get our instructions once we arrived there. And then they cancelled our visit and sent us home the morning after President Mwanawasa's stroke.'

Sarah shrugged. 'Whatever! But I don't think either of us would have been capable of killing someone.'

'Don't be so naïve.' Thomas' face looked strained. The way Sarah dismissed his concerns irritated him. 'I agree we'd not be first choice, but what if they needed backup if the operation went wrong? Maybe we'd be the scapegoats and accused of being rogue agents.'

'Thomas you're paranoid, but if you believe that, don't talk to Jedson about it. He seemed distant on this trip. And don't talk to anyone else about it because you never know who you can trust.'

That night Sarah had difficulty sleeping. She'd slept that afternoon, and her mind kept going back to the questions Thomas raised. He was always anxious at work. Perhaps he was right about his suspicions. Thirty months remained on her contract, but Thomas would have forty-two to serve if he renewed his. Sarah resolved to warn him not to say anything about leaving at the end of it. One didn't know how the COU might react. Thomas appeared a lot more relaxed when they wandered around Sharm el-Sheikh by themselves, but he always seemed tense around Jedson.

With the hint of the first light of dawn, Sarah drifted off to sleep. It would be days before her sleep pattern returned to normal.

CHAPTER 9

29th June 2008

The radio pips signalled the hour, and the recognisable accent of the newsreader followed. 'It is Twelve o'clock GMT. Hello this is ... with the latest news headlines from the BBC...'

Sunday, twenty-ninth June 2008. Greg Sanders jumped out of his chair to turn up the volume on the radio. He always listened to the BBC World Service and said, 'It was the best place to get news of Africa'. But what came next shocked him.

'Dammit, Ian, did you hear that? Did you hear the news?'

Greg's son Ian looked up from the mess of papers and reports scattered across the dining table. His father paced in small circles, thumping his right fist into the palm of his left hand. 'What news, Dad?'

'The Zambian president had a stroke.'

'Levy Mwanawasa had a stroke?'

'Yes, you know, the Zambian president, dammit!'

'Why are you so upset, Dad?'

'Don't you follow the African news? Mwanawasa was due to speak at the summit meeting of the African Union in Sharm el-Sheikh in Egypt.'

'Yes?'

'He was chairman of the Southern African Development Community (SADC). He didn't accept Mugabe won the presidential election in Zimbabwe.'

'Yes, and?'

'Well, he planned to speak against Mugabe's claim to have won, and he hoped to get other African leaders at the summit to back him. Who'll confront Mugabe now?'

'Oh! I see.'

'Mwanawasa was one of the good guys who stood against corruption. He said Mugabe had turned a blind eye to the election violence, and he'd turned the country into a "sinking Titanic". The neighbouring countries have to deal with the flood of refugees.'

'Yes, Dad, the stroke was bad luck.'

Greg stopped pacing and his light-blue, penetrating eyes fixed on Ian. 'Bad luck? Is that what you call it? A bloody disaster is more like it. Morgan Tsvangirai won that election. Why else would the ZANU-PF thugs go on a rampage against his MDC supporters? Tsvangirai only agreed to a second round of voting because of pressure from the other African leaders. But then, the ZANU-PF violence forced him to withdraw, and the next day he took refuge in the Dutch Embassy. What sort of election is that? African leaders don't want to see what's happening in Zimbabwe. Mwanawasa would have forced them to see. Mugabe must have been dreading the summit. There's something fishy about that stroke. Why now?'

'Dad, it's not Mwanawasa's first stroke. The leaders sit in alphabetical order at the summit, and he would've been right next to Mugabe. Perhaps the strain got to him.'

'Rubbish! The timing is too convenient. I don't believe in coincidences. Too many of Mugabe's critics have met a sticky end.'

'You can't say that without proof. We don't know what's happened. With luck, Mwanawasa will soon recover.'

'Humph! By then it'll be too late. It's already too late. With Mwanawasa out of the picture, no one else will stand up to Mugabe. They'll all breathe a sigh of relief and carry on as normal.'

'Yes, I'm sure you're right.'

'They used to call Rhodesia the breadbasket of Africa, but now Zimbabwe is a basket case. We gave them a beautiful country that exported food. Now they need food aid. Zimbabwe has gone backwards.

Rampant inflation, corruption and the brain drain. What else can go wrong? It was a land of opportunity.'

'Yes, Dad, but not a land of equal opportunity, was it? That led to the Bush War.'

'There was an opportunity for anyone willing to work hard and take their chances. Plenty of blacks did well under white rule. There wasn't apartheid like in South Africa. The races didn't mix, but by choice, not impractical laws. The economy was strong when we whites ran the country.'

'Dad, in South Africa they call the former Rhodesians the *Wenwes* because they're always saying, "when we".'

Greg curled his lip in disgust. 'A man I met through work the other day told me he'd travelled through almost the whole of black Africa in the mid-seventies. Aside from the scenery and wildlife, he'd not been at all impressed. But he said when he set foot in Rhodesia, "It was like finding a diamond in a donkey's arse".'

'I wonder what he'd say now.'

'We hoped for peace after black rule in 1980, but only two years later, Mugabe sent the Fifth Brigade into Matabeleland and massacred twenty thousand Ndebele civilians. Then, the new century kicked off with the farm invasions, and thousands of black farm workers lost their homes and their jobs. People had nothing to eat. Next, at the start of winter in May 2005, they bulldozed the houses of the urban poor. Most of them were MDC supporters. I tell you Ian, Africa's a disaster with famine and corruption wherever you turn.'

'Come on, Dad, they're not all so bad. Take Botswana and Namibia, they've done well?'

'They're exceptions.'

'It's a start, isn't it?'

Ian flipped the file in front of him closed and ran his fingers through his short brown hair. 'This work is getting me down, and I'm tired of it. I've not had a break in five years, and the projects keep piling up on my desk.'

'The young of today are soft.'

'Yeah, yeah, you old folk had it tough, but I'm exhausted and tired of writing business reports for clients. I need more stimulating work. You know, like being a journalist in a war zone.'

'That's a dangerous job, and often you don't even have to be in a war zone for it to be dangerous.'

'At least it would be stimulating.'

'I can tell you what would be even more dangerous,' said Greg. 'The ZANU-PF people in Zimbabwe are dropping like flies.'

'What do you reckon is happening?'

'Isn't it obvious? They're knocking each other off, aren't they?'

'A lot of those accidents are because of bad roads and poorly maintained cars.'

'Come on, Ian, you've seen how many mysterious deaths there've been. Zimbabwe's neighbours have bad roads and poorly maintained cars. Have their politicians suffered so many fatal accidents?'

'So, who's responsible?'

'They say it could be Mugabe or, more likely, his cronies. He's put them into positions of power, and if he goes, they go.'

'Yes, they might be charged with crimes against humanity.'

'Even if Mugabe is not directly responsible for the deaths, he's not blameless. All the suspicious deaths have happened on his watch.'

'Of course, his political opponents blame him,' said Ian. 'It's the same in every country. Don't fall for all those conspiracy theories.'

'It's a lot more than just his political opponents who question the official version of the deaths. People see his record against the Ndebele, the white farmers and his Shona opponents, so it would be no big deal to bump off a few troublesome individuals.'

'People are quick to think the worst. There's no proof he bumped off anyone.'

'Someone must've done it. Since they politicised the police and judiciary, it's difficult to separate fact from fiction. Whenever there's factional conflict in ZANU-PF, we get these fatal accidents.'

'It might be a coincidence.'

'True, but we only hear of the high-profile deaths or injuries,' said Greg. 'There's bound to be others. Mugabe started well but look what happened. As soon as he faced a serious political challenge, everything changed. Look at the forced evictions of the commercial farmers and the damage to the economy. There was no compensation, even for those who bought their farms with government approval. Mugabe's cronies got the farms, and they know bugger all about farming. The "war veterans" even murdered or evicted the black farm workers. Like hell they were war veterans; a lot of them were too young for the Bush War. Those farms are lying in ruin, and the farm machinery is rusting in the fields, and there're no jobs and no food unless you support ZANU-PF. And that's why even the blacks are fleeing to neighbouring countries. Thank goodness we left before all that happened.'

Ian saw his father's growing agitation and tried to calm him. 'It takes time for a country to settle. The next generation of leaders might sort things out.'

'Oh yes? Look at the rest of black Africa. They've had plenty of time to improve, but they've only got worse. The leaders who'll sort out Zimbabwe have yet to be born.'

'It's not only Africa, is it? All countries have a problem with corruption. We even have it here, but I agree Africa might be the worst case. But when you think about it, they've the least experience of democracy.'

Greg remained unconvinced. 'There was no future for whites in Zimbabwe once Mugabe took charge.'

'Then, why did we wait almost eight years to leave?'

'We left as soon as possible. We didn't want to go to a cold climate, and we wanted an English-speaking country that had a good standard of living. It was easier said than done.'

'Do you see now, Dad, you older folk should have been more open to compromise? It's no wonder the blacks wanted to get rid of you.'

'Rubbish! My farm workers didn't want me to go.'

* * *

Farming life had been good to sixty-year-old Greg. A tanned, leathery skin showed his years in the African sun, tending his beef herd and the crops on his farm close to Bulawayo. Blond hair disguised the encroaching grey, and years of hard physical work moulded his lean frame. In his youth, he was handsome and popular with the daughters of the farmers in the area.

Typical of a lot of white Rhodesians, Greg was conservative in his views but objected to being called a racist. He was happy to be labelled paternalistic. Like most whites in the country, he believed the blacks were better off under white rule. After a few years under ZANU-PF, a lot of blacks held the same view.

By his twenty-second birthday, and mature for his years, Greg ran his own farm and married Norma, the pretty, dark-haired girl from a neighbouring farm. Like his parents before him, he'd grown up in the farming community.

Greg always claimed he'd switch off the lights at the airport when he left, meaning he'd be the last person to leave the country. So, he surprised many of his friends and acquaintances when he and his family left for Australia.

For Greg, the genocidal Gukurahundi campaign was the last straw when Mugabe's Fifth Brigade set upon the Ndebele. Greg was close to his Ndebele farm workers, but helpless to do anything to aid them. His experiences in the Bush War hardened him, but he couldn't stomach what was happening in Matabeleland, and he made plans to leave.

The black farm workers liked Greg and were sad to see him go. His manner was impatient, but fair, and he cared for the welfare of his workers. When in trouble, they always went to him for help or advice. The Ndebele farm workers soon saw through his hard exterior, but they respected him as a leader.

In Australia, Greg soon found sales work for a farm machinery supplier. His skills suited the role, and he enjoyed the drive to rural properties to visit his customers for a yak over a cup of tea.

Greg had not mellowed through his years in Australia, and Ian grew up with his father's stories of the old days. This left him reflecting many of his father's views, though he wouldn't admit to it. At first glance, Ian appeared a little serious. He was patient by nature and happy with his own company. A mischievous streak, spiced with an enquiring mind and good sense of humour, made him a rebel who enjoyed a contrary view and going against the flow. He delighted in the verbal duals with his father.

Ian was thirty-six years old and grew up in the slip-slop-slap sunscreen era. It showed in his smooth, clear skin. Sparkling blue eyes capped off his masculine good looks. His tall, athletic figure belied his years in a desk job. Squash twice a week after work and tennis on Sunday afternoons kept him fit, and his job in the CBD allowed him to walk to many of his clients' offices. He was a picture of health and in his prime.

A demanding job meant long hours and taking work home to his St Kilda Road apartment close to the city. He often visited his parents for dinner at their home in Bentleigh, on the south side of Melbourne. After dinner he'd review his day at the office or work on an urgent report. But often a news item would distract him and lead to a verbal joust with his father. It gave Ian the opportunity to tease with provocative comments on contentious issues.

'You know, Dad, with all its troubles, Zimbabwe would make a great setting for a novel. Maybe I'll visit and get inspiration for a book.'

'Have you forgotten what it's like there? Don't you remember what happened at our farm? Haven't you been keeping up with the news in that country?'

When Ian used his debating skills and applied too much pressure on Greg's view of the world, Greg would try to change the subject. He would start by talking about Ian's work and how well he'd done. If that didn't do the trick, Greg's second line of attack was Ian's private life. 'You're thirty-six years old. How long is it since your last steady girlfriend? You can't spend your whole life sitting in the office and writing reports. It's time you thought about your future. You're getting on in years, you know? Soon, no suitable young woman will have you. Do you think swanning off to Zimbabwe is the answer?'

'Teatime,' said Norma Sanders. She came into the room carrying a tray of tea and biscuits. The family had been in Melbourne for twenty years, and Norma liked the lifestyle. She did not miss the constant drama of life in Zimbabwe, but Greg did. To him, the problems in Australia all seemed minor with few life and death issues. 'But then,' as Norma often reminded him, 'Wasn't that the whole point of bringing the family halfway round the world?

CHAPTER 10

July 2008

JOHN picked up the phone. It was the boss calling. 'Good morning, Captain. How was the tour?' The deep voice was authoritative and direct. For security, they always used indirect references to the names of people and places. 'Good morning, Sir. It was a good experience for team LA4, but they played no active part in the operation. The male is ready, but he continues to question the purpose of the tour. The female is not ready. She seemed to view it as a holiday.'

'The problem with the educated ones is they always ask questions. You must watch them to make sure they don't become a threat. What about the others?'

'Teams A1 and E2 were fine, as always. No complaints there, Sir.'

'Yes, a satisfactory result. All's well that ends well. Did you play any part in the outcome?'

'Do you want me to answer that question, Sir?'

'No, perhaps not. Now, about that other matter, it is agreed his loyalty is in doubt.'

'Is that a green light then?'

'Yes, but we don't want another motor accident. It would look suspicious even if genuine.'

'No, Sir, this one will be different.'

'Good.' The phone went dead.

Captain John held the receiver for a moment before putting it down in the cradle. That's how all the calls ended, never any goodbyes. The boss just hung up the receiver.

John pondered over the discussion. Thomas in team LA4 was developing into a good operative, but he asked too many questions. The best operatives followed their orders without question. Thomas persisted in asking about his team's role in Sharm el-Sheikh. He wouldn't let the matter drop, like a dog with a bone. Questions threatened the COU, and they could become a threat to him if he did not drop his quest for answers.

Sarah in team LA4 seemed loyal and supportive, but did she understand the true nature of her work? John didn't expect a woman to be as effective as his male operatives, though she added another dimension to his unit.

John smiled to himself. He would let Sonny Mutezo handle the 'other matter'. Sonny, in his mid-forties, looked half that, and his high-pitched voice seemed to confirm a young age. In the past, John found him useful, ruthless and without pity, like a pit bull on a postman.

The Fifth Brigade provided John a rich source of recruits. Sonny caught his eye early in the Gukurahundi campaign, where they both made their reputations. Hard, cruel men made up the brigade, but Sonny stood out even in that brutal company. He delighted in the torture and killing of the Ndebele women and children, the old men and the young.

The genocidal campaign was a coming of age for Sonny, and John was wary of him. One day soon, he would have to cut him off before the younger man's notoriety threatened to overtake his own. This was the way of Africa. While he still had the strength, the old lion needed to kill or drive off the young lion. If he did not, the young lion would one day challenge his position as head of the pride.

John was ambitious in both his work and personal life. He didn't like dealing with uneducated people like Sonny, but it was a necessity for now. He recruited Thomas and Sarah as part of his plan to raise the quality of his operatives. John wanted a better class of person in the COU, but the plan was slow in developing, and its success, uncertain. Soon, Thomas and Sarah would have to face a real test of their commitment. Disposing of Sonny might be just the examination he needed for his young recruits.

In his home life, John made a good start. His attractive young wife bore him two children, a girl, Suzie, and a boy named John Junior, of whom he was most proud. He owned a nice home with three servants, including a garden boy, a cook, and a nanny for the children and housework. The children attended the best schools, and John's servants kept his house and garden in an immaculate condition. The front room proved an ideal setting for his collection of antique French clocks, which stood witness to his good taste. He loved the finer things in life and always dressed in imported suits. The best tailors in London and Milan listed Captain John on their books.

When he was ready, John would enter politics. In the interim he would develop his contacts and bide his time. Many people feared him, and he liked that. Once they realised they were not his quarry, they'd become loyal supporters. To some, he represented a benign figure, firm but fair. They hoped to learn from John, but where would his lessons take them? He savoured the idea of shaping fine young talent.

John's farm lay west of Harare, ninety-six kilometres out on the Bulawayo Road, between the small towns of Norton and Chegutu. The war veterans chased the white owner off the farm, but with his contacts, John had no difficulty seeing off the thugs. He rehired the best of the black farm workers and appointed one as farm manager. There was no place on his farm for the semi-retired and older workers, to whom the former white owner promised a comfortable retirement. The war veterans caused minor damage, but the farm operated much as before the invasion.

Other farm invasions saw the eviction of not only the white farmer but also their black farm workers, who became homeless and unemployed. With his approach, John soon won over the farm workers' loyalty. They dropped their allegiance to the white farmer, for whom, many worked for twenty or thirty years. John harboured thoughts of providing military training at the farm for his COU operatives. It could be the genesis of a private militia. The farm was big enough for such a venture to go unnoticed by anyone likely to question his motives.

* * *

John swivelled in his chair, took out the bottle of Scotch and poured himself a large tot over ice. He held it up to the late afternoon light slanting through his office window and admired the colour and clarity.

Yes, John was happy in his business and personal life. He took pride in how he structured the COU. His fee for each job varied according to the task, and payment in US dollar notes came from an unknown source. Whoever paid the bills knew how to spend. His expenses, and the cost of the operatives, came out of his own pocket. It was a good system for him, for he made a handsome profit, and thanks to the secrecy surrounding the COU he paid no tax. The COU was not an official government department, and he ran it as he saw fit.

The voice at the end of the phone was his sole point of contact. John hadn't met the man he referred to as *the boss*, and he didn't know whether his orders originated from an individual or a committee. It didn't matter as he liked it that way. It felt like he was running his own show and he might well have been if he had multiple clients. But for now, his only concern was to keep the boss sweet.

John downed the remnants of his drink. Time for one more. He dropped two fresh ice cubes into his glass and poured himself another Scotch.

CHAPTER 11

19th August 2008

LEVY Mwanawasa died on the nineteenth of August 2008, just seven weeks after his stroke. The news of his death at the Mercy Military Hospital in Clamart, near Paris, came as a shock to his supporters.

Greg Sanders threw his hands up in disgust when he heard the news. 'This whole business stinks. Four days after his stroke, they said he'd died. Even Thabo Mbeki (the South African President) called for a moment's silence. Then, the Zambian High Commission, in Pretoria, called it a hoax. Next, we hear conflicting reports about his condition. The opposition wanted a team of doctors to go to Paris to assess him. Only three weeks ago, they said he was making steady progress. Now, they tell us Mwanawasa has died. There were rumours he died in Egypt, but they held back the news. Many people believe they flew his body to Paris, and he's been dead all this time. What a fiasco!'

Ian sat back in his chair and looked at his father. 'After his car accident in 1991 they set up a commission of inquiry to investigate whether it was an attempted assassination, so he had enemies even back in those days.'

'Bugger it, Ian. No one else will pick up where Mwanawasa left off, least of all the other African leaders.'

'Yeah, Dad, but we're in Australia now, so it's not our problem anymore.'

'That's not the point. Zimbabwe might now become a problem for the whole of Southern Africa. Mwanawasa tried to prevent that. Already, the neighbouring countries are facing a refugee problem. With a collapse of the infrastructure, disease threatens the whole region. Yes, we don't live there anymore, but that doesn't mean we shouldn't care. Zimbabwe's gone from being one of the best countries in Africa to one of the worst. You were too young to appreciate its heyday.'

'No, I wasn't too young; I was sixteen. I remember the *garden boy*, and the *house girl* who did the cleaning and laundry and helped with the cooking. After black rule, the house girl became a *maid*, and the garden boy became a *gardener*. They were both older than you, Dad, as I recall, and all the servants became *domestic workers*. But I'd like to see for myself what's happening in the country now.'

'You'd be mad to go to Zimbabwe. Apart from all the election violence and trouble, the shops all have empty shelves and goods are scarce. People queue at the petrol pumps, sometimes for days, and they even pay others to wait in the queue for them. What would you do with yourself, wasting your time there?'

'I've thought about writing a book, and I'm sure someone could use an experienced business consultant.'

'Are you kidding? What firms would need business consultants? The decent businesses have left the country. Anyway, what's this book you want to write? You've never been interested in writing.'

'A novel set in these difficult times with the country's growing pains might make an interesting story.'

'Hah! Zimbabwe is shrinking, not growing. Where you get these fanciful ideas? You have a good job in Melbourne, and you want to give it up and go on a wild goose chase across Africa. The African nationalists had a slogan, *"Africa for the Africans"*. Let's leave it that way, shall we? And what would your mother say?'

'She would say what she always says, "Why don't you find a nice girl and settle down and start a family?"'

'That's not a bad idea. It's later than you think.'

'Yes, but all I've done is study and work. I need something more exciting, more fulfilling. We're not here to spend our lives at work.'

'Perhaps, your mother can talk sense into you.'

'The country has problems, but I'd like to see the situation for myself. Writers do their best work with first-hand, on-the-spot experience.'

'Oh, so you've not written a single word, but you're a writer now, are you? Anyway, we came to Australia to escape that on-the-spot experience.'

'I'm dead serious, Dad.'

'So am I, Son. Why go looking for trouble?'

'I'm not looking for trouble, but I want to visit the country and see my birthplace through adult eyes.'

'You were born in Rhodesia. That country no longer exists.'

Ian did not respond, and they both sank back into their own thoughts.

* * *

Greg was angry about the fate of Zimbabwe. Ian shared many of his father's feelings, but he'd invested fewer years there, while his father spent most of his life in that country. Greg fought in the Bush War and found it difficult to forget the things he'd seen. He bristled when he heard about the corruption and the violence, but still held hope of justice and peace for his former homeland.

While young Ian was aware of the ongoing Bush War, his focus was on school, sport and friends. He remained unaffected by events until his best friend's father died in a landmine explosion on one of his army call-ups towards the end of the Bush War. It brought home to Ian, the realities of life in Rhodesia. The Bush War ended in December 1979, but violent crime grew because of the abundance of firearms in the country. A lot of the handguns were stolen from white households that kept them for home protection.

One Friday evening, Greg came home with the news they were all going to Australia. To Ian, the country represented kangaroos, koalas, cricket and the Sydney Opera House. Norma relished the prospect of shops without shortages. For Greg it was bittersweet. He didn't want to leave Bulawayo, but how else might his family lead a normal life?

* * *

Ian broke the silence. 'UDI (The Unilateral Declaration of Independence) was the wrong move. What did it achieve?'

'Fifteen more years of civilised, corruption free rule, that's what.'

'But look at the cost. People died in a war that any clear-headed person could see was a lost cause from the beginning.'

'We would have preferred a different outcome,' said Greg. 'Although he never said so, I suspect Ian Smith fought on, giving people time to make their plans to stay or get out on their own terms.'

'He never left,' said Ian, 'that is, until he retired to Cape Town for health reasons.'

'That's true, and as for those international economic sanctions... What a joke! They led to a golden age in Rhodesia, and we manufactured a lot of new products. The country was at war, so when they put international sanctions on us, we ignored their patents. Industry advanced in leaps and bounds. Several countries ignored the sanctions and supplied us with whatever we needed.'

'Ah yes, but they charged a premium price, didn't they?'

'Yes, they did, but our economy was strong, and we rode those premium prices with ease. But then, South Africa withdrew its support, and that threatened our supply lines.'

'Yes, Kissinger and Vorster spoilt the party. First, America threatened South Africa, and then, together, they threatened us.'

'Would you two like tea and cake?' Norma Sanders entered the room carrying a large tray. In Zimbabwe, a maid would have served the tea. Now she carried out all the domestic duties herself, but this hadn't troubled her in the slightest. She was an attractive woman with dark hair and young looking for her age. Norma settled into the Australian way of life much quicker than Greg or Ian. She left the troubles of her homeland behind and seldom spoke of the old days, accepting her new life with good humour. She was used to Greg's irascible ways, and she knew what he'd gone through and how each twist and turn in Zimbabwe's post-independence traumas tore at him.

'I don't miss having servants,' said Norma. 'Not having servants gives us freedom in our own home. We can leave our drawers unlocked now. In Africa, things would often go missing from unlocked cupboards or drawers.'

'Did all the servants steal?' said Ian.

'No, not all, but many did. Who could you blame when more than one servant had access to the house? If I made a big fuss when a piece of jewellery went missing, it would often reappear. Your father used a ball-point pen to mark and date the levels in the Scotch and brandy bottles.'

Ian laughed. 'Ah yes, the evaporation test!'

'We had many loyal and wonderful servants, but others were a headache.'

'Yes, I can see your ad for a house girl,' said Ian. 'Headaches need not apply.'

'We didn't advertise,' said Norma, laughing. 'It was all word of mouth. The system worked well, but if I had to fire the relative or friend, because that's often who they were, you had a sulky house girl on your hands for a few days. But things would soon return to normal.'

'Never employ relatives or friends. It isn't worth the hassle,' said Ian. 'So, you were happy to be rid of the servants?'

'There were pros and cons,' said Norma. 'Servants were a privilege on the one hand, but a big responsibility if they got into trouble. The long-serving servants were like family. It was heartbreaking to leave them.'

'Were you tempted to bring any of the servants with you when you came to Australia?'

'No, not possible,' said Norma. 'They wouldn't want to leave their families.'

'We knew of people who wanted to bring their old house girl or cook with them,' said Greg, 'but the Australian immigration wouldn't allow it.'

'It was very sad,' said Norma. 'One family we knew had their house girl for twenty-five years. When they left Zimbabwe, she seemed in perfect health. She was devastated to see them go and died within three months of them leaving. It wasn't their fault, but they felt responsible.'

'In the old days,' said Greg, 'if you interrupted an African burglar in your house, they would run away. They were seldom violent. These days, it would be dangerous to challenge a burglar. A lot of them are armed, and sometimes they even coerce loyal, old servants to help in robbing their employers.'

'Wow!' said Ian, with a mischievous smile, 'It sounds fascinating, but I'd like to see it for myself.'

'There you go again,' said Greg, 'with your damn silly ideas. You'd soon find out how fascinating it was. The whites who ran into trouble in Zimbabwe all agree the jails were fascinating, but none of them stayed in the country after their release.'

Norma smiled. The banter between Greg and Ian, when they crossed swords, amused her. She recognised Ian's penchant for contentious comments and Greg's tendency to take the bait. There was never any ill will, and soon enough, they'd be laughing and joking together, but Greg held onto his strong views with a passion. Ian also kept his view of things, but he was a little more open to debate. With his easy-going manner, it was sometimes hard to tell what he thought.

'Ian, if you go to Zimbabwe,' said Norma, 'when will you meet a nice girl and settle down and start a family? Time is passing. You won't be young forever.'

'Mum, if it happens, it happens. If you go searching for something, you never find it.'

'Well,' said Greg, 'you won't find it in Zimbabwe, that's for sure.'

'Aren't there enough nice girls here in Australia?' said Norma.

'Yes, but I haven't met them because I've been too busy at work.'

'If you want to write a book, why can't you write it here? Why must you go to Africa to write it?'

'I want to set it in an exotic location. Zimbabwe with all its troubles would be ideal. If I'm there, the book will be more authentic.'

'How long would you stay in Africa?'

'I don't know, maybe six months of research and six months to write the book. I could do the editing back here.'

'What about your job? Will they keep it open for you?'

'I was telling Dad that my life seems to have been all study and work, and I'm sick of it. It's time for a change. I'll search for something else when I return.'

'Life is about looking to your future,' said Greg. 'It's about building a career and taking care of your family, not swanning around following a wild dream.'

'Well, Greg, if that's what Ian wants—'

'The trouble is he's spoilt. He's got too much money, and he thinks life is a game. That was the good thing about Rhodesia. Young men had to do national service, and it made men of them, responsible men.'

'It's a different world today, Greg. Young people have a lot more opportunities. Perhaps Ian should have done this long ago. But it's not too late—'

'At his age, Norma, we were long married and had a child. We had a working farm that fed us and put a roof over our heads.'

'I've been working hard ever since I left university,' said Ian. 'It's time for my gap year.'

'I think it's exciting,' said Norma. 'Have you set a date for the trip? When are you thinking of going?'

'Well, I suppose, after I've finished my current projects at work.'

'Hah!' said Greg, 'Projects overlap. A new one starts before the last one finishes. Don't worry, Norma, he'll never have the chance to get away.'

CHAPTER 12

November 2008

SUNDAY night, and for Ian Sanders that meant dinner at his parents' home. While Norma did the dishes, Ian chatted with Greg. 'No, I'm serious, Dad, I've thought about this for a while. Yes, I have a good job, but something's changed. The CEO (chief executive officer), was happy with me, and I've brought in a lot of business over the last six years. Now, he takes every opportunity to find fault. It's comical how he invents ways to criticise me. Maybe he feels threatened, though I can't imagine why he should. I'd never be interested in his job. Two of my former secretaries said he was jealous of my success, but I never believed it until now.'

'The board must know what you've done for the business?'

'No, I'm not sure they do. Most of the board members, including the chairman, are new. If Thornton hasn't told them, how would they know? He's scared of the chairman, and I suspect he's one of those who takes credit and passes blame. He's changed since the new chairman took control of the board. Thornton used to rely on me for support, but now he's critical of me, almost as though he's hoping I'll get fed up and leave.'

'Why don't you speak to the chairman about it?'

'The chairman is the problem. I'm sure he's ordered Thornton to get rid of me. He calls the shots even though he knows bugger all about the business. Thornton fears losing his job, so he does what he's told. I blame him for not making the situation clear to the board.'

'What about the other directors? Wouldn't they have something to say?'

'No, apart from the Finance Director, they're only there to make up a quorum.'

'It will be their loss if you go.'

'Thornton is weak, and the chairman is overbearing. That, together with a compliant board, is a recipe for disaster. These days, it's no pleasure working there.'

Ian was sure his concerns were valid, so it came as no surprise when a fortnight later the receptionist said, 'Mr Thornton wants to see you. Is half past two OK?'

Paul Thornton, in his late fifties, looked pudgy, sitting behind the desk in his big office. The personnel manager sat to one side, and when Ian looked at her, she averted her eyes. Thornton said, 'Ian you would be aware the GFC (Global Financial Crisis) has taken its toll. Business is down from last year.'

'Uh-huh,' said Ian.

'We have to cut costs.'

'Um,' said Ian.

Thornton shifted in his seat. 'Profits are down, and we can't afford you any longer. The board would like you to finish up today.'

Ian looked Thornton straight in the eye but said nothing. Thornton's right eye twitched. 'We considered other positions for you in the company, but there's nothing suitable.'

The corners of Ian's mouth curled in a wry smile. The letter was burning a hole in his jacket pocket. 'My department has a positive cash flow, but the allocated admin charges are too high. Almost all the increase in those fees is because of board projects and the various consultants you've engaged. None of those costs benefit my department.'

'Yes, well, the board's decided, so it's out of my hands. You will receive your annual leave and pay in lieu of notice.' Thornton shook his head and whistled through his teeth as if to suggest the amount was excessive. 'It's quite a large figure when you include your pro rata long service leave.' He leant back in his chair and crossed his fingers with thumbs raised, looking smug. The men locked eyes, in silence.

After a pause, Ian reached for the letter in his jacket pocket. 'The board has also agreed on an ex gratia payment. In total it comes to a hundred grand.' Ian let the letter fall back inside his jacket pocket. 'Thanks,' he said, trying not to sound too sarcastic. If he gave the letter to Thornton now, he could miss out on the ex gratia payment. Writing his resignation letter was fun, and he looked forward to giving it to Thornton, but it wasn't worth risking the ex gratia money.

Thornton's instructions were to get rid of Ian as cheaply as possible and with little or no fuss. Ian's lack of response and direct eye contact pressured Thornton. He'd hoped to get away with paying the minimum legal entitlements, and it annoyed him he felt compelled to offer more. He knew the extra payment would come out of his own bonus.

Ian made a lot of money for the business, but now, they wasted it on a dozen consultants and fancy new offices. He was happy to be going. The puzzled look on the faces of Thornton and the personnel manager amused Ian. He guessed they wondered why he took the news so well. Stupid bastards! He'd be glad to be rid of them, even without the ex gratia payment.

* * *

The news of Ian's redundancy surprised his secretary, Louise Ross. For several weeks, he'd talked of leaving, and she'd suggested, in that case, she might also leave. Louise worked with Ian for six years and was a friend and confidant, though they'd not socialised outside work. Now and then, Louise invited Ian to a party or drinks at her house, but he'd always declined. He didn't mix business with pleasure, and for him, the former came first. Louise was in her forties and about eight to ten years older than Ian. He'd not viewed her as anything other than a capable secretary. Pretty, with blond hair and innocent blue eyes, her fair skin threatened to age early in the hot Australian sun.

Often, when Ian explained some detail of work to Louise, she would stand next to his chair to get a clearer view of the computer screen. Sometimes, she stood so close, her hips would brush his shoulder as he sat at his desk. For Ian it passed unnoticed. When he told Louise about his redundancy, she insisted he drop by for a drink at her place on his way home. Why not? He needed a drink.

Ian knew where Louise lived. He once dropped her home when her car was in for repairs overnight at the garage. He'd never been inside her house before, and it surprised him how cosy it looked. She left the office half an hour before him and started a fire in the huge open fireplace. The weather was unseasonably cool, and the fire made the open-plan living area inviting. Louise changed into a loose kaftan gown and looked most attractive. It was a different look from the business suit and glasses she wore to work each day. She switched on her sound system, and Richard Burton's silky-smooth voice introduced Jeff Wayne's War of the Worlds.

'Where are your girls?' said Ian, enquiring about Louise's two preteen daughters. 'They're staying at my mum's place for the next two weeks. She loves having them, and it gives me a break. Take off your jacket and tie and sit on the cushions in front of the fire.' Louise poured a beer for Ian and a gin and tonic for herself. 'Why don't you take your shoes off and warm your feet? Isn't it cosy? I love sitting here in the evenings.' Louise laid cushions on the floor, creating a gentle slope up to the low settee.

Ian lay back on the bank of sloping cushions with his head and shoulders resting against the sofa. Louise lay on her stomach, resting on her elbows on the cushions beside him, chatting about his plans, office gossip and the music playing in the background. Ian was relaxed and comfortable. Louise fixed his gaze with her innocent blue eyes. 'Ian, may I kiss you?'

He hesitated. Well, what's a kiss between friends? 'Er, yes, why not?' She moved closer, and their lips met. Her breath was fresh, and her lips were soft and warm and searching, and they lingered. It wasn't the kiss he'd expected, but he liked it.

They broke apart and chatted for a few minutes. Then Louise said, 'May I kiss you again?' This time he put his arms around her and held her to him, during the long and hungry kiss. They melted into each other, warm and cosy and delicious. Ian stroked Louise's back. 'Do you like your back tickled?'

'Mmm, yes I do.' Ian slid his hand down the back of Louise's loose-fitting kaftan. Darn! She wore a singlet.

The music stopped, and Louise got up to change the disc. She sat down on the cushions next to him. 'Would you like me to take off my camisole?'

'Yes, that would be nice,' he said, imagining she would go to her bedroom to remove it, but she stayed seated next to him. Louise undid the string bow at her front and let the kaftan fall to her waist. She wore a thin white camisole with a delicate knitted pattern. 'Mmm, nice vest, he said.' Louise pulled the camisole over her head, and her long blond hair fell in a copper coloured cascade in the firelight. 'Mmm, nice chest,' said Ian, looking at Louise sitting there in her lace bra.

'Oh well,' said Louise, unclipping her bra, 'in for a penny, in for a pound.'

'Mmm, nice breast,' he said. They both laughed.

'I know I have nice breasts. I've always had nice breasts.'

Louise's breasts were magnificent. Ian took them in his hands and drew her gently to him, resuming their kissing in a passionate orgy of lips, breasts and hands. Louise let her right hand carelessly come to rest on Ian's groin, where there was no disguising the effect she had on him. Was it deliberate? He supposed it must have been when moments later, Louise brought her hands up to his belt buckle. 'Let's see what we have here,' she said, as she undid his belt and buttons at the top of his trousers. She slid open his fly and went down on him with her head bobbing greedily.

Soon he was ready. 'Be careful,' he warned, 'I might...'

She ignored him or didn't hear.

Louise ran her tongue around the edge of her lips. She had a mischievous smile at the corners of her mouth. 'There you are, that wasn't so bad, was it? Now, what were you saying?'

In no time, Ian was ready again. This time Louise lifted the hem of her kaftan and straddled him, guiding him home with a slow gentle movement of her hips. Ian held her beautiful breasts and used his tongue and lips to gorge himself on her erect nipples. They'd both been through a dry spell and soon came together in a shuddering climax.

'You'd never have let this happen if you hadn't been leaving,' Louise said.

Yes, she was right, and he'd never have known what he missed.

At half past two in the morning, Louise walked Ian to the gate where he'd parked his car. 'Thank you for coming.'

'Thank you for having me. Oh, we might have swopped our lines.' They both laughed. Ian opened the door and stepped into his car. 'Thank goodness it's Saturday, and we can lie-in in the morning.'

Louise was on Ian's mind a lot that weekend. She'd been magnificent. The other girls he'd known just lay there and passively accepted what came. Louise was the first sexually aggressive woman he'd met. He realised she'd planned the whole thing. For her it worked like clockwork, but he didn't mind at all.

After that night, Ian was a regular visitor to Louise's house.

CHAPTER 13

December 2008

SAM Kagonye wanted at least one son, but his wife bore him two daughters. 'Two children are enough,' said his wife Esther. If he couldn't have a son, he decided he would call his second daughter Samantha, the nearest thing to his own name. Esther, his wife, would have none of it. 'They will shorten her name to Sam, and I'm not having two Sams in the house at the same time.'

'OK then, let's call her Clementine.'

'Don't be silly.'

Sam was a gentle soul, and often his only means of disagreeing with his wife was through suggestions he knew she wouldn't accept, but it seldom worked. As usual, Esther's view prevailed. After much debate, they settled on *Sarah*. Esther narrowed it down to the name she favoured from the beginning.

Jemma and Sarah adored their father, and he loved them. Sam and Esther brought them up to be fine young women. Both parents were tall and slim and blessed with good looks which the girls inherited.

Esther was an English teacher when they first met. Sam admired her clear thinking. Progressive in their outlook, they did not follow the old ways. They brought up their daughters to be open-minded. Esther stressed upon the girls the need to be well spoken, and she did her best to improve their command of English. Sam was their moral compass, and he instilled in them the need for good morals, ethics and principles. 'A reputation is hard won but easily lost,' he would tell them.

Jemma, though bright and intelligent, didn't attend high school past midway through the first year. She was gentle and trusting, too trusting in Sarah's opinion. Her time at Wits influenced Sarah, and it gave her a harder edge. Both girls possessed enquiring minds but an element of distrust sharpened Sarah's.

The family lived in a small two-bedroom house in Hatfield, an old African suburb in the southern part of Harare. Sam caught a bus to the city each morning and then walked from the bus terminus to the party offices where he worked. Six months earlier, Sam bought an old Mini Minor that spent much of its time in the workshop for repairs. Somehow, they kept it going, but when it was in for repairs or petrol was unavailable, Sam took the bus. It gave him the opportunity to catch up with his old acquaintances.

The country's direction since majority rule in 1980 disappointed Sam. At first things went well. Even the whites were happy. It all changed when Mugabe saw the MDC as a threat to him. ZANU-PF won the year 2000 elections by a narrow margin. In response, Mugabe encouraged the war veterans' invasion of white-owned commercial farms. He hoped it would shore up his popularity, but he allotted the farms to his cronies, most of whom knew nothing about farming. They evicted the white owners and their black farm workers, so the farms became derelict. The country could no longer feed itself. People starved and needed international food aid. The eviction of Mr Marais and the black farm workers from their farm between Norton and Chegutu (formerly Hartley) upset Sam. 'Thank goodness my parents didn't live to see what's happening to this country. They would have been heartbroken to lose their old home.' The violence surrounding the 2008 presidential election was worse than ever and was a turning point for Sam. He spoke to Esther about it.

'The economy is in dire straits. If it gets any worse, we'll soon be a failed state. Look what's happening now. The beatings, mutilations and killings are too much for me. I can't stomach it. What happened to one man one vote?'

'Don't talk like that in front of anyone else. It could be dangerous. You have a good job in the party's admin department. Focus on your work and forget about the politics.'

Sam knew his wife was right, and he followed her advice. He took care to show no outward signs of his reservations about the country's direction. But it was hard to keep up an act, and often he had to bite his tongue. Sam was not in the best frame of mind, and his work colleagues soon picked up on the change in him. Moses Mutasa, one of Sam's admin assistants, caught him off guard one evening. 'Sam, what do you think of the party's plans for the future?'

The question concerned Sam. 'We have wise leaders who know what's best for the country. Why do you ask?'

'It seems you're a little less keen these days. You have been missing drinks after work, and you don't attend all the meetings like you once did.'

'That's a stupid thing to say,' Sam snapped. He regretted the sharpness of his tone, so he tried to make light of it. 'You will have the answer to your question when you reach my age. I feel tired these days, and my wife hasn't been too well.' The question troubled Sam, and he worried his response might have sounded like an excuse. If Moses Mutasa questioned Sam's commitment to the party, who else might? What if Moses expressed his doubts to someone else? Rumours can spread like a bush fire, but Sam couldn't see how anyone would have known his concerns about the party's direction. He only spoke of it to Esther.

After his discussion with Moses Mutasa, Sam made sure he attended every meeting open to him. He also joined his colleagues for drinks after work more often. But he did not want Moses to think his comments forced him to react. That might look even more suspicious. Sam's concerns grew when he perceived his invitations to the higher-level meetings had decreased. Was he being sidelined? The country's circumstances should have called for even more meetings, not less. Over the next few days, Sam tried to put the whole thing out of his mind, but it kept on coming back. It would pop into his head at odd times during the day and night, and he felt the building pressure.

Sam consoled himself with the thought Sarah was doing well. Last month she was in Sharm el-Sheikh, and now, at Wits, in Joburg, on a two-week Portuguese refresher course. He understood how the party worked. If he were under a cloud, they wouldn't be investing in her.

Thursday afternoon, two days before Sarah's scheduled return, Sam sat in his office, waiting to pick up his car from the garage at half past five. The car was costing him money, and he regretted not having saved a little longer to buy one in better condition. The phone rang as he was about to leave. It was the garage. They did not have the required spare part. 'Can you leave the car overnight and pick it up tomorrow?'

'Yes, OK, I'll catch the bus home.'

Sam worked on and left his office a little later than usual. By the time he reached the bus terminus it was dusk. He recognised Amos Moyo, an old friend who lived close to Sam.

'Hello, Sam, slumming it again I see.'

'Yes, Amos, car trouble as usual.'

They'd been friends for at least ten years. Often, Sam would stop and give Amos a lift home if he saw him walking along the street. It wasn't a regular thing because their working hours didn't always coincide. This evening, they chatted away at the bus terminus and on the bus. The troubled times gave them plenty of topics to discuss.

When they alighted, it was dark. They crossed the busy main road and walked down the dimly lit street towards Sam's house nearby. The street was about a hundred metres long with a single street light at the half-way mark. The large jacaranda trees met overhead and moved with the rhythm of the breeze. Near the street light, they cast ghostly, swaying shadows onto the road surface, but the greater part of the street was in darkness. Set back from the avenue of jacarandas, bushes grew on both sides of the street. Ahead of them, beyond the street light, a group of youths kicked around a tin can in an impromptu game of soccer. Two of them used knobkerries to hit the tin as if on a golf driving range. It was in one of the darker spots. Why didn't they play under the street light? Idle youths were always a potential source of trouble, and Sam and Amos were on their guard, but one youth surprised them when he spoke.

'Where are you old men going?'

'We're going home for dinner, and so should you,' said Sam.

'Ah! You're Sam Kagonye, are you not?'

'How do you know my name?'

'It doesn't matter.' The youth turned to Amos. 'And what is your name, old man?'

'I'm Amos Moyo.'

'Off you go, Amos. I want to talk to my friend Sam here.'

'I must wait for him.'

'No, you mustn't, old man.' And with that, the youth struck Amos a hard blow on the ankle with the knobkerrie.

Amos struggled to walk, but terrified, he somehow hobbled off at a fair pace.

Esther heard the urgent knocking at her door.

'Mr Moyo, what is it? You are puffed out and shaking.'

'Mrs Kagonye, a gang of youths have held up Sam a block down the road. I'm afraid they might harm him. They hit my ankle with a knobkerrie and said I had to leave.'

The news alarmed Esther. 'Jemma, quick, come with me, your father might be in trouble. Mr Moyo, please call the police.'

Amos Moyo still stood at the front door, shuffling his feet. 'I'm not a coward, Mrs Kagonye, but there's nothing I could do.'

'Hurry, Mr Moyo. Go home and call the police.' Esther threw down her tea towel, grabbed Jemma's arm, and ran out on to the street, leaving the front door wide open.

In their haste, neither Esther nor Jemma thought to find a weapon of sorts to take with them. They ran as fast as they could to the spot Mr Moyo told them. When they arrived, they found Sam lying in the middle of the road, bleeding from cuts to his head and face. Five youths stood around him. Two of them held knobkerries.

'Stay away from my husband,' Esther yelled. Jemma stood beside her, aghast.

'Ah! The family has arrived,' said a young man, holding a knobkerrie. 'This is the punishment for traitors.'

'He is not a traitor. He works at the ZANU-PF offices in the city.'

The young man smirked, looking at Jemma. 'You must be my reward. Come with me.' He grabbed Jemma by the arm, but Esther rushed at him and scratched his face with her nails. The young man shouted with pain and dropped Jemma's arm. Suddenly, a police car turned into the street from the main road. A youth shouted something, and in an instant, they all dissolved into the darkness on either side of the street.

The police car arrived by chance and not in response to Amos' call. The police did not seem too concerned about Sam's condition. 'Go to the police station in the morning, and make a formal statement,' they said to Esther. Amos had called for an ambulance when he arrived home. It arrived forty minutes later and 'rushed' Sam to hospital.

Esther and Jemma made their own way to the hospital and spent the whole night waiting in the emergency department with Sam. Sick and injured people, lying on stretchers and trollies or on the floor, filled the crowded emergency department. Others were in wheelchairs or sitting on benches. Some bled, and others groaned or cried out in pain, and a few appeared to have died. Worried relatives did their best to look after them. It was a picture of hell. Injured people were coming in, but the nurses still went off on their tea breaks. There was no sense of urgency, and the staff moved without haste. They appeared tired and overwhelmed. The hospital was short of staff and short of equipment and medicine.

At ten in the morning, hospital orderlies took Sam into the operating theatre, and Esther and Jemma waited and worried. Would he be OK? He was still unconscious when they wheeled him away.

At last! Late in the morning a young doctor came out to speak to them. Esther and Jemma stood up as the doctor approached. It was terrible news. Sam died on the operating table from a fractured skull and internal injuries. 'Even if he survived, he would never have fully recovered,' the doctor said. 'Maybe it's for the best.' Esther took the news in the stoic African fashion, but Jemma couldn't hold back her sobs and tears.

'What is Sarah going to say?' Jemma sobbed, holding on to Esther's arm. 'She will come back tonight all happy from her trip, and then she will get the terrible news.'

Esther did not have an answer.

CHAPTER 14

December 2008

SARAH raged at the news of her father's murder. It brought back memories of Kemi at Wits. She vowed never again would she or a loved one be a helpless victim. Nothing would bring her father back, but he wouldn't go unavenged.

Her father was her guiding light and the source of her beliefs and values. He supported the party and so did she. She'd accepted her job with the COU because she supported her father's views, but now her mother spoke of his reservations about the party's direction.

Esther worried that somehow, he must have betrayed his true feelings to someone other than her. Sam wouldn't have been so stupid as to talk about his views to anyone else, but how did they discover his qualms? The youth called him a traitor. A throwaway comment, maybe, or perhaps the youth tried to justify his actions? But how did he know Sam's name?

Sarah swung between grief and rage. Who attacked her father? A random attack seemed unlikely. So many high-ranking party officials died in mysterious circumstances.

'Jemma, have you seen those youths before that night? Would you recognise them?'

'I've only seen them that one time, but I would recognise the leader, the one who spoke in a high voice like a girl. Mama scratched his face when he grabbed my arm.'

'Tomorrow is Saturday, so we have the whole weekend to find them. We'll visit the places and areas those sorts go.'

The next day, after a sleepless night, the girls searched for the youths who'd attacked their father. Esther warned them to be careful, and she worried that they might recognise Jemma.

'Don't worry Mama,' said Sarah. 'We're not silly. We'll be careful.'

At work, Sarah told Jedson about the attack, but he did not seem too interested in the news, and he mumbled his condolences. She found his response puzzling and put it down to him being busy in his work. He seemed preoccupied, but she found his lack of empathy disappointing.

Sarah found Thomas supportive, but their hidden relationship often proved to be a stumbling block. She did not tell him about her search for her father's killers because he wouldn't approve. If her search somehow exposed their relationship, they might both be in trouble.

The girls spent the next two weekends in an unrewarding hunt for the killers. 'If we don't find them soon,' said Sarah, 'the youth's scratches will heal and make it even more difficult to identify him.'

On the Monday after the second weekend of fruitless search, Jemma came home from work excited and impatient for Sarah's return that evening.

'Sarah, Sarah, guess what! I'm sure I saw the gang leader this evening, the one with the scratches. He walked past the bus terminus at a quarter to six, and that's when I saw him. I followed him, and he entered a house nearby. He might have come home from work.'

'Can you meet me after work at the bus terminus tomorrow evening? I will be there at half past five, and then you can show me the house. We'll wait for him to come home, and you can take another look at him to make sure it's the right person.'

The next evening, the two girls met at the bus terminus as arranged. Both wore baseball caps pulled well down to cover as much of their faces as possible. A five-minute walk from the bus terminus, they turned into a street and Jemma said, 'That's it, the house with the high grey wall.' Sarah stepped back in disbelief. It was her workplace.

'Are you sure, Jemma? Are you positive that's the house? Didn't that man at the gate stop him when he tried to enter?'

'No, when the youth arrived, he waved to him.'

'Are you sure it was him? Did he have scratches on his face? Let's wait here, and you can have another look at him when he comes.'

By six o'clock there was still no sign of the youth, but Sarah saw Jedson leave. Was he connected to the youth with the high-pitched voice? Might the youth be the leader of the gang that attacked their father? Did Jedson know of the attack beforehand or before she told him? Was she sent on the Portuguese refresher course in Johannesburg to get her out of the way? Why didn't Thomas also attend the course?

'Jemma, we must wait here each evening until he comes again. This area is so busy no one will notice us standing here.' Sarah's mind was in turmoil that night, and she struggled to sleep as the questions swirled in her head.

The youth didn't turn up that week. Could Jemma have been mistaken? But she'd pointed out the COU offices. It was too much of a coincidence.

* * *

After the death of her father, Sarah found it hard to approach her work with any great enthusiasm. She didn't understand Jedson's strange lack of interest in her father's murder. But he seemed so nice, and she found it hard to believe he would involve himself in such a diabolical act. With the secrecy in the COU, Jedson may well have known nothing about it.

Sarah understood the need for secrecy but found it excessive. Secrecy was fine as far as outsiders went, but within the COU itself? That was taking things too far. Captain John and those working in the rear of the building even used a separate entrance at the back of the property. Only team LA4, it seemed, regularly used the front entrance. Jedson parked his car in the front yard. Sometimes one or two other cars parked there, but Sarah never saw who drove them. With her office door always closed, she felt isolated. The extreme secrecy kept her off balance. Was that its real purpose? She didn't know what to think.

Would she follow orders without question? Sarah was, now, not sure. She knew the COU dealt with dissidents. Were they behind the mysterious deaths of high-profile figures? Now that her family was on the receiving end of an attack, it made her think twice. Her father's loyalty to the party did not save him. Could she inflict such trauma on any other family?

Christmas approached; the first without her father. Sarah loved the family meals and relaxing together over the Christmas break. It was always the four of them: Sam, Esther, Jemma and herself. This year would be different. Sarah couldn't shake off her depression.

On the Friday morning before Christmas, Sarah sat at her desk when Jedson walked into her office. 'Sarah, the country is going through a difficult period, and the government is short of money. All departments must make cost cuts. I'm afraid I cannot afford to keep you on the team any longer. Today is your last day.'

The news shocked Sarah, but also gave her a sense of relief. She valued the experience and training in her job, and she'd miss that. She would also miss working with Thomas though they didn't work together as often as she'd expected. But Sarah worried where her job might lead, and now she felt a great weight lifted from her shoulders. She wouldn't miss the quiet, dull office. Another concern was Thomas' second contract which he'd signed only earlier that week.

Was Jedson's budget the real reason behind her termination, or was it somehow connected to her father? The gang of youths accused him of being a traitor. It was just a few days since she and Jemma began their vigil at the COU. Perhaps someone noticed them watching the building? They'd taken care to stay out of sight of the guard at the entrance.

As one door closes, another opens. She always tried to find the positives in every situation. She needed the money, but finding work in Harare, in the current economic climate? Where would she start? Even before she got home with the news, Sarah planned for her changed circumstances. Where might her language skills come in useful? If the government wasn't cutting costs, the Ministry of Foreign Affairs would be a good choice. The better hotels, with their international visitors, might be a possibility.

After the weekend, Sarah approached the leading hotels about a job. But as she feared, the hotels were not hiring. Her language skills could be useful on the front desk when the foreign tourist numbers revived. The supply of fresh water was a problem, and cholera raged. It was a bad time for hotels, and they suggested she come back in a few months when conditions might have improved. Occupancy rates were steady thanks to an increase in the number of domestic guests, but her language skills were no advantage there. The Monomotapa Hotel needed a room maid. The job required a fit person, and that suited Sarah. Because of the secrecy surrounding the COU, she couldn't get a work reference from her former employer. From the hotel's perspective, she couldn't show any work experience. She had little choice when she took the job. She was to report for duty on the Monday after Christmas, so she would miss only one week of work. The rate of pay was much lower than she'd earned at the COU, but it would do for now.

Starting time for Sarah would be seven in the morning. Six-and-a-half hours of the day was for making up guest rooms. Lunch and tea breaks would take up one hour, and the final hour of the day was for refilling the service trolleys in readiness for the next morning. Finishing time was half past three in the afternoon.

* * *

Half past five in the evening, and Sarah and Jemma once again watched the COU offices. Sarah reflected on the job interview that morning. The mundane nature of the work concerned her, though the position held the prospect of future opportunities. Suddenly, Jemma tugged at her sleeve.

'Sarah, there he is. That's the one who spoke to Mama and me and then grabbed my arm. Watch if he goes into that building again.' He did. The girls were not close enough to see if the youth showed any sign of the scratches Esther inflicted three weeks earlier.

'Jemma, you go home now, and I'll follow him when he comes out. It would be dangerous if he recognised you.' Jemma was reluctant to leave, but Sarah insisted.

Within thirty minutes, the youth emerged from the offices and turned left into the street. The area close to the COU offices was still busy with people going home. Sarah walked parallel to the youth as he strode along the pavement on the opposite side of the road. But when he crossed to her side, she fell back to a safe distance. If he were with the COU, he would be familiar with tailing techniques, and he would also be quick to recognise if someone followed him.

After half a dozen blocks, Sarah broke off for home, but it frustrated her when the youth again did not appear for the rest of the week.

CHAPTER 15

January 2009

DAY one in a new job can seem endless as the minutes drag. It was the same when Sarah started at the COU. At last, it was half past three, but there were still two hours to kill before her watch at the COU offices. There'd been no sign of the youth since the last Monday, but today he was back. It seemed he only came on Mondays. When he entered the offices, Sarah walked to where she'd left off when she last followed him. Then, when he appeared, she again followed him for a short distance before breaking off and going home. In this way she remained unnoticed.

It frustrated Sarah when the youth did not appear the next Monday, but she realised she needed to be patient, and sure enough, he turned up the following week. She continued her tactic of following the youth for a short distance for another two Mondays. Then at last, she was familiar with the entire route and identified where the youth lived.

Sarah noted the address and turned for home. She'd walked two blocks, when a gang of young men approached her. One produced a knife, another a bicycle chain, and a third carried a knobkerrie. The biggest didn't appear to be armed, but he seemed to be the leader. 'Where are you going, girl?'

'I'm going home.'

'First you must pay a toll to the Dragons. This is our area, and anyone who passes through it must pay a toll.'

'I haven't any money.'

'Girls don't need money.'

The expectant gang of young men smirked as they surrounded Sarah. The unarmed young man did the talking. 'Where do you live?'

Sarah ignored the question while she considered her options. If she tried to force her way past the one with the knife, she might be stabbed. A heavy blow from the knobkerrie could be fatal. The bicycle chain was a more ponderous weapon which she might elude if she was quick. The leader did not carry a weapon, but he looked the biggest and strongest.

'Have you fucked four men before?' said the leader grabbing his crotch. The gang planned to rape her. Sarah girded herself to run, but her legs felt weak and trembled, and her throat was dry, and her heart banged inside her chest.

'We'll take you to a quiet, dark spot and give you a good time.'

'Like hell you will.' Sarah did not feel as brave as she tried to sound.

The leader took a step towards Sarah and reached out. In a flash she acted. She lunged between the youth with the knobkerrie and the one with the bicycle chain, too close for the former to swing the club. Sarah struck him hard, just under his ribs. He cried out and dropped the knobkerrie. The youth with the chain swung at her, but it caught the youth with the knobkerrie and wrapped around his head with a loud, swishing crack. He screamed in agony and fell to the ground. With her left hand, Sarah gave the youth with the chain a rabbit punch to the side of his neck. He dropped the chain and pulled away; his eyes wide in panic. Sarah broke through the circle, but a hand grabbed the collar of her jacket. She turned to face the leader.

'What's going on here?' A booming voice called out nearby. The gang members' heads turned as one to look at the intruder. In a flash, Sarah brought her right knee up to crash into the gang leader's crotch. The man yelped in pain and doubled over, just as Sarah's left knee smashed into his nose. Blood splattered over his face and he shrieked in pain and shock.

The gang turned and fled with their leader loping in agony after them. Sweet timing triumphed over brute force once Sarah's COU training kicked in to end the confrontation. Only the youth with the knife escaped unscathed. Sarah flushed with her success, brimmed with a newfound confidence. In the space of a few seconds she'd gone from being a scared young woman to a ferocious beast.

Two men came to Sarah. 'Are you OK? Did those boys hurt you?'

'No, you came at the right time. Thank you.'

'We'd better walk with you until you're out of this area, in case they come back.'

'Don't worry, they won't be back.'

Despite her protests, the two men insisted on accompanying Sarah back to the main road. She thanked them again and made her way back to the bus station to catch a bus home. The bus station after dark was not the safest place for a young woman alone. She'd faced more than enough excitement for one day.

Sarah resolved not to go back to the area unarmed. If she met that gang of bullies again, she would be ready for them. The incident scared her, but it also gave her a new confidence in her ability to protect herself. The COU training stood up to the test, and she knew now she'd been a good student. Sarah also realised she was ready to face the man who'd killed her father.

* * *

In her school years and while at university, Sarah concentrated on her studies. She had little in the way of domestic chores, and her mother and older sister did most of the housework and cooking. Now and then Jemma would object to Sarah's exemption from housework. 'Education comes first,' her parents had said. This response stung Jemma who'd missed out on high school.

'But Sarah needs to know about housework.' Jemma would protest.

For Sarah, working in the hotel was a new experience, and she set about the work with a ferocious energy. The hours and physical work were no problem, but she found it hard to deal with the lack of intellectual stimulation. Sarah was the brightest of the lot, but she didn't react when the more experienced maids treated her like an ignorant junior. Cleaning baths and toilets, making beds, emptying bins and tidying up after guests was not part of her career plan, but the harder and better she worked, the quicker she might advance. She'd read of people who'd started out in the lowliest of jobs and ended up running the company. Perhaps the hotel business might be right for her. With luck, she could move on to the reception desk and further. One step at a time. Focus on the job at hand.

Sarah soon learnt the routine, and her physical strength and agility made the job a breeze. Soon enough, she had her own row of guest rooms, and before she knew it, she was a senior room maid. She ignored the petty jealousies this aroused in a few of the longer serving maids.

Despite her good progress, Sarah found it difficult to focus her mind on her new career. There was a distraction, a big one. Ever since her father's death she'd been plotting to avenge him. That was her number one goal and focus. She could think of little else.

CHAPTER 16

January 2009

SOON, Ian would leave Australia. He booked and paid for his flight. Had he been too hasty? Louise never tried to dissuade him from going though he was sure she held strong feelings for him. He supposed they would pick up where they'd left off when he returned.

Ian reflected on how important dates crept up on one. First, departure was an age away, weeks away, days away, and then, oh no! It's tomorrow.

Ian's mother, Norma, always encouraged and supported him in his plans, but she was nervous about him going back to Zimbabwe in such troubled times. His father, Greg, was more concerned about him wasting his time and money. If he'd known about Ian's relationship with Louise, he would have had no hesitation in using it to encourage him to stay. Ian rented out his furnished apartment through a reliable estate agent. It was an ongoing source of income for him, and Greg would keep an eye on things while he was away. With his affairs wrapped up, it was time to go. Ian had never been without a job before, and he would have been lying if he denied having qualms about the step he now took.

Ian kissed Louise goodbye the night before his flight. Cell phones, Skype and the internet made it easier than it might otherwise have been. Before he knew it, he stood with Greg and Norma in the Tullamarine international departure terminal. Ian and his parents arrived early and headed the queue when the check-in counters opened. He travelled light with only a carry-on backpack, and this gave Greg and Norma the comfortable feeling he was going on a short holiday. Ian was flying to Perth on Qantas, and from there he would catch a South African Airways Airbus to Johannesburg. The trip was about fifteen hours of flight time and a five-hour stopover in Perth. Twenty hours in total. With plenty of time before Ian's flight, they went to buy coffee.

'Now don't forget to walk around and move your feet when you're sitting.' said Norma, 'You don't want to get DVT.'

'Son,' said Greg, 'when you're in Bulawayo, don't forget to have a look at our old house. See what they're doing to it.'

Norma looked at her watch. 'Looks like it's time to go. The stopover in Perth is almost five hours, and you'll arrive in Johannesburg around four in the afternoon, exhausted I expect.'

Ian picked up his backpack. 'Don't worry, Mum, I will call you once I am through immigration and customs.'

Greg shook his hand, 'Take care Son.' Norma looked like she would cry. Ian was travelling to a distant and dangerous place with no set return date. One last wave and he turned and walked through to the security check.

Greg took Norma's arm. 'Don't worry love, he'll be back soon. Once he's over there, he'll find out his fancy ideas are not all that exciting.'

Norma looked up at Greg. 'No, I want him to succeed and grow. He's spent too much time studying and working, and now he needs to find a balance in his life and broaden his horizons away from the comforts of home.'

Greg frowned. 'Yes, Dear, but he needs to settle down, don't you think? If he takes too much longer, we'll miss out on grandchildren. His steady girlfriends have never lasted. But it's true what you say, kids stay around home too long these days. At least he's lived on his own. That's more than we can say for some we've met. But wasting his time in Africa, what's that going to achieve? That secretary of his he introduced us to, she seemed nice.'

Norma smiled. 'Oh no, Dear, she's much too old for him, and she already has two children. I don't think Ian's ready for that.'

* * *

Ian found his seat in business class and stowed his backpack and mid-blue, crush-resistant sports jacket in the overhead locker. He wore black stretch jeans, black walking shoes and a white polo shirt. In his backpack he carried a lightweight, navy blue windcheater, a pair of beige flannels, blue stretch jeans and a light-blue, crew-neck jumper. Two business shirts, another two polo shirts and a pair of dark brown business shoes completed his wardrobe.

A well-dressed woman stowed her hand luggage in the overhead locker they shared. She was business class in every sense of the word. Ian was conscious of his casual attire.

'Hello, I'm Ruth Bernstein,' she said, shaking Ian's hand. She had a lovely smile and a friendly face. 'Is your trip for business or pleasure?' She looked in her late forties and clearly a seasoned traveller.

'I'm visiting friends in Joburg and then flying on to Harare where I'm planning to research and write a novel set in Zimbabwe.'

'Oh! Be careful with your book. They don't trust journalists. How are you financing your trip? There're no jobs there these days.'

Ruth explained at length the troubles in the country. Ian followed events in Zimbabwe through the media, but Ruth filled in the gaps.

'You will need to be alert. Corruption is rife, and you don't know which government officials you can trust. Watch out for the police and don't think you can rely on the courts. Even the Anglican Church has its problems. The Anglican Bishop of Harare, the Right Reverend Chad Gandiya, and his supporters must hold their services in the open air. A rival bishop broke away from the main body and started his own branch of the Anglican Church. With the help of the police and security services he took over the church and all its properties, leaving ninety percent of the Anglican congregation without a church. The rival bishop, a great supporter of Mugabe, called him a second Moses. The reward for his loyalty was one of the invaded commercial farms. There were claims he even ordered the murder of clergy who did not support him. That's the Zimbabwe you will find.'

Ruth knew when to chat and when to keep quiet. She was full of interesting news about Zimbabwe. Much of it spread through local channels of gossip rather than the media. Even if it made the local media, it was not mainstream stuff. It occurred to him that Ruth might be a contact who could give him local perspective and lend credibility to his novel. Ian always enjoyed the meals and refreshments on international flights. He watched a movie, walked down the plane's aisles and took a short but restful nap. The attentive air hostess kept him supplied with water to drink.

The tiredness brought on by the stress of air travel soon receded, and he took Louise's letter out of his jacket pocket. She made him promise not to open it until airborne.

My Dearest Ian,

We've had a wonderful two months together, and you know I love you. I'm sure you must have wondered why I never tried to encourage you to stay in Australia.

You will recall I talked of the possibility of getting back together with my husband for the sake of my two girls. When you and I got together, I put the idea on hold. I separated from my husband two years ago, and now I must decide before it's too late and the girls have grown up and left home.

I believe it's only fair to both you and me, to let you be free to follow your dream. You couldn't do that if our relationship hung over you as a constant distraction.

The future is open for us both. Who knows what it may hold? I wish you every success and happiness.

My love always,

Louise xx

Louise's letter did not come as a complete surprise as she'd talked in the past about the girls needing their father. Ian read the letter twice more to see if it held any prospect of them getting back together. No, it seemed final.

This was not Ian's first disappointment in love. He'd experienced the same hollow sensation in his stomach before, and it was part of the reason he made his work his life. He was familiar with the course his feelings would take. First, could he prevent what was happening? Perhaps an urgent phone call or email might get her to change her mind. Then a sense of helplessness would follow. There was little he could do. Next there would be anger. She'd used him. Disbelief would follow. Didn't she realise how much he loved her? Loneliness and longing would be followed by a growing acceptance that would lead to a sense of release. Finally, indifference would take hold, and that would bring freedom. Louise would be just a pleasant memory.

This was the process Ian expected to go through over the next few days, weeks, or months. But there would be cycles within cycles. He'd already gone through the whole sequence in a matter of minutes. Ian felt hurt and didn't like it one bit. He'd been careless about his social life and focussed on work at the expense of all else, but losing his job was not as bad as this.

After reading the letter, jumbled thoughts raced through Ian's mind. He'd buried himself in his work after his last failed romance, and he knew it was a mistake. So much wasted time! Soon, the thrill of his new adventure came crowding back into his mind and pushed aside thoughts of Louise for the time being. He put the letter back in his pocket to read again later.

A voice was saying something. Ian realised Ruth was talking to him. 'You should meet my husband. We used to live in Bulawayo, and he still has business contacts in Harare. Perhaps he could give you one or two introductions.'

That was a promising start. He didn't plan on doing any work other than writing his book, but extra money would come in handy.

Ian and Ruth didn't have common acquaintances. There was a ten to twelve-year age difference, and Ian left Zimbabwe in his teens. Their families moved in different social circles. Ian's father was a farmer, and they'd spent much of their time in the bush. Ruth and her husband were part of the Bulawayo business community.

The plane touched down in Johannesburg in the late afternoon. Other flights landed, and long queues formed at the immigration counters. The bored looking officer didn't speak a word. He stamped Ian's passport and looked up at the next person in the queue. Ian joined Ruth at the carousel, but they didn't have long to wait. Her suitcase was one of the first to emerge on the conveyor belt. They walked into the customs area where their luggage passed through an x-ray machine, and the officer waved them through to the arrival hall. Soon they were out in the covered parking area where Ruth left her car. She'd offered Ian a lift to the Rosebank Hotel where he was due to meet David, an old school friend with whom he would stay during his time in Joburg.

This was Ian's first visit in twenty years. The route into the city looked different with a lot of new warehouse buildings. But there was also a familiarity as they left the airport and drove past Isando and Bedfordview. Before long they drove onto the raised motorway that bordered the south and west of the city. They passed the iconic Ponte City Apartments, a huge cylindrical building that was a landmark from almost all points of the city. An open back bakkie raced past, packed with African building labourers, happy and singing after a hard day's work. 'They couldn't do that in Australia,' said Ian.

The raised motorway provided a grand view of the CBD. It looked a lot older than Ian remembered. They drove past Johannesburg Park Station on the right. It had gained a bad reputation for crime since majority rule. 'Whites don't go into the CBD anymore.' said Ruth, 'It's too dangerous. And the station is one of the worst spots in the city. Rather go to Pretoria if you want to catch a train. Almost all the white-owned businesses have moved north of the city to Sandton and Midrand.'

Before dropping Ian off at the Rosebank Hotel, Ruth gave him her phone number and address. 'Come for dinner on Monday night and meet my husband, Solly.'

Ian thanked Ruth and said goodbye before walking up the hotel steps. There, in the lounge, David waited for him. It was twenty years since they last saw each other, but they reconnected in an instant. They were mature men and no longer teenagers, but the intervening years evaporated over their first beer together.

CHAPTER 17

January 2009

THE Bernstein's lived in a grand old house, surrounded by a large garden with tall trees and manicured lawns, in Parkwood, close to Zoo Lake in Johannesburg. An African maid met Ian at the front door. She showed him through to a large, high-ceilinged, magnificent room at the back of the house. A floor to ceiling picture window looked onto a huge, floodlit atrium full of tropical plants.

Ruth came in and greeted Ian, pecking him on both cheeks. She was welcoming and looked most attractive. A small balding man, around fifty years old, stood beside her. 'This is my husband, Solly. Darling, meet Ian. I've told you about him.' When they settled in the plush armchairs, a second maid brought out a tray of dry sherries for them. Ian thought Ruth seemed too good for her husband, in a physical sense at least.

Solly was all business, but he had a good sense of humour. 'My solicitor in Harare is Manfred Schwartz and Associates. He is sharp. When he saw the time for black rule had come, Manfred made his black secretary and his black tea boy twenty-five percent partners in his firm. The associates in the firm's name are the secretary and the tea boy. She is competent, and I believe he makes a good cup of tea,' said Solly, laughing. 'Without Manfred, there's no business, so with fifty percent of the partnership he still has full control. Having two black partners brings in a lot of business. He gets plenty of government work, but not much else. The breweries have survived, but most other larger companies have closed. Manfred only accepts payment in US dollars, so inflation and the value of the Zimbabwe dollar is of no concern to him.'

The maid came in to call them for dinner. 'I would suggest you get hold of all the US dollars you need for your stay in Zimbabwe. Did you know they printed a one-hundred-trillion-dollar bank note? There are billionaires in Zimbabwe who can't afford a loaf of bread.' Solly found the idea amusing though he empathised with the plight of the population. 'The government uses food as a weapon. You must support ZANU-PF if you want food aid. Matabeleland bore the brunt of the food shortage because it's an MDC stronghold.'

After dinner they retired to the atrium room for coffee and port. Solly sank back into his plush armchair. 'When you are in Harare, make sure you look up Manfred Schwartz. I will warn him you may be in touch. There's nothing concrete mind you, but all my business up there goes through him. One of my business associates is keen to invest once things settle down in Zimbabwe. In due course, we'll review the market opportunities, so keep in touch. If you came to Joburg, there'd be a lot more opportunity.'

After a nightcap, Ian said goodnight to Ruth and Solly. The Bernstein's maintained the lifestyle they enjoyed in Zimbabwe. Much of the white diaspora was less fortunate. They became accustomed to having servants in Zimbabwe, but now they needed to manage for themselves. But the Bernstein's employed a chef, two maids, and at least two full-time gardeners.

Ian's friend, David, rented a house in Sandton, not too far from the Wanderers cricket ground. He'd taken a few days off work to coincide with Ian's visit. This gave them the chance to catch up on old times and meet with two other friends from schooldays. They all warned Ian visiting Zimbabwe was not a good idea, but it was too late to turn back now. Ian liked the idea of a troubled country. An unsettled Zimbabwe was what he needed as the background to his book.

Ian joined his three old school friends for a coffee at the Rosebank shopping centre. They tried their best to persuade him not to go. 'Have you heard about the cholera in Zimbabwe?' said David. 'It started in August last year, and this year it has spread to the neighbouring countries. Up to now it has infected almost one hundred thousand people, and over four thousand have died.'

'It started in the urban areas,' said Peter, stirring the third teaspoon of sugar into his coffee. 'The collapse of Harare's urban water supply was the start of it. Poor sanitation and the lack of garbage collection was a problem, as was the shortage of chlorine and other chemicals to treat the water. Harare switched off the water supply in December and elsewhere even earlier.'

Tony sat forward in his chair. This was big news, and he was keen to add his bit. 'The city folk spread the infection to the rural areas. The death rate was high because of starvation and HIV and AIDS. Most people can't get treatment inside the country. You know the medical school and three of the four major hospitals in Zimbabwe have shut, and medical staff has left the country in droves.'

'If it's spreading to neighbouring countries, it'll come here, so I might as well meet it there. I'll be careful not to go near water unless it's bottled or boiled first.'

'It would be a good idea if you boiled the water and then used a facecloth to wash yourself,' said David. 'My Dad said it's what they did in the Bush War. You couldn't risk a shower or a bath in Harare even if the taps were working.'

'Why are you going to Zimbabwe anyway?' said Peter. 'South Africa's much better.'

'There's also violence here. Is Zimbabwe any worse? I'm going there to write a book.'

'Is it an auto-biography based on your experiences?' said Tony, putting his cup back on the saucer. 'I've read a few, and most are ordinary.'

'No, it's a novel; fictitious from beginning to end.'

The friends looked puzzled. 'Why are you doing that?' said Peter and Tony in unison.

'Why not? Maybe because it's there; Zimbabwe, I mean. It's a place I know, and its troubles make it a place of interest. People want to read about it. The problem is I've been away twenty years. That's why I must go there.'

'You know there's no petrol?' said Tony.

'That's OK, I'll walk.'

'What about your career?' said Peter.

'If I'm lucky, writing might be my career. I'm tired of meetings and writing reports.'

'That's fine, but now is a bad time for what you're planning.' Tony and David agreed, but nothing would stop Ian now.

He changed the subject. 'One other thing, the coffee here in Joburg needs attention. If you don't know what I mean you should visit Melbourne.' The comment drew boos from his friends.

Tony said, 'Real men don't drink coffee; they drink Castle lager.'

'Then what on earth are we doing sitting here,' said Ian. They all laughed and headed across the road to the Rosebank Hotel. Ian was not fickle, but with all the beer and merriment with his friends, thoughts of Louise were fading, for that afternoon at least.

David's house was in a large crescent with boom gates at either end, but that did little to make the street any more secure. 'The boom gates are useless. The guards are alone, and they're too frightened to stop a carload of suspicious-looking characters. And sometimes they're in league with the criminals.'

'The gated community across the road looks safe.'

'No, it's not. Two months ago, intruders murdered a man in his apartment. The guards and the password protected gate couldn't keep him safe. No one saw or heard anything.'

On David's side of the road the houses were on their own separate blocks. This meant, aside from the boom gates, they needed to make their own security arrangements. Ian was uneasy each night when

David went through his locking up routine. It was the downside of living in South Africa. At night, there were three distinct areas in the double-storey house. A wrought-iron door at the top of the stairs separated the upstairs and downstairs sections. Anyone breaking into the downstairs office area was free to take what they wanted. Upstairs, a second wrought-iron door isolated the sleeping quarters from the rest of the house. The bedroom wing was close to impregnable at night. If they somehow broke in, they would still have to face David and his 9mm Browning, MKIII High Power handgun.

It was much like the night-time security arrangements and routine Ian's parents followed when they lived in Bulawayo. Each night a locked wrought-iron door separated the living area and kitchen from the sleeping quarters. The wings of their L-shaped house framed a large, curved front veranda. There was no wall or covering overhead, and the iron round-bars ran from the edge of the veranda and met overhead in the corner of the roof. One metre from the floor, the round-bars passed through an iron flat bar for reinforcement. From the road, the front veranda looked like a giant, round bird cage. The family often took tea there, and at such times, Ian could empathise with his mother's budgie sitting in its small round cage in the living room.

Ian brought David duty-free Cognac from Melbourne. David poured a glass for himself and one for Ian. 'So, you're still going ahead with your trip to Zimbabwe?'

'Yes, I must. I've already invested too much in this venture to abandon it now.'

'Well, if you go in with your eyes open, you should be OK, I suppose. A lot of innocent people have had major problems and ended up in jail.'

'I won't do anything silly, and I won't get involved in anything political. I want to get the feel of the country and write my book.'

'That's a joke. Since when, have you stayed out of political debate?'

'From the moment I land in Zimbabwe.'

'Yes, that's wise. I believe the jails aren't much fun. They can be slack about remembering prisoner release dates.'

'I'll be careful.'

'And whatever you do, don't make any notes to which they can take exception. If you want to write anything negative, memorise it, or write it in obscure language that can't be used against you. You can always finish your book outside the country.' David's parting words before going to bed were food for thought.

Ian lay awake for a long time, tossing and turning. He made a mental list of the difficulties he would face in Zimbabwe. The country was violent and politically unstable, and the currency was worthless. The politicised army and police, along with other government authorities, couldn't be trusted. There was a cholera epidemic, and the country's health system was in a state of collapse. There was no tap water in Harare, and there were constant power cuts. The potential problems were disconcerting but could be gold for his novel. With that positive thought, he drifted off to sleep, but a nagging feeling of apprehension remained at the back of his mind.

Zimbabwe always looked worse from outside, but locals got used to the troubles. They became immune to the fears others might have. Were his friends being alarmist? He would soon find out.

Chapter 18

26th January 2009

THOMAS became more and more restless at work, and it pleased Sarah. The more restless he became the better their relationship seemed to get; a little like the days before the COU. Thomas was glad Sarah was out of the COU, and he looked forward to completing his contract. Sarah warned him not to show any signs of his dissatisfaction at work. Jedson seemed supportive of Thomas and often took him for a drink after hours, but that worried Sarah.

'When you're out drinking, be careful what you say, and don't ask questions that might raise suspicions. Look what happened to my papa. You may think you can trust Jedson, but you never know who says what to whom and how it might be construed. What if he repeats what you say to Captain John?'

'Don't worry. I'll be careful.'

But Sarah did worry. Thomas still seemed obsessed by the purpose of their visit to Sharm el-Sheikh.

'And don't keep on about the election violence,' said Sarah. 'It will only get you into trouble.'

'I don't support the opposition, but I'm not for the violence against them.'

'Agreed, but making your views known to others can only lead to trouble.'

Until her father's murder, Sarah approved of how the regime ran things, but now she felt uneasy. Her mother believed her father's murder was because he held the same views Thomas now expressed. If it were true, how could she still support the government? But changing her support to the MDC was unthinkable.

Thomas offered to help Sarah find her father's killers, but she feared for his safety and kept him out of it. Their relationship was in breach of the terms of his employment contract, and he might be dismissed, or worse. Sarah asked Thomas if he'd ever seen Sonny Mutezo, but he didn't know of Sonny or his visits to the COU offices. To make sure Thomas didn't involve himself, she said nothing more to him about the matter.

Sarah trailed Sonny for almost six weeks before she found out where he lived. On the following Monday, Thomas left his office at five o'clock as usual. His scheduled home time preceded the others by thirty minutes to ensure he didn't bump into those who worked elsewhere in the building. At the bus station, Thomas realised he'd left his cell phone in his desk drawer. At first, he thought he'd leave it overnight but then remembered he was due at the army barracks for weapon training in the morning. His watch showed half past five. It was a short walk to the office, but he'd wait for a quarter of an hour to allow the others time to leave. They left by the back gate, but he didn't want to risk a chance encounter.

* * *

At five minutes to six Captain John looked at his watch. Sonny Mutezo was late. He should have arrived at ten to six; twenty minutes after the other operatives left the premises. John was strict about time and obsessed about keeping his operatives separated.

He wanted a Scotch, but he didn't drink until the day's end. The shadows lengthened, and the sun lost its bite. John liked to be out of the office before sunset, but if Sonny was much later, he wouldn't have time for his customary single malt. In the office, John drank alone, never sharing his precious Scotch with any visitor, let alone subordinates. Ah, footsteps in the passage. That must be Sonny.

'Hello, Boss, sorry I'm late. I was checking up on our results from last night. Good work, yeah?'

'Yes, the target died in hospital this morning.'

'Boss, remember the one we did two months back?'

'You're talking about Kagonye?'

'Yes. Why did we target him? You said he was a traitor, but his family said he was a big deal in ZANU-PF.'

'His family saw you?'

'Er, yeah, his missus and daughter turned up just as we finished the job.'

'If they saw you again, would they recognise you?'

'No, they were in a panic, and we left when they arrived.'

'I hope you're right. If you get caught by the police, I can't help you. As far as anyone is concerned, the COU doesn't exist and neither do you.'

'Don't worry, Boss, no one will recognise me or any of the gang. Do you believe he was a traitor?'

'Maybe. Who knows? I get my orders the same way you do. I get a name and address, sometimes a photo, and that's it. We know what they want us to do, and we do it. They seldom say why.'

'Yeah Boss, but he seemed like a nice old bloke.'

'It's dangerous to wonder why they select certain targets. You're not going soft on me are you, Sonny?'

'No Boss.'

'You should be sorry for his family. They're the ones who suffer the real pain.'

'Do you feel sorry for the families left behind, Boss?'

'Yes, sometimes, but never for the targets. There's a reason they're selected.'

'Any more targets for me, Boss?'

'Not yet, Sonny, but there may be a big one coming up soon. I'll phone you as soon as I have confirmation. Sonny, I hope your gang doesn't get up to mischief when there's no target to keep them entertained?'

'No Boss, they'd have me to answer to if they did.'

'We wouldn't risk using them again if they got into trouble with the police, and then you'd need a new gang.'

'It would be hard to replace them, but don't worry, I'll make sure they behave.'

* * *

By the time Thomas returned to the office it was almost six o'clock. The guard at the gate viewed him with suspicion. Thomas explained the reason for his return, and the guard seemed satisfied and let him pass. When Thomas entered the building, he noticed the door in the passage leading to the back of the house was wide open. He went into his office, opened the top right-hand draw, took out his cell phone and switched it to silent. The open passage door seemed to invite Thomas, arousing his curiosity.

Voices came down the passage, a man's voice and a clear, high-pitched voice. Thomas tiptoed down the corridor in his rubber-soled shoes. The man's voice was not distinct. Thomas moved closer, but just then the man dismissed his visitor.

Thomas hurried back to his own office and pulled the door behind him, leaving it ajar, just a chink. Like Sarah's office, there were no longer any windows looking onto the front yard, but through the narrow crack, Thomas observed a young man pass his door and exit the building. Sarah asked him about a COU operative with a high-pitched voice. She said the youth visited the offices on Monday evenings, so he must be the one Sarah mentioned.

* * *

A few minutes after Sonny left, the phone rang. John picked up the handset.

'Good evening, Captain, you did a good job. Are there any loose ends from Friday?'

'Thank you, Sir. No, no loose ends from Friday, but there may be one from the job we did eight weeks ago. The target's family saw our operative and his gang, but our man says they wouldn't recognise him or the others if they saw them again.'

'Captain, what sort of debrief did you have with your operative? There's something wrong if it takes eight weeks to find out there may be a problem.'

'I can't imagine why he took so long to report it, Sir.'

'How can he say they wouldn't recognise him? Tell me what happened.'

* * *

Down the corridor, the phone rang, and someone answered it. So once more, Thomas closed his office door and crept back towards the voice to listen. He moved a little closer than before and could hear one side of the conversation. The voice was clear now, and Thomas couldn't believe his ears. It was Jedson talking. 'His wife and older daughter saw them. The younger daughter was on a Portuguese refresher course in Joburg.' Thomas realised they talked about Sarah and her family. 'I don't see how she'd find out but if she did, we'd handle it. She doesn't work for us anymore, so it wouldn't be difficult to make her disappear. No, the wife and the older daughter are no threat.' Thomas strained to listen. The voice was softer now, and Thomas moved even closer.

'Her father's loyalty wasn't in doubt at the time I hired her, Sir. He held a senior position in the party and attended high-level meetings.'

Was the telephone discussion finished? There were no goodbyes, but the silence and the rustle of papers suggested the phone call must have ended. From the half he'd heard, Thomas gleaned the gist of the conversation. As he stepped back from the office door, the wooden strip flooring creaked. To his ears it sounded loud, and he hoped no one else heard it. Thomas hurried to the front door and into the yard. The fresh air was a welcome relief, and once out of the front gate, he realised he was sweating from the tension.

* * *

John hated how the calls always ended. The line went dead, with no goodbyes or any other niceties. He resented the rudeness and imagined it a way of reminding him that the caller, whom he'd never met, was his superior. Was he really his superior? For all he knew, it might be a jumped-up little clerk who reported back to the real authority that determined the next target. When talking to his operatives, John referred to the voice on the phone as *the boss*.

The creak in the passage outside his door interrupted John's thoughts. He stopped and listened, then got up from his chair and walked into the passage. There was no one in the open plan office, so he ran to the corner and looked down the passage towards the front door. Was it his imagination, or did he see the last movement of the front door closing? He ran down the passage, opened the front door and peered out. The guard stood on duty at the gate. 'Noah, did someone leave the office in the last couple of minutes?'

'Yes, Sah, Mr Thomas just left. He came back to pick up his cell phone.'

'How long was he here?'

'About ten minutes, Sah.'

John thought the creaking floorboard must have been Thomas, snooping. It wouldn't have taken him ten minutes to pick up his cell phone. Had Thomas overheard any of his telephone conversation with the boss? The murder of Sarah's father was common knowledge. If Thomas overheard part of the conversation, he might figure out the rest. What would he do with that information? What if he told Sarah? They'd been work colleagues. What if they communicated outside work hours? What should he do? He'd sleep on it and decide in the morning. But it could become a major problem for him. The boss criticised the way he'd handled things. If this slip in security got out, he doubted he would survive in his role. There was no way he would let anybody compromise his lucrative position as head of the COU.

In future he'd be more careful in his dealings with the boss. John resented criticism, and it felt he was walking on thin ice. Did the anonymous voice, the boss, work for the government's interests? The boss ordered the demise of many senior members of the governing party. Provided they paid, it didn't matter one way or another to John. But if he couldn't prove he worked on behalf of the government, it might put him in a tricky situation. The boss warned him he could expect no support if discovered. John gave Sonny the same warning a little earlier.

John's mind drifted back to when he started in the business, the day the anonymous voice approached him. That voice was his only contact with his paymaster. Someone must have recommended him for the role. Who might it have been? A chilling thought came to John. What if his paymaster was a clandestine fifth column, remnants of Ian Smith's white regime? Was it possible? A lot of the high-profile deaths worked in the governments favour, but then others... What if they branded him a traitor? If the boss wanted to replace him, he could be vulnerable to such accusations. Secrecy was more important than ever, and he wondered how he might strengthen it even further.

Too late for a Scotch in the office, but he'd go home and have one before dinner. Not quite the same as having one in the office before driving home. In the office, he could relax and dream about his work and where it may lead. At home, he would have to listen to his wife prattle on about shopping and her visit to the hairdresser. Even worse, his kids would compete for his attention with stories of no interest to him. It was like having to listen to Akashinga in the office.

Akashinga was John's enforcer. He provided the COU with brawn, not brains. His bulk and power made him a formidable figure, and the other operatives were wary of him. Odd then, that Akashinga was such a weak personality. He looked up to John with dog-like devotion, and he was not at all assertive with his fellow operatives. If he'd any brains, he would have been John's right-hand man. His value was that he did what John asked of him. He never questioned his instructions, but he often misinterpreted them. John's ability to bully such a beast gave him a real sense of power, which he relished. Akashinga was affable, a nice guy, a mindless killer but in all other respects a nice guy. The other operatives laughed at him behind his back. Despite his overt bullying of Akashinga, John liked him. He didn't respect him, but he liked him. Everybody liked him.

As John drove out of the gate, he stopped and spoke to the guard.

'Noah, come here; I want to talk to you.'

'Yes, Sah?'

'After people leave the office in the evening, you mustn't let them back in without my permission.'

'Yes, Sah.'

'If someone wants to come back in, you must phone me and tell me, and I'll tell you what to do.'

'Yes, Sah.'

'Do you understand?'

'Yes, Sah.'

John sped out of the gate, swung right and almost ran down a passing cyclist.

* * *

Thomas tried to ring Sarah several times, without luck. The wait for the bus and the journey home, seemed much longer than usual. He needed to talk to Sarah and warn her and give her the other big news. Thomas prayed the security guard would say nothing about his return to the office. The guard seldom spoke to Thomas, only nodding as he entered or exited the premises. Thomas hoped he didn't speak to anyone else either. He was sure no one saw him leave the building.

On his way home, Thomas passed Sarah's house and knocked on the front door, hoping to talk to her.

'No, she and Jemma are out together. They said they may be home late.'

'Mrs Kagonye, please tell her I need to talk to her. It's urgent. I'll call her in the morning if I can't speak to her tonight. It's important she keeps her cell phone with her at work, so I can reach her.'

'They're not supposed to carry their cell phones at work in the hotel, but I will give her your message when she gets back.'

CHAPTER 19

26th January 2009

ONCE Sarah discovered where the leader of the gang that killed her father lived, she resolved not to waste any time. She would confront him the next week. 'Jemma, you must come with me next Monday, and we'll find out if that youth is the culprit; the one who led the gang that killed our father. I need you there for a positive ID.'

Jemma feared the prospect of confronting the youth, but Sarah was, as usual, most persuasive. Sarah picked out the loneliest and darkest spot on the youth's walk home. She took off her raincoat that concealed the knobkerrie she carried, and she and Jemma sat on the low brick wall of a deserted house and waited. It was always dark on the second half of Sonny's journey home. Tonight, he was a little later than usual, and it was pitch-black with no moon. When he appeared the street was empty, and a week street lamp cast ominous shadows on the road surface.

'Hello, Pretty Boy,' Sarah called out in a solicitous voice.

'Are you talking to me, Whore?'

The high-pitched voice made the hairs on Sarah's neck prickle. This must be him.

'Sorry, I've made a mistake. I mistook you for a man, but your voice tells me you are a girl or a little boy.'

Sonny stopped and looked at Sarah.

'I'm forty-four years old, stupid bitch. You'll soon find out if I am a man, and it'll be a lesson you won't forget.'

He advanced towards Sarah with an evil smirk on his face. Jemma stepped out of the shadows to Sarah's left. 'Like the lesson you taught our father?'

Sonny stopped. He hadn't noticed the other woman sitting to one side. 'You!' he said. Sarah swung the knobkerrie she'd been holding behind the low wall and hit him on the left temple. Sonny collapsed in a heap and lay there with his eyes wide open in surprise. Sarah and Jemma saw the faint, healed scratch marks on his face, and they knew he was the culprit.

'Quick, Jemma, help me lift him over this wall. No one will see him behind there.'

Jemma stood in shock, shaking, with her mouth open. Their father's murderer was dead. A touch on the arm brought her to her senses, and she helped Sarah move the body. It might be many hours before anyone noticed it, tucked up close to the wall, and realised he was dead.

Before they left, Sarah took one more look at Sonny Mutezo's still body and his face. A chill came over her when she recognised him as one of the two men she'd seen in the passageway in her second week at the COU. He'd been helping to carry the body bag that bright afternoon when Jedson chastised her for leaving her office door ajar.

Sarah's sporting skills at Wits came in handy. If Sonny Mutezo's temple was a squash or hockey ball, she would have hit it in the sweet spot. No noise, clean hit, little blood. He must have been through the same combat training she went through in the COU, but how easily she'd dealt with him. Sonny was arrogant and made the mistake of underestimating her. Sarah made a mental note to never underestimate a potential enemy, no matter how outwardly benign.

Life was precious, and Sarah thought she should feel something other than her loathing for Sonny Mutezo. She was so calm and remote. Was she like him? What if Jedson asked her to kill someone? Would she do it? They'd have to deserve it. Sonny deserved to die; he was her father's killer. Had Sonny's team leader asked him to kill Sam?

Did Sonny believe Sam deserved to die? The questions in Sarah's head made her think about her work at the COU.

Jemma trembled. 'Sarah let's get out of here quick before someone comes. I don't like this place.' She now knew just how strong her sister was. Jemma had never considered what may occur when they confronted Sonny. The finality and calmness of her sister's actions sent a shiver down her spine. She would never have been able to avenge her father, and she was thankful for Sarah. What would they have done without her? But her sister's violence shocked Jemma. 'What'll Mama say?' she said, in a nervous, piping voice.

'Mama won't say anything because we won't tell her about it.'

'But Sarah, what if someone saw us?'

Sarah wiped the knobkerrie on the grass to remove as much blood as possible and then put on her raincoat to hide it from view. Two blocks from where they left Sonny's body, Sarah and Jemma noticed two policemen standing on the street corner. Jemma shuddered. There was no way to avoid them. Sarah ran straight towards the policemen. 'What are you doing Sarah? Let's cross the road, quick.' Sarah ignored Jemma's pleas.

'Help police,' said Sarah sounding breathless, 'a gang of boys attacked a man in a garden down the road. Call an ambulance.'

'Where Miss, where did this happen?'

'Two blocks down that road, the empty house with the low, white brick wall. They attacked him in the front garden. The gang that did it call themselves the Dragons.'

'Yes,' said the policeman, 'we know them.'

'Quick,' said Sarah, 'before they get away.'

The two policemen ran off in the direction Sarah pointed out while she and Jemma stepped out in the opposite direction towards the bus station.

'Sarah, should you have blamed that gang for killing the man? They'll be in big trouble for that.'

'Yes, that gang goes around making other people's lives a misery. You can bet they've committed many crimes. Anyway, they'll all have alibis, unless at the time they were doing something just as bad or even worse. Either way they had it coming to them.'

'Yes, but—'

'I bet you they've committed many rapes and even murders. We've performed a good service for the community.'

Jemma could never beat Sarah in an argument. Sarah was way too smart for her. But Jemma didn't agree with blaming the gang. If she was a witness at their trial, she could never lie and say she saw the gang attack the man. But she didn't need to worry. African law enforcement didn't work like that. The police were unlikely to apprehend the gang and even if they did, it probably wouldn't end up in court. A talking to, or a beating, was the probable outcome. A small bribe from the gang members' families would settle the issue. Everyone would be happy with the outcome, and African justice would be served.

Sarah had no illusions about how the system worked. If you wanted justice, you had to get it for yourself.

CHAPTER 20

27th January 2009

IT was an early start for Thomas at the army barracks. The time seemed to drag. Weapon training was fun, but today, all he thought about was contacting Sarah. He would phone her on his way back to the COU offices. At last! Weapon training ended.

When Thomas left the barracks, he tried to phone Sarah. 'Damn!' The cell phone battery was flat. He'd charged it the night before, but sometimes it did not seem to charge properly. Thomas caught the bus into the CBD and then walked as fast as he could to the COU offices. As soon as he got in, he put his cell phone on charge and dialled Sarah on the fixed line. Almost half past eleven, she would still be on her lunch break. Ah! It rang. Sara answered. 'Sarah, thank heavens I've caught you! I need to talk to you. It's very important. Can you meet me after work?'

'You mean at home this evening?'

'No, I'm helping my father in the shop this evening, but it's urgent we speak.'

'What's it about Thomas?'

'I can't talk on the phone. Meet me in Harare Gardens after you finish work. I'll wait for you near Herbert Chitepo Avenue. It's more private on that side of the gardens.' Thomas couldn't say much. Someone might have tapped the phone and be listening. As he put the handset down, his door opened and in walked Jedson.

'Thomas, Captain John has asked me to release you to help one of our other teams on a special job this afternoon. Go with Akashinga, Samson and Elijah and give them a hand. They're waiting for you in the car out front.'

'Sir, I'm meeting a friend at half past three.'

'Don't worry; you'll be back by then. Introduce yourself to the boys.'

Thomas unplugged his cell phone from the charger and hurried out to the car. Two men sat in the back. Thomas hopped in the front passenger seat next to the bull-necked, bald driver. Akashinga introduced himself, but the other two barely acknowledged him. Thomas didn't like the looks of them.

'What's this job we're doing?' said Thomas.

'Captain John wants us to dump some stuff for him,' said Akashinga.

'Where are we going?'

'We're going to Beatrice, about sixty kilometres from here.'

It soon became clear to Thomas that this wouldn't be a social trip, and before long he too lapsed into silence. Thomas sat looking through the windscreen, watching the roadway racing past under the car. What were they going to dump? If they were papers or files, wouldn't it be better to shred them in the office? Why, at a moment's notice, did he have to introduce himself to the others? The COU had gone to such lengths to keep them apart. Something didn't seem right. Had someone seen him in the office last night? Was this related to that? Thomas shivered at the thought though he was hot and sweaty under his polyester shirt.

At Beatrice, near the Mupfure River, they turned off the main road. The Beatrice Gold Belt was a suitable name for the area. Gold had been mined there for one hundred years, but in the year 2000 operations ceased. The four mines, now all closed, left disused mineshafts that filled with water in the rainy season.

'This is it,' said Akashinga, suddenly sounding cheerful. He stopped the car on the edge of the road. Thomas tried hard to conceal his fear.

Here he was, in the middle of nowhere, with three unfriendly individuals. Why had they brought him here? He was ready to make a break, but where would he run?

They all jumped out of the car and Akashinga opened the boot. Inside were two large heavy-duty hessian sacks. 'Captain John wants us to dump these down the mineshaft.' With the help of Elijah, he took hold of a sack and lifted it out of the boot. 'Thomas, you help Samson with the other sack.' Relief flooded through Thomas like a fresh mountain stream flowing through his veins. He needn't have worried. He was there to help with a physically demanding task. Thomas felt foolish now as he peeled the sticky shirt away from his skin. His anxiety and the warm day made him sweaty. The sacks were heavy, and the four men struggled with the weight. Thomas' arms ached by the time they reached the barbed wire barrier that surrounded the mineshaft. It was almost three hundred metres from where they parked the car. They found a gap in the barrier surrounding the mineshaft and squeezed through with their heavy loads. Now nothing stood between them and the dark, gaping mouth of the shaft.

First, Akashinga and Elijah took each end of their heavy sack and lifted it. They swung it backwards and forwards, first slowly and then with increasing momentum. Akashinga counted each forward swing; 'one, two, three, four.' On the fourth swing they heaved it into the open mouth of the mineshaft. There was silence for about three seconds followed by a loud splash far below them.

Akashinga took out his cell phone from his pocket and looked at it. 'This phone is dead. Has anyone else got a phone?' Elijah and Samson shook their heads. 'What about you Thomas?'

'There isn't much of a charge,' said Thomas, handing his phone to Akashinga.

Now it was Thomas and Samson's turn to dump their sack. Thomas took one end and Samson the other. 'What's in these sacks?' said Thomas. 'They're heavy.'

Chapter 21

27th January 2009

Ian saw little of the airport on his arrival in Joburg a few days earlier. Ruth offered him a lift to the Rosebank Hotel, and they'd hurried through the arrival hall to the covered parking area, where she'd left her car. Now on departure, Ian was early, and he undertook a leisurely exploration of the terminal. It was unrecognisable from the one he'd passed through on his way to Australia twenty years earlier. The building was modern and clean, a world-class facility, full of the buzz so typical of major airports around the world.

O.R. Tambo, the busiest airport in all of Africa, and the first to receive the huge Airbus A380. Modern shops and cafes lured visitors to spend, and they splashed out in the duty-free shops on alcohol, perfume and expensive watches. The scary stories Ian heard about Zimbabwe deterred him from joining the spending frenzy. He planned to save his US dollars, restricting himself to a cup of coffee and a bottle of Cognac.

The departure experience differed from when he'd arrived. Then, Ian queued to meet an immigration officer, who didn't look at all pleased to welcome him. Next the stern customs officer seemed to view him as more of a nuisance than someone who helped keep him in a job. The process turned out to be trouble free, but the irony of the situation struck Ian. The customer service could be better. Didn't they know their government spent a fortune on tourist advertising to attract foreign visitors? On this occasion, the immigration officers acted friendly and chatty, almost relieved to see the visitors go. Many other international destinations also greeted visitors with sullen immigration officers. Fiji was a rare example of a country that knew how to welcome visitors. Customs and immigration played a big part in this.

It was a beautiful morning with the sun shining and a few puffy, white clouds scattered across a deep blue sky. The South African Airways mid-morning flight to Harare would take one hour and forty minutes. The flight was smooth and the cabin crew attentive. Ian enjoyed the inflight tea and sandwiches and looked through the window at the passing scene. Late January was well into the rainy season. Rain washed the air clean, and the crisp and clear sight from thirty thousand feet looked like the satellite view on Google Maps. The green landscape in Zimbabwe bore witness to the good rains that helped spread the cholera epidemic.

* * *

'What are you doing here?' the surly immigration officer asked.

'After twenty years overseas, a visit is long overdue.'

The official paged through Ian's passport. 'Haven't you former Rhodesians seen enough of Zimbabwe?'

'It will be different, seeing the country through adult eyes.'

'Ah yes, through adult eyes it will look different.'

'There are still many places in Zimbabwe I haven't visited.'

The official stamped Ian's passport with a loud whack. 'Be careful. It is easy to get into trouble here,' he said, handing back Ian's passport.

'Thank you, I'll remember that.'

Next came customs. The bored looking officer viewed Ian with suspicion.

'Do you have anything to declare?'

'I have a bottle of Cognac.'

'What about drugs?'

'No, I don't use drugs,' said Ian, with an edge to his voice.

The customs officer waved his hand over Ian's backpack. 'Empty it.'

Ian bristled, but he held his tongue. One by one the customs officer examined the items laid out on the table. He opened all the zips and Velcro fastenings and ran his hand around the inside of each pocket. He ran his fingers along all the seams of Ian's clothing, and he opened the wash bag and squeezed out a small amount of toothpaste and tasted it. Ian could contain himself no longer 'Do you have much drug smuggling here?' The customs officer gave Ian a cold stare but didn't answer. He opened the bottle of Cognac and smelt it. 'There's not much you can smuggle in a sealed glass bottle,' said Ian.

The customs officer ignored him. 'Start your laptop.' The officer looked through Ian's documents and pictures folders. 'Why have you brought a laptop on your holiday?'

'This is my diary for the trip.'

'Are you a journalist?'

'No.'

'Give me your camera.'

This was worse than Joburg. After almost an hour and a comprehensive search of all his possessions, the customs officer walked away without a word, leaving Ian to repack his bag. Ian considered it lucky he'd only brought a few items in his backpack. If he'd also carried a suitcase, he'd have been there all day.

The terminal was modern and clean but almost deserted. Of the major airlines, only Emirates and SAA flew into Harare. Even with no check-in luggage, Ian was the last to exit the quiet building. Outside, there were no people or taxis. Ian waited at the sign that read Taxi Rank, and after about thirty minutes a car pulled up in front of him. The elderly, male, African driver offered Ian a lift into town.

By the time they arrived at the Monomotapa Hotel it was half past two in the afternoon. From their chat Ian learned that most of the remaining whites were elderly folk trapped in the country by their economic circumstances. Expatriates, on short-term contracts or working for NGOs or foreign embassies, accounted for most of the few whites of working age. Foreign tourists were down to a trickle, and few white faces appeared on the streets of Harare. The country's white population, which once numbered two hundred and eighty thousand, was down to thirty thousand or fewer. The elderly African driver waved Ian goodbye. 'I preferred the old days, but don't tell anyone I said that.'

Ian laughed. 'Yes, my father says the same thing, but he doesn't live here anymore.' He thanked the man for the lift into the city and turned towards the hotel entrance.

* * *

The polite hotel receptionist seemed pleased to see Ian. There were empty rooms, but due to the water supply crisis and the cholera epidemic, not all were available for guests. The city's hotels used various coping methods, including disinfecting the water and finding alternative sources of supply. Some hotels even used water from their swimming pools. Water needed to be boiled and treated with aqua tablets before drinking. Bottled water was the best bet. This wasn't the return to Africa Ian expected.

The large, clean and comfortable room overlooked Harare Gardens at the rear of the hotel. In the guest rooms a notice warned of the water shortage and the need to be thrifty. The water was working, so Ian enjoyed a quick shower to freshen up after the flight.

Ian needed to buy a prepaid SIM card for his cell phone. He took the lift downstairs to the hotel lobby and asked the concierge for directions. Already late afternoon, the streets were busy with workers and street vendors going home. Many of the buildings Ian recognised from a visit to the city with his parents, years earlier. Several new buildings graced the skyline, including the Reserve Bank of Zimbabwe tower, now the tallest building in the country.

Back in the hotel, the early evening warmth lured Ian to the lobby bar for his first taste of ice-cold Zambezi beer. He'd expected it to be bustling, but it was quiet with no sign of the after-work crowd. Four

African men sat with their beers, chatting at a table, and three attractive African women sat alone, sipping their drinks.

The first sip of beer slid down Ian's throat, conveying pure ecstasy. He closed his eyes and let the cold liquid trickle all the way down his oesophagus.

'Are you visiting for business or pleasure?'

Ian opened his eyes and looked at the speaker, one of the attractive African women he'd seen sitting alone when he walked into the bar. She wore a peacock blue, high-neck, figure-hugging dress with slits up the side to her thighs. The dress looked familiar. Ah yes, it was like the one worn by the woman in Vladimir Tretchikoff's famous *Blue Lady* painting.

'A bit of both,' said Ian.

'Is this your first visit to Zimbabwe?'

'No, I was born here.'

'Shush! You'll be labelled a racist.'

'My family supported Ian Smith, but we weren't racists.'

She smiled. 'Many black people admired him though few would admit it. He was a good leader for the whites but slow to recognise not all blacks were on the lunatic fringe.'

Ian laughed. 'Yes, it may have been a lost opportunity. Are you with the MDC?'

She lowered her voice. 'It is dangerous to talk politics in Zimbabwe if you are not a ZANU-PF supporter.'

Ian pulled out a bar stool for the young women. 'Can I buy you a drink? My name is Ian.'

'I'm Hazel,' she said sitting down next to him. 'A lemon, lime and bitters please.'

Ian noted the barman knew how to make a proper lemon, lime and bitters. It was not the bottled variety he'd sometimes seen back in Melbourne.

'And what work do you do Hazel?'

She hesitated. 'I'm a hairdresser. I do those intricate knotted patterns African women wear in their hair, and I can also do western hair styles for people with longer hair.'

'Are you meeting someone here this evening? When I entered, I noticed you sitting alone at a table.'

'No, I came for a quiet drink.'

It dawned on Ian that Hazel must have come to the bar to meet men. She had made the approach to him, and it was likely she was a prostitute. Where should he take the conversation next? He didn't want to waste her time when he had no intention of using her services. Honesty was the best policy. 'Hazel, I don't want to keep you from anything, but if you're content to sit and talk for the rest of the evening, that's fine with me.'

'You're a real gentleman, Ian. You've worked out what I do for a living. In the evenings, I make many times the money I earn in my day job. But I'm happy to talk to you.'

'Well, would you like dinner at Le Francais?'

The whole trout looked inviting, but Ian decided against it. They settled on rib-eye fillet steak on the bone with garlic sauce and chips. Ian and Hazel chatted away like old friends in the hotel's cosy French-themed restaurant, covering a wide range of topics. Hazel proved to be good company, but perhaps that wasn't surprising; being good company was her business.

Ian learnt that Hazel came to the lobby bar two or three times a week. It helped her support her mother and two children after her husband had abandoned her three years earlier. Since then she'd not heard of him and didn't know if he was alive or dead. By day, she worked as a hairdresser, and she hoped to open her own salon soon. She didn't like doing what she did in the evenings but needed the money. Under no circumstances would she ever agree to unprotected sex, and this stand limited her earning capacity. 'But no amount of money,' she said, 'can substitute for health. There are many prostitutes on the street. Some, especially the young ones, will forgo a condom for a higher price. But then, they have no future. They live for today. It's crazy.'

After dinner and coffee, Ian needed to sleep. The morning flight and the late-night chats with David back in Johannesburg were catching up with him. As he walked away, Hazel said in a low voice, 'Don't forget, if you need room service, call my cell phone number. I'll bring up whatever you want.' They both laughed, and it reminded Ian of the good sense of humour most Africans possessed. Ian smiled; he'd received worse offers. His plans for Hazel were not of a carnal nature, but she might prove to be a great source of information and lend local colour to his novel.

When he lay down on the bed, Ian tossed and turned but sleep eluded him. Perhaps he was too tired or his mind overactive with the start of his new project. Meeting Hazel was a stroke of luck. Through her he might meet others who could be helpful for his book. His story of writing a travel book was a cover. Ian intended to write a novel set against the background of Zimbabwe. He knew he would have to be careful in what he wrote because it could get him into trouble. How many warnings did he need? On his first day in Harare, he'd already received two. They told him to keep his plans to himself and not be too open about his views.

Ian sensed the elderly driver who gave him a lift from the airport wanted to say more, but he was cautious, preferring to hint at things. Only when he said goodbye, did he summon up the courage to voice a mild criticism of the regime. A few brave people used oblique language to express their criticisms, but others who made direct criticisms paid the price. Hazel was slow to admit her support for the MDC, but when she did, she spoke in a hushed voice.

A more permanent base was essential. He couldn't stay in the hotel for too long. Ian needed quiet and secure lodgings where he could live and write in peace. He imagined a townhouse with a nice sunny courtyard and shady trees would be perfect. Tomorrow he would start his search for something suitable. Ian resolved that his life would be different; he wouldn't waste another day working for a greedy boss who just saw him in terms of dollars and cents. In the past, money drove him, but in future he'd work only to replenish his coffers, and his personal life and wellbeing would come first. He'd made this promise to himself once before, but it was so easy to slip into a daily grind. Never again, he swore, never again.

With no commitments in the morning, Ian felt free, free to do whatever he wanted. If he couldn't sleep, he might as well have another beer. He hopped out of bed, opened the minibar, took out a bottle of Zambezi and pulled a chair to the window to look at the night sky. The air conditioning struggled, but the cold stream of beer glugging its way down his throat chilled his core all the way to his stomach. Man! Who needs air conditioning when you can cool yourself from the inside out with an iced Zambezi?

The next time Ian looked at his watch it was half past three in the morning. It seemed like a few minutes ago that he'd pulled the chair to the window. He must have fallen asleep. He staggered across to the bed and rolled into it, tired and with his eyes burning. Before he drifted off to sleep again, his mind flitted over random matters, including his book, the accommodation he wanted, and Louise. What was she doing right now? It was one o'clock in the afternoon in Melbourne. Too tired to focus, the thoughts swirled in his mind. Each time he tried to concentrate on any single thought, the others crowded into his head.

With the first signs of dawn on the horizon, Ian slipped into a deep, much needed sleep. He'd planned to skip breakfast. Sleep was more important. He was too tired to dream, but he imagined he heard a door slam somewhere along the corridor. Some poor bugger must have had an early morning start.

Chapter 22

28th January 2009

Thomas' phone call troubled Sarah. What was so urgent that it couldn't wait until she got home from work? He sounded worried, even scared. Last night she and Jemma dealt with Sonny Mutezo. Was his call connected to that?

After finishing work at half past three, Sarah hurried to meet Thomas. He told her to wait in Harare Gardens about thirty metres short of Herbert Chitepo Avenue, opposite Colquhoun Street. There was no sign of him. He was late. Sarah checked her watch, ten minutes to four. Four o'clock, still no Thomas. Half past four, still no sign of Thomas. At five o'clock Sarah walked to the bus station to catch a bus home. He'd not called in at her house. Where might he be? He sounded desperate to see her. Where was he?

Sarah walked to Thomas' house. 'Mrs Chimedza is Thomas here?'

'No, my dear, he's helping his father at the shop this evening.'

'He said he'd meet me after I finished work this afternoon, but he never came.'

'Work often makes him late. As soon as he gets home, I'll tell him you called.'

Sarah did not want to worry Thomas' mother, so she didn't tell her the nature of his phone call. That evening, Sarah waited at home for Thomas, but she didn't hear from him. Why didn't he contact her if the matter was so urgent?

That night, Sarah worried and struggled to sleep. In his mysterious phone call, Thomas stressed she should not ring his mobile number because of his flat battery. If he was not alone, it also might also be awkward for him to answer her call. Perhaps the COU discovered she killed Sonny. Was Thomas trying to warn her? She woke from a restless sleep to find Jemma bustling about in the morning gloom, doing her early morning chores.

Sarah, so worried about Thomas, she skipped breakfast. She walked to Thomas' house before work, and his worried mother came to the door. He'd not come home last night or told her about any travelling plans. His passport was at his workplace, but he'd not taken any clothing or bags for a trip.

* * *

When she reached the hotel, Sarah changed into her maid's uniform and placed her clothes in her locker. Although the rules barred maids from carrying their cell phones while on duty, Sarah often did. Today, she needed to carry it in case Thomas called.

Sarah always did a second, last-minute check on her service trolley in the morning to make sure none of the towels and toiletries for the guest rooms had 'walked' overnight. Her cell phone rang, and she almost dropped it in her haste to answer. It might be Thomas, but no, it was Jedson. He sounded breathless and anxious and nothing like the calm Jedson she knew.

'Sarah, I must talk to you. Where are you?'

'Why, what's happened?'

'Thomas seems to have disappeared. He accompanied one of the other teams yesterday to help on a job. On the way back, they dropped him in the CBD because he said he had to meet a friend at half past three. But then he never came back to the office, and his mother says he didn't return home last night. Something worried him, and he said he needed to talk, but now he's vanished. I need to see you Sarah. Where are you?'

'Why do you need to see me?'

'It's hard to talk on the phone, Sarah.'

'I'm a room maid at the Monomotapa Hotel.'

'OK, I'll be there in half an hour.' The phone went dead.

Sarah pushed the service trolley down the corridor towards the guest room of the first early check out. Why did Jedson need to talk to her in person? She'd left the COU six weeks earlier. What could she tell him? Sarah's anxiety increased by the minute. Where was Thomas? Perhaps Jedson was also in danger, but revealing her relationship with Thomas wouldn't help find him. Jedson said something worried Thomas, and he wanted to discuss it. Did that relate to Thomas' call to her?

The room maids' schedule allowed a limited time to service each room, but today Sarah felt like she was running in soft sand and worked at a slow pace. She couldn't concentrate. Confused and worrying thoughts ate away at the back of her mind. Round and round, they raced. Perhaps they found out about her relationship with Thomas? Maybe Thomas somehow revealed his suspicions about their trip to Sharm el-Sheik? Did the COU know of Thomas' disquiet over the election violence? Oh, where was Thomas?

Half an hour passed with no sign of Jedson. Almost an hour later her phone rang. Ah, that must be Jedson. She pressed the receive button. 'Sarah, it's Stanley here, at the concierge desk. Uh-oh, he must know she carried her cell phone. Listen, I overheard three men in dark suits, asking reception where to find you. One is at reception now, but two of them have taken the lift to your floor. I thought I'd better warn you.'

Panic rose in Sarah's chest as the back of her throat closed, and her mouth turned dry. Three men in dark suits; Sarah feared what that meant. First, her father's murder, and now Thomas seemed to have disappeared. Jedson wanted to meet her, but three men in dark suits arrive. She had to act fast, but what should she do?

Chapter 23

28th January 2009

The sunny, late January morning lit the room. Ian bounced out of bed and did his usual morning exercises that kept him fit: push-ups, sit-ups and squats. Yesterday's fuzzy head no longer troubled him.

The water supply was on, and Ian hurried to shower before it stopped running. He stepped into the bath and pulled the shower curtain closed. The water was nice and hot, and the lightweight shower curtain flapped about, sticking to him. Once, in another hotel, he'd seen a shower curtain with weights sewn into the hem. That worked well to keep the shower curtain still, but it was the only time he'd ever seen it done. Ian resisted the urge to relax under the shower, fearing the spray might cut out at any moment. He shampooed his hair and soaped himself and was about to step under the shower rose to rinse off when he heard his room door open. Damn! It must be the room maid. He'd forgotten to hang out the Do Not Disturb sign, and the bathroom door lay open.

'I'm not ready to have the room made up,' Ian shouted from behind the shower curtain. 'Please come back later.'

The maid came into the bathroom. 'I'm sorry, Sir, but bad men are looking for me. Can I please hide in here until they leave?'

Ian hesitated. The intrusion irritated him, but he could hear the fear in her voice. 'Wait in the bedroom and shut the bathroom door. I'll be out in a min—' A loud knock at the door interrupted him. In a flash, the African room maid pulled aside the shower curtain and stepped over the edge of the bath and into the shower. She held her shoes above her head to keep them dry.

'What are you doing?' said Ian, in a startled voice, uncomfortable with the sudden closeness of the maid. He wore nothing but the soap suds, and those were fast disappearing under the spray of water.

'Please, Sir, don't tell them I'm here. If they find me, they'll kill me.' Her fear was plain to see, and he realised it must be serious if she'd get into a running shower fully clothed.

'Pass me a towel,' said Ian, pointing to the chrome towel rack on the wall behind the maid. The persistent, loud knocking on the door sounded urgent. Ian left the shower running and stepped out of the bath onto the mat and took the towel the maid handed him. He wrapped the towel around his waist, pulled the shower curtain closed and walked to the door leaving wet footprints on the carpet.

Ian opened the door and stood there dripping wet with his soaking hair plastered down across his forehead. Two African men, dressed in dark suits, stood in the doorway. One wore a moustache and was tall with broad shoulders and looked to be in his late forties. Behind him was an even taller, broad shouldered, clean shaven younger man.

'Yes,' said Ian, irritated by the intrusion, 'what's the problem?'

'Sorry to bother you, Sir, we're from hotel security. We're looking for the room maid who works on this floor.'

'How would I know where she is? I'm in the middle of my shower.'

'The maid's trolley is right outside your room, Sir. We wondered if she might be here.'

'No, I haven't seen her, and I'm not ready to have my room cleaned.'

'She might've sneaked in while you were in the shower, Sir. May we come in and check your room?'

Ian backed into the bathroom doorway and made an exaggerated welcoming sweep of his right arm, inviting them to enter. The men brushed past Ian and peered behind the bed and out of the window. They opened all the cupboard doors. Satisfied their quarry was not in the room, they walked up to Ian who stood in the bathroom doorway. They looked past him into the bathroom.

'I'm not likely to be showering with the room maid, am I?' said Ian, trying to make light of the situation.

'How long have you been staying in this hotel, Sir?'

'I arrived yesterday afternoon, and I've never even seen the room maid.'

The men smiled and the older one said, 'You had better get back to your shower, Sir. We must conserve water.'

'Yes, thank you.'

'If you see the maid, Sir, please phone hotel security. The woman has been stealing items from the guests' rooms, and we've had a lot of complaints.'

'Yes, I will. Thank you for the warning.'

As they left, Ian hung the Do Not Disturb sign on his door. He walked into the bathroom and pulled back the shower curtain in one quick sweep, startling the room maid. Her clothes were soaking wet except for her shoes which she still held over her head.

'It's not true what those men said, Sir. I haven't stolen from the guests. I don't know why they want me, but they might be from state security, maybe the CIO. Sometimes they can detain a person for no reason. People can disappear when state security takes them.'

'So I've heard. Your clothes are all wet. What are you going to do now?'

'Can I stay here until my clothes dry, Sir?'

'That could take all day. Here, put on these clothes.' Ian gave her one of his polo shirts and underpants to wear while her clothes dried. Still only wearing the towel wrapped around his waist, he returned to the bathroom to brush his teeth and dress. The hotel room-safe held his valuables and passport, but his watch and loose change were on the bedside table. He would keep an eye on them.

This will take forever, Ian thought. What a damn nuisance. But as he came out of the bathroom he stopped, blinked and blinked again.

The frightened room maid now looked relaxed and most attractive, sitting on the end of the bed in his polo shirt. And like Hazel, Sarah proved to be a good conversationalist. It surprised him to discover how well educated and well-spoken she was. To his even greater surprise, he found his thoughts returning to just how attractive she was, a real beauty. In Africa, the local whites didn't think about blacks in that way, but he couldn't take his eyes off her. 'Are you MDC?'

'No, my family has always supported ZANU-PF.' Sarah's reply disappointed Ian, though he wasn't sure why it should.

'My father worked for ZANU-PF, but in November a gang of youths attacked and killed him. Who knows why it happened? But soon afterwards I lost my job with state security. That's why I'm working here.'

'You worked for state security?'

'Yes, they are dangerous men. If they are looking for you it means big trouble.'

Ian smiled. It all sounded fanciful. 'Did you see them arrive at the hotel? Do you think they saw you coming into my room?' Ian now pondered the ramifications for him.

'No, a friend working on the concierge desk overheard them asking reception where they could find me, so he called me on my cell phone to warn me. I knew straight away they would be from state security, so I ran into the nearest room, yours.'

'If they are waiting for you downstairs how are you going to get past them?'

'I can't go back to the staff lockers to get my things, but if I walk out in my maid's uniform, they will see me. My sister works as a maid in an apartment block near here. Maybe I can phone her and get her to bring me a change of clothes.'

'It may look suspicious if your sister brings your things here. If she puts them in a shopping bag, I can meet her and bring your stuff to you.'

'Would you do that?'

'Yes, I will.'

Sarah called her sister on her cell phone and arranged for her to go home and collect her clothes. She'd meet Ian in three hours outside the Meikles hotel in Jason Moyo Avenue.

In the time they waited, Sarah spoke about recent events in her life. Between Sarah and Hazel, he could pick up unique first-hand information for his novel. He would be like a piece of blotting paper, soaking up all the details of life in current day Zimbabwe. What a great opportunity! Hazel, an MDC supporter, and Sarah, not only a ZANU-PF supporter but also a former employee of state security. He'd try to get more details from her if the opportunity arose.

Ian found it easy to recognise Sarah's sister, Jemma. Sarah told him what clothes she wore, but they were so alike he would have recognised her, anyway. She politely introduced herself and handed Ian a large white plastic shopping bag. Written on the bag was Edgars, the name of a local chain of clothing stores.

'Sarah tells me you work in an apartment block?'

'Yes, Sir.'

'Are there any vacant apartments there? I would like to rent one, but I've read they're difficult to find in Harare.'

'I will talk to the caretaker, Sir, and phone you. Can I please have your number?'

Everyone seemed to have a cell phone. After they exchanged phone numbers, Ian said goodbye to Jemma and made his way back to the hotel.

Even before Ian returned, Jemma phoned her sister and told her he'd asked about an apartment, and she thought she could help him.

'How long are you staying here?' Sarah asked.

'I'm booked in for another three nights.'

'Jemma says her employers are going overseas for six months at the end of next week. If you can wait a little longer, they might rent their apartment to you while they are away. Can you go tomorrow and meet them?'

While Ian was out meeting Jemma, Sarah tidied the room and put on her underwear, which had soon dried. Now, she laid out the fresh clothes he brought back from his meeting with Jemma and pulled off the polo shirt she'd been wearing. Sarah was not at all self-conscious standing there in her bra and pants, tall and slim with toned muscles and enough curves to hold Ian's attention. When she looked back at him and smiled, he flushed with embarrassment.

Sarah now wore a black pencil skirt, a white long-sleeved blouse, mid heeled black leather shoes, white framed sunglasses and a straw hat with a wide brim. She put on what Ian took to be an artificial pearl necklace and a zircon ring on the third finger of her left hand. The change in her appearance amazed him. The frightened room maid now resembled a polished, well-heeled hotel guest. Mmm, not bad! She looked terrific. It reminded him of the story of the frog that turned into a prince. He'd always found it fascinating how a simple change of dress and a little makeup made women look so different. But this one's transformation was like a chameleon.

Sarah packed her damp room maid's uniform into the shopping bag and was ready to leave. 'Thank you for helping me. You saved my life today.'

'Oh, that's OK.'

'Don't forget to see my sister tomorrow about the flat.'

'No, I won't forget.'

In the next instant she was gone.

* * *

Meeting Sarah took up a fair part of the day, and it was already mid-afternoon. Ian fancied a walk and looked in his wallet for Manfred Schwartz's business address. He did not intend to visit him just yet, but identifying his premises now might save him time later. The office was near the old Pearl Assurance building, one block from the hotel. At the next corner, Ian turned into the First Street mall. A long, patient queue of about a dozen Africans stood at the sole public telephone that Ian noticed on his walk. The African woman talking on the phone appeared to be in no hurry and not at all pressured by the queue waiting close behind her. The better hotels scrapped their public phones a long time ago, to prevent similar queues forming in their hotel lobbies.

Ian tried to buy a newspaper, but none were available in the afternoon. He ordered tea at a small café, where the waiter was happy to sell him his own copy of the paper. Most of the articles covered government initiatives and rural news. Ian finished his coffee, left the newspaper on his chair and strolled back to the hotel. The CBD's grid system made it easy for him to get his bearings.

Warmed from his walk, Ian made for the lobby bar, but there was no sign of Hazel. Two other women sat at the tables, but Ian didn't make eye contact and they did not approach him. After two beers he made his way to Monos restaurant on the hotel ground floor and ate a quiet meal alone. He was starving. Sarah caused him to miss breakfast and lunch, and now he relished his evening meal.

Back in his room Ian switched on the TV, but nothing interested him, so he wrote notes as a first step towards writing his novel. In Johannesburg, his busy social schedule prevented him from writing anything. The quiet social scene in Harare made it a good place to make a start on his novel, but he wasn't in a hurry. Work kept him busy in Melbourne and he'd neglected his social life. Johannesburg gave him a taste for fun and relaxation, and Ian now felt a little lonely. Last night, Hazel helped cushion his arrival in this city where he knew no one, but tonight he was all alone and at a loose end. It was only eight in the evening, so Ian caught the lift down to the lobby bar.

The change in the faces walking in the CBD struck Ian. In the past, white faces dominated. There were black faces too, but the whites didn't notice them. Now, in Harare, black faces were everywhere, and the white ones, absent. Even in the lobby bar, white faces were the exception. Ian chatted to a smart-looking young African man sitting near him.

'Are you on holiday?' the man enquired.

'I'm here to write a novel set in Zimbabwe.'

The young man sat up straighter in his seat and looked about him with mock concern. 'I'd keep quiet about that if I were you. Most whites who write about Zimbabwe get jailed or deported. Here's my card. If you get arrested, I can defend you.'

Ian looked at the card, Daniel Moyo, Lawyer. 'You're in practice here Daniel?'

'Yes, but I trained in the UK.'

'You came back to make your fortune?'

Daniel lowered his voice to a whisper. 'I don't know about that. You see how things are. My parents preferred it when the whites ran the country, and now I can see why.'

'So, you and your family are MDC supporters?'

'Shush man, are you looking for trouble? I'm serious this time. If you get us both arrested, who'd be able to defend you?'

Ian and Daniel spent a pleasant evening together chatting about their school days and everything they'd done since then. Ian imagined he could fit in with young, educated people like Daniel.

'You think it's strange I left England and came back to Zimbabwe to practice law, but man, what about you? A white man coming back to Zimbabwe; now that's really strange.'

'It's strange not knowing anyone here, but I was born in Bulawayo, and it seemed like I was coming home.'

'One thing I learnt in England is that home is not where your house is; it's where your family and friends are.'

Ian planned for an early night, but in the evening's haze of beer and chatter it slipped his mind. It was his first full day in Harare, and already he'd made new friends.

CHAPTER 24

29th January 2009

IAN woke early to a lovely summer morning. The sun streaming through the window promised another warm day. Today, he planned to get in touch with Jemma about her employers' apartment. He was impatient to get things moving and to make a start on his book. Somehow, staying in the hotel was not motivating him for the task.

The hotel was a lot less busy than when Ian last stayed there with his parents. It was newer back then, but now it was showing its age and in need of refurbishment, though it was still a fine hotel. Tourists and business visitors were thin on the ground, and the cholera epidemic would have made things worse still. Drinks in quiet bars and dinner and breakfast in quiet restaurants gave the city an isolated atmosphere. It was clear Zimbabwe was at its lowest ebb.

After breakfast Ian returned to his room and called Jemma. 'Hello, Jemma, Sarah told me to phone you about a flat to rent in the apartment block where you work.'

'Yes, Sir. The boss and madam are home today. If you come at eleven o'clock, you can meet them.'

Old houses and small blocks of flats made up the inner-city suburb named *The Avenues*. The apartment was a short walk of about six city blocks from the hotel. Ian soon found the neat two-storey building with its four flats on each floor. Jemma told him to go to number six upstairs. He knocked, and a young man opened the door. Ian introduced himself to Dennis and Mary Jones. They were expecting him and greeted him warmly.

The Jones turned out to be a young American couple in their early thirties, working in IT at the American Embassy in Herbert Chitepo Avenue. 'How on earth did you meet our housemaid?' Dennis Jones enquired.

'It was a chance meeting.'

Ian looked around the apartment. A short passage, between a bathroom on the left and the kitchen, led into a large single room. Double glass doors and floor-to-ceiling windows looked onto the balcony which ran the width of the apartment. Open curtains framed the leafy sycamore trees that lined the quiet street. A built-in cupboard backed onto the bathroom wall, and between it and the double glass doors stood a wooden dining table with four chairs. On the right, with its headboard against the kitchen wall was a huge bed with bedside tables. An armchair stood in the corner at the foot of the bed. The sparsely furnished studio apartment was bright and fresh.

'We will be away for at least six months,' said Dennis. 'After that, you can rent it by the week until we return.'

'It'll do for me,' said Ian.

'Everything you'll need is here, including bed linen and towels. We have few possessions here in Zimbabwe, and once we have packed our clothing for the trip, the apartment will be almost bare. The fridge will be empty of perishables, but you are welcome to use anything you find left in the kitchen cupboards.'

'That's the biggest bed I've ever seen.'

'Yes, that's a super-king-size bed,' said Mary. 'It's almost two metres square. We bought the bed here in Zimbabwe, but we had to buy the bedding on the internet. None of the shops here had anything near that size.'

'We were very lucky to find this apartment,' said Dennis. 'As you can see, it's freshly painted. The beauty of this building is the water supply. Each apartment has its own rainwater tank. You will have seen them as you came in past the secure fenced area at the side of the building. The summer rains keep the water tanks full, but in the dry winter season we must be frugal because you can run out of tank water. The mains supply is off at present, and you wouldn't want to drink it. Good luck with the electricity though; outages occur at the most inconvenient times. And there's one other little thing. The neighbours' young boy, in flat number seven, sometimes kicks his soccer ball against the wall between four and five in the afternoon. When we complained to his parents, it stopped for a day or two but then started again.'

'If it's only between four and five, it won't be too much of a problem. I write in the morning and after dinner.'

'Oh! And if you pay Jemma for the time we are away, we'll fix up the cost of the utilities on our return.'

Ian agreed to pay the rent and Jemma's wages for the next six months. His tourist visa was only for three months, but he planned to renew it when it expired. Dennis and Mary liked the look of Ian, and they shook hands on the deal.

'You were lucky to catch us,' said Mary, pouring the tea. 'We're leaving for the States at the end of next week, so you can move in anytime from Monday after next. We will leave the keys with Jemma. She also has her own key, so when we're at work she can lock up if she goes to the shops or goes home.'

'Yes, I thought she'd be here. Where is she?'

'No,' said Dennis, 'she was at home when you called her on her mobile. She phoned in to tell us what time you'd be coming here and to let us know she couldn't come in today. There's a problem with her sister.'

The news concerned Ian. Perhaps Sarah's pursuers caught up with her? He said nothing to Dennis or Mary, and he wouldn't risk phoning Jemma again in case it exposed his part in yesterday's drama. Jemma would tell him all about it when he next saw her.

It would be eleven days before he could move into the apartment. Aside from making notes for future reference for his novel, he felt there was not much else for him to do. Ian was in a holiday mood and justified putting off work on his book by telling himself the hotel was not conducive to writing. The apartment would be different, but until then he would spend his time exploring Harare. Wasn't that research for the book?

* * *

Ian returned to the hotel for a light lunch at the Gazebo Deli in the hotel lobby. There were more diners than usual, and it gave Ian the chance for a little people watching. From the way they dressed, he guessed they were office workers from the nearby high-rise buildings. Ian relaxed as the other diners hurried off as two o'clock approached. He fancied it would be easy to get used to this lifestyle. After a second cup of coffee, he set off for another walk around the city.

As he exited the hotel, Ian noticed the two Africans who'd come to his room, looking for Sarah. They were talking to a taxi driver and didn't see him pass. If they caught Sarah and interrogated her, would she tell them he'd hidden her in the shower? Would they recognise him fully clothed with his hair combed? He was a sight when they first saw him.

He'd start his walk with a visit to Manfred Schwartz. Ian found the building he'd seen on an earlier walk and took the lift to the third floor. The sign on the glass door said Manfred Schwartz and Associates. Ian pushed open the door and walked into the reception area. An African woman in a smart navy business suit, white blouse and horn-rimmed glasses sat at a desk behind the counter. 'Good afternoon, my name is Ian Sanders. Would it be possible to see Mr Schwartz?'

The woman stopped typing on her keyboard, looked up from the computer, lowered her glasses and inspected Ian at length. 'Mr Schwartz is away,' she said, without smiling. 'He won't see you without an appointment.'

'Please ask him to call me.' Ian gave the woman his mobile number and left. He stepped out onto the street and headed for the First

Avenue mall where he'd walked the previous afternoon. A large crowd of Africans gathered. Had there been an incident? Ruth and Solly warned him to stay away from gatherings as they often led to trouble.

Ian sensed that on this occasion it was a good-natured crowd. As he got closer, he saw they were all watching a man doing tricks on a bicycle. The man spun the bicycle round and round on its front wheel and then on its back wheel. He jumped the bicycle several times on the same spot with both wheels leaving the ground. Next, he walked the bicycle, taking alternate steps with the back wheel and the front wheel. Using this technique, he walked the bicycle over a nervous volunteer lying on his back on the ground. He stepped the bicycle over one leg and then the next, over the man's torso and over one arm, his head, and then his next arm. The man did all this without peddling. It was a skilled demonstration of balance and control. A hat passed around, and Ian wondered about the value of the money collected. Zimbabwe dollars were as good as worthless. Ian carried US one-dollar notes for just such occasions, so when the hat passed in front of him, he dropped in a note. The man bowed his head and put his hands together in a gesture of thanks.

The walk down First Avenue took Ian into Orr Street and past the railway station and then up Angwa Street back to the hotel. Ian was getting thirsty, and he decided there was no need to explore the whole city in one day. There were still eight weeks of summer before the idyllic weather in April and May. It was a warm and humid day, and Ian's mind turned to a beer at the hotel's lobby bar. With luck, Hazel would be there.

The progress he'd made in just two days pleased him. Hazel should be a good source of information for his book as should Sarah if he ever saw her again. Jemma was a simple house girl, so he was not sure how useful her contribution might be.

The day's heat slipped away as the setting sun turned the warm afternoon into a beautiful evening. The hotel's air conditioning did not work too well, but Ian felt comfortable in his light cotton clothing as he made his way to the lobby bar.

* * *

Ian was due to move into the apartment after the weekend, and even though he was not working, Friday always filled him with a sense of anticipation. The dark clouds looked heavy with rain, and Ian looked forward to the coming downpour with relish. The constant cycle of thirty minutes of threatening cloud, half an hour downpour and thirty minutes of brilliant sunshine delighted him.

Ian's cell phone rang. 'Mr Sanders? This is Manfred Schwartz. My good friend Solly Bernstein has told me all about you.'

'Hello Mr Schwartz. When can I come and meet you?'

'Are you free for lunch today, at the Gazebo Restaurant at the Monomotapa?'

'Yes, what time?'

At half past twelve Ian walked into the lobby bar and soon recognised Manfred Schwartz from the description Schwartz gave him over the phone. He was tall, with a medium build and balding. Light brown hair sprouted on either side near the back half of his head, looking like pampas grass and reminding Ian of a circus clown. The smart, light grey suit and fashionable, black leather shoes looked imported. He stood up as Ian approached and put out his hand. 'Call me Manfred. Welcome to Harare.'

He had a most engaging smile and Ian estimated he was in his mid-fifties. 'You're too modest Manfred. You're much better looking than you described yourself over the phone.' They both laughed, and their relationship was off to a good start.

'I'm sorry I was not there to meet you when you called at my office, but I was in Johannesburg. I spend a lot of time down there on business, and it gives me a break from all the crap over here. My wife lives in Joburg. That's where all her friends are. Although I'm resident here,

I spend more time down there. You met Jacinta; I believe? She looks after things for me in Harare, and we are in constant touch. How are you settling in here?'

'Not bad thanks. Both Joburg and Harare seem more tropical than I remember. But I was in my teens then, and maybe my memory is faulty.'

'No, I've also heard others say that. But if you want tropical, visit Victoria Falls. That'll put it in perspective for you. Did Solly tell you what he was doing in Zimbabwe?'

'No, he only said you look after his business affairs and to keep in touch with you in case work became available.'

'I might have something for you already. One of his clients is putting together a business case for when the politics here settle. I've looked at it, and it's not at all professional. Perhaps you could tidy it up to make it suitable for presentation to government and investors. Come to my office on Monday and we'll talk further.'

'Is Monday afternoon at say half past two OK? I'm moving into my apartment on Monday morning.'

After lunch, when they were saying goodbye, Manfred said, 'Oh! I almost forgot; Ruth will be here in late May. She's involved with the project and will have the final say, so you'll have a lot to discuss.'

As he walked back to his room in the hotel, Ian thought about his lunch with Manfred. The prospect of paid work pleased him, but the opportunity had come sooner than he expected. He hoped it wouldn't interfere with his novel as it would be easy to get sidetracked, and he needed to keep work and writing in perspective. There would have been little prospect of him writing a book if he was still working full-time in his job in Melbourne. For Ian, work was like fly paper or a cobweb, and once he got stuck in, everything else went by the wayside. He promised himself he would keep the novel as his number one goal, and this time, the fill-in would be work.

* * *

The eleven days in the hotel sped by, and before he knew it, it was time for him to move into the apartment. After a good last breakfast at the Monomotapa, Ian returned to his room to brush his teeth and finish packing his backpack. He checked the room to make sure he'd not forgotten anything. Ian took one last look at the view of Harare Gardens from his hotel window and then caught the lift down to the lobby to check out. 'We hope you enjoyed your stay, Sir' said the hotel receptionist. 'Please come again. You'll be most welcome.'

It was a lovely bright morning, and Ian enjoyed the short walk from the hotel to the apartment. In a country with a serious fuel shortage, not having a car was proving to be a blessing. As in Melbourne, walking was turning out to be his main form of exercise.

Ian approached the front door of flat number six and knocked. After a moment, Jemma opened the door and greeted Ian with a broad smile.

'Come in, Sir. Let me take your bag.'

'It's fine thank you, Jemma. It's not heavy.'

'Sir, I will make you tea.'

'Thank you, Jemma. My name is Ian. You can call me Ian.'

'Thank you, Sir Ian.'

'It's just Ian.'

'Yes Boss.'

For the time being, Ian gave up trying to resolve that issue. Jemma fussed around him, pointing out the armchair, encouraging him to sit. Ian thanked her but did not sit. He looked in the wardrobe and found it was spotless. Ian refused Jemma's offer to lay out his clothes. He would do that himself.

Jemma, meanwhile, walked out the front door, returning five minutes later with a pan of water bubbling away.

'Is that water safe?' said Ian, looking warily at the pan.

'This is bottled water, Sir. Miss Mary said I should use bottled water for your tea. We have too much bottled water in the fridge.' Ian understood the African use of the term *too much,* which was a common way of saying *a lot*. He walked to the huge refrigerator and opened the door. Sure enough, bottled water crammed the fridge. Dennis and Mary must have got it from the US Embassy. They couldn't have bought that much from the shops with their constant shortages. The size of the refrigerator suggested the need to stockpile when essential items were available in the shops.

'Why didn't you use the water from the rainwater tank?'

'Bottled water is better, Sir. The ice is also bottled water.' Ian heeded the warning to travellers to not ask for ice when ordering a drink, even in hotels. The source of the water was uncertain. Since arriving in Harare, Ian moved away from his preferred choice of Scotch on the rocks. Now if he drank Scotch, he drank it with soda, or he drank it neat. But now, in Harare's warm and humid weather, he turned to drinking beer.

'But Jemma, you went to the servants' quarters and brought back the boiling water in a saucepan?'

'Yes, Sir, the electricity is off again, so I had to use the fire the maids use.' Ian made a mental note to keep his laptop plugged in to the mains to keep the battery charged.

'Jemma, have tea with me!' said Ian, sitting down at the dining table.

'I have tea with the other girls, Sir.' Ian did not push the point further, but he wanted to chat with Jemma.

'How is Sarah? Is she all right?'

'Yes, Sir, she's fine. But she's not at home. She's hiding.'

'Sit down, Jemma,' said Ian, pulling out a dining chair.

'No thank you, Sir. I can stand, Sir,' said Jemma, shuffling her feet and folding her hands in front of her. She was uncomfortable being on familiar terms with her boss.

'Who is she hiding from, Jemma?'

'I think she is hiding from the CIO, Sir.'

'And what is she going to do?'

'I don't know, Sir.'

Ian saw it might take time before Jemma would relax and talk with confidence. All her answers were short and getting any information was hard work. He imagined a writer's life might be isolated, but he needed human company and conversation, even if it was with his housemaid. If he worked from his apartment, he needed Jemma to be more communicative. He could, in the evenings, visit the hotel and chat with Hazel if she was there. But to be stuck in the apartment with a quiet maid was a daunting prospect. It would add another perspective to his book if he could get Jemma to converse. Zimbabwe, seen through the lens of a housemaid, would be fascinating.

'Jemma, I want you to have tea with me each morning and each afternoon. Have your tea break with the maids, but afterwards, you must also have tea with me.'

'Yes, Sir.' Jemma looked nonplussed. This order from her boss was most unusual. None of her former employers had made such a demand. Important people didn't have time to talk to their housemaids. She would ask her mother and Sarah about it.

The next morning after tea with the maids, Jemma made tea for Ian, and he motioned for her to sit on one of the dining chairs. She obeyed, sitting with a straight back, drinking tea from her tin mug. Ian drank from a china cup and saucer. They made an odd couple; she in her work clothes and turban style headscarf and he in his casual wear.

After a week of formal and stiff conversation, Ian tried to break down the barrier a little further. 'Jemma, from now on I want you to drink from a china cup and saucer. Get one from the kitchen.'

Jemma looked shocked and giggled. 'I can't drink from the madam's cups, Sir. She will be cross.'

'Well, she's not here, Jemma, so what she doesn't know won't harm her. These cups are not special. If it makes her happy, I will buy her new cups when she gets back.'

'Which cup should I use, Sir?' said Jemma, picking up a chipped cup consigned to the back of the kitchen cupboard.

'Use any cup, Jemma. You needn't use the same one every day.'

The move to a china cup was a big step for Jemma. Ian's hunch proved right, and she became more relaxed and talkative. By the end of the second week, she was bringing back snippets of gossip she'd picked up at the tea breaks with the other African maids. Ian often heard them shrieking with laughter. He smiled at the thought of the African maids enjoying a good joke. They all seemed to have a wonderful sense of humour.

'Jemma, have you told the other girls you have tea with me.'

'No, Sir, I can't tell the other maids. If I tell them, they can be jealous and tell their madams, and sometimes they may not like me.' Jemma's response did not surprise Ian; the tall poppy syndrome was alive and well in African society. He did not want to disturb the balance of the prevailing social structures amongst the African maids, and he wanted to glean as much of the maids' gossip as Jemma would divulge. It would supply him with fertile material for his book. At least, she'd got past the unhelpful one-word answers.

After another week of morning tea, Jemma seemed relaxed in Ian's company. Although the tea breaks were taking up more of her time, she had no difficulty in keeping the small apartment spotless. It came as a surprise to Ian one morning when Jemma seemed more nervous than usual. He got the impression she was hovering around him while he was writing. 'OK, Jemma, what's the problem?'

'No problem, Sir.' Jemma didn't seem to have much to say. But when she came back from the maids' morning tea break, she sat down opposite Ian with an even straighter back than usual.

'What is it, Jemma?' said Ian. 'You seem quiet today. Are you unwell?'

'I am well, thank you, Sir.'

'Then what's wrong.'

Jemma stood up and stepped back from the dining table. 'It's my sister, Sir. Sarah is in great danger. A man visited the house where she is hiding and asked if anyone had seen her. The people who hide Sarah are scared, and they want her to leave. I don't think she can stay there anymore.'

'Can she go somewhere else?'

Jemma looked at the floor, unable to look Ian in the eye. 'Can she come here, Sir?'

The request surprised Ian. 'Here?' He hesitated to answer. 'Come for how long, Jemma?'

'I don't know, Sir. Can she stay until it's safe for her to go?'

'Where would she sleep?'

'She can sleep on the floor, Sir, maybe on the balcony.'

It was almost a month since Ian met Sarah. How long could she stay in hiding? He knew the police and CIO's reputations for intimidation and violence, and he understood there was no one else for Jemma to turn to for help. How could he refuse? Damn! Servants could be a nuisance. That's what his mother often said.

'Yes, OK. We can discuss the details when she gets here. When does she want to come?' Ian pushed his chair back and stood up, looking at Jemma as he waited for her reply. She shuffled her feet.

'Tomorrow, Sir,' said Jemma, making eye contact for the first time that morning.

Chapter 25

February 2009

The angry voice crackled at the end of the line. 'Good morning, Captain, is the unit falling apart?'

'No, Sir, I've just been doing a little spring cleaning.'

'Is that so? It looks worse than that from where I'm sitting.'

'I had to get rid of the girl from team LA4 after that business with the father. You know what they say about one rotten apple in the barrel. If the father's loyalty was in doubt, how could I trust her?'

'What about team A3, that's also fallen apart?'

'Well, Sir, team A3 operated as a gang on the streets. Only the team leader was one of our operatives. I never met the members of the gang. There probably was a dispute, and the others killed him, so the gang is now defunct. As soon as I find a suitable individual, they can set up a new street gang.'

'And what happened to the male member of team LA4?'

'He left without notice because of trouble with money lenders. Apparently, he's gone to South Africa.'

'Be a lot more careful in your choice of operatives, Captain.'

'Yes, Sir, but we're better off without him. You'll recall how he questioned the reasons for the Egypt trip, and he wouldn't let the matter drop. He came close to guessing the purpose of the operation, and he also questioned the purpose of the unit. I warned him several times to let the matter drop, but it seemed he had an ethical problem with us.'

'What if he talks to someone about the Egypt operation or about the unit?'

'Don't worry, Sir, he won't talk. He always followed the secrecy rules and wouldn't discuss us with anybody.'

'You're sure about that?'

'Yes, I am positive, Sir.'

'OK, but be it on your head if there's any leak about our activities.'

'We won't hear from him again, Sir, but there might be one loose end to resolve.'

'I don't like loose ends, Captain.'

'The girl we let go was his team partner, and it's possible he discussed his concerns with her. We might have to deal with her.'

'You mean she must go?'

'Yes, Sir, as soon as we find her.'

'As soon as you find her?'

'She worked at a city hotel but left both her job and home without notice or telling anyone. No one knows where she is.'

'You better find her, Captain, and quick, or your position will be a little shaky.'

'We'll find her, Sir.'

'What about the families, Captain? Would they have told them anything?'

'He wouldn't speak about us to any outsider, not even his parents, but I'm not sure about the girl. Once we find her, we can decide what to do next. The sister is a simple housemaid, and the mother is a retired teacher. I doubt they'd be any threat.'

'Find the woman, Captain. If she's a loose end, she's the number one target.'

'Yes, Sir.'

The phone went dead. Captain John slammed down the receiver. The idiot! After all the COU's achievements, they still believe it necessary to make threats and offer gratuitous advice. One little obstacle arises, and they question your work. The fools don't understand covert operations. During the Bush War, brute force worked. There was no need for subtlety. But in the COU one needed finesse, particularly if the target was once one of their own.

John swivelled in his chair and reached for the ice tray in the minibar. He dropped two cubes of ice into the crystal glass and poured a large tot of Scotch from the bottle he kept in the cabinet under his desk. He held it up to the light, but his mind was elsewhere. The fools didn't give him any advice when he set up dangerous missions where his neck was on the line. Did they think he didn't know finding Sarah was a matter of urgency? When he found her, she'd be sorry, and whoever hid her would be sorry too.

The elusive Sarah was an embarrassment to John. She must have guessed the COU wanted her, and now she avoided them. In future they'd take more care when screening potential operatives. No more independent thinkers. They were nothing but trouble, and their language skills were of limited use. Yes, they translated documents and stuff, but few arrests had come out of it. But if they'd known where some of their translations led, they might have objected on ethical grounds. That Sarah was a tough cookie, but Thomas was soft. In that regard, he may have been a bad influence on her. It was a mistake to send those two to Sharm el-Sheikh. They might even have refused to carry out his Plan B.

The glass was empty. Where did that Scotch go? John didn't remember drinking it though he tasted it on his tongue. He poured another large tot over two ice cubes. The bottle was getting low; time for another external operation to replenish his supply of duty-free, high-end Scotch. Captain John's loyalty to his country depended on his creature comforts. Right now, he wasn't feeling all that patriotic.

A single crystal glass stood on the bookshelf. John always drank alone in his office. He wouldn't waste precious Scotch on visitors, no matter how important. Tea, he would offer, but not Scotch, never Scotch. Though on one occasion he'd offered a Scotch to the young secretary seconded to him from foreign affairs. But she'd earned it, and her work wasn't too bad either. He'd been generous with his Scotch on that occasion, but then she'd been generous too. Damn! If things didn't improve soon, he could kiss goodbye to any chance of having a secretary like that again.

In the good old days, they could blame everything on the whites and Ian Smith. But twenty-eight years on, it was drawing a long bow. Blaming the whites was now the president's prerogative. It wouldn't be easy for him to do that. The COU's future was in his hands as the boss so unnecessarily reminded him.

'Akashinga, come here.' John shouted.

'Yes, Sah.' A broad, strongly built, balding man of average height came to John's office and stood in the doorway.

'Would you recognise Sarah Kagonye? You saw her in Sharm el-Sheikh.'

'Yes, Sah.'

'Remember when you and the others tried to pick her up at the hotel?'

'Yes, Sah.'

'You remained downstairs and the other two caught the lift to her floor.'

'Yes, Sah.'

'Sam and Elijah spoke to a murungu and searched his room.'

'Yes, Sah.'

'Have you ever seen the murungu?'

'Yes, Sah, Samson and Elijah pointed him out to me.'

'I am told his house girl is Sarah Kagonye's sister. Do you imagine that's a coincidence?'

'Yes, Sah. No, Sah.'

'Do you know Hazel? The murungu often meets her at the hotel.'

'No, Sah.'

'Well find her and talk to her. Ask her what she knows about the murungu and about Sarah Kagonye. If she knows nothing, then talk to the murungu about Kagonye.'

'Yes, Sah.'

'It is most important we find Kagonye soon.'

'Yes, Sah.'

'Now go.'

John leant back in his swivel chair planning the next step. If Akashinga couldn't find Sarah, he might have to make a move on her mother or sister. He didn't like the idea. His own relatives suffered in the Bush War, and he remembered the pain he'd felt. Sarah's mother and sister were ordinary Shona people. If they were Ndebele, he would have no such qualms. But he wouldn't let Sarah's disappearance come between him and his ambitions. If he needed to use her family to get to her, he would, as a last resort. Perhaps he should finish the remnants in the bottle of Scotch to celebrate his new plan. A bottle in reserve stood at the back of the cabinet under his desk.

Chapter 26

27th February 2009

Five o'clock in the evening. Ian had made plans to meet Hazel at the hotel, so he left Jemma to arrange for Sarah's arrival. 'Tell her to make herself a cup of tea. I should be back at about half past ten,' said Ian, putting his ballpoint and a sheet of blank paper into his pocket. He always took something to write on in case he needed to make notes for his novel.

Since they first met, Ian and Hazel saw each other half a dozen times. She was his first new friend in Zimbabwe. He enjoyed her company and looked forward to seeing her. The occasions helped break the monotony of his time spent in the apartment. Jemma's company was improving but talking to her could still be hard work.

Ian looked at his watch yet again, seven o'clock. One-and-a-half hours late; a first for Hazel. There was no sign of her as Ian drained his second glass of Zambezi beer. Two was his usual limit when he drank alone, so he tried to engage the barman in conversation, but there was no rapport. Only time builds the trust required for uninhibited conversation. No, he needed Hazel, but where was she? Tonight, the women in the lobby bar were missing. Ian spoke to the barman. 'Where are the ladies tonight?' The barman shrugged.

About half past seven an African woman walked into the bar area and sat down at a table. Ian recognised her from his earlier visits. After a few minutes, Ian downed the last of his third beer, paid the barman and crossed the floor towards the woman's table. When she saw Ian approaching, she got up to leave, but he moved swiftly to accost her. 'Good evening, I am a friend of Hazel's, and I was due to meet her here tonight, but she hasn't come. Have you seen here today?'

The woman tried to ignore Ian, but then looked down, avoiding eye contact, and said in a low voice, 'She's dead, Sir.'

'Hazel is dead? How, where, when? Are you sure?'

'Yesterday evening, Sir. Someone strangled her in Harare Gardens.'

'Do they know who did it?'

'No, Sir. She spoke with a big, bald, African man, and they left together, but no one saw her after that. I must go, Sir, it's dangerous for me to talk to you here.'

'But, but…' She'd gone before Ian could get his words out. The news stunned him. Why did it happen? Why in Harare Gardens? What did the African woman mean when she said it was too dangerous for her to talk to him there in the hotel lobby? Why wasn't it on the news? Now, he'd lost his appetite and wanted to get back to the apartment.

Ian strode out of the hotel. After a block or two he heard someone walking fast behind him, but when he slowed down, so did the footsteps. When he picked up his pace, he heard his footsteps echoed by another's. The person maintained a discreet distance. Was he being followed? There were no shop windows handy for him to see the person's reflection. When he came to cross the next street, he looked left and right, as if for traffic, and saw a dark figure in his peripheral vision.

A block from home, Ian made a detour and turned down a dark treed avenue. If the person followed him, he wouldn't lead him to his front door. Why would they be following him, anyway? Once around the corner he picked up his pace, but now someone walked right behind him. He heard their laboured breathing.

Ian turned to his left to look at his pursuer, but the person moved to his right. Before Ian could turn back, something scratched at his throat. He tried to get a grip of it, but it was too tight. He struggled to get away from his determined attacker, but the coarse rope garrotte cut off his breathing. Ian twisted and turned, trying to face his attacker, but the assailant turned with him in a macabre last dance. Ian realised he wouldn't survive unless he did something fast. His throat burned and hurt with a crushing sensation, and his head felt like it would explode. An intense choking sensation came over him. With all his concentration and strength, Ian lifted his right foot and kicked down as hard as possible on his assailant's shin. The man yelped in pain and for a second loosened his hold on Ian's neck. Ian slipped the deadly stranglehold. The rough rope scratched and burned his face when he pulled his head free. He swivelled around and swung out his right fist with all his strength, striking his assailant on the point of his chin. The man's huge bulk hit the ground like a sack of mealies. For a few seconds, Ian stood over the prostrate form of the bald man. The prone figure looked shorter than him but built like a gorilla. Africans were strong, even the thin ones. Ian didn't intend to stick around and test the theory. He ran.

The detour meant Ian needed to run the length of three blocks. When he turned into his apartment building, he struggled to catch his breath, and his heart thumped in his chest as if struggling to break free. The same person might have strangled Hazel. His hands trembled from the shock as he thought of poor Hazel struggling to get away from the attacker. Ian felt emotional, and he retched again and again before he finally brought up his beers. His temples throbbed as if they would burst. The pressure behind his eyes built up into a headache. The lump in his throat prevented him swallowing, and his eyes burned, and his breath came in sobs. He took deep breaths to calm himself, but his African dream was turning into a nightmare. Hazel understood the risks she took. Ian had known her for just a few weeks, but it shocked him to lose his first new friend in Zimbabwe in such a violent way. His narrow escape from a similar fate made him emotional. Tears welled up in his eyes and his hands shook.

At last, when his hands steadied, Ian took another deep breath, found the Yale key in his pocket, and opened the door of his apartment.

In the darkness, he searched for the light switch. The dull lightbulb flooded the room, and there she was, sitting in the armchair. Damn! He'd forgotten about Sarah. She'd arrived.

* * *

The timing couldn't be more inconvenient. This, the worst evening of his life. He narrowly avoided meeting the same fate as his friend Hazel, lying dead in a morgue somewhere. Ian needed time to adjust. Yesterday, unaware of the danger he and Hazel faced, everything seemed perfect. And now Sarah had arrived, shattering his privacy.

'What's wrong with your neck? It looks like you escaped the hangman's noose.' Now that Sarah mentioned it, his neck felt hot and itchy. Ian walked into the bathroom and looked in the mirror. A broad, half-inch wide red line ran right around his throat. The bathroom mirror reflected a multitude of scratches with slivers of sisal rope embedded in his neck. He washed with soap and water, but the sisal slivers proved hard to shift. Ian explained to Sarah what happened.

'Let me help you with those little bits of rope in your neck,' said Sarah, standing in the bathroom doorway. She produced a pair of tweezers from her bag and placed them in a small pan of water she boiled on the stove. She added a teaspoon of Dettol. After she sterilised the tweezers, Sarah let them cool and one by one removed the sisal slivers from Ian's neck. 'If you're not careful, you can get infected from those scratchy ropes.'

Ian had the foresight to buy first aid supplies in Johannesburg, and Sarah used cotton wool to apply TCP antiseptic to his neck. 'Keep those scratches clean, and we'll put TCP on them for the next couple of days. Can I make you a cup of tea?' Ian, shaky after his traumatic experience, needed the hot sweet drink. He didn't take milk or sugar in his tea, but that didn't seem to matter right now.

Sarah fussed around Ian and brought him another cup of tea. After she dabbed more TCP on his scratches, she wrapped a bandage around

Ian's neck, and he relaxed. The calm way she'd taken control of the situation, impressed him. It was good having someone take care of him.

'Were you a nurse at one time?'

'No, but I trained in first aid in my job.'

'You mean in your job with state security?' Sarah did not reply.

For the next couple of hours Ian and Sarah chatted about what happened since they last saw each other.

* * *

After Sarah left Ian's room at the hotel, she headed for the lift. It was empty, and to her relief, it did not stop at any of the floors. But when she reached the lobby, she noticed two men who fitted the description Ian gave. Sarah, with her heart in her mouth, walked past them, but they only gave her a cursory glance. Where was the third man? Stanley, at the concierge desk, warned her that three men enquired about her. No one intercepted Sarah when she walked out through the front of the hotel, and she didn't dare look back. Her Sunday best did the trick.

Sarah walked to the bus station to catch the bus. At two o'clock, far fewer buses ran compared to the five o'clock rush hour. She waited, trying to make herself inconspicuous in her smart clothing. At the hotel, disguised as a successful businesswoman or tourist was an advantage, but now at the bus station, she feared it might attract unwanted attention.

When Sarah arrived home, her mother, Esther, stood at the door, waiting for her. A well-dressed man visited earlier and enquired as to her whereabouts. It was too dangerous for her to stay there. The authorities knew where she lived. Seldom was Esther flustered, but she feared the man would come back. Sarah packed a small bag and hurried to Thomas' house. His worried mother, who now wore a constant furrow on her brow, welcomed her. 'Sarah, come in my girl. I can't imagine what's happened to Thomas. There's still no news of him.'

Thomas' mother rung her hands and tears came to her eyes. 'My husband is at the bus station making enquiries. It's difficult because he never told us where he worked.'

Sarah knew where Thomas worked, but she hesitated to make any comment. She did not want to alarm Thomas' parents by telling them about Jedson's phone call that morning. If she phoned Jedson, he might give her information about Thomas, but it could be a risk. When Jedson phoned her at the hotel, he said he would be there in thirty minutes, but others came instead. Who were they? Was the third man Jedson or someone else? Was Jedson also in danger? Sarah waited, hoping Thomas would get in touch with her or his parents.

After hiding for a fortnight with Thomas' parents, Sarah could wait no longer. She rang Jedson on her prepaid cell phone to seek news of Thomas. A dry mouth, and a tongue that seemed to stick to her palate, made her voice a scratchy whisper. 'Hello, Sir.'

'Sarah, where are you? I've worried about you.'

'Sir, why didn't you come to the hotel after you phoned me?'

'I did Sarah, but no one could find you.'

'After you phoned, three men arrived at the hotel, but I escaped.'

'I don't know about that Sarah. Perhaps someone overheard our phone call. Where are you? We need to talk.'

Sarah's heart was thumping when she asked the next question. 'Sir, what's happened to Thomas? Where is he?'

'He said he was heading south, and I assumed that meant South Africa. Sarah, where are you?'

'I'm in Johannesburg,' she lied, 'but no one here has seen Thomas.'

'What did you want to talk about, Sir, when you phoned me?'

'It's too dangerous to talk over the phone. Let's discuss it face to face. Where are you Sarah?'

'I have to go, Sir. Bye for now.' Sarah put the phone down before he had the chance to respond. She took deep breaths to calm herself. Her hands shook. Perhaps someone listened to their call and beat Jedson to the hotel. She got through to his mobile without difficulty, so she thought it unlikely he was in trouble with the authorities. But might he be working with them against her? First, someone in the COU murdered her father, then she lost her job, and now Thomas was missing. The COU was the common thread, and only Jedson from team LA4 still there, unaffected by events.

A week later, Sarah called Jedson again, but the result was the same. She didn't believe he would be a party to Thomas' disappearance, but if someone bugged his phone, strange men might turn up again. Perhaps she should warn him to be careful and tell him about Sonny Mutezo. Someone was working against team LA4.

Sarah spent her days reading and studying, trying to improve her Ndebele, her weakest language.

One morning, after Sarah had been with Thomas' parents for almost four weeks, a loud knock on the front door startled them. Sarah hurried into Thomas' room which she'd occupied since her arrival. Thomas' mother opened the door to a well-dressed man standing there. 'Good morning Mrs Chimedza, my name is Elijah. I worked with Thomas until they transferred him to another department.'

'Where is my son?' asked Mrs Chimedza, drying her hands on a tea cloth. 'Do you have news of Thomas?'

'Since his transfer, we've not had any news of him. They don't keep us informed about other employees. There's a rumour he might be in Joburg, but I'm not sure.'

'I would like to speak to Thomas' boss. Can you tell me how I can get in touch with him?'

'I'm sorry, I can't tell you his name or where he works. But I'll tell him you'd like to speak with him and then he can contact you.'

'Thank you.'

'Mrs Chimedza, do you have any idea where Sarah Kagonye is? She is also missing from her home.'

'No, I'm sorry, I don't. We haven't seen her for almost a month.' Later that night Thomas' parents asked Sarah to find another refuge. Hiding her might put them in danger, and they had good reason to be scared. Had Sarah's phone calls to Jedson given away her location? The net closing.

In the four weeks Sarah hid with Thomas' parents, no news of him came, and they all feared the worst. None of his clothes or any other items were missing. Thomas left for work one morning and vanished.

* * *

'Thank you for agreeing to hide me,' said Sarah. 'You're brave.'

Ian did not feel in the least bit brave after his experience earlier in the evening. It never crossed his mind, giving Sarah refuge might endanger him.

'You can put your things in here,' said Ian, walking to the built-in cupboard. 'I don't have a lot of clothes, so there's plenty of room.' He opened the door to show Sarah, but then he saw she'd already taken a shelf, a drawer and hanging space. She also didn't have too many clothes, and between them the cupboard wasn't even a quarter full. 'I'm glad to see you've made yourself at home,' said Ian, with the hint of an edge to his voice.

Ian gave Sarah first use of the bathroom. When she emerged, she wore a dusty blue, mid-thigh length T-shirt, stretched in all the right places, showing off her figure and her long, shapely legs. Sarah looked even more attractive than he remembered. Ian went into the bathroom to change into his pyjamas and brush his teeth and get ready for bed, but when he returned to the room, where was Sarah? He looked in the kitchen, and on the veranda, but then discovered her lying behind the bed.

'What are you doing lying on the floor, squeezed in between the bed and the wall? It's a huge bed. You can sleep on this side. There's plenty of room.'

'No, I'm fine thank you, I like sleeping on the floor.' Sarah had wrapped herself in a spare blanket from the cupboard and taken a pillow from her side of the bed.

'You needn't fear me. I won't touch you.'

'You're right. You won't.'

'The parquet floor will be cold.'

'I'll be fine, thank you.'

'It's a huge bed, big enough for four or five people.'

'I'm used to sleeping on the floor.'

'OK, whatever you want.' Ian got into his side of the bed and soon fell asleep. His last waking thoughts were Sarah seemed too confident for a fugitive relying on him for shelter.

Dawn broke, and Ian became aware he had company in the bed. Sarah crept in during the night. After going to the bathroom, Ian hopped back into bed. Sarah stirred, stretched and rolled out of the bed and walked through to the bathroom while Ian dozed. What seemed like a moment later, she placed a cup of tea on his bedside table. Sarah walked around to her side of the bed and climbed back in and sat sipping her tea. Ian noticed that she didn't need any invitation to use one of the china cups. Sarah saw Ian watching her and said, 'It got cold during the night.'

'I told you it would. What's the time?'

'It's half past six. Jemma will be here soon. Want to be first in the bathroom?'

The way Sarah took control of the apartment both impressed and irritated Ian. She'd not even been there twenty-four hours, and already she set the routine they'd follow. He saw that her initiative and organising ability might make life a little easier for him, but she did not seem to appreciate her status as the one seeking refuge in his apartment. Now she behaved like the mistress of the house and no longer the room maid, the servant he first saw. Ian was grateful that Sarah's sister found the apartment for him, but that didn't entitle Sarah to take control of running it. Ian gave orders to the African women working around his parent's home even before he'd reached double figures. But this one seemed to push him in the direction she chose.

When Jemma arrived, the two sisters chatted away like parrots in a bird cage. They tried to keep their voices down to conceal Sarah's presence. Ian shook his head. 'Noise,' he shouted. 'Everyone will hear you.' How loud would it be if secrecy wasn't essential? While the sisters chatted, Sarah helped Jemma with the housework. There was insufficient work for two maids in the studio apartment, so the ratio of chatter to housework was high.

Ian was not in the mood for venturing out with his abraded throat. The red rope burn was more painful and prominent than ever. Jemma watched in sympathetic silence while her sister dabbed the TCP on Ian's wound. He resolved to stay in and progress with his writing, and like everyone before her, Sarah warned Ian to be careful of what he wrote. Journalists were a marked breed in Zimbabwe, and she warned him not to write anything that could be misconstrued. 'Yes, Sarah, journalists are a marked breed in many countries. Zimbabwe is not alone in that regard.'

* * *

On Sarah's third or fourth day in the flat, she and Ian had their first political disagreement. 'You told me to stay away from politics,' said Ian, 'but you seem to want to debate politics with me.'

'I said, don't write about politics, but that doesn't mean we can't discuss it. We are amongst friends here.'

'And if you don't like my politics, are you going to report me to the authorities?'

Sarah smiled. No, she wouldn't do that. 'So, you believe colonialism was good for Africa?'

'Yes, I do.'

'Then, how do you explain why black Africa has reverted to tribalism?'

'The blacks weren't ready to rule. Ian Smith said he wanted a slow but steady build-up of an established black middle class. That would have led to a government based on merit and electoral qualifications.'

'S*low*, being the operative word,' said Sarah, pacing up and down and warming to the debate. 'Most blacks wouldn't have had a vote, and those that qualified would have become pseudo whites and might even have voted for Ian Smith.'

'Pushing a people forward because of their colour always leads to disaster. Look at Zimbabwe now.'

'Any policy holding people back because of their colour is what leads to disaster. Countries where the whites voluntarily handed over power to the black majority are in a better situation. Look at Botswana and Zambia.'

'So then, you agree this country is a disaster.'

'My father thought the country showed signs of going down from around the year 2000, and my mother thinks they murdered him for his views. She thinks he may have somehow let slip his dissatisfaction with the country's direction.'

'At least we're agreed on something.'

'But why did you whites wage war against the blacks?'

'The whites weren't fighting the blacks. Mugabe and Nkomo both talked up Marxism. Ian Smith said we were fighting Marxism, not the blacks. You know eighty percent of the Rhodesian regular army and police were black, don't you?'

'They were traitors.'

'I'll tell you who fought the blacks. In 1983, Mugabe sent the Fifth Brigade into Matabeleland. They killed around twenty thousand innocent civilians. That's more casualties than in the Bush War.'

'Yes, the Gukurahundi, but who said they were innocent civilians?'

'And, Sarah, it's not just the Gukurahundi against the Ndebele. Since the elections in 2000, there has been a campaign of violence against the Shona opposition. And remember the Murambatsvina in 2005 when Mugabe destroyed the homes of the poor slum dwellers. It was also the Shona who endured that. And let's not forget the white-owned farm invasions that made hundreds of thousands of black farm workers homeless and led to the food shortages and starvation for those who did not support him.'

'Was your father in the Bush War?' Sarah asked.

'Yes, he was. What about your father?'

'He didn't fight, but in his spare time he worked for ZANU in an administrative role. After independence he took on the job full-time and rose to a senior position which he held right up to the time of his murder.'

'You must wonder, Sarah, why they killed him. Did they catch whoever did it?'

'I caught the main culprit, and he paid for his crime.'

'What do you mean *paid*?'

'He's dead.'

'What! You killed him?' said Ian, joking.

'Someone had to do it. The police wouldn't have done anything. But whoever ordered my father's murder should also pay.'

Until now, Ian gave little thought to Sarah's circumstances, but now he'd a creeping realisation he may have involved himself in a situation he didn't understand. Who looked for Sarah and why? She claimed she didn't know. Might they have found out about her retribution against her father's killer? Nah, he didn't believe her. She was just trying to impress him. How could she kill anyone? Perhaps the security services wanted Sarah because of her father's situation, but then, why wasn't Jemma also targeted? Perhaps, something in Sarah's past made her a target? She'd never told him the precise nature of the work she did for state security. He'd assumed she was a receptionist or secretary. Maybe she'd seen a confidential report or overheard something. Clearly, she was too educated for the mundane job she'd held at the hotel. How long would she stay? The sooner she moved on the better.

CHAPTER 27

2nd March 2009

THE loud voice rang through the office. 'Akashinga, come here.' Captain John's face was black with rage.

'Yes, Sah.' Akashinga hovered in the doorway.

'Come in and close the door.'

Akashinga edged into John's office, closing the door behind him.

'You fool, Akashinga. You stupid fool. I never told you to kill her.'

'Sorry, Sah, it was an accident. I tried to make her talk, and I must've squeezed her throat too hard.'

'You idiot, it was lucky the murungu got the better of you, otherwise you might also have killed him.'

Akashinga hung his head. He felt a cold chill run down his spine. Everybody feared Captain John's formidable temper. They'd all seen the dreadful punishments he'd handed out and their irreversible consequences. Akashinga remembered the incident in the office a year back. A new operative dropped dead during one of John's interrogations. They presumed it was a heart attack. Sonny helped Akashinga carry the body out to the boot of the car parked in the front yard.

'I'm sorry, Sah, I thought if I scared them, they'd talk and tell me where Sarah Kagonye is hiding.'

'You thought? You thought? When have you ever done that? You're too stupid for such a complicated process.'

'Yes, Sah. I'm sorry, Sah.'

'It's my fault. I should never have sent a fool on a job that needed subtlety and finesse. You should have been diplomatic, used your charm, befriend them; not strangle them. Akashinga, you're a moron, an absolute moron. Do you know what a moron is?'

'Yes, Sah. Sorry, Sah.'

'Yes, I'm sure you have heard the word many times.'

The veins in John's temples pulsed. 'I'll decide how to deal with you later.' He enjoyed tormenting the trembling Akashinga.

'Yes, Sah. I'm sorry, Sah.'

John didn't fancy answering to his superiors, or the police, questions about the murder of a woman in Harare Gardens.

'Sorry is not good enough. Because of your stupidity we must now ease back on the search for Sarah Kagonye. The police are investigating the woman's murder, and if the murungu reported your attack on him, they might also investigate that.'

Akashinga paled and his lower lip quivered. 'I'm sorry, Sah.'

'What if he took a photo of you on his cell phone while you lay on the pavement? Have you considered that?' John was hitting his stride now and twisting the knife. 'Thanks to your stupidity the murungu could now also be a risk to us. If he's involved with Sarah Kagonye, they'll be on their guard. Now you've doubled the size of the problem.'

'Sorry, Sah,' said Akashinga, looking about to faint.

'What if the murungu asks questions about you? What if he asks whether a fat, ugly, stupid, bald man had been talking to the murdered women?'

'I'm sorry, Sah.'

'Sorry? Is that all you can say? Get out you fool. Get out of my sight.'

Akashinga fled John's office, relieved to be dismissed from his presence.

John leant back in his chair and put his hands behind his head. He needed to be careful now. The boss was paying too much attention to what he was doing. Didn't he realise a person can't work with someone looking over their shoulder?

John swivelled in his chair and reached for the ice tray and crystal glass. He took the bottle of Scotch from his desk cabinet and poured a large tot over two ice cubes. He would let things quieten down before making his move. From now on that fool Akashinga, and Samson and Elijah from team A1, would be busy keeping a watch on the murungu.

'Akashinga, come here,' John shouted.

Akashinga peered around the corner of John's office door.

'Come in,' said John, beckoning with his right arm.

The burly man entered John's office, taking little steps, ready to flee at any moment.

'The murungu is the key to our search for Sarah Kagonye.'

'Yes, Sah.'

'Shut up and listen. First, she disappears, leaving her cleaning trolley outside his hotel room, and then we find out her sister is his housemaid. I don't like coincidences. The murungu is the key.'

'Yes, Sah.'

'Now listen, between you, Samson and Elijah, I want you to keep a twenty-four-hour watch on the murungu's apartment. Note where he goes and what he does and who else comes to his apartment. Do you understand?'

'Yes, Sah.'

'Start at midnight tonight. Don't let him see you, and don't use the same car every day.'

'Yes, Sah. No, Sah.'

'And don't forget to tell Samson and Elijah it's your fault the three of you are on duty around the clock.'

'Yes, Sah.'

'That's all. Go now.'

Akashinga retreated from John's office, relieved to have received another assignment, no matter how tedious. Anything was better than one of John's dreadful punishments. Team A1, John's original team of operatives, soon learnt his fearsome reputation was no exaggeration. He could be charming, but he was a cunning, cold-blooded killer. That was how he got his nickname, The Leopard.

John's plan pleased him, but he would need to take care. If he did it right, he might yet come out of his recent run of setbacks with his reputation intact, if not enhanced. Keeping an eye on the murungu was a positive move. At least they weren't sitting back and doing nothing.

He eyed the bottle of Scotch. The label said *twelve-year-old single malt*. It would have to do. Twelve-year-old single malt was his baseline, and he would accept nothing less. Should he pour another tot before going home? Why not? He held the crystal glass up to the light and admired the clarity. John was aware colour was no indication of quality or flavour, but he considered the single malt to have a cleaner look than the blended whiskeys. He fancied he could feel the fumes and the flavour on the tip of his tongue. Maybe he'd tour the Scottish distilleries soon. John smiled. Somehow, he'd avoided the list of banned Zimbabweans prevented from entering the UK. But then, he wasn't yet a cabinet minister.

Laughter from the open plan office, where the six operatives from teams A1 and E2 sat, interrupted John's thoughts. Friday night drinks! Those fools were happy with cartons of Chibuku beer. Imagine wasting a good Scotch on them. John picked up his glass of Scotch and wandered into the open plan office. 'You lot sound cheerful. What's so funny?'

The men jumped to their feet at the sight of John. 'Nothing, Sir, we're just looking forward to the weekend.'

'Well, some of you are. Team A1 is on a twenty-four-hour watch. I might put you all on the twenty-four-hour watch, so you'll each do only four hours a day.'

The faces of the three team E2 members fell. Everyone was silent now. John smiled as he turned on his heels and went back to his office. He'd reminded them who was boss. It made sense to share the burden, but first he'd punish Akashinga and his colleagues in team A1 with a rolling six-hour shift.

CHAPTER 28

6th March 2009

THE sixth of March 2009, a day Ian and Sarah wouldn't forget in a hurry. Discussions about the poor state of the country and who to blame, were an everyday occurrence. Ian walked out of the apartment for a breath of fresh air after a terse exchange with Sarah. She was there only a few days when they first clashed, and Ian's patience soon wore thin. She was too damn pushy. When would she leave? Ian recognised himself voicing his father's arguments each time he and Sarah disagreed.

Sarah bristled after listening to Ian's views. At such times she enjoyed the calming effect of a cup of tea. She sat at the dining table, frowning and quiet. Jemma saw something troubled her.

'What's the matter, Sarah, are you angry about something?'

'Ian is a racist. That man blames the blacks for buggering up the country and doesn't accept that the whites are also responsible for what has gone wrong.'

'You disagree, but you are both right.'

'Do you mean we both made good points?'

'Yes.'

'Well, he should accept some of my points then, instead of always coming back with an answer.'

'But you always have an answer for all his points.'

'Why are you taking his side?'

'I'm not taking his side, but I'm saying, you are both the same. Both of you are always right.'

'If we disagree, we can't both be right.'

'Both of you think you're right. Together, you get the right answer.'

'What whacky logic is that?'

'What does *whacky logic* mean?'

'Oh, never mind.'

'Even if you disagree, you can't call him a white racist.'

'Ian is a white racist and blames the blacks for everything.'

'If he was a white racist, he wouldn't let you stay here. Most people wouldn't shelter you if they knew the security services were looking for you. He's putting himself in danger.'

'He probably has an ulterior motive.'

'What does *ulterior motive* mean?'

'He hopes I'll be so grateful I'll let him have sex with me.'

'Sarah, he's never ever tried to touch you. If you think he wants sex with you, how can he be a white racist?'

'How can you be so logical if you didn't finish school? Anyway, I've seen the way he watches us when he thinks we're not looking.'

'But Sarah, we watch him when he's not looking.'

'Don't be silly, I'm engaged to Thomas. You may watch him, but I don't.'

'Ian's a nice, kind man.'

'You like him, Jemma, don't you? You more than like him.'

'He's good to us.'

'The way you run around him makes me sick. If Papa was alive, he'd be shocked you love a murungu, and so would Mama.'

'Mama and Papa always said the colour of the skin is not important, but what's inside a person's heart.'

'Oh boo! Wait until I tell Mama you're in love with your white boss.'

'I didn't say I loved him. I said he has a good heart. But don't tell Mama, Sarah.'

'I've noticed how you look at him. You haven't looked like that at a man since your husband, Edward, died. You're a silly fool if you imagine Ian would have any time for you.'

'What do you mean?'

'Jemma, one day I'll put you through high school, and then we can hold a proper conversation. What I mean is he is an arrogant murungu with racist views, and he would never be interested in his black house girl. Even though you're pretty, you'll have no chance with him. All you will get is disappointment. To him, you are just a silly ignorant kaffir.'

'I don't believe that. Ian's a good man. I never said he would be interested in me. All I'm saying is he respects us and treats us like equals.'

'He invites us to drink tea with him, but don't be fooled by that. He's writing a story about Zimbabwe, and he's using us to help him write his book. That's why he asks all about our lives and how things changed since black rule.'

'What's wrong with that? Isn't it a fair price for putting his life in danger by helping you?'

'Ian's life's not in danger. If the authorities found out they would just deport him.'

'Or, Sarah, they might put him in jail, and who knows what would happen to him there.'

The serious discussion suddenly turned frivolous. 'On one point I agree with him; you are a silly ignorant kaffir, Jemma.'

'Sarah! How rude you are. The boss is never rude.'

'Well, it's true,' said Sarah laughing. 'You're a silly ignorant kaffir. I'm black, so I can say that.'

'The boss is white, but he'd never use those words. You're a silly bitch, Sarah. I'm your sister, so I can say that.'

The two women shrieked with laughter, rolling about on the king size bed and hitting each other with pillows.

Suddenly, the door opened, and Ian walked into the apartment. 'Am I missing something?'

Sarah ignored Ian's question, but Jemma snapped back into her housemaid role. 'Can I make you tea, Sir?'

'Thank you, Jemma. Sarah, have you heard the news? Susan Tsvangirai has died in a collision with a truck on the Harare-Masvingo Road.'

'What, when, where?'

'The radio said the accident occurred about forty-five kilometres south of Harare. Morgan's injured and is in hospital.'

'What happened?'

'The Tsvangirais were in the middle of a three-vehicle convoy when an oncoming truck crossed onto their side of the road and side-swiped them. Their vehicle rolled three times.'

Morgan Tsvangirai had been prime minister for less than a month. Lots of people suspected the accident was an assassination attempt. There'd been tough negotiations with Robert Mugabe, and the other African leaders put pressure on them to compromise. A fragile power-sharing arrangement resulted.

'Unbelievable,' said Ian, 'He gave his maiden speech to parliament only two days ago.'

'Accidents happen,' said Sarah.

'Are you serious? After all those delaying tactics with Mugabe dragging out the election results, no one will believe this was a genuine motor accident.'

'It might just be a coincidence.'

'Sarah, I know the roads need repair, and the vehicles should be better maintained, and this country has a lot of bad drivers. But how come the black politicians were safer on the roads before black rule?'

'That's a racist statement.'

'No, it's not racist, it's a fact.'

'You whites are all racist.'

'Face it, Sarah. In 1997 Mugabe supporters tried to throw Tsvangirai out of a tenth-floor office window. Then in 2007 the police assaulted him, at a prayer rally of all things, and he had to be hospitalised.'

'That prayer meeting was a political rally in disguise.'

'If people could meet freely and peacefully, there'd be no need for disguising political rallies.'

'There's no such thing as a peaceful political meeting in Zimbabwe.'

'You said it, Sarah. What happened to your father is no different to what's happening now.' Sarah was silent at the mention of Sam. Was this a rare occasion when he'd have the last word? Ian noticed Sarah's eyes glistening. 'I'm sorry, but I'm trying to be honest.'

'My father was always loyal to the government. It must have been a mistake.'

'Sarah, it sounds like your father was a principled man who didn't agree with the election violence.'

'It's not fair. There was no need to kill him just because he didn't support violence.'

'Sometimes life isn't fair, Sarah.'

For the first time, Ian saw tears rolling down Sarah's face. He'd always seen her as tough and unyielding, but now he saw her softer side. He shouldn't have brought Sam into the discussion; it was a low blow. Ian wanted to hug her and tell her it was OK, and he didn't mean to upset her, but somehow, he couldn't. Maybe she was right. Perhaps he was a racist. 'I never met your father, Sarah, but from what you've told me, I respect him.'

'Thank you, Sir.'

Sarah's response surprised Ian. She only called him *Sir* in mock respect when she tried to manipulate or irritate him. It was probably a slip of the tongue in a vulnerable moment. A slip for which he was sure he'd pay later. Jemma came back into the room carrying the tea tray, smiling and cheery like a ray of sunshine. 'Here are nice biscuits Mama has made, Sir,' said Jemma. 'Mama makes the best biscuits.' Jemma had put a smile on their faces, and Ian caught Sarah's eye across the table. They both recognised a subtle shift in their relationship. Perhaps they'd now be more honest with each other. Both their masks had slipped a little.

'Thank your mother for the delicious biscuits please, Jemma.'

'Yes, Sir. Thank you, Sir.'

'Does your mother know Sarah is staying here?'

'No, Sir, Sarah told me not to say anything, except that she is safe.'

'And the less she knows the safer she'll be,' said Sarah.

'But I wish I could tell her,' said Jemma.

'One day you might,' said Ian.

Chapter 29

1st – 2nd April 2009

April arrived, and Sarah had been in the apartment for a month. Ian had adjusted to her being there. She was good company when he wasn't busy with his writing. The arguments continued, but they were benign affairs. Ian still thought Sarah should be more appreciative for her refuge. But if he was honest, he'd have to admit her presence came with some benefits, and it left Ian free to concentrate on writing. Jemma and Sarah kept the apartment spotless and Ian's clothes washed and ironed. The two sisters deliberated over what meals he might enjoy. In effect, two maids worked for him. On balance, it was a good deal, though he'd never tell Sarah that.

Jemma brought in the morning tea, and Sarah switched on her cell phone to call her mother. 'Oh! There's a message for me. My God! It's from Thomas. He wants me to meet him at the bus station at five o'clock tomorrow evening.' Sarah shook with excitement. 'He's come back at last. Wait till I see him; he'd better have a good explanation.'

'Hang on, Sarah,' said Ian, 'how do you know it's Thomas? It might be a trap.'

'It's his cell phone number.'

'Anyone could use his cell phone.'

'It must be him. How would he know my number? Tomorrow, I'll meet him.'

'Sarah, someone from the COU may have found his phone with your name and number stored in it. We want it to be Thomas, but let's think about it. Check with his parents if they've heard from him. If not, then ask his father to meet him. If it is him, his dad can phone you and confirm it.'

'But I need to be there. If I'm not there, I might miss him.'

'Well, you can wait somewhere nearby. Would the COU recognise Thomas' dad?'

'I don't think so, but I'm not sure.'

In the evening Sarah phoned Thomas' parents to tell them about the SMS. They were sceptical as they'd not received any message from him. But they were as keen as Sarah for it to be Thomas, and George Chimedza agreed to be at the bus station to meet him. George was a pleasant, stout man of average height, and it would be easy for him to blend into the throng in rush hour. He would call Sarah on her cell phone with any news.

Half past four the next evening, Sarah sat at a table in a café two blocks from the bus station. Dressed like a housemaid, she hoped to make herself inconspicuous in the evening crush of people going home. She looked at her wristwatch once again. Time seemed to stand still. Where had Thomas spent the past three months? She hoped Mr Chimedza wouldn't be late. Each time anyone came into the café, Sarah averted her eyes. Everyone at the nearby COU premises would have seen photos of her.

George Chimedza arrived at the bus station a few minutes before five, and he scanned the crowd. There was no sign of Thomas, but if he was in hiding, he'd not turn up any earlier than necessary. The bus station teemed with people, and George stood to one side and waited, looking at the faces as they passed.

Five o'clock came and went with no sign of Thomas. George moved his position, but his son was nowhere to be seen. He took out his cell phone to call Sarah, but as he dialled her number, a youth snatched the phone and ran off into the crowd. There was little hope of George catching him.

Sarah looked at her watch. The hands showed half past five. Why hadn't George phoned? She could contain herself no longer and made her way to the bus station. The scene was a jam of people. Sarah saw a handful of faces she recognised. She blended into the crowd, trying not to attract attention by standing too long in one spot.

At last she spotted the familiar face of George Chimedza and made her way towards him, but then she observed a tall man in a suit, surveying the crowd. He was only a dozen paces in front of her. A few metres to her left, another tall man in a suit searched the crowd for someone. Might they be looking for her?

Sarah turned and walked away, desperate to melt into the throng. As she reached the exit, she looked back and caught the eye of one of the tall men. She detected a flicker of recognition in his eyes, and he shouted something. Both the tall men now pushed their way through the crowd towards her. Sarah ran across the street and around the corner. Halfway down the block, Sarah ran across the road and into an alleyway. She decided her best chance of escape was to zig-zag. At the end of the alleyway, she turned into the street, crossed the road and ran down the next corner. Sarah pictured the men right behind her, and she dared not slow up to look around as she ran on as fast as she could.

In an alley, five blocks from the bus station, Sarah slowed to a walk and turned to check if anyone followed. There was no one. Her heart thumped, and she struggled to draw breath though she was fitter than most, but it was months since she'd run so fast. She exercised indoors every day, but the three months in hiding eroded her fitness. Sarah continued her zig-zag strategy as she walked back to the apartment.

Jemma and Ian waited for news, but when Sarah walked in, they knew without asking. Sarah paced around the apartment like a caged tigress, taking a long time to settle.

Days later, Sarah heard George's side of the story, through Jemma. Thomas didn't turn up, but George couldn't contact her without his cell phone and her number stored in it.

* * *

Back at the COU, Captain John berated his team A1. 'Why do I have to rely on such fools? How did you lose her yet again? This isn't the first time.'

'Sir, it might have been someone else,' said Samson.

'It was Kagonye, I'm sure of it. Why else would she run when she spotted you? Don't make excuses for your failure.'

'The crowd hemmed us in,' said Elijah. 'By the time we pushed our way through, she had gone.'

'You should have been waiting on the edge of the crowd, not in the middle of it, you idiots. And what about you, Akashinga; don't you have anything to say?'

'I never saw her in the big crowd, Sah.'

'You are too short and fat, Akashinga, that's why. Get out all of you! Get back to your stake-out of the murungu's apartment.'

Captain John needed a drink. He took out the ice tray from the fridge in his bookcase and dropped two cubes into his crystal glass. Then he reached for the bottle of Scotch at the back of the cupboard under his desk.

CHAPTER 30

April 2009

SOON it would be Easter. The long weekend ran from April tenth to thirteenth. 'What are you doing for Easter?' Sarah asked.

'I must meet with my business clients in Joburg to discuss the project they gave me.' Manfred provided good legal advice for the hotel project, but now Ian needed to discuss the more basic business and marketing issues. 'And I can catch up with friends while I'm down there.'

'How long will you be away?'

'I'd be away for about ten days. Will you manage OK?'

'Perhaps Jemma could stay here with me. It would be a holiday for her.'

'I'm not sure Jemma would see it that way. Would you like to spend your holiday at your workplace?'

'It would be fun for us to stay here together.'

'OK, it's up to you, if that's what you want.'

Jemma was happy with the idea she and Sarah would stay together at the apartment while Ian was away.

* * *

Ian caught the South African Airways lunchtime flight to Johannesburg on the Thursday before Easter. David was waiting at the airport to meet him. That night they sat up late, catching up on all the news since Ian's last visit when he was en route to Zimbabwe.

'Be careful. Apart from the risk you run in sheltering a fugitive, can you trust her?'

'There's nothing for her to steal. I keep my passport and money with me all the time, and if she stole my computer, I'd still have my USB backup.'

'What if she turned you in to the authorities to save her own skin?'

'No, she wouldn't do that. She's already suffered too much at their hands to do any deal with them. Besides, they want her, not me.'

'Well, it's your neck on the line, but you need to be careful. You're putting too much trust in her.'

'Don't worry, I'll be careful.'

'And how can you shelter her in a studio apartment?'

'It has a huge super-king-size bed with enough room for four or five people.'

'You're mad! I wouldn't tell anyone else about it if I were you.'

'No, I won't, but what's the big deal?'

'Australia has mushed your brain. Most folks down here wouldn't understand you sharing your apartment, let alone your bed, with an African woman you hardly know.'

'After living with her for two months, I know her well enough. And I've told you there's nothing in it. There's no relationship involved. Do you realise how big an eighty-square-inch bed is? I stay on my side and she stays on hers. We're in the same room, but we're miles apart. In the hotel, two big men searched my room for her. I wouldn't want them looking for me, I can tell you.'

'Look after yourself first. If you don't watch out, you'll be next on someone's radar. This organisation she was with before she worked at the hotel; how do you know they're legit? She might've been a member of a criminal gang. Maybe she was a gangster's moll. Don't laugh, I'm serious.'

'Look, I admit she has stayed longer than I expected. But what would you have me do; throw her out and let her be murdered by thugs? For the time being, I'm stuck with her.'

'You told me that someone strangled the woman, Hazel, that you met at the hotel, and the next night someone tried to garrotte you. Doesn't all that tell you something?'

'It tells me Sarah is in real danger; that's what it tells me.'

'You're crazy. It's time for you to leave. I warned you it'd be easy to run into trouble.'

'My book isn't finished.'

'The CIO may have a longer reach than you imagine. The Zimbabwe diaspora claim the CIO is operating amongst them, right here in Joburg, so you better be careful.'

Ian's visit to the Bernsteins proved helpful to his work on their client's project. Ruth reminded Ian she would be in Harare in May and would follow up on the project with him then.

With the business side of his visit complete, Ian now relaxed and caught up with his friends. Zimbabwe was a land of shortages, but Johannesburg was a land of plenty. Ian caught up on all the dishes he'd been missing for the past three months. A good curry house and a good Thai restaurant were amongst the eating places on his list.

* * *

Back in Harare, Sarah and Jemma enjoyed the novelty of being together in the apartment overnight. Although they saw each other on weekdays, there was always plenty to talk about, and they chatted into the early hours. For Sarah it was the same four walls she'd been looking at for the past two months. On the third day, Saturday, they hit upon a new idea. Jemma always kept a spare set of work clothes at the apartment in case she needed to change if her clothes got extra dirty or wet. The plan was that Jemma would leave for home at lunchtime. At five o'clock Sarah would leave the apartment dressed in Jemma's spare set of work clothes. That way they'd both spend a few days at home with their mother, Esther.

It was almost nine weeks since Sarah last saw her mother, and she was high with anticipation. The sisters realised it might seem strange for the maid to leave work twice on the same day. But they reasoned if anyone was watching the apartment, they would assume they missed seeing the maid return after lunch. That was precisely what Akashinga thought when he saw Sarah leaving at five o'clock that evening. Between them, Akashinga, Samson and Elijah became aware by Sunday evening that both the murungu and the housemaid must be away, and the apartment would be empty.

The sisters and their mother, Esther, relaxed together at home. Sarah enjoyed Jemma's cooking, but no cooking could match her mother's. Although Jemma assisted Esther with the cooking, Sarah felt her mother's presence somehow made all the difference. It was a wonderful, relaxing week for the three of them. Sarah spent the entire time indoors, but the change of scenery did her a world of good.

Soon it was time to return to the apartment. Ian was due back that morning and Sarah looked forward to seeing him again. She put it down to missing the verbal battles that came like waves in a heavy sea. There was little to debate with Esther as they shared similar views and arguing with Jemma was too easy. They agreed Sarah would go back first, dressed in Jemma's work clothes, and Jemma would turn up for work as usual the next day.

Sarah enjoyed the walk from the bus station to the apartment. The early morning air was crisp and cool, but the sun was warm on her skin. It was Monday, a week after Easter and the commuter traffic buzzed past her. Sarah's thoughts were a million miles away when she turned into the apartment block. She walked up the steps to the first floor and put the key in the lock and entered the apartment. She stopped, aghast at what she saw. The place was a mess with chairs knocked over and the drawers and cupboard lying open. The super-king-size mattress from the bed lay on the floor with the bedding strewn around the room. Cutlery lay scattered in the kitchen sink and on the floor.

Someone had been there. Sarah spent the rest of the morning cleaning up the mess and couldn't believe how a sparsely furnished apartment could be in such a chaotic state. It was a big job, and when she finished, she put the kettle on to make herself a cup of coffee.

'Mine's white with no sugar please.'

Sarah's heart jumped. She hadn't heard Ian enter. 'Goodness, you gave me a fright!'

'Why so nervy? Is it because I haven't been around to protect you?'

Sarah gave a weak smile at Ian's joke and told him what had happened.

'Do you think it might have been vandals?' he asked.

'No, vandals cause damage. There's no damage, just a terrible mess. Someone has searched the apartment.'

Ian put a finger up to his lips to silence Sarah, and he pointed to the light fitting and under the dining table. They spent the next hour looking for any hidden listening device. 'All clear,' said Ian. 'Now how about that coffee you promised.'

'The great white master has returned,' said Sarah with a wry smile.

Ian leant against the kitchen counter while Sarah prepared the coffee. 'Would anything here give them cause for suspicion?'

'No, I took all my stuff with me to get a change of clothes, but your stuff was here. It looks like they didn't touch your computer.'

'So, you left nothing here? No items of clothing or makeup?'

'Not a single thing.'

'That was lucky. It's a good reminder we should always be packed and ready to move at a moment's notice.'

The neighbours on both sides went away for Easter and returned late on Easter Monday. Sarah was in the apartment until five o'clock on Easter Saturday. The intruders must have searched the apartment sometime between Easter Saturday night and Monday afternoon. Outside those times, the neighbours would have heard them. With Sarah living in the apartment, Ian couldn't report the incident to the police.

'We must keep a close eye out from now on,' said Ian. 'Someone might watch the apartment.' 'Oh! I almost forgot. I've got something for you and Jemma and for your mother.'

'Earrings, thank you. We love earrings.'

'You and Jemma have pierced ears and often wear earrings, so I thought you might like them.'

'We will let our mama choose first, and Jemma and I will share the other two. We share everything. Thank you. Our mama will love these.'

CHAPTER 31

May 2009

IAN read the business plan for the new Flying Eagle Hotel Group. The ambitious idea was to train Zimbabwe's low-cost labour to a high standard, giving visitors a world class stay. Poor tourist accommodation and high prices were now the norm in Zimbabwe. In the campsites, there'd been no maintenance carried out for years, but prices rose in line with neighbouring countries. The grills on the braais were missing, and often there was no fuel to run the power generators. Tourists could face a lack of power, an uncertain water supply and bed bugs. They would leave with a bad impression of the country. Only hotels in Victoria Falls maintained a high international standard. Competition from the Zambian hotels over the river made that essential.

Many of the hotels in Harare needed an upgrade, but the investors kept their wallets shut. Who'd invest in an unstable country? The presidential election was a farce. Mugabe wouldn't concede defeat, and the country was in turmoil. In February, ZANU-PF and the MDC formed 'a government of national unity', but it was fragile from the start. The memory of the election violence endured, and investors waited to see what happened next.

* * *

Manfred Schwartz warned everyone that Ruth Bernstein would arrive in the morning. Ian refreshed himself on all the salient points of the business plan. Manfred's associates were in a state of high expectation.

Ruth's visit was important to them. Frida braided her hair and wore a smart mid-blue business suit. Her horn-rimmed glasses set off her image well. Nelson, the tea associate, looked smart in polished black leather shoes and a light grey Armani suit that Manfred gave him when he replaced it with a new one. Ian felt under-dressed in his white business shirt, beige slacks, mid-blue sports jacket and dark brown shoes. The looks he got from Frida and Nelson that morning did little to reassure him. Ian breathed a sigh of relief when Manfred arrived in a brown suit with an open-necked, floral patterned business shirt.

Frida did not warm to Ian in the ten weeks he'd worked part-time at Manfred Schwartz and Associates. Nelson was friendlier when Frida was absent. Neither of the associates seemed to notice how friendly Manfred Schwartz was towards him. If they did, it did little to change their attitude.

Ian found space in the meeting room. Manfred occupied one office, and Frida or Nelson used the other on an as-needs basis. The second office doubled as a filing room. Frida sat at the reception desk, and Nelson seemed most at home in the kitchen when not filing. Frida saw herself as the senior associate, and she ordered Nelson around as if he were the tea boy. That was the term she used for Nelson on one of the few occasions she deigned to speak to Ian. She couldn't see why the tea boy's share in the business should be equal to hers. Ian did not know how to respond to that comment, but he contained his grin until after she left the meeting room.

A knock on the meeting room door alerted Ian to Ruth poking her head around the corner. 'Hello, Ian, how are things going? When I've finished with Manfred, I'll come and see you. We must share this space. There's nowhere else for me to sit. I hope you don't mind. Anyway, we'll be working together most of today.'

Ian didn't mind at all and welcomed the prospect of intelligent company in the office. Manfred was often away, and the stilted conversation with Frida and Nelson was draining. Ruth came in after half an hour. 'Tea's on its way,' she said. 'How's progress with the project?'

Nelson brought in morning tea on a silver tray. He took pride in the way he presented it, and Ian always looked forward to it. Lunchtime came around before they knew it, and Nelson came into the meeting room with tea and tasty sandwiches, which they ate while they worked.

Ian impressed Ruth with his ideas in the business plan. 'This is good work you've done here, but Mr Joshi won't go ahead with these plans until the country is more stable. He made his fortune by making good decisions, not by risk-taking. But either way, the effort we're putting in will come in useful. Joshi will wait until he's comfortable, whenever that may be. There's also a backup plan to put these ideas into effect in Botswana or Namibia or even both.'

Ian saw in Ruth a shrewd business brain. She reviewed each of his ideas to make sure they complied with the aims of the project. He looked on while she assessed his strategies, and it crossed his mind that brains and beauty complemented each other well. Ruth would be in her early fifties, but she was still attractive. Her questions were incisive and working with her proved to be a real pleasure. They bounced ideas off each other, and between them they honed the strategies for the project. How refreshing it was, compared to the stifling environment he'd worked in back in Melbourne. Her clear skin, short brown hair and neat figure were a bonus that hadn't escaped his notice.

At a quarter past five there was a knock on the door and Manfred's smiling face appeared around the corner. 'Frida and Nelson are going now, and I'm following them.' Ruth walked out to the reception area to say goodbye to them and arrange with Manfred for a lift to the airport in the morning. She returned a few minutes later. 'It always pays to keep in with the staff, no matter how junior because you never know when they may come in useful. One day when there's no one else, we may have to rely on them.' After working on for another half an hour, Ruth said, 'Are you in a hurry to get home this evening?'

'No, I knew your visit was brief, so we can work as late as you want.'

'Actually, I was thinking about dinner. We're finished for now, so I thought we'd go for a sundowner and chat over dinner. We can talk business if you like, but to be honest my mind needs a rest.'

'That sounds good. Where do you fancy?'

'I'm staying at the Meikles. It's a good hotel. The cocktail bar has a nice ambiance, and La Fontaine restaurant overlooks Africa Unity Square. It's a short walk of half a dozen blocks from here.'

Ruth used her own keys to the office and went through the locking up procedure. Ian could see she was close to the Schwartzes.

By the time they reached the Meikles, it was dusk. They entered the hotel between the sculptures of the two sitting lions at the front entrance. '*Lions sejant*,' said Ruth. 'That means they are sitting on their haunches with both paws on the ground.'

'They remind me of the lions in front of the Hong Kong and Shanghai Bank in Hong Kong,' said Ian.

'Yes, but those are *lions couchant*. That's when the lions are lying down with both paws out front and their heads raised.'

'Are you interested in heraldry?'

Ruth laughed. 'Not really, but these lions at the front of the hotel aroused my curiosity, so I looked it up on the internet.'

As Ruth promised, the hotel projected a grand image, enhancing its reputation as the best in Harare. Ruth excused herself to return to her suite to freshen up before dinner. Ian found a table for two in the Explorer's Club in the lobby. The waiter assured him the ice in the drinks was safe. Ian ordered a Scotch on the rocks and sat observing the after-work drinkers winding down from a day in the office. Most, including the women, wore business suits. Others, like Ian, dressed in a more casual style. The warm Harare weather made an open-necked shirt acceptable business wear. Ian entertained himself with the comings and goings from the popular bar.

'Hi there, lost in thought?' Ruth was back, wearing a shimmering, bottle-green cocktail dress that ended a little above her knees. On her feet she wore black, medium heeled, open toe shoes. She looked cool and elegant and smelled nice.

Ian sprang to his feet and pulled out a chair for her. 'What can I get you to drink?'

The waiter brought Ruth's vodka and tonic with ice and a slice of lemon. 'So, you're planning a trip to Bulawayo soon?' she said. 'I have a car here in Harare, but I need it in Bulawayo. Would you be interested in driving it down for me? There's plenty of petrol in the tank, so you could use it while you are in Bulawayo, and then drop it off just before you leave. It doesn't matter if you use most of the petrol because I have a private source of supply down there.'

Ian and Ruth chatted away over dinner about a variety of subjects including their past lives, their interests and their hopes and ambitions. 'Solly lives for his business ventures. In Cape Town, he has a major interest in a commercial fishing venture. In Durban, one of his interests is in property development of coastal resorts and wildlife resorts along the border of the Kruger National Park. That's how we got involved in this project. He has a girlfriend in Cape Town and another in Durban. Solly has a lot of business interests in those cities and spends a lot of time in them, so I suppose it makes sense he has girlfriends there. He's never tried to hide it from me. What about you? How's your social life?'

Ian shifted in his chair. 'I've only been here three months.'

'That's plenty long enough,' she said, with a knowing smile.

The La Fontaine restaurant lived up to Ruth's glowing testimonial. The meal was delicious and the service excellent. 'I don't like to recommend restaurants because so often when one goes back a second or third time, they're different. Something changes; either the owner, or the chef, or the menu. But this place has never disappointed me.'

Ruth put down her coffee cup. 'Manfred keeps one set of car keys. The other set I keep with me. I'll give you those for when you take the car to Bulawayo. He'll give you a lift back to his place to pick up the car just before you go on your trip. You can take the keys now, but I've no petrol to spare up here, so you can't have the car until you're ready to leave. You'll need the full tank for the drive down to Bulawayo and any running around you do there.'

After putting the restaurant bill on her room tab, Ruth said, 'Come and get the car keys. I have them in my travel bag in my suite.' Ian stood up and pulled back her chair, and they made their way to the lift. Ruth pressed the button for her floor, and she smiled at him. It differed from her usual smile, almost conspiratorial as if there was an unspoken understanding between them. Although ten to fifteen years older than him, Ian found Ruth increasingly attractive.

The suite was luxurious, with a view of Africa Unity Square. Ruth kept it tidy, almost as if it were unoccupied. 'Here are the car keys,' said Ruth, coming out of the bedroom. 'Would you like a Cognac?' After a little more chat about the hotel project, Ruth drained her glass. 'Well, if you want sex, we'd better get down to it. Manfred's picking me up early in the morning.'

Ian hesitated for a moment. After hearing of Solly's arrangements, her offer was not entirely unexpected, but the businesslike manner of it surprised him. This was the most direct approach he'd ever received. Either way, it was a perk he couldn't resist. 'Erm, I don't have a condom.'

'Do you have HIV?'

'No,' said Ian, sounding a little more indignant than he intended.

'Well, neither do I.'

Ruth slipped off her shoes. Her tanned legs didn't need hosiery. She unzipped the back of her dress and stepped out of it, leaving it on the back of a chair near the king-size bed. She unhooked her bra and put it on her dress and lay back on the bed in her lace panties. Ruth looked at Ian, who, to this point, had only taken off his shoes and socks. He'd sat on the edge of the bed entranced, watching her undress. Now, he unbuttoned his shirt and hung it over the back of a chair in the corner of the bedroom. He unzipped his trousers and placed them on the seat of the chair. Ruth pulled off her panties and tossed them onto the chair next to her dress. Ian stared at her neat triangle of pubic hair as he pulled off his underpants and put them on top of his trousers.

He sat on the bed and then turned and lay down next to her, propping himself up on his left elbow.

'Once won't be enough for me,' said Ruth.

'No problem,' said Ian, stroking her stomach. He lowered his head and took her right nipple between his lips, gently rolling his tongue over it. Then he moved to her left breast.

Soon, both of Ruth's nipples were hard and erect. 'Let's get on with it,' she said, 'It's getting late.'

Ian eased himself into position and teased her for some moments before pressing home. Ruth gasped, and before long, she shook with anticipation.

'I want to come now. Can you come with me?' Ruth whispered.

'Yes, I'm ready.'

'Now, now, come now,' Ruth's voice was unsteady, rising and desperate as her body shook. They came together in a lusty union, the strength of which surprised them both.

They lay side by side while Ian explored Ruth's body with his right hand. Soon he was ready again, and she, more than ready. As he entered her, she said, 'Fuck me. I mean really fuck me.' Ian was happy to oblige.

'My God! What are you doing to me?' she said, as they came together once more.

They lay, recovering from the emotion and physical release. 'I wish we could go on all night, but I'm catching the early plane out. There'll be other occasions for us. I'll make sure of it.'

Ian stepped into the shower, expecting Ruth to join him. But she just stood, watching him soap himself. He looked at her, and she anticipated his question. 'I'll shower after you've gone. That way, I can enjoy the feel of our sex a little longer.'

A cool breeze sprung up as Ian walked back to his apartment in a happy mood. What a night! Ruth was fantastic, and her parting words promised more of the same. His trip to Zimbabwe and his work at

Manfred Schwartz and Associates was looking more and more promising.

As he walked back to the apartment through the deserted streets, Ian looked at his watch, half past two in the morning. Since his frightening episode with the attempted garrotting, he'd been wary of walking out at night. Ian slid the key into the keyhole and opened the door and entered the apartment. He crept into the room but jumped when Sarah suddenly sat up in bed. 'Where have you been? It's almost three o'clock.'

'No, it's only half past two.'

'I worried about you.'

'You knew I had to work late.'

'It's dangerous to be walking around Harare late at night. You should know that.'

Chapter 32

3rd – 5th June 2009

Sarah was restless, couped up in the apartment like a canary in a cage, but she wouldn't go out for fear of being seen. Her debates and discussions with Ian gave her plenty of intellectual stimulation, but she was a woman of action. She exercised every day in the cramped confines of the apartment, but this was not enough physical stimulation for her.

Ian walked to the CBD or to Manfred Schwartz's office in Samora Machel Avenue. This gave him a break from sitting at his laptop all day. The time spent chatting with Sarah and Jemma was productive, and it gave him an insight into the African mind. Ian felt his book was coming on well, or at least his research notes were.

Jemma returned home each night. She spent her evenings with her mother and her days with her sister. For her it was a happy arrangement, but for Sarah the same four walls confined her day after day. Prior to coming to Ian's apartment, she'd spent almost a month in a similar situation with Thomas' parents. Sarah's frustration and irritability sometimes showed. Like a caged lioness, she paced up and down, sitting, standing up, sitting again and standing once more before resuming her pacing.

Ian looked up from his laptop. 'Sarah, can you please relax? I can't concentrate with you marching up and down the whole time.'

Sarah sat down with a huge sigh. 'Would you like tea?'

'If you are having tea, I'll join you.'

Minutes later Sarah brought in the tea and put down a cup in front of Ian. 'How far are you into your book?'

'Not as far as I would be if you didn't keep interrupting me the whole time.'

'Can I help you with the book?'

'You're already helping me with the book.'

'No, I mean can I research or write for you. When you go out, I would write, instead of doing nothing.'

'Yes, if you like, you can write. I will go over it and if it fits, I'll include it in the book.'

'Can we be joint authors then?'

'Ian snorted. I'll think about it.'

'Can you put my name first?'

'No. Now you're playing with me.'

'Do you want to play table tennis?'

'We don't have a table tennis table Sarah.'

'We can use the dining table with a rolled-up towel as the net.'

'No, I don't think so.'

'Well, what else can we do?'

'Sarah, I have a good idea. Find something sensible to occupy yourself. That should keep you busy.'

'No, I want to do something active; run and jump, or something like that.'

'Would you like to go for a walk when it gets dark?'

'Do you realise how dangerous it would be? You can be in big trouble for harbouring a fugitive. If they caught me, they'd kill me, and they might even kill you. The least that would happen to you would be a lengthy jail sentence, followed by deportation.'

Sarah's comments gave Ian something to turn over in his mind. 'OK, how about doing more push-ups and floor exercises?'

'I've already done that today. It's getting boring.'

'Well then, do some speed cooking.'

'What's that?'

'It means you make a delicious dinner with as much speed and energy as possible. I'm getting hungry.'

'Very funny, but yes, OK, if it makes you happy.'

Each day Sarah and Jemma would discuss the night's dinner. Jemma would help Sarah cut up the meat and vegetables, and later, after Jemma left for home, Sarah would cook the meal. Cooking was the one area Sarah needed coaching. At home, Jemma or their mother always prepared dinner. Sarah skipped that part of her education because she was always away from home or busy with other activities. Between them, the sisters came up with tasty meals for Ian. The biggest problem being the shortage of ingredients, both local and imported.

The loud clattering in the kitchen sounded like preparations for a banquet, and it set off Ian's saliva glands. It reminded him of one of his mother's meals; an entrée of smoked salmon laid on half an avocado with sliced red onion and capers, followed by a main course of twice roasted duck with rice, roast pumpkin and green peas. That's the dinner Ian imagined, though Sarah served him something less ambitious, a simple but tasty meal of bangers and mash with green peas. Well, at least he'd got the green peas part correct.

Sarah's cooking had made great strides, and Ian complimented her. 'So, locked away in a one roomed apartment isn't a total waste of time.' Sarah did not agree but accepted the compliment.

After dinner, Sarah put forward other ideas that might help to absorb her excess energy. They were not much better than her table tennis suggestion. 'I'm going for a bath,' said Ian. 'Let me know if you get a worthwhile idea.'

Ian relaxed in a deep, hot bath, enjoying the water he'd treated with Radox bath salts. Where did they get Radox in a country of endless shortages? Maybe Dennis and Mary Jones brought it in from South Africa or overseas.

The bathroom door swung open and Sarah walked in with a mug of tea. Ian sat up quickly, drawing up his knees. 'What do you want? Don't you ever knock? I'm having a bath.'

'I've brought you tea. You said to let you know if I got a worthwhile idea. Well, I've had a great idea.' Sarah placed the mug on the flat corner of the bathtub.

'Can't it wait until after my bath?'

'Wait, I'll get my tea. I need to talk to you.' Sarah walked into the kitchen and returned with her mug. She shut the door behind her and sat down on the closed lid of the toilet seat.

'What if I were on the toilet?' said Ian, irritated by the intrusion.

'No, I looked through the keyhole, so I knew you weren't.'

'What!'

'Just kidding,' said Sarah, leaning forward, eager to talk about her good idea. 'Besides, I heard you splashing in the bath'

'So, it's OK for me to come into the bathroom when you're having a bath is it?'

'No, it's not OK.'

'Why isn't it? You seem to come in on me whenever you feel like it.'

'Ladies need their privacy. Men are different. Anyway, it's no big deal. I've seen it all before?'

'What do you mean?'

'Don't you remember our shower together in the hotel?'

'You mean when you stepped into my shower. You were so scared, if I showered in a dinner suit, you wouldn't have noticed.'

'I was being realistic, not scared. If those men had found me, they'd have killed me. But I did notice. I'd never seen a naked white man before then. It was nothing special.'

'Anyway, what's this great idea of yours?'

'Well, I can't be in hiding forever. So, when you go on your planned trip to Bulawayo and the Victoria Falls, can I come with you? From there I'll get across to Botswana or Zambia.'

'What about the roadblocks? There're a number on the road to Bulawayo, and I'm sure, also on the Victoria Falls road.'

'How about the train?'

'Hmm, maybe, but it's too soon to worry about that now.'

Sarah leant forward, bright-eyed and smiling. 'Would you like me to wash your back?'

'No! Off you go! Out! Now!'

Ian heard travelling by train these days was much like catching a bus. The first-class carriages were seldom full, and you needed to buy the ticket at the station on the day you travelled. Lack of demand meant the ticket office often only opened in the afternoon. If on schedule, the Bulawayo overnight train departed at eight o'clock.

* * *

Next morning, when Jemma took her tea break with the other housemaids, Sarah sat down in front of Ian. 'I've been thinking.'

'Oh no, again?' said Ian, looking up from his typing.

'Yes. I haven't seen my mama for a long time.'

'Yes?' said Ian, peering over the rim of his cup.

'You say Jemma and I look so much alike. If we swapped clothes one evening, I could go home and visit my mama. Anyone who saw me leave would think I was Jemma.'

'Right?' said Ian, dragging out the word.

'Jemma would have to stay here with you overnight.'

'Oh! What does Jemma say about that?'

'She thinks it's a good idea.'

'Why can't you do what you did over Easter? One of you can leave at lunchtime and one in the evening?'

'No, our mama doesn't like that. She said the lady across the road noticed she had both daughters home for the holiday. That lady doesn't know I'm in hiding, but if she saw us both there, who else might have?'

'OK Sarah, I wouldn't want to stand in the way of you seeing your mother.'

'Thank you, Sir.'

Hmm, it had been a while since she called him *sir*. She was trying to stay in his good books. 'It will also give you a chance to get out of here and get fresh air and exercise.'

The plan was soon in action. The next day Sarah, full of anticipation, interrupted Ian at his writing more than ever. 'You know, tonight I will see my mama for the first time since Easter; the first time in two months.'

'That's a long time. You'll have a lot to talk about, won't you?'

'Yes, but I won't tell her about our plans for Victoria Falls. The less she knows the better.'

'Does she now know you're staying here with me?'

'No. That would be too dangerous.'

'But she must realise Jemma knows where you're staying. How else could you swap?'

'That's all she knows.'

At five o'clock that evening Sarah and Jemma swapped clothes. The transition they both made surprised Ian. They almost seemed to have also swapped personalities. Sarah now looked every bit the housemaid, and if she didn't speak, Jemma fitted into the role of the educated, modern young woman. Sarah questioned Jemma about the route she walked, which bus she caught, where she sat on the bus and what time she left for work each morning. It was getting late. The two women hugged each other, and Sarah disappeared into the descending dusk.

After dinner, Ian got down to writing. Sarah's incessant interruptions slowed his progress, but now was an opportunity to get work done. He was finding his rhythm when Jemma brought him a cup of tea. 'Would you like a biscuit, Sir?'

'No thank you, Jemma.'

Jemma disappeared into the kitchen to fetch her own tea and then sat down in the armchair in the corner. A few minutes later she got up and took her cup to the kitchen and then came and retrieved Ian's cup. After washing up she sat down in the armchair again. Jemma scrabbled through her bag and then walked into the bathroom to brush her teeth. She returned and put her toothbrush away and went back into the bathroom to change into her nightwear.

Ian studied the screen of his laptop but was becoming more and more aware of all the activity. He pondered the phrasing of a sentence. Jemma came out of the bathroom wearing what looked like an eau-de-nil, mid-thigh length, stretch T-shirt. She walked around the super king-size bed and put her things in her bag on the floor and then sat down in the armchair. After a few minutes she got up and stood in front of Ian's desk. 'Would you like more tea, Sir?' A thought flickered through Ian's mind. She looked good in that T-shirt, like the smoky blue one Sarah wore. The sisters looked like twins.

'No thank you, Jemma. You relax now.'

Jemma returned to the armchair, but a minute later she passed Ian; this time heading for the kitchen. Ian watched her for a second or two and then tried to focus on his work. A moment later, Jemma again stood in front of Ian. 'Would you like me to bring you a beer, Sir?'

'For Pete's sake, Jemma, settle will you! I can't concentrate with you moving around the whole time.'

'I'm sorry, Sir.' Jemma sat back in the armchair.

A moment later, Jemma headed back to the kitchen and returned with a glass of water, which she placed on her bedside table. 'Can I get you a glass of water, Sir?'

'All right, Jemma, if you must. Thank you.' The T-shirt stretched in all the right places. It showed her breasts which looked just the right size and shape, with her nipples invitingly erect. Perhaps she was cold. She had a nice flat stomach, and a round, firm bottom like a perfect peach, shapely but not ample enough for African tastes.

Ian looked back at his laptop screen, trying to find his place again. Jemma passed with his glass of water and put it down on his bedside table. As she walked by, he noted her curves moving in a fascinating, rhythmic coordination. Would she be wearing anything underneath her T-shirt? Probably not. Hell! She looked delicious. He'd not before seen her in this light. He snapped shut his laptop lid. Damn! He'd no chance of concentrating on his work now. He hoped she didn't notice him ogling her. She might get the wrong idea. Between the two sisters and the boy next door, kicking the soccer ball against the wall, when would he ever be able to work in peace?

At bedtime, though there was plenty of room between them in the super king-size bed, Ian couldn't shake the thought he shared his bed with the housemaid. It was an imposition, and he hoped his friends would never find out. Sharing his bed with Sarah was different. She was his equal in every way and giving her shelter from her enemies in state security was a necessity, a life or death matter. He could justify that. It was different to sharing a bed with his housemaid, his servant.

In the dark apartment, there was still enough ambient light from the public passageway for Ian to see Jemma's white teeth and big bright smile. 'Go to sleep, Jemma,' said Ian, turning to face away from her.

* * *

In the early hours, Ian woke with a start. He'd been dreaming of approaching footsteps that stopped at his front door. Now he was wide awake, listening to a tapping sound he couldn't quite make out. Ian threw back the bedcovers and padded to the front door and looked through the magic eye. A tall African stood there, looking back at a second man at the edge of the magic eye's view.

The tall man stooped to look through the magic eye. The apartment was in darkness, and he didn't see Ian staring back at him. Ian's mind raced. Who were these men? Might they have caught Sarah and now come for him? Why were they in the passageway?

Ian crept into the kitchen and climbed up onto the kitchen counter and peered down through the high, narrow, horizontal window near the ceiling. The high viewpoint made it difficult to see the man's face. Ian only saw the trouser leg and shoes of the second man and the tip of a walking stick. Ah! That accounted for the tapping sound he'd heard. The passageway lights automatically switched off at midnight, and it was too dark to identify anyone. After a short while the men left. Who were they? What did they want? Ian found it difficult to sleep after that. Someone must be interested in the apartment or, more likely, the occupants. He would remind Sarah they had to keep their bags packed in case a quick getaway was necessary. They wouldn't have time to grab their belongings if they needed to leave in a hurry. From now on they'd live out of their backpacks, as if travelling. They also needed to remember someone might watch all their comings and goings.

CHAPTER 33

8th June 2009

MONDAY morning, and Ian looked at his watch. Eight o'clock, she's late. He'd expected her by half past seven at the latest. Ian and Jemma finished breakfast, and he paced back and forth between the bedroom and kitchen of the studio apartment. He sat down at the dining table and tried to read yesterday's paper, but he couldn't concentrate, not even on the headlines.

Sarah left at five o'clock on Friday evening. What if the police or security services caught her? What if she'd talked and told them he'd been sheltering her for the past three months? They might already be on their way to the apartment to arrest him. Ian moved to open the door but changed his mind. Someone might have the apartment under surveillance. He'd give her more time. There could be a simple explanation for her late arrival.

Ian filled the electric kettle to boil water to make yet another cup of tea. He'd already drunk three cups. Why another, his stomach already sloshed with too much liquid? Perhaps he should pack his backpack in case he needed to leave in a hurry. He sat down, stood up, walked to the front door, paced around the room, and sat at the dining table again.

Ian remembered Jemma, who'd been sitting quietly in the armchair in the corner of the room. She hadn't said a word. What thoughts passed through her mind? 'Is Sarah often late, Jemma?'

'No, Sir.'

'OK, well, let's have a cup of tea while we're waiting.' As Jemma stood, they heard a loud knock on the apartment door. They looked at each other, but neither rushed to open it.

Ian peeped through the magic eye. Sarah, almost an hour late. He swung open the door. 'Where have you been? We worried about you.'

Sarah came in and put down her bag on the kitchen counter. 'I thought a man was following me, so I didn't come straight here. I purposely took a long time and bought vegetables on the way to make it appear I was on a shopping trip.'

'Did he follow you here?'

'No, when I left the grocery store, he'd gone.'

'Jemma worried about you.'

'Didn't you worry about me?'

'Yes, if you didn't turn up, I might have had to help Jemma with the housework. But you're back now so it's all OK.'

Sarah smiled at Ian's little joke. She told them all about her weekend visit to her mother. 'Perhaps we can swap again sometime soon?' Ian did not respond to her question.

* * *

Ian marvelled at the two women. So alike yet so different. They were both attractive and of similar height, build and colouring. Separated, it was hard to tell them apart, but together, the differences were clear. At twenty-seven years of age, Jemma was two years older than Sarah, but to Ian, Sarah seemed more mature.

Jemma completed junior school, but her parent's poor circumstances forced her to leave high school early in her first year. She stayed home and helped her mother with household chores. When she turned sixteen, she got a job as a housemaid with a family in The Avenues. Jemma took her values from her parents, but her life experiences came from the company she kept with the other maids.

Sarah, the lucky one, grew up in a time when her father's finances improved, and he afforded her the education he'd not been able to give

Jemma. Sarah passed through high school and graduated with an honours degree in languages from Wits. The way she spoke marked her as a well-educated young woman. Fluent in French and Portuguese, she also spoke basic Ndebele and good English with only a trace of an African accent. At Wits, Sarah mixed with people of different races and cultures, tasted their foods and debated a wide range of ideas. She was a modern young woman who communicated on many levels.

The two women were close, and although younger, Sarah took it upon herself to watch over Jemma's welfare. She used her best efforts to make up for her sister's lack of education. Jemma reciprocated in other ways. Calm and thoughtful, her counsel often caused Sarah to stop and think twice. The sisters supported each other. They made a good team.

Jemma was quieter and more accepting than Sarah. She married at twenty-two years of age. Her husband had a good job in a government department, and she gave up work to set up their new home. Jemma worried when she didn't fall pregnant, and then the doctors gave her the devastating news. She would never have children. Despite this, they were happy together. When Jemma was twenty-six years old, her husband fell ill. The doctors carried out tests, but the cause of his illness remained a puzzle. In Zimbabwe AIDS was often the first suspect, but both Jemma and her husband tested HIV negative. One doctor said someone might have put an evil spell on him. After about six weeks Jemma's husband died. By that time the evil spell theory had gained currency, and no one wanted to carry out a post-mortem. Jemma never found out the cause of her husband's death.

It was common practice in Zimbabwe for the husband's brother to take the widow into his family. But Jemma's husband came from Mozambique, and she'd never met his family. Jemma, the childless widow, returned to her parents' home, and they welcomed her back.

As with Jemma, Sarah got her values from her parents. But Sarah was sassy and ready to argue almost any topic. She shared Ian's love for playing the devil's advocate and possessed good debating skills honed at university. Her time at Wits reinforced her old prejudices and gave her some new ones. Inevitably, she and Ian would disagree on many subjects. Sarah held strong views but kept an open and enquiring mind. Ian often felt on the verge of changing her point of view, only to end up with his hopes dashed.

Ian stopped typing on his laptop and watched the two women doing the housework. Jemma had changed back into her work clothes. When he looked at her, he saw an African housemaid, a servant. He first saw Sarah as a hotel room maid, much like Jemma. Now she seemed so different, an intellectual equal, able to hold her own in their frequent debates. Perhaps that's why he found her so irritating. But to Jemma, he was the boss, and she never questioned anything he said. Ian found that to be one of her endearing traits. Jemma may well have been as intelligent as Sarah, but she had little education. The thoughts went around in his head. Perhaps he should give her the benefit of the doubt and change his view of her. The different way he related to the two women was subtle. But when he considered it, Ian realised he treated Jemma like a servant and Sarah as an equal.

The country overflowed with millions like Jemma, people who'd not improved themselves because of lack of opportunity. Many blacks left their school days behind too early. Could the whites have made a better job of providing black schooling? The blacks outnumbered the whites by twenty to one. As always, funding was the problem. The whites were slow to change and the black leaders impatient. This led to the worst possible outcome for the country. Both sides missed opportunities, so all the people lost. Following black rule, the situation with schools, health and jobs worsened. How might the country tackle its problems? Did the answer lie in schooling for the masses? Ian looked at his notes and thought he might include all those questions and arguments in his book.

'Tea, Sir,' said Jemma, cutting across Ian's thoughts.

* * *

As usual, at eleven o'clock Jemma joined the other maids in the apartment block for morning tea. Sarah's presence was a secret, so she did not join her sister and the others. Ian and Sarah sat at the dining table with the tea and raisin toast Jemma had prepared for them. On most days, morning tea was a time for lively debate, but today things were quiet. Ian focussed on his book, and until he drained his first cup, he hadn't noticed that Sarah seemed withdrawn. 'More tea?' she asked quietly.

Ian looked at Sarah. 'Yes please.' Sarah poured his tea in silence, a silence that now attracted his attention. 'Jemma seems a little quiet this morning. Is there a problem?'

Sarah's eyes flashed. 'What's wrong? You embarrassed her. She tried to be friendly, and you rejected her.'

'When did I reject her? I didn't reject her.'

'Last night.'

Ian sat back in his chair. 'I didn't reject her. I told her to go to sleep.'

'Yes, and you embarrassed her.'

'I didn't mean to upset her,' said Ian shifting in his chair, 'but is it normal for a housemaid to expect to get cosy with her boss?'

'She wasn't trying to get cosy with you, but your reaction to her made it look like that.' Sarah paced around the room, 'You're a racist, the same as your father.'

'That's not fair. A racist wouldn't let either of you sleep in their apartment and in their bed.'

Sarah stopped and looked at Ian. 'Don't tell me that if she'd been a white woman, you wouldn't have responded differently. I knew you'd been with another woman that night you claimed to be working late. I bet you anything she was white.'

Ian gripped the edge of the dining table, and the white of his knuckles showed through his skin. 'It wouldn't be right for me to take advantage of my servant.'

'That's bullshit,' said Sarah, throwing up her arms in disgust and turning away.

Ian leant back on the two rear legs of the dining chair. 'And to be honest, you can't blame me for being cautious about HIV in Africa. I haven't any condoms, which means I wouldn't have done it even if I wanted to sleep with your sister.'

'No condoms? That's careless of you,' said Sarah, standing in front of Ian with her arms folded. 'Did you have condoms the night you slept with the white woman? I told you, Jemma can't have children. She tested negative for HIV when her husband died, and she hasn't been with another man since then. We are both HIV negative. Not all African women are HIV positive you know.'

Ian threw his head back in frustration. 'Aren't I the lucky one? I have two Zimbabwean women who are HIV negative. So now, if I sleep with either of you, I won't be a racist anymore.'

'Don't be sarcastic,' said Sarah with hands on her hips.

'Just a joke,' said Ian putting his hands up in surrender, 'just joking.'

'You better be joking,' said Sarah, wagging her right index finger at Ian. 'If you tried to touch me, you'd regret it.'

Ian was being facetious, but Sarah's last comment angered him. He snapped shut his laptop and stood up, noisily pushing away his chair with the back of his legs. He strode into the kitchen and switched on the electric kettle. For once, the electricity worked. Ian felt angry and frustrated with his odd domestic arrangement, and it slowed his attempts to progress with his book. The silly little fool! I'm taking a big risk giving her shelter from heaven knows who, and she acts as if she's doing me a favour. Who does she think she is?

The water boiled, and Ian had calmed down. The arrangement with Sarah and Jemma gave him a unique opportunity to study the close workings of the African mind. Perhaps his reaction to Sarah's threat was childish. When people argue, they say things they don't mean. After a few minutes, Ian came out of the kitchen and handed Sarah a cup of tea; a peace offering, but he was to be disappointed. All he received in return was a curt, 'Thank you.'

After their exchange, Sarah, like Jemma, was quiet. Ian rolled his eyes. Women! They're sulking because I didn't take advantage of a vulnerable woman. They've got to be kidding.

'Oh, and my father is not a racist either. A person may prefer to mix with their own kind, but that doesn't make them a racist.'

'All you Rhodesian whites were racists. That's the reason you wouldn't let us black Africans have the vote.'

'We're not going through that argument again, are we? We weren't against blacks having the vote. What we wanted was an educated, black middle class with an interest in keeping up the standards of the country. Only time could achieve that.'

'What about the uneducated and ill-informed whites then? Should they have had the vote?'

'No, but we had to draw the line somewhere. We wanted an electorate based on merit and qualifications, not one based on affirmative action.'

'That's an unworkable principal. No one runs a country that way.'

'Pushing people forward because of their skin colour leads to disaster. Look at the state of this country.' Ian stood up, warming to the debate. 'You accuse the whites of racism because we wanted to defend the civilised society we built. Blacks are just as capable of racism as the whites. The farm acquisitions are based on race. Watch or listen to your president's speeches.' Ian paced up and down the apartment. 'Two wrongs don't make a right. You keep accusing me of being a racist, but every time we debate anything, you bring race into it. You're every bit as racist as I am.' He stopped pacing and paused for effect. 'But then, I'm not a racist, so that lets you off the hook.' Ian plonked himself down in his chair, satisfied with his little speech.

Now it was Sarah's turn, but before she could respond, the door opened, and Jemma walked into the room. She saw the look on their faces and smiled uncertainly. The debate would keep. Sarah couldn't believe Ian thought her sister shouldn't qualify for the vote. Ian liked

Jemma. She was gentle and caring, but he doubted she would have the ability to cast an independent vote, free from manipulation.

Sarah found Ian's point of view hard to accept, while he worried the debate strengthened her view that he was a racist. Surely, she didn't believe that. He wouldn't back down this time. But the problem, he realised, neither would she.

In most cases Ian and Sarah stuck by their differing views. They agreed to differ, and bit by bit their respect for each other's views grew. This allowed for plain speaking in their debates. As much as they provoked each other, they both enjoyed the joust. Triggers for debate were everywhere, and race played a big role in most of them. No matter the topic, it always came back to race. Their robust debates led to short-term frustration, and usually there were no hard feelings, but today they were both angry.

Chapter 34

8th June 2009

Five o'clock, home time. Jemma spent just one night in the apartment, but it seemed much longer, almost like a holiday. It was ages since she'd last stayed away from home. Would there be other occasions when she and Sarah might switch roles? For Jemma, the experience was a thrill though she was embarrassed the boss might think her too forward. Sarah said, Ian was not cross, but she still worried she'd offended him.

Ian and Sarah both looked angry when she returned from morning tea with the other maids. Jemma realised they'd been arguing about something, and she hoped she was not the cause. She didn't like the heated debates. She liked a peaceful environment. At least, Ian acted normal and polite towards her through the rest of the day. That's what she liked about him.

Jemma walked two blocks from the apartment when a man called out from a parked car. 'Sister, which way is the hospital?'

Jemma walked over to the car and leant towards the open rear window to give the man directions. Suddenly, from behind, a hand covered her mouth, and an arm wrapped around her waist. Jemma tried to scream, but the person holding her was strong. The man inside the car opened the door, and they bundled her into the back seat. Jemma found herself squashed between two large men. 'What do you want with me?' Her voice weak and croaky as she trembled with fear.

'Quiet! Keep your head down, woman!' The two men pushed Jemma forward, forcing her face down onto her knees.

'What do you want? Please don't hurt me.'

'Shut up, or you will get hurt!'

Jemma shrieked as the car sped down the road. 'Keep quiet!' In her panic she didn't think to count the blocks they drove or try to memorise the turns they made. She prayed they wouldn't harm her.

Soon, the car slowed and stopped somewhere in the city. It was a short trip, and Jemma could hear passing traffic.

The man who'd pushed Jemma into the car grabbed her arm and pulled her out. The driver ran around the car and grabbed her other arm. Between them, the two men dragged her up a short flight of steps to the front door of the house. They moved fast, and Jemma struggled to keep her footing as they hauled her like a sack of mealies into the building.

Once inside, they went into the first room on the right and dumped her onto a hard, wooden chair. A man picked up the phone and dialled a short number. 'We've got her in the front office, Sir.'

Jemma glanced at the men. 'Look down! Don't look at our faces!' one man shouted. Jemma quickly hung her head and sat trembling, looking as if she was shivering from the cold.

Two minutes later the door opened, and someone entered. After a short silence, the newcomer cupped Jemma's chin and lifted her face and looked searchingly at her. Jemma saw a pleasant face with a neat moustache. 'What is your name, woman?'

'Jemma, Jemma Kagonye,' she answered in a quavering voice.

The man turned to the others. 'Go back to your desks. I'll talk to you later.' As the men filed out of the office, the newcomer smiled at Jemma and lowered his voice. 'The boss asked me to interview you because I'm the only one who worked with your sister. I didn't want to talk in front of them,' he said in a reassuring voice. 'My name is Jedson Ziyambi, and I'm a friend of your sister. Where is she? I need to see her. I'm worried about her safety.'

'She's in Joburg, Sir, but I don't know where.'

'If she gets in touch with you, please tell her to contact me. It's important.'

'Yes, Sir, but I haven't seen my sister for months.'

'Please accept my apologies for your treatment. The boys can be overzealous. I'll explain to the captain it's all a big mistake. I'll get someone to drop you wherever you need to go.'

'Just to the bus station please,' whispered Jemma. The man picked up the phone and spoke to someone.

Within a minute a man entered. He was not one of those who abducted her. 'Take this young lady to the bus station. Use the van. Put her in the back.'

The panel van's windows were blacked out. This time, Jemma tried to keep track of the direction they were travelling, but there were so many turns she got confused. They were making sure she couldn't trace her way back to the house.

* * *

Captain John's face was as black as thunder. 'Samson, you fool! You guaranteed it was Sarah Kagonye you tailed, but it was her sister. I told you her sister worked for the murungu.'

'Sorry, Sir, but when I followed her to the grocer's store and on to the apartment, she looked like the photo you gave us. They're so much alike.'

'Don't make excuses you fool. And what about you two?' said John turning towards Elijah and Akashinga. Couldn't you see she wasn't Sarah Kagonye? Why am I wasting my time training idiots who never seem to learn?

'Sorry, Sir,' said Elijah, 'but shouldn't we have found out from her where her sister is hiding? She looked afraid and ready to talk.'

'No, she wouldn't have told us the truth, and you all know my policy to not involve a target's family members. And you, you fool,' said John turning back to Samson, 'you've only made things harder for us through your stupidity. If she knows where her sister is, she'll tell her about this evening.'

'Must we still keep watch on the murungu's apartment, Sah?' asked Akashinga.

'Yes, more than ever now. Samson is on double shifts for the rest of the month. Now get out, all of you. Get out of my sight.'

As they walked back to the open-plan office, Akashinga said to Elijah, 'That's not so bad. If Samson's on double shifts, it means less work for us.'

Elijah gave Akashinga a long, patient look.

Chapter 35

30th July 2009

A beautiful sunny winter morning, not too cold with a fresh, gentle breeze; one of those mornings that made one feel alive. Despite several new buildings, Harare looked a little more worn than Ian remembered. No longer did it have the sparkling new look of the nineteen-eighties, though it remained an attractive city. Ian strode out with a spring in his step, but something niggled at him. That bloody Sarah! Fancy, her calling him selfish!

Since Jemma's brush with the COU, Sarah pestered Ian to bring forward his trip to Victoria Falls. She was keen to leave the country soon and hoped Ian's trip would be a way out for her. But the timing wasn't convenient, and he dismissed the idea. He was busy at work, and behind with his book. A trip at Christmas made more sense, but Sarah accused him of selfishness. Deep in thought, Ian didn't notice the police car pull up next to him.

A policeman sitting in the front passenger seat wound down his window. 'Good morning Mr Sanders. Please get into the car. We need to talk to you at the police station.'

Ian went across to the open window, hesitating. The hairs bristled on the back of his neck. 'Why, what's the matter?'

'We'll ask the questions, Mr Sanders, at the police station. Why do you whites always question everything?'

Ian looked in the car and saw a scruffy African sitting in the back seat. He didn't look like a policeman. 'Do you have proof of identity?'

The policeman showed Ian a card identifying him as Inspector Dennis Mpofu. The card looked authentic, but Ian was cautious. 'How long will it take?'

'The quicker we get back to the police station, the quicker it will be.'

How long had the police kept track of him? Perhaps, it was them who searched his apartment at Easter when he was in Joburg. 'Must it be now? Can't I come later? What's the problem?'

'We are just following orders, Mr Sanders. This country has enemies, and we must be vigilant. But for you, it's a random check we do on tourists.'

'How do you know I'm a tourist? How do you know my name?' Ian realised the police must have an active file on him.

'There are not too many tourists in Zimbabwe these days, Mr Sanders, so it's easy to keep track of them. Please get into the car. We must hurry.' The inspector's voice now had an unmistakable edge to it.

The inspector's face hardened, but Ian persisted. 'Where is the police station?'

The policeman tapped his fingers on the dashboard and his voice thickened. 'It is near the railway station. Do you want me to arrest you for resisting the police? Please get into the car.'

The tone of the inspector's voice was threatening, and Ian thought it best not to test his patience further. He got into the police car, leaving the door lock in the open position and his seatbelt undone. If they didn't head towards the railway station, he might try to make a run for it. But how far would he get? He'd heard about other abductions. His friends warned him that people disappeared in Zimbabwe.

The scruffy man sitting in the back seat smiled at Ian, but he didn't say a word.

'How are you enjoying your stay in our beautiful country, Mr Sanders?' said Inspector Mpofu, his manner now pleasant.

'It's most enjoyable thank you.' If they weren't already aware, Ian wouldn't admit to being born in the country. A lot of blacks regarded the local whites as racist.

'How long are you planning to stay?'

'At least a year, I hope. I want to tour all the sites in Zimbabwe.'

Ian relaxed a little when he saw the railway station on his left, and he felt the tension at the back of his head ease. He realised he'd been screwing up his eyes, and he opened them wide to relieve the tension further. A short distance past the railway station, the police car slowed and turned into Inez Terrace, and then left into the courtyard of a four-storey brick building. Irrelevancies crowded into Ian's mind. The brickwork on the building looked fine, but the windows looked rusted and dirty. He noted the razor wire on top of the open storm mesh gate. The top hinge looked damaged and about to break. Ian's mind raced yet found time to focus on trivial details. A large group of African men waiting at the gate. Why were they all there?

The inspector led Ian up a flight of steps to the rear entrance. Inside the building, Ian noticed a strong musty smell, the smell of Africa. Did they ever open the windows for fresh air? They passed the reception counter and turned into a passageway busy with people scurrying about, police in uniform and others in street clothes. People stood or sat in a row of chairs, looking bored or half asleep, waiting for someone to attend to them. Inspector Mpofu showed Ian into a room on the ground floor. 'Please wait here, Mr Sanders. The chief inspector will be with you in a minute.'

Ian sat fidgeting in an uncomfortable metal chair in the spartan interview room. The wait seemed interminable. What was the delay? No one bothered to offer him a drink. He surveyed his surroundings for the umpteenth time. The walls, a gloss mint green, a typical government, bureaucratic colour like in his school classrooms back in Bulawayo. A brown wooden desk like the ones the teachers used. The high ceiling, fly-spotted walls and the rough wooden floor, rutted with age and wear, all reminded him of his schooldays. On the wall under the window stood a large plumbed-in, old style water heater like the ones in the classrooms. He didn't remember them ever being turned on, but no one seemed to notice. The large windows made the room bright. The bars on the windows concerned Ian, but most houses also had them. Why had they brought him here? Was it part of their strategy to keep him waiting? They knew his name. Were they keeping an eye on the apartment?

A plain beige manila folder caught Ian's eye. He'd not seen it before now. It lay on the desk in front of the empty seat where the chief inspector would sit when he arrived. How did he miss it? The mind played funny tricks in stressful situations. Ian sat up straight, trying to read the words on the cover, upside down — *Ian Sanders–Confidential.* The file, half an inch thick; what might it contain? Ian struggled with conflicting thoughts. A quick peek would take a second. No sound in the passageway penetrated through the heavy wooden door, and Ian worried there would be no warning if anyone approached. It appeared to be a busy thoroughfare when he arrived, but now only silence. What if they caught him looking at the file?

Ian stood up and walked halfway around the desk. This was crazy! What could they have on him; nothing much? He'd done no wrong, so he should ignore it. He sat down, but the file seemed to draw him in with a pulsating magnetism. Perhaps he could turn the file around and read it across the desk. He stood, turned the file and sat down again. Whoever put it there might have faced it the wrong way.

Total silence outside the door but if he didn't act soon, he might miss his chance. Ian took a deep breath and jumped up and flipped open the cover. He stared at the blurred, A4 sized enlargement of his passport photograph copied by immigration when he entered the country.

A click at the door. Ian's heart jumped. Somebody was coming. In his haste to close the file, he pushed it off the desk, and the papers slid across the floor like an open fan. Sheets flew in all directions, and to his horror, one slipped under the door. He raced around the desk to gather up the papers. It took seconds, but it seemed much longer. No one came into the room. So many papers in his file but… they were blank sheets of A4 paper. Were they trying to frighten him? Ian replaced the file and sat down once more. Was the sheet that slid under the door also blank? He heard his own heart thumping in his chest. Then, he noticed he'd placed the file with his name facing him. He leapt up and turned the file. Now it looked the same as when it first caught his eye. But did he put his photo back in the file, facing the right direction? Ian jumped up again and looked under the front cover of the manila folder. A blank sheet greeted him. He flipped through to the back of the file and there he found his photo. He brought it to the front of the file and placed it facing the chief inspector's chair. Ian sat down once more, breathing heavily. He'd made a hash of something so simple.

The tension headache at the back of Ian's head returned. He again screwed up his eyes with the strain of waiting, waiting for what? More than an hour passed since his arrival at the police station. Tired of sitting, Ian stood up and walked to the window. Just then the door opened, and a thick-set policeman of medium height walked in, carrying several sheets of paper in his left hand. Did they include the sheets that slipped under the door? 'Mr Sanders, I am Chief Inspector Charles Chamisa; sit down please.'

Ian didn't like the looks of the stern sounding man. 'Why am I here Chief Inspector?'

Chief Inspector Chamisa ignored Ian's question. 'Mr Sanders, what is your business in Zimbabwe?'

'I'm here on holiday, but I'm hoping to write a book about all the country's tourist attractions.'

'So, you're a journalist then?' said the chief inspector, raising his eyebrows.

'No, I've not written anything before now, but I thought a travel book might help pay for my trip to Zimbabwe.'

'Are you aware you must submit anything you write to the government censors for approval to publish?'

'That's OK, I'm happy to do that,' Ian lied. He suspected Chamisa made it up to discourage him, but he planned to be long gone by the time his manuscript was finished.

'If you write any criticism of our president or make any adverse comments about our government, you will be in deep trouble.'

'I don't intend to say anything negative or controversial Chief Inspector. It's a travel book advising potential tourists about the best sites and places to visit.'

'Mr Sanders, you were born in Bulawayo. Haven't you seen enough of Zimbabwe? Why did you want to write a travel book about this country? There are plenty of brochures telling tourists about the best places to visit.'

The authorities knew of his local origins and must have investigated him. 'I want to give it a personal touch, but I've been out of Zimbabwe for twenty years and needed to update myself. Now I'm between jobs, I thought it the perfect time for a visit.' Did they know about Sarah? Was that what this was all about?

Chamisa frowned. 'What is your connection to the Mthwakazi Freedom Front - the MFF - Mr Sanders?'

The sudden change in direction took Ian by surprise. 'The MFF, what is that?'

'On your flight from Perth to Johannesburg you sat next to Mrs Ruth Bernstein.'

'Yes.'

'She and her husband are supporters of the MFF. You have carried out work for her husband's accounting firm. Is that not true?'

'Yes, I'm assessing a business venture for one of his clients. The Bernsteins didn't mention the MFF.'

'How is it you're so close to the Bernstein family?'

'I'm not close to them. I met Mrs Bernstein on the plane. When I mentioned my former work as a business consultant, and my visit to Zimbabwe, she invited me to meet her husband. She said he needed professional help from time to time.'

'Oh! You say you are not close to them, but you spent time with Mrs Bernstein in her hotel room. Forgive me if I've got the wrong impression.'

'I've only met them once or twice.'

Chamisa, stony faced, stood up and walked to the window. 'Mr Sanders, what is your connection to Sarah Kagonye?'

'Who is she?' Ian realised he was squeezing the fingers of his left hand and tried to relax by putting his hands on his knees. Had Chamisa read his body language?

'Mr Sanders, she was the room maid on your floor at the hotel. Her sister is your housemaid. That's too much of a coincidence, don't you agree?'

'I never met the room maid at the hotel. They always cleaned the room in my absence. Was she the one hotel security searched for on my first morning at the hotel? Two men from hotel security knocked on my door and asked if I'd seen her, but no one cleaned my room that day.'

'How did you find your apartment, Mr Sanders?'

'Oh! Clean and tidy thank you.'

'This is no joking matter, Mr Sanders. I understand your European sense of humour but trying to be clever now will not help you.'

'Sorry, Chief Inspector, I meant no disrespect. I went for a walk in the inner-city suburbs and saw an apartment block I liked, so I knocked on the caretaker's door and asked if any apartments were free. By chance one was available, and now I'm renting it for six months while the occupants are travelling overseas. The housemaid works for the owners of the apartment, not me. I was lucky to find an apartment so soon.'

'Yes, lucky, Mr Sanders, almost too lucky to be true. Suitable apartments in Harare aren't easy to come by these days.'

Chamisa looked Ian straight in the eye. 'Now, what can you tell me about the whereabouts of Sarah Kagonye?'

'I told you, I've never met her, and I wouldn't know what she looked like.' A frightening thought crossed Ian's mind. What if the police were searching his apartment while he sat here lying to Chamisa?

What if Sarah was already in custody? Was that why they'd kept him waiting so long? He prayed they'd not found her.

'What strikes me, Mr Sanders, is that after a short time in Africa, you've already met three of our country's most wanted dissidents. If you are withholding any information about these people, it will go badly for you. You might spend more time in this building than you would care to imagine. Tell me if I'm wrong, but I don't think Chikurubi Prison is where you planned to spend your time in our country. But I suppose it might give you good material for your book.'

'Chief Inspector, I will call you if I come across anything of interest to you.' But Ian had no intention of seeing or talking to the chief inspector again.

'This is not a light matter, Mr Sanders, and you could end up in serious trouble. We will keep a close eye on you and your movements. You can go now, but don't leave Harare without letting me know where you are heading. I am sure we will talk again soon. Sign the attendance book on your way out.'

'Before I go, Chief Inspector, I would like to tell you something. About four months ago when I walked home from the Monomotapa Hotel, someone tried to strangle me with a length of coarse rope.'

'Why didn't you report it?'

'With all due respect, Chief Inspector, people warned me to avoid the police in Zimbabwe if I wanted to keep out of trouble.'

'That was not good advice. You should have reported it at once. It was your civil duty to report something like that.'

'Well, I'm reporting it now. I understand someone strangled a young woman in Harare Gardens. The next night, someone tried to garrotte me. Do you think they're connected?'

'Sources tell us the young woman was friends with a white man. Was that you, Mr Sanders?'

'I met her on my first night in Harare. I thought she might give local colour to my book.'

'You must make a full statement, Mr Sanders. Two of my detectives will interview you.'

Damn, he should have kept his mouth shut. But he owed it to Hazel to help the police find her killer. Ian remembered the young lawyer, Daniel Moyo, and his offer of legal representation. But it was early days for that, and it might look suspicious and make matters worse if he asked for his lawyer.

Two detectives came in to get his full report. A surlier pair he couldn't imagine. Their manner was curt and disbelieving. Mid-afternoon! At this rate, he'd be at the police station till nightfall. Two hours later, Ian worried he might not get out of the police station that day. 'So, you assaulted the man and did not report the assault,' said one detective?

'I defended myself,' said Ian, speaking in a slow, emphatic voice. 'If I hadn't, you would have had two strangulation murders in two days. Imagine all the paperwork.' Ian's last point seemed to strike a chord with the two detectives. It was a relief when they at last finished and Chief Inspector Chamisa returned.

'You seem to be trouble, Mr Sanders. I don't think you should stay in Zimbabwe too much longer. You can go for now, but the only suspects are you and the unidentified, burly black man you claim attacked you.'

'Surely you don't suspect me, Chief Inspector?'

'When there's trouble wherever you go, Mr Sanders, what better suspect could we have? You would be an easy conviction, guilty or not. A burly black man describes half the men in Zimbabwe. Why didn't you take a photo of him with your cell phone when you had the chance? If we get any leads on this person, we will call you to identify him. Remember, we are keeping a close eye on you. Don't forget to sign out when you leave the building.'

'Yes, thank you, Chief Inspector. Will I be able to get a lift back to my office?' said Ian, with mischievous earnestness.

Chief Inspector Chamisa smiled for the first time, but it was a cold smile. 'Most people in Harare wouldn't want a lift in a police car, Mr

Sanders. That's one way you can disappear. The man sitting with you in the police car this morning… No one will see him again. I wouldn't push my luck if I were you.'

Ian felt the chief inspector was trying to scare him, but he saw it was not a good time to be smart. 'No, sorry, Chief Inspector, I was joking. I'll enjoy the walk back to my office. Thank you.'

With that, Ian walked out of Harare police station and breathed a sigh of relief. If they'd known Sarah stayed at the apartment, they wouldn't have let him go. First Jemma and now me. What next? The bastards hadn't even offered him a cup of tea. He needed a strong coffee on the way back to the office, something to settle his nerves. This was one occasion Nelson's tea wouldn't do the trick.

Chapter 36

31st July – 7th August 2009

JEMMA put the tea tray down on the dining table for Ian and Sarah. 'I'm going for tea with the other girls now, Sir.' Sarah rolled her eyes, but Jemma smiled in return.

'Thank you, Jemma.'

After Jemma left, Ian said, 'I don't think I'll ever be able to stop Jemma calling me *sir* or *boss*.'

'Oh, come on, you love it! It makes you feel like the big white boss from the old days before black rule.'

'I've tried a lot of times to get her to call me Ian, but it makes her uncomfortable.'

'It makes me uncomfortable when she calls you *sir* or *boss*.'

'When I was in the hotel, when we first met, you called me *sir*.'

'That was part of my job then.'

'It was part of your job because you were the room maid. Over here Jemma is the housemaid, so it's part of her job.'

'If it makes you happy, that's fine by me. If she's happy to call you *sir* or *boss*, it's not my business to object.'

Finally! Ian had the last word debating with Sarah. That didn't happen too often. But then he became suspicious. Was she up to something? Ian was sharp, but Sarah always seemed to be two steps ahead of him. He took another sip of tea, and Sarah said, 'Are you still planning to go to Bulawayo next weekend?'

'Yes, I'm staying at the Rainbow.'

'For four days?'

'Yes, they asked me to drive the company car down to Bulawayo and leave it there. I'll drive down on Saturday morning and get the train back on Tuesday evening. It's a good opportunity to see Bulawayo again.'

'I was hoping to see my mother for a few days next weekend.'

'We can't leave Jemma here on her own for four whole days.'

'No, we can't. Is there any chance you might take her with you? I'll pay her expenses.'

'Oh yes, with what?'

'I have money.'

'Can't you make it another weekend?'

'No, my Uncle Charles is visiting my mother next weekend. It's my best chance to see him, and it's very important that I talk to him and soon.'

'Who's Uncle Charles?'

'He's my godfather and my papa's best friend.'

Ian thought for a moment. He'd try to get a single room for Jemma. He was planning on spending a few days on his own, but what the heck. 'OK, if I can change the hotel booking, it should be fine.'

When Jemma returned from morning tea, Sarah smiled. 'The boss says it's OK for us to swap next weekend, but you must go to Bulawayo with him.'

'So, you two planned this between you?'

Jemma looked embarrassed. Sarah smiled her sweet smile. 'You are one of the nicest white racists I've met. Thank you.' It was one of the nicest things Sarah ever said to him. She'd always given him the impression he should feel privileged to be sheltering her.

He phoned the hotel to change the booking. 'I'm sorry, Sir, the hotel is full. There's no vacancy for those dates. We are booked out for a conference.'

Damn! Sharing the apartment was one thing but sharing a hotel room was another. Ah well, no one in Bulawayo knew him, and he was on his own. 'What size bed have you booked for me?'

'It's a king-size, Sir, but if you prefer you can have twin share. Do you want me to change your booking from single to double?'

'Yes, OK, thank you. Twin share will be fine.' Ian switched off his phone. 'Sarah, make sure Jemma brings a swimming costume with her. It's a pity it's not summer, there's a beautiful public pool down there. But I hear the Bernsteins have a great heated indoor-outdoor pool at their old house in Bulawayo, and we can swim there if we want.'

'Jemma can't swim.'

'Don't worry, I'll look after her.'

* * *

After work on the Friday before the Bulawayo trip, Manfred Schwartz took Ian back to his house in Gun Hill to pick up Ruth's car. The house was an impressive, African-themed, single storey construction. The large grounds comprised manicured lawns and fir trees along the front fence. Ivana, Manfred's small dark-haired wife, gave Ian a warm welcome.

'How about a nice cold Zambezi?' said Manfred. 'Ivana, bring us beers, will you?' Ivana returned from the kitchen carrying a plate of snacks and two beers.

'This is a lovely house,' said Ian.

'Towards the end of white rule in Rhodesia,' said Manfred, 'there were plenty of bargain houses available. Even people of modest means were able to afford top properties. We already had a nice house, but we couldn't pass up this one.' Ian's gaze followed the sweep of Manfred's hand around the room.

'Yes, my parents had a nice house in Bulawayo, but they sold it when we left for Australia.'

'There were lots of bargains on offer when the whites were leaving. Then with black rule and Mugabe making a few conciliatory statements, the prices shot up again. So now, we have this house and one, a little less grand, in Joburg. As I told you, we spend a lot of our time down there.'

Ian told Manfred about his visit to the Harare police station. 'They were aware of my visit to Ruth's house in Joburg, and they also knew I sat next to her on the plane. When you next see her and Solly, you must warn them someone is spying on their activities. Perhaps the maids listen in on their conversations. Somebody is monitoring their every move, and it's all reported back to the police or CIO here in Zimbabwe.'

'That doesn't sound good. Yes, I will warn them. That business about the Mthwakazi Freedom Front—the MFF—is a worry. It could land them in big trouble.'

'So, it's true they're involved with the MFF?'

'No, I'm not saying that, but even the accusation makes it dangerous for them, whether it's true or not. If Ruth visits again, they could detain her for heaven knows how long. Solly doesn't like coming up here, so he sends Ruth instead, but now I'm not sure that's safe anymore. I'll warn them when I next see them. A phone call would be risky because you never can tell who's listening on the line.' The phone rang, and Manfred got up from his chair. 'Excuse me, I'll take the call in my study. Ivana will look after you.'

'You must join us for dinner sometime,' said Ivana, 'perhaps when we are next up here.'

'Thank you, I would like that.'

'The problem is I'm not here too often. I only come up to reinforce my status as number one wife and owner of this house.'

Ian laughed. What was Ivana hinting?

'No, I'm serious about that. What do you think of Manfred's associates?'

'They're OK, though they could be a little more approachable.'

'Nelson is Shona and Frida is Matabele. They don't like each other. Manfred believes in divide and conquer. No matter the issue, one of them will always support him. Without Manfred, there would be no business, so he has no fear of them undermining him. He would still have de facto control of the business even if he was to become a minority shareholder.'

'Surely, he wouldn't want to hold less than fifty percent of the partnership?'

'No, but there's talk that the government wants all businesses to be majority owned by black Zimbabweans.'

'If that's the case, Manfred's arrangement is smart.'

'Tell me, how does Frida treat you?'

Ian smiled. 'She's always cool and arrogant, and she acts as though she owns the business and treats Nelson as if he's the tea boy.'

'Do you know why she's so arrogant? Manfred has an apartment in the Avenues where he keeps Frida. When I'm not here, he moves in with her. That's why I must come up here periodically to reinforce my status as wife and owner of this house.'

'Oh! I see.' Ian was lost for words after Ivana's last comment.

'Sometimes, he's even brought her here. What they don't realise is that my Shona cook, who has been with us for twenty years, tells me everything. Andrew is my spy, and he resents Frida,' said Ivana, with a twinkle in her eye, 'but he and Nelson get on well.'

Ian blinked. Perhaps it was not the African maids working in the Bernstein's Johannesburg mansion who leaked information about their affairs. Before he had the chance to respond, Manfred returned, and Ian decided it was a good time to leave. He thanked Manfred and Ivana for their hospitality and made his excuses. 'I should go. I don't want to tell Ruth that I damaged her car because I drank too much.'

'No,' agreed Manfred, 'I wouldn't like to do that either. Oh, and there're cartons of photocopy paper in the boot of the car. Just leave them in the boot when you hand the car over in Bulawayo on Tuesday afternoon.'

'Thanks again for the drinks,' said Ian, through the driver's window as he eased Ruth's car down the long driveway. He hadn't driven for six months and it made him a little more cautious than usual. 'Good luck on your trip to Bulawayo,' Manfred called out. 'I hope you don't have too many roadblocks.' Ian waved back as he drove the car out through the gate before disappearing behind the fir trees lining the front fence.

It was a short drive back to the apartment. The Volkswagen Polo was in tip-top condition with almost new tyres because of the limited use Ruth made of the car on her occasional visits. The shortage of foreign currency meant that a lot of luxury cars in Zimbabwe drove on bald tyres.

Ian got back to the apartment close to seven o'clock. Jemma had prepared dinner and was waiting for him. She had her hair braided in readiness for her big trip to Bulawayo. She looked most attractive, and Ian couldn't let it pass without comment. 'You're looking pretty Jemma, and your hair is nice.'

'Thank you, Sir.' Ian would have sworn she blushed.

Chapter 37

8th August 2009

It was the Saturday of the Heroes and Armed Forces Day long weekend, and Ian and Jemma were up early for a half-past-five start. 'Sir, I've made tea and sandwiches for the trip,' said Jemma, holding up the thermos flask she'd taken from the kitchen cupboard.

'Good girl, now let's hurry.'

Ian clicked the apartment door shut behind him, and he and Jemma padded along the corridor and down the stairs to the front entrance. He hoped no one saw them leave. Prying eyes and wagging tongues would draw unwelcome attention and could mean trouble for them down the line.

They left the building and hurried to the car, parked around the corner in the street below their apartment. It was a crisp morning. Neither of them noticed the big African asleep in the back seat of the old car, parked three spaces down from the building entrance. Ian wiped the windows and rear-view mirrors with a cloth he found in the door pocket. 'Are you ready, Jemma?'

'Yes, Sir.'

'No, you're not ready. You must put on your seatbelt.'

Ian looked at Jemma fumbling with the seatbelt. He took it from her and clipped it home.

'Thank you, Sir.'

'Always put on your seatbelt, Jemma.'

'Yes, Sir.'

That little incident made Ian realise Jemma may not have travelled in a car too often. 'Didn't your father take you for drives in his car?'

'Yes, Sir, sometimes.'

'And didn't he make you wear a seatbelt?'

'No, Sir, his car only had seatbelts in the front for him and Mama.'

Ian switched on the car heater. He loved the silence of the deserted streets so early in the morning. Daylight comes fast in Zimbabwe, and it was bright soon after a quarter past six. In no time they were on the open road, leaving the Harare skyline behind them. 'Would you like a sandwich, Sir?'

'Thank you, Jemma.'

They were both hungry. In their hurry to get going, they hadn't had breakfast. 'Yum, you make delicious ham sandwiches Jemma.'

'Thank you, Sir.'

Ian liked his tea black without sugar, but in the morning cold Jemma's sweet white tea hit the spot. He felt much better after that, and Jemma was happy her efforts pleased him. She knew how Ian liked his tea, but in her hurry to get things ready, she'd added milk and sugar, the way she liked it.

Jemma couldn't sit still. It was her first long car trip and travelling to Bulawayo was a real adventure for her. She'd dressed for the occasion in tight blue jeans and a clingy, white sweater and a delicate pair of strappy, white sandals on her feet. Through her ears she wore the hooped, gold earrings Ian brought back from his Easter trip to Joburg. If nothing else, she was at least decorative. She looked nothing like the maid who cleaned his apartment and did the washing and ironing and helped prepare his meals each day.

The fuel shortage meant few cars on the road. Soon they approached Lake Chivero, which Ian knew as Lake Mcllwaine. As they neared the village of Norton, they saw the first roadblock. The policeman eased himself from the old metal chair and waved Ian to stop. He sauntered up to the car window. 'Good morning, Sah, where are you travelling today?'

'We're going to Bulawayo for the long weekend.'

'Is this your wife with you?' said the policeman, leaning over to peer into the car.

'No, she's my housemaid.'

'Why are you taking your housemaid with you, Sah?'

'She's never been to Bulawayo, and she'd like to see it.'

The policeman asked a lot of questions. He looked at Ian's Australian driving licence and asked who owned the car. He even had an issue with the car's registration plates. 'They're too dusty. You must clean them.' Next, he raised doubts about the condition of the vehicle even though it looked almost new.

Soon, the policeman ran out of questions. Ian could almost hear his mind whirring, trying to find an excuse to charge him a toll. Ian saved him the trouble and handed him a US dollar note. The policeman smiled and said, 'Thank you, Sah, have a good trip.'

Sixty kilometres down the road, they arrived at a second roadblock near the small village of Chegutu. This time, a surly policeman confronted them.

'Open the boot. I must search it.'

The policeman looked through their backpacks. 'What's in those boxes?'

'They're cartons of photocopy paper I have to deliver for my employer.'

The policeman used a knife to slice open the tape on the lid of a carton and took out a ream and tore open the packaging. As stated on the carton, it was plain white A4 80GSM photocopy and print paper. He threw it down into the boot of the car. Ian took out a one-dollar US note, and the policeman took it without a word and walked away. Ian put the ream of paper back into the carton and drove on his way.

A deep blue sky and bright sun soon replaced the morning chill, and Ian switched off the car heater. It promised to be a warm day.

The state of the road meant that the four-hundred-and-forty-kilometre drive to Bulawayo would take about six-and-a-half hours. Ian remembered when the same trip with his parents took only four hours.

Evidence of the farm seizures bordered the open road. Once, well-tended farms lined the route, but now, tall, dry grass had overgrown the properties. Farm machinery lay rusting in the fields and broken fences and derelict farm buildings a common sight. The countryside seemed abandoned with few signs of life, animal or human. 'There's a nice farm,' said Ian, as they drove past one of the few well-tended farms belonging to whites who had somehow kept in with the regime.

'It's nice, Sir.'

Near the small town of Kadoma, the policeman at the roadblock insisted Ian should pay a dollar per head. After bargaining, he accepted the single dollar Ian gave him.

At the roadblock near Kwekwe, a policeman sliced open the second carton for inspection. As with the first carton, the package contained a ream of plain white photocopy paper. The policeman took out a pack from the second layer and tore it open. But before he had the chance to examine it another vehicle pulled up at the roadblock. 'Tchah, another one so soon,' he said in disgust, throwing down the ream of paper into the boot. He slammed down the lid of the boot and held out the palm of his left hand, 'Two dollars on weekends.' Ian gave him a dollar. The policeman took it and walked to the other vehicle without saying a word.

Ian drove on, 'I didn't like the looks of that last guy,' he said to Jemma, who had shrunk down into her seat. 'I smelled the drink on his breath.'

'No, Sir, a bad man.'

At the roadblock on the outskirts of Gweru, a young policeman waved them to stop. He looked inside the car and saw Jemma sitting in the passenger seat.

'Who is this woman, Sah?'

'She's my housemaid.'

'Are you taking her for work in Bulawayo?'

'No, she's just visiting for the long weekend.'

'Sah, it's illegal to transport prostitutes between cities? This is a serious matter.'

'I am not a prostitute, you rude boy,' Jemma shouted. 'Has your mother not taught you any manners?'

'Sorry, Madam, I didn't—'

'You should be courteous and helpful to the public, not bully them.'

'Yes Madam. Sorry.'

Ian feared that Jemma's outburst might create problems for them, but the policeman seemed intimidated. Ian hadn't seen her like that before now. She had fire when she needed it. The policeman did not have the nerve to ask for the usual one-dollar toll. 'Thank you, Sah. You can go now, Sah.'

Ian smiled at the turn of events. 'That was brave of you Jemma. I can see I will have to mind my manners with you.'

'Oh no, Sir, sorry, Sir,' said Jemma, a little flustered in case she'd done the wrong thing.

'It's OK, Jemma. He needed to be told.'

'Yes, Sir.'

The roadblocks proved to be a perverse blessing as they gave Ian a little relief from the long drive. Jemma was not the sparkling company Sarah might have been if she'd accompanied Ian on the drive to Bulawayo. English was Jemma's second language, and her work as a housemaid had done little to develop her communication skills. This did not stop Ian from pumping her for information about her life, her parents and her view of things. At first Jemma seemed shy in the unfamiliar surroundings of the car and the open road. Ian found it difficult to get much out of her. Later, although she seemed to like the focus of the questions being on her and her family, she responded with short, monosyllabic answers. 'Jemma, do you have any family apart from Sarah and your mother?'

'No, Sir.'

'Don't you have any aunts and uncles?'

'No, Sir. We have Uncle Charles, but he is not really an uncle. He was my papa's best friend.'

'And where are your grandparents?'

'They are dead, Sir.'

By the time they reached Gweru's city centre, Ian's persistence in asking open-ended questions seemed to be working. Jemma expanded on her answers as her confidence grew. It seemed her outburst at the unfortunate policeman at the Gweru roadblock also helped burst the bubble of shyness that shrouded her.

The flask of tea and the ham sandwiches had long since run out. 'Are you thirsty, Jemma?'

'Yes, Sir.'

'OK, let's stop for tea at the Midlands Hotel.' It was years since Ian's last visit to Gweru, but the old Boggie Clock at the intersection by the corner of the hotel remained an unmistakable landmark. A pioneer woman built the landmark in the main street of the town, in memory of her husband. There appeared to be no one else at the hotel, and the tired-looking waiter seemed surprised to see them. 'You are open, aren't you?' Ian asked.

'Yes, Sah,' said the waiter recovering from his surprise.

Saturday, and the streets of the town looked deserted. In fact, the road from Harare was almost devoid of traffic. 'The roads used to be busy on weekends and on long-weekends,' said Ian. 'People would visit relatives or go camping in the bush near dams and rivers for a weekend of fishing. The African buses would be crowded, and the roofs piled high with luggage.'

'There's no petrol, Sir.'

'Yes, and it's bad for business. Look, the hotel is empty.' The waiter brought the tea on a large wooden tray. It had been a long time since Ian had seen a silver teapot, sugar bowl and milk jug set, all with hinged lids. The thick white china cups and saucers were standard hotel issue.

For Jemma, having tea with her boss at the hotel was like being on a date. What would Sarah say about this? A trickle of other guests dropped in, and Jemma welcomed each curious glance in their direction.

'Here's the milk and sugar Jemma.'

'No thank you, Sir.'

'But you always have your tea with milk and sugar.'

'I want to try tea like yours, Sir.'

'You may not like black tea without sugar if you're not used to it.'

'I will try, Sir.'

She noted how Ian drank his tea and copied him, giving others the impression it was a routine occurrence. Ian soon saw what she was doing. 'Jemma, if you hold your little finger out when you are drinking from a cup, it will make you look like a lady. But you mustn't do it when you are drinking from a mug.' He showed her what he meant, and thereafter Jemma always drank her tea that way.

Ian and Jemma returned to the car refreshed and eager to reach their destination. Ian remembered the open ream of paper the policeman at the Kwekwe roadblock threw down in disgust. He opened the car boot to put it back into the carton. The sheets, spilt from the torn package, lay scattered across the boot. Ian gathered them up and—discovered print on the reverse side. In large block letters he read, *Mthwakazi Must Be Free.* At the bottom of the page an MFF logo depicted a rising sun and the name, *Mthwakazi Freedom Front.*

The bastards! They risked his neck to deliver their flyers. Why didn't they warn him? Was this why Ruth offered him her car? Manfred should have told him the cartons contained sensitive material.

Ian put the sheets face down in the torn packaging, in the second level of reams. Now what should he do? Even though he could truthfully plead ignorance if they found the flyers, it might not do him much good.

They set off on the last stretch to Bulawayo. Ian didn't talk to Jemma about what he'd discovered in the boot. She was a Shona, and he didn't know how she would take the news of the MFF flyers. If push came to shove, how would she respond to a police interrogation? He worried about the flyers and further roadblocks.

With Ian's pensive silence, Jemma became chattier and even initiated parts of the discussion. She didn't appear to have too much interest in politics though he gleaned from her comments she worried about the country's direction. It seemed she only wanted to talk about her sister. 'Sarah is clever, Sir.'

'Yes.'

'Now our father has gone, she makes the important decisions for our family.'

'Uh-huh.'

'She is pretty, Sir.'

'Mm-hmm.'

Ian smiled to himself. Now, he gave the one-word answers.

'Do you think she is pretty, Sir?'

Whoops! Here come the open-ended questions. 'Yes, she's pretty, just like you.'

Jemma blushed. Damn! He'd answered without thinking. He did not want to give her any wrong ideas about why she accompanied him on the trip. Ian and Sarah agreed they could not leave Jemma alone in the apartment over the long weekend.

'Sarah is prettier than me, Sir.'

Darn! How to respond to that comment? He might just ignore it, but when he looked at Jemma out of the corner of his eye, he saw she waited for a reply.

'You are both pretty. When you dress the same, it's difficult to tell you apart.' The corners of Jemma's mouth betrayed a small, shy smile. Ian knew what Sarah's response would have been; 'You whites think blacks all look alike.' That would have started another debate about race and the country's ills. Ian's arguments with Sarah were not vitriolic. They both respected each other's points of view, but boy, she could be wearing. She'd make a good barrister. She could argue a lion pride off its kill. The emphatic way Sarah put her case in their debates made them seem like arguments.

'Look, Sir, another roadblock.' Halfway between Gweru and Bulawayo, in what seemed like the middle of nowhere, the next roadblock came into view. This time Ian was tense. Earlier, he'd been blissfully ignorant of what he carried in the boot of the car. Two policemen approached on either side of the vehicle. They signalled Ian and Jemma to wind down the windows.

'How far have you driven today?' the policeman on Ian's side of the vehicle asked.

'We've come from Harare.'

'Have you passed through any other roadblocks?'

'This is the seventh.'

'Open the boot.'

Ian got out of the car, dreading the policeman would find the MFF flyers.

The policeman searched their backpacks in the car boot and pulled out Jemma's lacy underwear. He held up a pair of her panties and said something to the other policeman. They both chuckled. 'Honeymoon weekend,' he said under his breath. While the search continued, the second policeman stood at the front of the car staring at Jemma.

'What's in those cartons?'

'It's photocopy paper. The policemen at the other roadblocks opened them.' Ian cursed himself for not dumping the flyers when he discovered them in Gweru. Manfred and Ruth had not warned him about them. Why shouldn't he dump them? He didn't owe them anything.

The policeman took out a pack from a carton and grunted when he saw it was open. He called out to the policeman staring at Jemma, and the two of them turned and walked back to their chairs. As an afterthought, the policeman who had searched the boot called back to Ian, 'You can go.' Ian waved, closed the boot and hopped back into the car and drove off before the policemen changed their minds. Ian looked in the rear-view mirror and saw the policemen watching them drive into the distance. Perhaps he'd looked in too much of a hurry to leave.

One more roadblock passed; how many more to come? 'Tell me, Jemma, if the authorities are looking for Sarah, why didn't they go to your house and ask you where they could find her?'

'Someone did, Sir, after Thomas disappeared and Sarah left her work at the hotel. Our mama told the man she didn't know where Sarah had gone. They have been watching our house and waiting to see if she comes back.'

'And when she has gone back, they think it's you.'

'Yes, Sir.'

'How do you know they've been watching your house?'

'My mama has seen strange men in the area. They stand across the street or to one side. She has seen them often, for three months now.'

'You must be careful. They may lose patience and try to catch you again and force you to talk.'

'I will be careful, Sir, but you also must be careful.'

'Yes, someone searched the apartment at Easter, so we know they have us under surveillance.'

'When Sarah and I were at home with our mama over Easter, we never left the house. But the lady across the road said it was nice for my mama to have her two daughters back home again.'

On the edge of Bulawayo, another roadblock came into view. Ian's heart was in his mouth once again, and he'd still not dumped the flyers. A big sergeant waved them to stop. He had an amiable face and a moustache that suited his huge frame. 'Good day, Sah. What is your business in Bulawayo?'

'Good day, Sergeant,' said Ian, putting on a cheerful voice. 'We're here on a weekend visit. We're going back to Harare on Tuesday.'

'Open your boot please, Sah.' Ian got out of the car, opened the boot and lifted the lid. 'What are in those cartons, Sah?'

'It's photocopy paper I'm delivering. The police at the other road-blocks inspected them.'

The sergeant opened the lid of a carton. He took out the first open ream and examined it. Then he noticed the second open ream underneath the first.

Ian's right eye twitched, no matter how hard he tried to control it.

The big sergeant opened the second ream and fanned the paper with his thumb. He suddenly stopped and put the ream back in the carton and replaced the top ream and lid. 'As you said, Sah, just photocopy paper.'

'Yes, thank you, Sergeant.'

Just then a second policeman called out, 'Sergeant Dube, you're wanted on the radio.'

'Enjoy your stay, Sah,' said the big sergeant, waving Ian through and turning back towards the man who had called him. Ian was sure Sergeant Dube had seen the message on the flyers. Perhaps he was also a member of the MFF?

Ian drove on his way. Getting through the last roadblock lifted a weight off his mind. The policemen at the last two roadblocks didn't demand money. Perhaps the police in Matabeleland received their pay. There was no official roadblock toll, but the policemen tried all means to supplement their meagre wages. The government was broke, and the army, police and civil servants often not paid for weeks or months on end. To Ian, paying the police at the roadblocks was a minor matter, but he worried after discovering the MFF flyers in the car boot. The policemen did not believe Jemma was his housemaid, and they gave him knowing smirks before letting them pass. This at first irritated Ian, but after he'd discovered the MFF flyers, he could think of little else.

'Well, here you are Jemma, in beautiful Bulawayo. Have you ever seen a lovelier city?'

'No, Sir.'

'No? You surprise me. I thought you'd say Harare is lovelier.'

'Harare is lovely too, Sir.'

'If you think Harare is prettier, Jemma, you must say so. Stand by your own opinion.'

'Yes, Sir.'

'Have you ever seen a lovelier city than Bulawayo, Jemma?'

'Yes, Sir.'

'Where have you seen a lovelier city, Jemma?'

'Harare is prettier, Sir.'

'Do you think so?'

'Yes, Sir.' Ian looked at Jemma and raised an eyebrow. 'No, Sir.'

They both laughed. Jemma was getting Ian's sense of humour.

'The answer, Jemma, is *yes, Sir, Harare is prettier.* If you don't tell me the truth and answer honestly, how can I ever believe you?'

'Yes, Sir.'

'So, Jemma, have you ever seen a lovelier city than Bulawayo?'

'No, Sir.'

They both laughed. This time the joke was on Ian.

CHAPTER 38

8th – 9th August 2009

LUNCHTIME, and Ian and Jemma had arrived in Bulawayo. They drove past the old Kumalo Aerodrome on their right and turned left into Robert Mugabe Way (Grey Street). Ian drove down the length of the CBD straight to his favourite light-lunch spot. The Eskimo Hut takeaway backed onto the edge of the International Trade Fair grounds. Ian was pleased to see it still open after his absence of twenty years. They ordered hamburgers and sat in the car under the shade of the trees and ate their lunch. Afterwards, they bought the Eskimo Hut's famous soft serve ice cream in cones. The building looked tired now, and the asphalt car park seemed to have degenerated into a dirt surface.

Check-in at the Bulawayo Rainbow Hotel was at two o'clock, and Ian and Jemma arrived right on time. The circular hotel foyer looked grand with African motifs on the wood-panelled walls. An elegant sweeping staircase leading to the mezzanine floor curved along the far wall of the foyer. The dark and light honey-tone décor would have fitted well into a top Joburg hotel. A crystal chandelier hung in the middle of the foyer above a large, round, polished table, on which stood an artistic arrangement of dried flowers. They walked up to the long two-toned wooden reception desk. 'Do you have any single rooms?' Ian asked.

The male receptionist looked up from the computer screen. 'Not for this weekend, Sir.'

'I'm booked under the name of Sanders.'

'Yes, Sir, I have your booking for one double room.' He looked at Ian and then at Jemma, standing to one side.

'That's right, Sanders and Kagonye.'

'Porter, please take Mr and Mrs Sanders luggage up to their room.' Ian did not correct the receptionist, and Jemma couldn't hide her broad grin.

They took the lift to the third floor. The room faced west with views over the city. It wasn't too big but pleasant enough, and they travelled light, so that wasn't a problem. Ian requested twin share, but a lone king-size bed greeted them.

'How do you like the room Jemma?'

'It's beautiful, Sir.'

'It's west facing, so the afternoon sun should warm the room. On winter nights it can be cold here in Bulawayo.'

Tired after their early start and the long drive from Harare, Ian and Jemma would have welcomed a rest. But they were keen to see as much of Bulawayo as possible during their short stay. For Ian it was a nostalgic trip back to his childhood twenty years ago. For Jemma it was a big adventure. She took off her sandals and put on runners.

'What should we do this afternoon?' said Ian. Jemma shrugged in response. 'Should we drive through the city and suburbs?'

'Yes, Sir.' Jemma liked Ian asking her opinion as it made her feel important.

The phone rang. Hotel reception suggested Ian should park his car in the hotel's car park behind the building. Someone noticed a white man parked his car in the street where it was at risk of being stolen or damaged. The good citizen told the hotel who deduced the driver was Ian, their only white guest. Ian thanked reception and went down to the car with Jemma.

They drove east, out of the CBD, down Leopold Takawira Avenue, formerly Selborne Avenue, the prettiest thoroughfare in the city. The road separated Central Park on the right-hand side and the Bulawayo

Theatre, Centenary Park and the National Museum on the left. They headed for Hillside Dams, a popular beauty spot, a quarter of an hour from the CBD. A scenic walk joined the upper and lower dams.

'What do you think of Hillside Dams Jemma? They're not as big as Lake Chivero.'

'They are very nice, Sir. It's like we are in the country, but we are close to town.'

After their walk around the dams, Ian and Jemma headed back to the hotel. Stretching their legs after the long drive made them tired and hungry, so it would be an early dinner in the hotel followed by an early night. At the end of a long day, they were asleep as soon as their heads hit the pillow.

It seemed to Ian he'd just closed his eyes, but it was daylight already. The night flashed by, but they'd slept well and woke refreshed. The king-size bed was a lot smaller than the super king-size they'd shared back in Harare. Jemma lay right next to him. How did people manage with double beds?

* * *

Sunday morning, and Ian planned to take a walk around town and see the shops and buildings he remembered from his childhood. After breakfast they brushed their teeth, put on their baseball caps and stepped out into a perfect, early spring morning, sunny but not too hot.

Avenues of trees provided shade, and when they reached the CBD, the wide pavements and awnings gave them cover. The city looked clean but ageing, and otherwise little changed in Ian's twenty-year absence. Development in Zimbabwe took place in Harare, and Bulawayo was ignored.

The concept of home, or hometown, intrigued Ian. Although the streets and buildings were familiar, he was a stranger in his hometown. With family and friends scattered around the world, he didn't know a soul. The nearest thing to a friend in Bulawayo was Jemma, his housemaid. Now that she was more confident and chattier, she was good company. He knew all too well from his many business trips the loneliness of travelling and eating on his own. Jemma relished the new title of Mrs Sanders.

'It is funny, Sir, when they call me madam, but I'm the same as them.'

'Well, you look like a madam, Jemma, dressed like that.'

'I think it's because I'm with you, Sir.'

'Yes, I suppose so.'

'You don't mind, Sir?'

'Don't mind what, Jemma?'

'That they think I'm your wife.'

'No, I don't mind Jemma, it's funny. But it's not usual for a wife to call her husband *sir*.'

'For me, it is better, Sir.'

'OK, Jemma, if that's what you want.'

After a lunch of fried eggs and chips at a quiet café, they walked past Haddon and Sly department store opposite the city hall. The windows were almost empty, but once, they overflowed with products. The last time Ian saw these windows, one held a display of colourful swimming costumes. 'We should go to the swimming baths. It's beautiful there. If you haven't got a costume, we can buy you one tomorrow.'

'I have one, Sir. Sarah lent me her costume.'

They returned to the hotel and took turns in the bathroom to put on their swimming costumes under their street clothes. They walked the two-and-a-half city blocks to the Olympic sized pool in Samuel Parirenyatwa Road (Borrow Street). 'Why do all these streets have to have the full name of the person they're named after?' said Ian. 'It makes them so unwieldy. What's wrong with plain old Parirenyatwa Road?' Jemma smiled. Ian imagined the response Sarah might have given. It would have ended in another debate that would have stretched his patience.

The sign above the entrance said Municipal Swimming Bath. Underneath was the date 1926. The pool was not open for swimming, but the front doors were ajar, and a cleaner mopped the entrance.

'Can we look around?' said Ian. 'I've been telling my wife how beautiful the baths are. This is her first visit to Bulawayo.' It amused Ian to carry on the little charade. Jemma too, seemed happy about it.

'Yes,' said the cleaner, 'you can look.'

The pool appeared neglected, possibly due to the cholera epidemic. The surrounding grass was yellow, not its former lush green. Ian remembered the baths as a light blue sapphire in an emerald setting, but it didn't look like that anymore.

'The women's change rooms are the cubicles on the left,' said Ian. 'The men's change rooms are on the right.'

'Why can't men and women use the same rooms?'

'Those are the rules, Jemma.'

'Africans are not so worried about seeing each other naked.'

'Yes, Sarah has given me that impression,' said Ian, admiring the plants and the tall green trees that surrounded the baths, giving it privacy. The closed refreshment kiosk brought back memories. Ian could still taste the flavours of the sweets he'd once bought there: the sugar mice with their string tales, sweet cigarettes with their red tips, and his all-time favourite, the tiny, drum-shaped, pink cashews.

'The baths must be beautiful when they are open,' said Jemma.

'Yes, they are,' said Ian, 'but let's move on to the Bernsteins' swimming pool.'

Once again, they drove past Centenary and Central parks and headed to Khumalo, a suburb favoured by Bulawayo's once sizeable Jewish community.

Tobias, the African caretaker, came running to open the high wrought-iron gate when Ian tooted the car horn. Manfred Schwartz had forewarned Tobias he might have visitors. The gravel driveway crunched under the tyres as Ian drove up to the front of the double storey house. The facade of the building gave it a grand old Victorian appearance. Boston ivy grew part way up the walls between the tall windows on the ground floor. Tobias took Ian and Jemma through the garden to the rear. The sight of the magnificent, giant atrium came as a surprise. 'This is the most beautiful garden I've ever seen,' said Jemma.

'Yes.' Ian agreed.

Unlike the Johannesburg atrium, filled with tropical plants, the Bulawayo atrium contained a large blue swimming pool with crystal clear water. The surface rippled and sparkled in the sunlight that streamed through the glass roof. Large open skylight windows near the roof kept the air temperature comfortable.

Tobias gave Ian and Jemma fresh towels and showed them to a changing room in a corner of the atrium, where it joined the house. Ian used the room first, hanging up his street clothes on the pegs lined up on one wall. While he waited for Jemma to change, he sat on a pool lounger and surveyed the well-maintained private back garden. A borehole on the property helped it avoid the effects of the dry, winter season.

Jemma gave Ian a shy smile as she emerged from the dressing room. As she walked over to him, her body moved with an easy sway, making it hard for him not to stare. She wore a striking one-piece swimming costume and looked spectacular. The bright yellow fabric, splashed with black, set off her milk chocolate skin to perfection. Ian had always thought Jemma attractive, but now she looked magnificent. 'That's a nice swimming costume, Jemma.'

'Yes, thank you, Sir. It's a nice costume. Sarah bought it in Egypt.'

The perfect fit reminded Ian how alike the sisters were.

Jemma couldn't swim, so they selected pool loungers near the shallow end to lay down their towels. 'Are you ready for a swim?' said Ian.

'Better you go first, Sir,' said Jemma, with a nervous smile.

Ian stood up and walked to the pool. He sat on the edge with his legs dangling in the water. It was the same comfortable twenty-two degrees Celsius as the air temperature inside the atrium. Ian jumped into the pool and swam with leisurely strokes to the other end and back again, twenty times.

'Come on, Jemma, it's your turn now.'

Jemma hesitated and then stepped into the pool at the shallow end. The water came up to her waist, and Ian led her a little deeper. 'Don't worry I will stay right next to you.' Before now, Jemma had only paddled in shallow water and never tried to swim. She feared putting her head under water and clung to Ian like a little girl, with one arm held tight around his neck. Her fear of the water was more powerful than her natural reserve.

'Come on, Jemma, to swim you have to get your face wet.'

'But I can't swim, Sir.'

'Don't worry, I'll hold you.'

'No, Sir.'

'Let's go to the shallow end of the pool. Put your head underwater to get accustomed to it.'

'No, Sir.'

Ian tried to persuade her to duck her head under the water, but she wouldn't do it. Then he held her tight around the waist and ducked under the water himself, and she'd no choice but to go under with him. Jemma came up coughing and spluttering, and despite her squeals of protest, Ian repeated the dose several times. He enjoyed himself though it was not clear if she did. Tobias came running and chuckled at the spectacle. Ian held Jemma tight to prevent her struggling, and now she clung with both arms around his neck. But when he felt himself stirring, Ian let her go, leaving her in the shallow end. He swam another forty lengths to 'relax'.

'You are very naughty, Sir,' said Jemma, trying hard not to smile.

'Sorry, Jemma, but it's the only way you'll learn to swim.' Now they both laughed, and Ian guessed she wasn't really upset.

With Ian in easy reach, Jemma soon grew braver and made fast progress. After their swim they dried in the sun and put on their street clothes over their swimming costumes. 'We'll come back again tomorrow,' said Ian to Tobias, as they walked back to the car. An hour in a pool in the African sun, at high altitude, can burn even a black skin on a winter's day.

It was half past three in the afternoon, and Ian was thirsty. Back at the hotel, they stopped in the bar lounge on the ground floor. Ian ordered a Zambezi beer for himself and a lemon lime and bitters for Jemma. The ice-cold drinks went down well while they relaxed in the comfy chairs. Ian offered Jemma a sip of his beer, but after the sweet lemon lime and bitters she did not like the taste. He found it fun giving Jemma all the new experiences she would never otherwise have.

'Let's have another drink,' said Ian. 'Would you like to try white wine, Jemma?'

'Yes, thank you, Sir.' Ian ordered a Zambezi for himself and a glass of Riesling for Jemma. After the first sip, Jemma screwed up her face, but soon her mouth adjusted to the flavour.

'Jemma, how do you like the wine?'

'The wine is nice, Sir.'

'That wine is not strong. Others are much stronger.'

'No, I like this one, Sir.'

'After two or three glasses, the wine will loosen your tongue.'

Jemma looked alarmed. 'Loosen my tongue, Sir?'

'What it means is that no matter what question I ask, you will tell me the truth.'

'Oh! That is not good, Sir.' They laughed together. Ian found it fun to tease Jemma. Her lack of worldliness made her seem so innocent. 'Will the beer loosen your tongue, Sir?' asked Jemma with a cheeky smile.

Two rounds later, they headed for their room. Unused to alcohol, Jemma was giggly and exhilarated. Ian too was carefree because of the drink and his anonymity in the surroundings. He held Jemma's arm as they walked to the lift. She wasn't drunk, but it seemed the natural thing for him to do. Going up in the lift, Jemma leant her head on Ian's shoulder, and he put his arm around her waist. Both their inhibitions were down, and they did not notice the curious looks from the other couple in the lift. The morning walk around the city and the sun and chlorine at the pool affected Ian. Also, they missed lunch, and it was not usual for him to drink alcohol on an empty stomach so early in the afternoon.

'I'll lie down for a little while, so you can change first,' said Ian, as Jemma disappeared into the bathroom.

'OK, Boss,' she said.

Ian lay back on the bed and closed his eyes for a few moments to rest. A glorious drowsiness came over him, and he was half asleep when he felt someone sit down on the edge of the bed, next to him. He opened his eyes to see Jemma in her swimming costume, sitting with her back straight, hands in her lap and smiling at him. Ian gave a half-smile and closed his eyes again, falling back into a wonderful state of drowsiness.

A sense of something caused Ian to open his eyes again. Jemma stood right next to his bedside, looking down at him. She was still in her swimming costume. 'Do you want to fuck me, Sir?'

It was like a splash of cold water in his face. For a moment, the question stunned him. Ian's mind raced, and he couldn't speak. Was this his shy, quiet housemaid? The first time she swapped places with Sarah and shared his bed, he'd put an early end to any carnal thoughts. Sarah rebuked him for not responding to Jemma's unspoken but clear invitation. Why should it be different this time? He tried to clear his head, his mind in turmoil. Yes, he wanted to fuck her. She was beautiful. But it would be social suicide for him to screw his black housemaid.

It would have been social suicide in the old days, but all his friends and acquaintances had gone. No one would ever know. But Jemma might tell Sarah, and somehow that worried him. But last time Sarah criticised him for not screwing her sister. What if he caught something? What about HIV? Sarah said Jemma was clear, but how could she be certain? What if she was wrong?

Sarah said he was a racist. He didn't hesitate when he got the same invitation from Ruth. But this could complicate his relationship with both Jemma and Sarah. No, he couldn't do it. He'd not slept alone in his bed for weeks, but there'd been an *invisible wall* between him and the sisters, and he'd not laid a finger on either of them. He would lead Jemma back to her side of the invisible wall, to her side of the bed. She must have read too much into the charade of playing Mrs Sanders.

'Do you want to fuck me, Boss?' Jemma said again, looking at Ian as if he hadn't understood the question. She stood too close now.

Ian's mind zigzagged with indecision. 'No! No thank you, Jemma.' He remembered the old saying, *never shit on your own doorstep.* It made sense. Ian sat up on the edge of the bed. He reached up to Jemma to move her back, to give him room to stand up, to lead her back to her side of the bed.

His mind was like a pinball machine, bouncing back and forth between lusty desire and common sense. He could have this gorgeous woman. Forbidden fruit; a juicy plum waiting to be picked. Local whites never touched black women. It was social suicide, but then who'd know? Everyone he knew had left town.

Now Ian's mind was in meltdown. His hands were on Jemma's shoulders, and he would move her back, back to her side of the bed. A fraction of a second can change everything, a fraction of a second to decide. His hands slipped the leash of his mind. No! wait! Stop! He never meant to peel her like a ripe banana. Her yellow and black costume lay on the floor, like a banana skin at her feet.

There she was, stark naked, and it was all down to him. She must have noticed his arousal at the swimming pool. He thought she hadn't, but she must have. Her perfect, smooth skin looked like melted chocolate. She was irresistible, and Ian, spellbound, sat there immobile, like a dummy. What to do? It was too late now. No, it's never too late to stop and apologise. She was his African maid. She would laugh off the whole incident. But he seemed paralysed, unable to speak or act.

CHAPTER 39

9th – 12th August 2009

JEMMA saw the confusion on Ian's face. He moved to stand up, but she stopped him, placing her right hand in the middle of his chest. She took hold of his T-shirt and pulled it off over his head and gently pushed him back onto the bed. Jemma undid Ian's belt and the button at his waist and slid down the zip of his fly. She pulled off his jeans and dropped them on the floor.

The swing of her beautiful breasts that accompanied each of her movements fascinated him. There was still time for him to end what he'd started. He meant to say no, stop, wait, but his tongue seemed to stick to his palate, and his mouth was dry. He lay there silent, not resisting. Jemma slipped her fingers inside the top of his swimming costume and pulled the drawstring to undo the bow and ease down his costume.

Ian lay naked across the bed, looking back into Jemma's eyes. They were confident and determined; a look he'd not before seen in her. The corners of her mouth and eyes betrayed a small smile. Jemma knelt on the bed and straddled him in one quick move. He looked up at her magnificent breasts, his breath tight. Jemma's eyes never left his as she moved her hips in a slow rhythmic motion that drew him into her. Ian looked down at her flat stomach and watched as she ground her pubic mound against him. Spellbound, he looked into her eyes, and she held his gaze.

When he reached up for her magnificent breasts, her eyes still watched his. It was as if she tried to stare him down or look deep into his soul. Each time he tried to shift his gaze to her beautiful body, he felt compelled to look back into her eyes, which never seemed to waver. The slow, sensuous movement of her body against him melted his remaining qualms. When at last he took a deep breath, sighed and closed his eyes, they both came together in a glorious orgasm.

When Ian opened his eyes, he looked straight into Jemma's. Her eyes remained fixed on his. It was a strange and sensual experience. Did she shut her eyes when they both came? He knew she'd climaxed with him because she was flushed and breathing heavily, and he'd heard her moans resonate his. Jemma lowered herself onto Ian's chest, and they lay there together in silence.

As he became aroused again, Ian tried to take control of their love-making. He took hold of Jemma's shoulders and swung her over onto her back. Now he was on top, but when he began his slow, deliberate movement, her mouth still held its faint smile, her eyes almost defiant, boring through him. Jemma wrapped her legs around Ian's back and moved with him in an echo of his thrusts. Hell, she's still in control! Ian found it difficult to hold her gaze, and he blushed. What was he doing? This was his servant, his housemaid.

In the short space of an hour, Jemma closed the gap between master and servant. She controlled the pace and intensity of their union.

Afterwards, Ian lay beside her, his chest heaving with exertion and excitement. Jemma played with Ian's thick bush of pubic hair, running her fingers through it one minute and gently tugging on it the next. The length and texture fascinated her. It was nothing like the Africans' tight, spring-like curls.

How this gentle woman could be so assertive in bed, intrigued Ian. He imagined Sarah being like that, but Jemma! He smiled to himself. Was that all there was to it? Could a lusty fuck with a beautiful black girl break down a lifetime of racial prejudice? No, that was unfair.

Jemma was ladylike, gentle and caring, and that's what changed his view of her.

They showered together, exploring each other with a slow and intimate lathering. Afterwards they dried each other and then dressed together in the bedroom. They no longer needed to retreat to the privacy of the bathroom to dress. By now the effect on Ian of the Zambezi beers had passed.

They stepped out of the lift and made their way to the bar lounge. 'You can't call me *sir* or *boss* anymore. You must call me Ian.' Jemma smiled. She looked ravishing in a deep red cocktail dress and black, strappy, leather sandals.

'Sarah and I share all our clothes,' said Jemma, reading Ian's mind.

'You look beautiful,' said Ian, settling into one of the comfortable armchairs. It was Sunday, and a healthy crowd filled the bar lounge. This time they both settled for a lemon, lime and bitters and relaxed with their drinks, surveying the guests at the other tables. No one paid them the least attention as the alcohol flowed and the lounge grew noisier. Soon, they proceeded to the restaurant where a waiter showed them to a table in the corner of the room.

They sat, waiting for their order. Jemma reached across and took Ian's hand, tracing the back of his fingers with her fingertips. For her, a bold expression of intimacy. A remarkable transformation from the shy housemaid that left Harare with him a day earlier. Here was a self-assured young woman no longer out of her depth. Through her own initiative she'd made herself her master's equal, and Ian thrilled at the change.

It surprised him when he watched Jemma eating her dinner. He'd half expected her to eat in the African fashion of chewing with her mouth open and talking with her mouth full. 'Jemma, where did you learn to eat like that? You have beautiful table manners.'

Jemma looked up and smiled. 'Sarah told me I must eat with my mouth closed when eating in a restaurant.'

'Well, not only when you're eating in a restaurant. You should eat with your mouth closed all the time. But it's not only that. You have good table manners, and you know how to hold a knife and fork.'

'My mama and papa taught me, and I'm copying you, Sir.'

'Remember what I said, Jemma? No more *sir* or *boss*.' Jemma smiled.

She excused herself and went to the ladies' room. 'Ian Sanders,' a loud voice called out, 'fancy seeing you here.' Two couples were leaving the restaurant, but then, a man from the group walked across to Ian's table.

Ian got up to shake hands. 'Cobus Prinsloo, you haven't changed in twenty years. How are you?' Jacobus Prinsloo, a classmate from Ian's high school days, stood grinning at him.

'We're up from Joburg visiting friends.' Then lowering his voice, he said, 'But, Ian, I never took you for a kaffir lover. You were as racist as me.'

'It's true,' said Ian, 'you really haven't changed. In fact, you haven't evolved at all. Still the same old Neanderthal, I see.'

Cobus laughed. Damn! So much for anonymity; the news of his dinner date would travel fast. When Cobus returned to his group waiting at the exit, he turned back and shot Ian a sly smile. But Ian didn't care anymore. He was with a beautiful woman and proud of it. Education, money or the colour of one's skin didn't make a person, but what was in their heart. He knew Jemma to be a polite, caring and gentle soul, and that's what counted.

After dinner, they made love again in their hotel room. They slept naked, cuddled together, and made love again in the morning before breakfast. They were insatiable.

The next morning, they drove out to the Bernsteins' house for another swim. Old Tobias seemed pleased to see them and welcomed them with a cheerful smile. He'd enjoyed chatting with Ian the previous day. With only his wife for company, it must have been lonely looking after the big house. It was a responsible job, and he was keen to show Ian his diligence. The garden and the house were immaculate and the pool pristine. Tobias encouraged Ian to visit as often as he liked. 'No notice needed, Sah.'

This time, secure in Ian's company, Jemma's confidence swelled, and she was eager to swim. Now that she put her head under water, her swimming ability advanced in leaps and bounds, right in front of Ian's eyes. Ian taught himself to swim when he was ten years old. He swam underwater in the shallow end of the Borrow Street Baths before he could swim at the surface. 'If you're in the deep end of the swimming pool,' Ian said, 'you can always push yourself off the bottom and take a gulp of air at the surface. You can work your way to the shallow end or the side of the pool if you keep doing that. If you don't panic, you won't drown.' By the time they left the baths, Jemma could swim breaststroke for a short distance. Her new swimming ability thrilled her, and Ian shared her excitement.

After the swim they returned to the hotel and parked the car. It was again time to explore the city on foot. They walked the grid of streets and avenues that made up the city centre. As in Harare, the mix of faces on the street differed from that of Ian's childhood in Bulawayo. Ian and Jemma walked for almost two hours before returning to the hotel to pick up the car. They headed to the Eskimo Hut for lunch and then drove along the quiet jacaranda lined avenues to the train station. Ian parked the car. 'I'll see if I can buy the tickets for the train to Harare tomorrow evening. I won't be long.'

'Can I come with you please, Sir?' It seemed Jemma did not want to miss out on anything, as she enjoyed the charade of being Ian's wife.

There was a short queue at the ticket office, and they were soon at the ticket window.

'Two of your best first-class, sleeper tickets for Harare tomorrow evening please.'

'You must buy the tickets tomorrow, Sir. You can't book a compartment today.'

Ian and Jemma drove back to the hotel and passed through the boom gate into the car park. Outside on the street there were plenty of free parking spaces. As always, parking in Bulawayo was easy, and the fuel shortages made it even easier. But lingering doubts remained about the safety of leaving a car too long in the same space. Often young men would offer to guard the car in the driver's absence. Many people worried about the potential consequences of refusing such an offer.

Ian and Jemma 'relaxed' in their room in the afternoon and it proved to be more fun than going out. In the evening they had a quick meal at the Bonne Journee restaurant and then hurried back to the hotel. Neither of them wanted to waste a moment of their time together.

* * *

The hotel agreed to a late check-out at eleven on Tuesday morning. Ian and Jemma drove straight to the station to buy the train tickets.

'There is a coupé available, Sir.'

'Thank you, a coupé will be fine.'

'Name, Sir?'

'The name is Sanders, Ian and Jemma Sanders.' Ian could have sworn Jemma grew five centimetres when he said that.

The train to Harare left at eight in the evening, so Ian planned to hand in the car at five that afternoon. He found the name and telephone number of the contact Manfred gave him, and he made the call. On the third try, Ian got hold of Lazarus, who gave him directions for that afternoon. In the meantime, there were six hours to kill. They put their backpacks into the boot and drove down Twelfth Avenue past the tennis courts of the Bulawayo Athletic Club (BAC) on the edge of *The Suburbs*, an area of grand, old colonial style houses close to the city. They drove around the Ascot racecourse and passed the Bulawayo Central Hospital and the Lady Rodwell Maternity Hospital where Ian was born. 'All these places are interesting for me Jemma, but boring for you.'

'Oh no, Sir, it's also interesting for me.' The novelty of driving around town with Ian was still fresh for Jemma.

'Let's drop in for a drink at the Holiday Inn,' said Ian. A quick look around the bar lounge confirmed Cobus Prinsloo was not there.

Jemma thought the hotel marvellous. 'Can we stay here next time, Sir?'

'If you keep calling me *sir* or *boss*, next time I'll ask them to put you in the servant's quarters. What makes you think there'll be a next time?'

Jemma looked alarmed at his response. Ian at once felt bad. 'I'm joking Jemma. Yes, we can stay here next time.'

The relief on Jemma's face was palpable. 'Thank you, Sir, I mean thank you.'

Ian smiled, was she finally getting the message? It seemed incongruous for the woman he slept with to call him, *sir*, *boss* or *master*.

'Tell me Jemma, what would your friends say if they knew about our weekend?'

'Some wouldn't like it, Sir. Others would say *well done*.'

'Why is that?'

'The ones who don't like whites would be unhappy. The others would say *well done* because winning your boss is always a good prize.'

Jemma's reply was honest. She'd not attempted to be at all evasive in her response.

'And what would your friends say, Sir, if they knew you were with me?'

Jemma's honest response deserved an honest answer. 'Most would say I was crazy.'

'Is it difficult for you to be with me, Sir?'

'No, Jemma, I'm proud to be with you. You're a good person, and I like you very much.'

'Thank you, Sir; I also like you very much.'

'Ian smiled. Now Jemma if you call me *sir* once more, I will ask the hotel to serve your tea outside at the back where the waiters are.'

This time, Jemma laughed.

Ian laughed along with her. This was their deepest discussion yet.

* * *

At five o'clock Ian drew up in front of an old Besser brick factory in the Belmont light industrial sites. As he parked, the small factory's roller door opened. An African man beckoned to Ian to drive into the dark little building. Lazarus, a big, friendly, middle-aged man, greeted Ian with the three step African handshake and nodded to Jemma. 'Did you bring the flyers, Brother?'

Ian nodded, 'They're in the boot.' Lazarus, it seemed, assumed Ian to be a member of the MFF. 'The police opened the cartons, but they didn't notice they held flyers.'

'The police are lazy. We rely on their laziness and their greed for a dollar to not carry out proper searches.'

'They almost discovered the flyers at one roadblock, but another car arrived and distracted them. It was a near thing.'

'But you got through OK. That's what matters,' said Lazarus, unloading the cartons and hiding them behind a counter at the back of the small premises. 'If they found the flyers, you would have to pay them more.'

'Is it that simple?'

'It depends on the policeman. Sometimes they can cause trouble. Then it's difficult.'

'At the roadblock outside Bulawayo, a big sergeant stopped us. I'm sure he saw the flyers, but he said nothing.'

'Yes, we have friends in the police in Bulawayo.'

'Is Sergeant Dube one of them?'

'Please, no names Brother, it could get him into trouble.'

'No, I won't tell anyone else.'

'Come, I'll take you to the station, so you have time to eat before you board the train.'

The railway station was a short drive from the factory. Quiet roads made every drive in Bulawayo seem short. It was two hours to their scheduled eight o'clock departure.

On the way to the station, Lazarus stopped at a shop and suggested Ian buy sandwiches and drinks for the train. 'They don't have dining cars anymore.' At the station, Ian and Jemma made their way to the empty first-class waiting room and ate their sandwiches.

The cramped, first-class coupé had a grey leatherette bench seat, the back of which converted into the upper bunk. Grey Formica panels lined the walls, and the stainless-steel wash basin managed a trickle of cold water. A mesh security screen allowed the single window to be open for fresh air.

To Jemma the overnight train to Harare was an adventure as she hadn't been on a train before, let alone in sleeping class. Soon after departure, the conductor knocked on the compartment door to inspect their tickets, and a few minutes later, the bedding attendant came to make up their beds. 'Gee it's small,' said Ian, sitting on the lower bunk, looking at the opposite wall less than a metre in front of him. The newfound intimacy with Jemma made the cramped space tolerable, and they spent much of the night together on the lower bunk.

Ian crawled into the upper bunk around midnight but found it difficult to sleep as his thoughts drifted back over the weekend. When he and Jemma first had sex, he'd consumed three Zambezis in a short space of time, and Jemma had two glasses of white wine. They'd drunk more than usual and on empty stomachs. He was sure the alcohol played a part. But after that first occasion, they had sex at least half a dozen times where alcohol played little or no part. Would it have happened if not for those Sunday afternoon drinks?

They'd crossed a line. But where would they go from here? What would Sarah say? She'd made it clear she wasn't available, so it didn't matter what she'd say. Ian delighted in the substitute. If the sisters were rolled into one, the gentle and caring Jemma with the educated and sophisticated Sarah—that would be something!

If Jemma was awake, what was she thinking? It's funny how one can be so free and liberated in surroundings where no one knows you. Their weekend together was like a sea cruise, an unfamiliar cocoon where they could do what they liked, and nobody knew or cared. Once they'd broken the ice, nothing could hold them back. Would the routine in the apartment return to normal? How would Jemma behave towards him? She'd tell Sarah all about the weekend, and then how would Sarah react? The thoughts swirled in Ian's mind, making him uneasy, but it was too late to worry now. If his friends found out, they'd never understand. Ian wasn't sure if he himself understood. He'd grown up in a society where there'd been little mixing of the races. He cursed his luck, bumping into Cobus Prinsloo.

Ten in the morning, they rolled into Harare railway station. Jemma was a little quiet. Maybe overnight she had similar thoughts to Ian or picked up on his qualms. The train ground to a halt with a squealing of brakes and wheels on the steel tracks. Jemma came up to Ian and gave him a tender kiss on the lips. It surprised him, and he was unsure how to interpret the kiss, the first they'd shared, despite a full weekend of sex. But her manner was quiet and serious, and it disturbed him.

'Jemma, you go home and rest. People will have seen Sarah arrive at the apartment and think it was you. Come in tomorrow.'

'Yes, Sir. Thank you, Sir.'

Ian was a little disappointed. The confident young woman, who'd been his charming companion for the weekend, had reverted to servant mode. She wore her work clothes which she must have taken with her to Bulawayo. She was back in familiar territory, playing a familiar role. But now, he saw her differently. When she turned and walked away, he watched her disappear into the crowd. To him, she looked beautiful even in her work clothes. Ian walked in the opposite direction back to the apartment. It was always a little sad when a blissful trip ends with a goodbye. He'd see her again tomorrow, so why did he feel flat? Would things be the same?

As he headed for home, an odd blend of excitement and shame swept over Ian. He felt guilty for taking advantage of Jemma. He'd seen her as forbidden fruit, but now, the thought of another bite of the apple was a thrilling prospect. Was it guilt for what he'd done or because Cobus Prinsloo saw him? Before the weekend, he would have despised any local white who behaved the way he had. Was that how Cobus Prinsloo now viewed him?

Ian opened the door of the apartment with his key. There was Sarah, already changed out of Jemma's work clothes back into her own more fashionable gear.

'I'll put the kettle on,' she said. 'Tell me all about your weekend. Did you have a good time? How did Jemma like it?'

'There's nothing much to tell.' Ian related the details about the roadblocks, the hotel, the meals, the Eskimo Hut, Bulawayo and the Hillside Dams. He also told Sarah about the swimming baths, Jemma's newfound swimming skills and the train trip back to Harare. He didn't say a word about what else they'd done.

'Given you had a car, it doesn't seem like you did very much,' said Sarah.

'There wasn't much time. Bulawayo is spread out, and half the day is gone by the time you drive anywhere.'

To Ian, Sarah seemed unconvinced. Had he not left something out? Perhaps his guilty conscience made him imagine she disbelieved him. 'Surely, you could have done more sightseeing than that? Didn't you even go to see your great white founder's grave in the Matobo Hills?'

'There would have been plenty of people visiting Cecil Rhodes' grave. I'm sure he wouldn't have missed us.'

'I'll get Jemma to tell me more tomorrow. She has a good memory for details. Men are hopeless at recalling events.'

Ian flushed. It promised to be a long day.

Chapter 40

13th – 17th August 2009

THURSDAY morning dawned bright and beautiful as it often did at this time of the year. Ian felt refreshed after a good night's sleep. Sarah was her usual bubbly self. Jemma arrived right on time at half past seven. The sisters hugged each other in delight. 'I want you to tell me all about your weekend,' said Sarah, as she disappeared into the bathroom and closed the door.

Jemma put the kettle on for tea. Ian stood in the kitchen doorway. She saw him and smiled her shy smile and carried on with her domestic duties. When Jemma arrived, she'd said, 'Good morning, Boss.' There was no hint of intimacy, perhaps because of Sarah's presence. Now Sarah was in the bathroom, and Ian uncertain as he watched Jemma make breakfast. What would she say to Sarah? He felt constrained from any show of affection, and it was as if their weekend never happened.

Everything was back to normal; Jemma the polite, shy housemaid and Sarah her protective, feisty sister, stalking around the apartment like a caged lioness. When Jemma joined the other housemaids for morning tea, Ian said to Sarah, 'How was your weekend?'

'Most enjoyable, thanks,' said Sarah, sitting forward in her chair. 'Remember, I said my mother would have visitors over the weekend?'

Ian buttered his raisin toast. 'Yes, risky when you're in hiding.'

Sarah cupped her hands around her mug of tea. 'No, my father's best friend and his wife would never say or do anything to harm my family.'

'I hope you're right.'

'Uncle Charles would never harm us. He used to give my father lots of helpful information.'

'What sort of information?'

'All sorts. Uncle Charles is a chief inspector in the police and knows everything that goes on in Harare. He said he'd try to warn me if I was in any danger.'

'What's his surname?' said Ian, taking a sip of tea to disguise a sudden creeping apprehension.

'Chamisa, Charles Chamisa.'

Ian banged his cup down into the saucer. 'Charles Chamisa was the policeman who interviewed me at the police station and referred to you as one of the most wanted dissidents in Zimbabwe. Did you tell him you stayed with me?'

'No, I said I stayed with a friend.'

'Now he'll realise that everything I told him was a lie. I could be in big trouble.'

'No, I didn't tell him where I was staying, and he said it was better he didn't know.'

'What else did you tell him?' said Ian, shifting in his seat.

* * *

Sarah left for home on Friday evening, walking through the streets crowded with people going home for the long weekend. She looked forward to spending time with her mother. In the past nine weeks, she'd spent only one night at home when she and Jemma swapped places.

It was dark when she got home, and her mother waited at the front door for her. Esther prepared a nice meal, and there was much to discuss.

'Tell me about this person who shelters you?'

'He's a murungu. Doesn't that tell you everything?'

'No, does he treat you well?'

'Yes, he'd be scared to upset me.'

'Scared? Why would he be scared?'

'Well, perhaps not scared, but I can tell he's unsure how to handle me. And he knows I will always beat him in an argument.'

'It's not always good to win an argument, Sarah. Sometimes you should let the other person win. That is showing respect for them.'

'I can't let a murungu beat me in an argument.'

'When you say he's unsure how to handle you, do you mean because you're a black person or because you're a woman?'

'Both; he's unsure how to handle me because I'm a black woman.'

'Has he ever made advances?'

'He wouldn't dare. I would kill him.'

Esther laughed. 'You don't have to kill him to put him in his place, Sarah.'

'No, I'm joking, but there's no harm in letting him think I would. He didn't even try to take advantage of Jemma when he had the chance.'

'Yes, I worried about her spending the night away from home. But Jemma told me her boss is very nice.'

'Tchah, that Jemma sees the good in everybody. I've warned her life's not like that.'

'But it's good to see the best in everyone.'

'I suppose so, but I've seen too much to believe that.'

The discussion continued through the weekend with Esther trying to find out every little detail of the strange existence Sarah led.

'I would like to meet this man and thank him for helping you.'

'You might meet him one day, but I don't want him to get the idea he's doing me a great big favour. I'm sure he already sees himself as a saviour.'

'But he is doing you a great big favour and at great risk to himself.'

'Yes, but he needn't know that.'

'I'm sure he already does.'

'The varungu have done enough favours for Africa, thank you.'

'That's what your father used to think and look where it got him.'

Sarah didn't respond directly. 'Oh, well.'

'You can't go on hiding forever, Sarah, even if you like staying with your white friend.'

'I don't like staying with my white friend. I only want Thomas.'

'My dear, you must face the likelihood that Thomas is dead. Why else would he not contact you or his parents? Although they don't say so, I'm sure his parents believe he's dead.'

'I need to have it confirmed before I'll accept it. Thomas could take care of himself. Maybe he's also in hiding somewhere.'

'Uncle Charles and Mrs Chamisa are coming for tea on Monday. Why don't you discuss things with him? He always helped your father.'

Esther and Sarah spent a relaxing weekend together, chatting about old times and the situation in the country. Esther enjoyed having her daughter back, and Sarah relished her mother's cooking. All too soon, Monday dawned. Sarah helped Esther prepare snacks for the visitors, and they were ready in plenty of time. At half past three, the visitors arrived. Esther answered the knock. 'Mr and Mrs Chamisa, welcome.'

Charles Chamisa was his usual relaxed and jovial self. Off duty, he was not the stern chief inspector Ian met. Esther and Mrs Chamisa slipped away to the kitchen to catch up on gossip and make the tea.

Alone now, Charles Chamisa turned to Sarah. 'How are you, My Girl? We've worried about you.'

'I am well, thank you, Uncle, but I'm concerned,' said Sarah, getting straight to the point. 'Do you know why the authorities are searching for me?'

'It must be connected to your father. What other reason can the authorities have? The instructions to apprehend you came from up high.'

'They attacked my father when we were both away—you in the country visiting your family, and me in Joburg on a Portuguese refresher course.'

'Yes, I was furious when I returned and discovered how little the police had done. If I'd been here, it would have been different. These gangs terrorise members of the community, and most people are too scared to report them.'

'The police must have a hard job managing those gangs.'

'Yes, but the other day, one gang killed its own leader in an internal power struggle. They must have ambushed him or surprised him because he only had one blow to his left temple. They left his body behind the front garden wall of an empty house.'

'Really?' said Sarah, raising her left hand to her mouth to feign shock.

'Two female witnesses saw the whole thing, but they have disappeared. It's a clear case though. They are a violent gang, and many people feared them. We'll make sure they spend a long time in jail. The community is better off without them.'

'Oh, that's good,' said Sarah, trying to conceal her grin behind her hand. 'Were the gang members known to the police?'

'Yes, and their dead leader was a well-known thug with a long record of violence.'

Sarah couldn't believe her luck. If the gang stood accused of killing its leader, it must be the same gang that helped him kill her father. Revenge is sweet. Wait until Jemma hears about this.

'Uncle, have you heard of the COU?'

'No, what is that?' said Uncle Charles, sitting down in one of the worn but comfy armchairs.

Sarah sat on the edge of the sofa and told him about her job with the COU and her sudden termination.

'Do you have a payslip to show me?' said Uncle Charles, leaning forward. 'Perhaps they're connected to another department.'

'No, they always paid us in cash. They said payslips would compromise the secrecy and high security of the unit.'

'So, you've no way to prove you worked for them,' said Uncle Charles frowning, 'or even to prove they exist? They might not be a government department. They might be a gang of criminals. In the past, the government has used criminals and thugs to do its dirty work. Look at the "war veterans" who attack the opposition.'

Sarah sat up straight. The way Uncle Charles spoke surprised her. Till now, she'd never heard him even hint at any criticism of the regime.

'And I've never heard of this man, Jedson Ziyambi.' Uncle Charles shifted in his seat to look straight at Sarah. 'Listen, My Girl, I can't make any enquiries about him or the COU. It would only raise suspicions. But I can keep an eye on your situation. If you give me your cell phone number, I'll try to warn you if I find out you're in any immediate danger.'

Sarah gave Uncle Charles her prepaid mobile number. 'I'm staying with a—'

'No, my dear, don't tell me,' said Uncle Charles, holding up the palms of his hands to silence Sarah. 'It's better for both of us if I don't know where you're staying. That way I can't compromise you.'

'OK, let's say I'm staying with a friend.'

'Even that's too much information.'

Esther and Mrs Chamisa walked into the room with a tray of tea and snacks. 'What have you two been talking about?' said Mrs Chamisa.

'We talked about Sam and the old days,' said Uncle Charles. 'Those were the days, eh, Sarah?'

* * *

Later that evening, Esther and Sarah enjoyed a quiet dinner together. The next morning, Sarah would return to the apartment disguised in Jemma's work clothes.

'You must come more often,' said Esther, 'if Jemma doesn't mind swapping.'

Sarah's eyes flashed. 'Oh, Jemma won't mind. She loves her white boss.'

'Do I detect a little jealousy there, Sarah?'

Sarah looked at her mother. 'I'm not jealous. Why would I be jealous?'

'It sounded for a moment you might be a little possessive of Jemma's white boss. That's understandable since you spend more time with him than she does.'

'I want Thomas,' Sarah protested. 'No one else can replace him, least of all a murungu.'

Esther looked down into her soup and smiled.

Sarah had the last word, but her mother had given her something to ponder.

* * *

Ian left out the details of his weekend with Jemma, and Sarah left out the details of her discussions with her mother. She deflected Ian's questions about Esther by focussing on her discussion with Uncle Charles.

'But doesn't your mother wonder what arrangements we have here for sharing a studio apartment? Did you tell her we share a bed and where Jemma sleeps when you swap places? Any mother would worry about her daughters sharing a bed with a strange man she's never met.'

Sarah related her discussion with Uncle Charles. 'So, I don't think he'll be a problem. In fact, he could be helpful to us.' Her news made Ian apprehensive. The risk he took sheltering her was becoming plain.

'Your Uncle Charles might work out you are hiding with me.'

'Maybe,' said Sarah. 'Perhaps that's why he didn't want me to tell him where I was staying. Can't you see he's on our side?'

'Hell, I hope so,' said Ian, dropping his head and rubbing his temples. 'You're putting an awful lot of faith in your Uncle Charles. The person I saw at the police station didn't seem to be on our side.'

'Your tea's cold, Sir. Would you like me to make more hot tea?' Ian looked up at his polite housemaid. Jemma was no trouble at all.

* * *

Saturday morning, and Ian planned to walk to the Monomotapa for a coffee. It would be his first visit to the hotel since Hazel's murder, and he needed a break from the annoying Sarah. How much longer would she be staying? She made his relationship with Jemma more difficult, though he felt guilty to think of it like that.

As Ian opened the apartment's front door, the caretaker walked by in the corridor. She nodded to Ian, but then her eyes flicked past him. Ian saw out of the corner of his eye that Sarah stood in plain view in the apartment. Jemma would have waved or called out a greeting, but Sarah had never met the caretaker. Though less than a second, the incident niggled at the back of Ian's mind, and then he forgot about it.

For the rest of the weekend Ian worked on his novel, and then on Monday he walked to Manfred Schwartz's office. Frida worked at her computer in reception. Ian now saw her in a new light after what Ivana Schwartz had told him. 'Good morning, Frida. Is Manfred in today?'

Frida was at her arrogant best. 'Yes, but he's busy.'

'It's important that I see him soon.'

'I'll tell him.'

Ian waited, pacing up and down in the boardroom. He was angry and couldn't concentrate on work. Just as he sat down, Manfred entered. 'Morning, Ian, how are you?'

'I'm fine, but it's not any thanks to you.'

'Ah! You're referring to the flyers?'

Ian stood, 'Yes I am. Do you realise the danger you put me in with those flyers in the boot of the car? There were eight roadblocks, and at three of them they looked inside the cartons. It was a miracle the police didn't notice the printing on the reverse of those "blank" sheets. You were aware they questioned me at the police station about this damned Mthwakazi Freedom Front (MFF) of yours.'

'I only found out about your brush with the police when you picked up the car. If I'd known beforehand, I wouldn't have put the cartons in the boot. Once you told me about your visit to the police station,

I thought it best not to tell you about them. That way you wouldn't appear nervous at the roadblocks.'

'Thank you for your concern about my safety, but when I told you about my visit to the police station, you could have taken the cartons out of the car.'

'No, I couldn't have had the cartons at my house any longer. The police watch me like a hawk. They've searched the house a few times already.'

'I discovered the flyers in Gweru, and I had to pass through the last two roadblocks knowing they were in the boot.'

'Well done my friend. It's a credit to you. Thank you for not dumping them. Oh, and our "new recruits" impressed Lazarus no end, you and a young lady, I understand?'

'If you want to smuggle anything else, let me decide whether I want to take part.'

'Yes, I will, and I apologise if it upset you, but you've no idea how important it was for us to get those flyers to Bulawayo.'

'Why can't they print them there?'

'That would be ideal, but we're under scrutiny in Bulawayo. It hasn't yet occurred to the authorities, the flyers come from Harare.'

'Have you told Ruth about the police picking me up and that they knew all about my dealings with her?'

'No, not yet. It's too dangerous to talk on the phone. I will tell her when I see her in Joburg. If you excuse me, I'm expecting an important phone call.' Manfred walked to the door. 'Oh, and it's best not to mention anything about the flyers to Ivana or anyone else.' He closed the door behind him as he left.

He didn't want Ivana to know about the flyers. Was that why he couldn't take the cartons out of the car boot or keep them any longer at the house? A moment after Manfred left Ian alone in the boardroom, Nelson entered with a cheery smile. 'Good morning, Sah. Can I get you a cup of tea?' Why was Nelson suddenly so friendly? Had Ivana said anything to Nelson about his visit to the house to pick up Ruth's car?

Ian detected a divide between Ivana and Nelson on one side and Manfred and Frida on the other—not the ingredients for a happy outcome. Was Ivana or Nelson informing the police about the Bernstein's activities and Manfred's involvement? Ivana and Nelson both had motives to betray Manfred and the MFF. Did the web reach as far as Ruth and Solly's servants in Johannesburg? Was Manfred a double agent? With all the work he did on behalf of the government, he might also have a motive to inform on Ruth, Solly and the MFF. They were like a den of vipers. It was obvious from his visit to the police station someone reported back on his activities. That last thought troubled Ian. It was like being in quicksand. No matter which way he turned, he was sucked in deeper. He didn't want to get involved. All he wanted was to write his book.

CHAPTER 41

20th – 21st August 2009

SARAH's cell phone rang. Ian never phoned her. Perhaps it was Jemma, but she'd only just left the apartment. What could she want?

'Hello.'

'Don't speak, just listen.'

'Uncle Charles!' Sarah sat down on the edge of the bed.

'They've found out where you are and they're coming for you and your friend this evening. He's wanted for sheltering a dissident; that's you, and he's also wanted for the murder of a black prostitute in Harare Gardens. I'm sure he didn't do it but that won't save him. They've made arrests in Bulawayo, and they say your friend is a member of the MFF and has a female accomplice; that's also you. Get out now.'

'He's not yet back from work.' Sarah's voice shook. 'I can't leave without him.'

'Forget him. He's in bigger trouble than you are.'

'No, I can't just leave after all he's done for me.'

The phone went dead.

Sarah was in shock. What should she do? For a minute or two, she sat stunned. Then, she sprang into action, packing both her and Ian's backpacks, leaving none of their personal items in the apartment. Soon, no trace remained of who occupied it. Jemma could claim the food items as her own. The minute Ian came home, they would leave. Where was he? The one evening he needed to be home early from work, there was no sign of him. Sarah paced up and down between the veranda and the front door. The first-floor apartment with only one exit would be a trap. She tried to call Ian's cell phone, but it went straight to his recorded message. Next, she tried the office fixed line, no answer. Hurry Ian, hurry, for heaven's sake, hurry.

* * *

Ian tidied the files on the boardroom table. He'd worked a little later than usual to complete an important section of the business plan. Tomorrow he would begin a new section, but it would be much simpler and downhill from here to the finishing line.

Manfred was not at the office, much to Ian's disappointment. He'd hoped to discuss points of the plan with him. 'No, Manfred's not sick,' said Frida, 'He had to go to Joburg, and he didn't say when he'd be back.' Her voice had an edge that resonated with suppressed anger.

The business plan was about eighty percent complete. Ian reviewed his progress with satisfaction, but then he heard loud voices in the reception area. Frida came into the boardroom looking pale. 'The police are here for you.'

Ian swallowed. 'Me? Are you sure?'

'You'd better hurry.' Frida was desperate for the police to leave.

Ian hesitated before stepping out of the boardroom into the reception area. Two policemen stood there. 'Yes, can I help you…?' The policemen turned towards him, stopping Ian in his tracks when he recognised one of them. 'Chief Inspector Chamisa…' he said, in a faltering voice.

'Mr Sanders, come with us.' Ian's heart sank. Sarah should never have trusted him. Charles Chamisa was a stern, brutish looking man, even worse than Ian remembered. He must have discovered Ian lied to him when they first met.

Without further ado, Chamisa and a young constable marched Ian down the building fire escape, not bothering to wait for the lift. A parked police car stood in the alleyway at the bottom of the fire escape. Chamisa and the young constable had no other police backup. For a moment, Ian considered making a run for it. Madness! The police had his home address, and where else could he go? Manfred wouldn't appreciate him turning up at his house. And it would only make matters worse if he didn't cooperate. He'd done nothing wrong other than shelter Sarah. He didn't know she'd been a COU operative. Ian imagined the police would have picked her up by now. A cold shudder ran down his spine, and his stomach churned as he concentrated on preventing his hands from shaking.

Ian stepped into the back of the police car with the young constable beside him. Chamisa drove. Ian stared at the passers-by, wondering if he'd be in jail on trumped-up charges. When would he be free again? When would he next see the evening crowd going home from work? But they weren't heading for the police station! He shuddered when he remembered what Chamisa told him about people disappearing after rides in a police car. Ian didn't want to show any sign of fear, but he shivered as if in a freezing wind, and his muscles seemed to melt.

Before Ian could work out what was going on, the police car pulled up outside his apartment. 'Go!' said Chamisa. Ian looked up in surprise. He tried to open the car door, but his shaking hand struggled to find the handle. The young constable leant across and pulled the door handle for him. 'Move!' said Chamisa. 'Go!' Ian tumbled out of the police car, falling to the ground in his hurry. He stood up in time to see the police car race away. Cold and sweaty from his ordeal, Ian hurried into the apartment.

'Thank heaven you've arrived,' said Sarah. 'We must leave now. I'll explain to you on the way.'

'Where are we going?' said Ian, when Sarah handed him his backpack.

'Anywhere away from here; the police are coming for us.'

In the gathering dusk, they raced out of the apartment and across the street and then crossed over Samora Machel Avenue. As they reached the corner diagonally opposite the apartment, two police cars skidded to a halt outside the building. Several policemen tumbled out and ran into the apartment block. Ian and Sarah increased their stride as they hurried away from the scene. Ian's jangled nerves settled, clearing his mind for the first time since Chamisa surprised him at the office. 'Let's get to the railway station and catch the Bulawayo train. It's the best way out of town, and there won't be roadblocks.'

Despite the rush of adrenalin and the jangled nerves, Ian found the situation amusing. The police had raced to their apartment to apprehend them while they raced to the railway station, only two short blocks from the police station. Their breath laboured from the exertion and they giggled about their predicament. 'Just like the Keystone Cops,' said Ian, and they giggled even more. Nervousness can express itself in strange ways.

'I told you Uncle Charles would be on our side.'

'I thought,' said Ian, struggling for breath, 'he came to arrest me.'

They made their way to the railway station using quiet side streets wherever possible.

Thirteen city blocks at a brisk pace, enough to puff out anybody, but despite her extended period in hiding, Sarah proved to be much fitter than Ian. True, she'd exercised in the apartment, but he'd the advantage of walking the city each day. He made a mental note to keep in better shape in future and tried to keep his mind off the strain of pushing himself to keep up with Sarah.

At the station Ian bought two tickets under the names of Ian and Sarah Jones. The cheap fare allowed him to pay with cash. If Ian used his credit card, his real name would be on record for the police to follow his trail. They secured a two-berth coupé. 'You're lucky,' the man in the ticket office said. 'The sleeping class is often full if you leave it to the last moment to book.' Almost seven o'clock—still an hour before departure.

The pair waited in the shadows cast by the dull platform lighting, urging on every minute. Ian feared that any moment a group of police might spill onto the station platform searching for them; the police station, only a three-minute walk. Surely, when the police found no sign of them at the apartment, they'd look at all the means of leaving Harare? Wouldn't they check the railway station, bus stations and airport?

As they say, *a watched kettle never boils.* The wait seemed interminable and time crawled, with no sign of the train.

Ian noticed a man staring at them before approaching with a serious expression on his face. Was he a plain-clothes police officer? Ian's mouth was dry as the man walked straight up to him. 'Do you have a cigarette, Boss?' No, he didn't have a cigarette. Neither he nor Sarah smoked. To Ian, it seemed every second person on the platform looked at them. Did they all want cigarettes? Were they curious at the site of a black woman with a white man, or was it his imagination? Further along the platform, a uniformed policeman stood and chatted with a group that appeared to be waiting for the train.

'Relax,' said Sarah. 'If you look nervous, you'll attract attention. No one's staring at us. No one cares about us.'

'Let's hope this train comes soon.'

When the train at last pulled into the platform, Ian and Sarah boarded and locked themselves into the cramped coupé. The endless waiting process started all over again. Now they waited for departure. They left the lights off and pulled up the window shutter. They could see out onto the station platform, but the window mesh screened them from prying eyes. It was stuffy in the small coupé because they'd left the window closed, but they wouldn't risk drawing attention by opening it now.

Every footstep in the passageway outside their coupé seemed to pose a threat. Somebody stopped by their door, but after a short pause, the footsteps moved on down the corridor. Ian hoped that anyone who looked for a white man and a black woman would not check on Mr and Mrs Jones; a faint hope, given that few whites travelled on the train these days.

After what seemed like an age, the horn of the diesel locomotive at last sounded, and the train jerked and trundled out of the station, too slowly for Ian's liking. They jumped at the loud knock on the door. 'Tickets,' said the conductor. Their hearts beat fast; they'd had enough excitement for one day.

If the coupé seemed cramped when he'd travelled with Jemma, it was even worse now. In the confines of the coupé, brushing up against Jemma was fun. They'd enjoyed the contact. Ian's relationship with Sarah was different, and the confined space proved uncomfortable. Now they discovered the coupé lights didn't work. Both experienced physical and emotional tiredness and they fell onto their bunks early. Sarah chose the top bunk, claiming she could manage it better than Ian.

Lying in the darkness, sleep was the last thing on Ian's mind. 'Jemma will wonder what has happened to us. Shouldn't we phone her or your Mama and tell them what's happened?'

'Uncle Charles will tell them, but it's not a good idea for us to phone them. The police might already be at our house waiting for us.'

Sarah told Ian about Uncle Charles' phone call. 'When I told him you were at work, he must have gone straight to your office to get you. If you had walked home, I'd have been in custody and the police would have greeted you.'

'At least he could have said he was giving me a lift home. Your Uncle Charles doesn't like me.'

'He doesn't trust whites. Same as you don't trust blacks.'

'I never said I didn't trust blacks.'

'Well, you didn't trust Uncle Charles, did you?'

'He had a threatening manner. That's why I said he didn't like me.'

'Get real! Would you expect a policeman to like someone who's suspected of murdering a prostitute and who's a member of an underground organisation like the MFF? And that person is also hanging around his best friend's daughters. Why would he like you or trust you?'

'Excuse me,' said Ian, leaning out of his bunk to look up at Sarah. 'I'm not hanging around his best friend's daughters. They're hanging around me.'

'You know what I mean.'

'You should have told me more about your shady past with the COU. At least that would have allowed me to assess the risk I took.'

'If you'd known, would you have helped me?'

'I might have thought twice about it.'

'I never even told Jemma or my mother about the COU. Why should I have told you?'

'You used me,' said Ian.

'Yes, I did. I had to use you to survive. It was safer for you, my mother and Jemma to know as little as possible. If you knew everything about me, imagine how nervous you would have been when they questioned you at the police station. They'd have sensed your guilt and locked you up for good measure.'

'Fancy them thinking I murdered a prostitute in Harare Gardens.'

'If you didn't hang around with prostitutes, you wouldn't be under suspicion. But Uncle Charles doesn't believe you did it. He said you wouldn't have the balls for that.'

'I don't hang around with prostitutes. Hazel helped me with my book. And I don't believe your Uncle Charles said anything like that.'

Sarah smiled in the darkness. By not responding to Ian's last comment, she'd had the last word.

As Ian was about to drift off to sleep, Sarah said, 'Fancy them thinking I was your female accomplice in the MFF. How dare they say that! I'm a Shona.'

Ah, that was the last word.

Despite their anxiety, they both slept well and woke refreshed and ready to go by the time the train pulled into Bulawayo. Ian felt somehow safer in his old home town. Harare had got too hot for them. They disembarked from the train and walked through the railway station and out onto the street. 'We should stay at the Bulawayo Rainbow, where Jemma and I stayed. It's near the city centre and not too far to walk to the railway station.'

'Fine,' said Sarah, enjoying the freedom of walking in the street without having to worry about being recognised. The sun warmed their skin, and they relaxed after the night's tension. They breathed in the fresh morning air, heavy with oxygen. This was the Bulawayo from Ian's school days. He'd been here with Jemma less than a week ago, and it was with a twinge of regret he realised he'd not be seeing her again. Here he was, making his way out of the country, while Jemma, back in Harare, would wonder where they were. What was she doing right now? Probably, she'd be cleaning the apartment though there wouldn't be much work to do until Dennis and Mary Jones returned from their long overseas trip. Sarah had messed things up for him.

'What are you thinking about?' said Sarah.

'Oh, nothing much,' said Ian, trying to sound nonchalant.

* * *

After exiting the station, they walked past the old power station with its giant cooling towers on the left. The row of shops on the right looked as dirty and rundown as the railway carriage they'd just left. It would be another six blocks of shops and light commercial businesses before they reached the inner residential area on the eastern edge of the CBD.

Ian always loved arriving in Bulawayo by train early in the morning. It was seven o'clock and the early spring air smelled fresher than ever, now that manufacturing had fled the city. A lack of foreign exchange strangled industry through a shortage of raw materials, machinery and equipment.

They walked along the broad tree-lined streets. This part of town had few pavements. The properties fronted onto bare, hard earth with space for two cars parked side by side between the tall jacaranda trees. Quiet roads and the old and neglected buildings were a sure sign of the decline in the city's formerly bustling economy. Most of the larger and medium-sized companies had closed, and Ian felt nostalgic seeing the fate of his old home town. Since black rule, the government ignored the city, and when Sarah first passed through Bulawayo, it was already well into its decline. Sarah viewed it as a small run-down city that didn't compare with the glitz of Harare. But behind Harare's facade, the rot was as bad as Bulawayo and the other smaller towns in Zimbabwe. Ian didn't notice the decay on his holiday visit—only a week earlier—when he'd seen it through different eyes. Fleeing the country sharpened his senses, and he saw the city as it really was; again, a pang of regret. It was Sarah's fault he was leaving the country so soon.

'You're not cross with me, are you?' said Sarah.

'No, I'm not cross.'

'You're quiet. I hope I didn't offend you with something I said.'

'You didn't offend me. It's just sad to see Bulawayo looking so tired.'

'Yes, the Ndebele have neglected this place. Why can't they look after their city the way we Shona have cared for Harare?'

'Do you want me to answer that question?'

Sarah smiled. Ian knew she baited him. She was good at that.

CHAPTER 42

21st August 2009

THOUGH they'd not booked ahead, checking in at the Bulawayo Rainbow Hotel presented no problem. The polite receptionist greeted them. 'Welcome, Sir, Madam. Back so soon?'

'Yes,' said Ian, 'we enjoyed our last stay so much we've returned. Do you have a double room with a king-size bed for us?'

'Yes, we do, Sir. Will an east facing room be OK?'

'Yes, that will be fine.'

In the lift, Ian said, 'They thought you were Jemma.'

'Why didn't you ask for twin share?'

'I didn't think of it.'

'Do you want to ask them to change it?'

'Oh, it doesn't matter now. I'm so used to sharing with you.'

'I don't want to impose.'

'You're not.'

'So, you admit I'm not a burden, and you're happy to have me with you?'

'I wouldn't go that far,' said Ian, looking away from Sarah to hide his grin.

'My mother worried you might be a dirty old man.'

'What! I'm not old, and I've never tried to take advantage of you either.'

'You're twelve years older than me. And you've never tried to take advantage because I've held you in check.'

'Don't make me laugh.' Ian worried what Jemma may have told Sarah about her weekend with him at the hotel. At first it seemed improbable that Jemma hadn't told her, but the sisters acted as if nothing happened. Ian relaxed in the belief that his weekend with Jemma was their little secret. If she'd told Sarah, so what! But not knowing how much Sarah knew made him uncomfortable. Sarah gave Ian a little smile he couldn't interpret.

The room looked east towards the Ascot Centre and a flat, featureless horizon. It was larger than the room he'd shared with Jemma, which was fortunate. Somehow, Ian needed more space when he was with Sarah. The bed also seemed larger than the one he and Jemma shared on their visit. So that one was queen-size.

Ian and Sarah stood on the balcony of their fifth-floor room, looking at the roofs of the low-rise apartments in the neighbouring city block. Beyond that, the city matrix gave way to the large trees that stretched passed the Bulawayo Municipal Swimming Baths and Milton Junior School and on into the suburbs. 'Well, what now?' said Ian. 'I was planning to visit Victoria Falls, but leaving via Botswana might be quicker and easier. Zimbabwe is dangerous for us to hang around too long.'

'Yes, but I'd like to see Victoria Falls. Perhaps we could go via Botswana and see them from the Zambian side.'

'Oh! So now you're planning on touring with me?' said Ian, leaning away from Sarah to look at her.

Sarah smiled. 'Who else with local knowledge will help you finish your book? Remember, you promised we'd be joint authors.'

'No, I didn't, and somehow, I doubt that'll happen. How can we cross the border if the police or COU are searching for us? I'm sure they'll have alerted the border posts.'

'Ah! That's another reason you need me here. Our passports will give us away, but I know someone here who can help us.'

Morris Ndlovu was the best forger in the country. The COU had used his services many times, and Jedson had often entrusted Sarah with organising false passports for him. 'I have his phone number and address from when I spoke to him on the phone and sent him photos of Jedson for his false passports. Once, I even organised a false passport for Thomas. I'll call Morris and see if he will make false passports for us.'

* * *

The house was on the western edge of the city centre in Lobengula Street, about fifteen blocks from the hotel. Half-past six in the evening and it was getting dark. Morris did not encourage visitors during daylight for fear of attracting unwanted attention. Sarah knocked on the side door of the house as he'd instructed.

The door opened on a security chain. 'Hello Morris, it's me, Sarah Kagonye.' The door closed to release the chain and opened again to reveal a smiling Morris Ndlovu. He was a bald, nervous little man with delicate hands and narrow eyes and a thin face that alternated between a smile and a frown. He looked as if he would blow over if someone sneezed.

'Morris, I need your help. My mission is top secret, and I need false passports for myself and my colleague here. We may also need visas for Botswana.'

'Yes, after you called, someone else phoned me yesterday and said you'd be wanting false passports.'

'Do you know who it was?'

'No, he didn't say.'

'Morris, this mission is top secret. Even Jedson knows nothing about it. Please don't say a word about this to anyone. If Jedson or anyone else asks if you have seen me, say no.'

'I understand,' said Morris, with a knowing smile, 'but if you're planning to go to Botswana, I should warn you there're several police roadblocks on that road. If you want to get to Botswana, go via Victoria Falls or Zambia.'

'OK, but then we would need visas for Zambia and Botswana.'

'The visas are no problem because you are both eligible to stay in Botswana for ninety days without a tourist visa. In Zambia, your friend will need to get a tourist visa upon arrival, but you can enter for ninety days without a visa. The passports are more complicated. If you want to bypass the border posts and make an illegal crossing into Zambia or Botswana, you will need exit and entry stamps in your passports. They will need to be the correct colour stamps and in proper date sequence. Go through the border post in the normal way, using the false passports. Then, once you are out of Zimbabwe, copy the stamps into your genuine passports. I'll make you the exit, entry and date stamps and give you a little of each of the inks they use. The usual colours are red, green, blue, purple or black. You can go straight to Botswana or go there via Zambia. That means you will have exit stamps for Zimbabwe and Zambia and entry stamps for Zambia and Botswana. I will also give you adjustable date stamps of the correct size for each country.'

'Morris, you are a good friend.'

'I will need both of your existing passports to help me do all this. Mr Sanders, your false passport must also have stamps for your recent travels and for when you came into Zimbabwe, but I'll do that for you. This will take time, Sarah. I'll be as quick as possible, but allow for at least three days. Now if you don't mind, I need your passports, and I must take your passport photographs.'

Ian felt exposed without his passport, but they'd little choice other than to put their trust in the diminutive forger.

'It's a worry that someone phoned Morris to tell him to expect me,' said Sarah.

'It shows that the COU or the police or somebody is covering all stops, and they've considered the possibility we might be after false passports.'

'I still find it hard to believe Jedson would help the COU find me.'

'Jedson or someone else,' said Ian.

'You were wrong about Uncle Charles. Maybe you're wrong about Jedson.'

'Come on Sarah, your Uncle Charles said he'd never heard of Jedson or the COU. Doesn't Jedson's involvement with the COU tell you something?'

'What about your family's involvement with the Smith regime? Should I not trust you then?'

'You wouldn't trust me if you listened to your mother. The cheek of it! Fancy suggesting I might be a dirty old man.'

They'd walked about three blocks. No moon and broken street lamps made the empty streets dark. It was a quarter past seven and most people would be at home eating dinner. Ian noticed three unsavoury looking African men leaning against the high wall of a building about half a block ahead of them. As they neared, two men moved into the centre of the pavement. Ian slowed his pace, but Sarah said, 'Keep moving and ignore them.' Ian walked about two metres behind Sarah. They were almost upon them when he noticed the glint of a knife blade held by the man leaning against the wall. The man kept it concealed behind him, intending to surprise them with the blade.

Had Sarah seen the knife? There was no time to react. Before Ian could shout a warning, Sarah grabbed the man by his throat and smashed his head into the brick wall with a force that shook it. The man dropped the blade and collapsed to the pavement as his startled companions stood frozen. Sarah lashed out with her right foot against the knee of one. With a sickening crack of bone, the man fell to the ground.

A smear of blood on the wall showed the spot where the man with the knife had rested his head. Now he lay silent on the pavement. Another writhed in pain, holding his knee and groaning. The third ran off as fast as his legs could carry him.

'Are you cut?' said Ian, staring at Sarah's bloody hand.

'Not my blood,' said Sarah, stooping to drop the knife through the grill of a storm water drain.

Sarah confessed to Ian on the night train to Bulawayo that she trained as an assassin with the COU. He'd not been sure if he believed her, but the speed and violence of her assault on the men shocked him. It was clear they were looking for trouble, and they found it when they tried to hem Sarah in on three sides.

They passed an old house with a low wall. Sarah noticed a tap in the garden and stopped to wash the sticky blood from her hands. Ian marvelled at her calmness while his heart was still thumping. The incident was over before he'd taken in what was happening.

* * *

Three days to kill and no car. It would be too risky for Ian to produce his driving licence to hire one. The fewer people who knew his real name, the better. The police might check car hire companies.

'Perhaps we should go to another hotel,' said Ian. 'The police may check the hotels. If they had the foresight to imagine you might go to Morris for a passport, why wouldn't they be checking the hotels for us?'

'We need to be within walking distance of Morris' house. There're not too many hotels that fit the bill. We would be noticeable in a smaller hotel, so it's best we stay here and keep our fingers crossed and our eyes and ears open.'

'Three days is a long time to ride our luck.'

'Yes, but you know the police aren't competent.'

'Is that a racist comment, Sarah?'

'No, I can say it because I'm black.'

'Can't one make racist comments about one's own race?'

Sarah ignored Ian's question. 'That phone call to Morris makes me think it must have come from the COU. The whole time I worked there, I never saw genuine cooperation with the police or anyone else. Rivalry and excessive secrecy are the COU's hallmarks. In my experience, they'd prefer a covert hit to a public arrest. Those men this evening were more the COU's style.'

CHAPTER 43

22nd August 2009

IAN worried the COU had discovered their plans and knew where they stayed. It would not be too difficult to locate someone in a city the size of Bulawayo. Until now, he felt relatively safe cocooned in the hotel, but the encounter with the thugs rattled him. 'Do you think those men last night were COU?'

'Not unless standards have dropped. Those guys were bullies and cowards, not fighters.'

'OK, if we must sit out three days, let's use them well. How about a visit to my great white founder's grave in the Matobo Hills?'

The hotel organised a car and tour guide to take Ian and Sarah to the Matobo National Park to visit Rhodes' grave. They enjoyed a relaxing drive into the golden yellow countryside, past the Matobo Dam and into the park itself. The spectacular granite hills stood with huge lichen-covered boulders precariously balanced on top of each other as if a giant hand placed them. Msasa trees gave the place a haunting beauty. The guide took them to see the San Bushmen cave paintings, said to be five to ten thousand years old. On many, the colours were faded, but on others, bright and clear. The paintings depicted animals and hunting scenes.

The car stopped at the bottom of Malindidzimu—the place of benevolent spirits. It was one of the larger hills and presented quite a long climb. A dry, shrivelled looking ground cover grew on the rock. 'That's known as the resurrection plant,' said Ian. 'Although it looks dead now, if you put it in water it instantly comes alive, looking fresh with small green leaves.'

Rhodes' simple grave was at the top of the hill. It was a granite plinth about thirty centimetres high with a bronze plaque with the inscription: *Here lie the remains of Cecil John Rhodes.* Ian stared at it in quiet contemplation. He couldn't prevent a lump in his throat, looking at the grave in this beautiful but isolated spot with its all-pervasive silence. The place had a lonely, brooding atmosphere exemplified by Rudyard Kipling's words written in honour of Rhodes, in his poem, The Burial:

The immense and brooding spirit still
Shall quicken and control.
Living he was the land, and dead,
His soul shall be her soul!

'The old Federation of Rhodesia and Nyasaland banknotes,' said Ian, 'had a watermark of Cecil Rhodes' face surrounded by those lines.'

'Before my time,' said Sarah.

'Before mine too, but those banknotes were legal tender for ages.'

'Some members of ZANU-PF want to dig up his remains and send them back to England.'

'That would be madness. Don't they appreciate history?'

'The Matabele want to keep him here,' said Sarah. 'They make money out of tourism, and it's sacred ground for them.'

'At his funeral,' said Ian, 'the Matabele chiefs requested that the firing party not discharge their rifles. They said it would disturb the spirits. Instead, they gave him the Matabele royal salute—*Bayete.* It was the only time they gave a white man that honour. They regarded him as a great chief. Rhodes selected this spot himself, and he called it "The view of the world."'

The sombre atmosphere pervading the site even affected Sarah. She sensed Ian's mood and avoided provocative comments. They also viewed the graves of Rhodes' colleague, Leander Starr Jameson, and Sir James Coghlan, the first Prime Minister of Rhodesia. Nearby was the large memorial marking the grave for the thirty-four soldiers of the ill-fated Shangani Patrol, led by Major Allan Wilson and Captain Henry Borrow.

On the way down from Rhodes' grave, Ian broke off a twig of resurrection plant to show Sarah the plant's amazing ability to revive in water.

Ian and Sarah returned to the hotel in the late afternoon. The tour had a subduing effect on them, and they agreed that neither white nor black rule met the great promise of Rhodes' vision for the country. It had been a warm early spring day, and they were weary. After freshening up with showers and clean clothes, they relaxed with drinks in the bar lounge and ate in the hotel. It was still two days before their passports would be ready.

It wasn't easy to keep a low profile in the hotel, and it tested both their nerves. The friendly hotel staff were everywhere, and Ian being the only white guest made it even more difficult. They ventured out in the early evenings for short walks, but they knew the risk they were taking. Sarah felt frustrated confined to the hotel room. She'd been in hiding for over six months. Ian's experience in keeping a low profile didn't match Sarah's, and he admired her resolve. They were fortunate they could discuss and debate many issues, and their arguments went back and forth, helping the hours to pass.

'It's fine for you whites to laud Cecil Rhodes, but he invaded our country and took it away from us, and we had to adopt your culture and laws.'

'Sarah, his efforts benefited many blacks. Take you for example. You're an educated, modern woman; a beneficiary of colonialism. Don't you see it's the legacy he left you?'

'Yes, but how did it help Jemma?'

'It's true that not everyone benefited to the same extent, but at least the Shona are not being subjected to Matabele raiders stealing their women and cattle. The whites stopped the practice. For Jemma and those like her, it's a foundation on which to build. Their opportunities will come.'

'But nothing has really changed, has it? A few blacks have replaced the whites. Those few blacks hold the power and wealth now. Black rule has not helped most of the blacks.'

'Sarah, if you look at health, education and job opportunities, most are worse off now.'

'That's true. Oh no! Being couped up for months is affecting my mind. It doesn't seem right we are agreeing on these things.'

Ian laughed. 'We are agreeing on things Sarah because you are intelligent and sophisticated, and you can see what's happening in Zimbabwe. In fact, even Jemma would agree on these things because she has common sense.'

'There would have been a lot more people with common sense if you whites had included us sooner in the politics and benefits of your western culture. But you kept us out because you were afraid of losing your privileged position.'

'Now, my mind is going, Sarah. I agree with you.'

They laughed and agreed that agreeing can sometimes be as much fun as disagreeing.

CHAPTER 44

22nd – 24th August 2009

THE next two days passed quicker than they expected, and soon it was time to pick up their passports. The scheduled pickup time was seven o'clock in the evening.

Another dark night. The moon was not due until after ten o'clock. Sarah and Ian stepped out at a good pace, and they arrived on time at Morris Ndlovu's house and knocked on the side door. Morris looked through the window, and when he saw them, he smiled and opened the door. 'Everything is ready. The passports look good.' He showed them into his cosy workroom with its dull lighting and switched on his bright work lamp. Signs of his work were everywhere—on his dining and coffee tables, his sideboard and on his workbench. Blank passports, photos, bottles of ink, pens and craft knives like the old Exacto modelling blades Ian used as a boy covered every flat surface. First, he gave Ian his genuine passport and then the false one. 'Tell me what you think.'

'Amazing! How can you tell which one is the real passport?'

'Ah! I keep track of the real ones by the false names in the fakes. Otherwise, your two passports are the same.' Sarah's false passport looked every bit as authentic.

'But how did you manage the fake Australian passport with the photo enclosed within the page? I thought Australian passports couldn't be forged.'

'That my friend is my trade secret.' Morris went through the items one at a time, showing the stamps used by the different border posts. 'Sometimes they use a different colour ink on different days. That's why I say at least one of you should try to go through the border post with your false passport. Then, you can copy the stamps into your genuine passports.'

Ian and Sarah agreed that Morris' work was exceptional.

'Sarah, I received another phone call from the same person who phoned to tell me to expect you. He asked if I'd heard from you, but I told him, no. I'm sure they're expecting you to go straight to Botswana. That's why you should exit via Zambia. There are many roadblocks between Figtree, Marula and Plumtree on the way to the Botswana border.'

'Thank you, Morris,' said Sarah, placing her hand on his arm. 'You've done a great job.'

Ian shuffled his feet. 'Thank you, Morris. Here's the four hundred dollars we agreed.'

'Thank you, Sir. Don't forget your rubber stamps and ink.'

Morris gathered up the various documents and stamps and ink and put them in a large white plastic bag. Ian and Sarah were in a hurry to leave. The phone calls Morris received worried all of them.

'Morris seemed to be a likeable fellow,' said Ian, 'but can we trust him? He seemed almost too keen for us to exit through Zambia.'

'Who can we trust?' said Sarah, setting a good pace. 'But he did a good job for us, and he didn't have to tell us about those phone calls.'

Ian walked fast to keep up with Sarah. 'If we go out through Zambia, we can catch the train tomorrow night.'

Sarah suddenly stopped. 'When we first spoke to Morris, he said the inks could be red, green, blue, purple or black. Do you recall seeing any black ink?'

'No, I don't.'

'Let's go back and ask him about it.' They'd walked about five blocks when they turned back. What a nuisance! But they agreed it was better than risking not having all the colours that the exit and entry stamps might need.

The house was in darkness. 'Morris can't have gone to bed so soon …' said Sarah peering up the dark driveway. They crept up to the side door. Sarah knocked. 'The door's open! That's strange. He was so cautious and kept it on the security chain even when we were inside the house.' She knocked again and called out Morris' name in a hushed voice. No answer. Sarah eased the door open, and for the first time she noticed its loud creak. The darkness seemed to amplify the sound. The interior was pitch-black without a single light anywhere. 'Perhaps the electricity has gone off again. That wouldn't be unusual. You stay here Ian and watch the driveway. We don't want to give him a heart attack if he returns.'

Sarah crept into the house and looked for a light switch near the door. She flicked the switch, and a single, dull bulb in the ceiling came to life. She caught her breath. The entire room was in a mess. Papers, work tools, drawers and chairs scattered everywhere. Sarah gasped. Morris lay on the sofa with a wire wound tight around his neck. His usually affable face, a mask of fear with blood around his mouth and eyes and deep scratches on his throat.

'Is everything OK?' called Ian from the door.

'No, you'd better come in here.'

Ian walked into the terrible scene. 'Bloody hell, we were away for only fifteen minutes.' He surveyed the room in horror.

'Shush, they might still be here,' said Sarah, picking up a knife from the floor. 'Try to find the black ink. I'll be back in a minute. Be on your guard.'

'Where're you going?'

Sarah didn't answer. She slipped into the dark passageway, closing the door behind her, and waited in the blackness for her eyes to adjust. Then with the stealth of a leopard she moved down the passage, straining her ears for any sound. Sarah was wary and took her time to breathe the air in each room before judging it to be empty. One room had a strong, musty smell, and she jumped when a cat raced out between her legs. Ten minutes passed before she gave the all clear. 'There's no one here.'

'Are you sure there's nobody hiding under a bed or in a cupboard?'

'There's no one.'

'How can you be so sure?'

'Don't ask.'

'We'd better get out of here. I found a small bottle of black ink on the sideboard. It's the same shape bottle as the other colours Morris gave us, so it must be part of the set.'

Sarah checked to make sure Morris was dead. 'Poor guy,' she said, as she closed his eyes. She wiped the knife handle on the bottom of her T-shirt and put it back on the table. She picked up one of Morris' work cloths and wiped all the surfaces and things she or Ian touched. 'OK, let's get out of here. Keep an eye out for any sign of somebody watching or following us.' Sarah again used her T-shirt; this time to close the side door. 'There's no point in leaving it open for someone to notice and raise the alarm. We should try to get away from Bulawayo before someone discovers Morris.'

Ian and Sarah changed their route back to the hotel. He was glad of her company. In the circumstances, there was nobody he'd rather have by his side.

They walked in silence for a while, and then Sarah said, 'Morris was so careful about opening his door. Perhaps he knew the person who entered. Or perhaps he realised he'd not given us the black ink and opened the door thinking we'd come back for it.'

'I wonder if they followed us to the house or waited there for us.'

'It's more probable they turned up just after we left. But why murder poor old Morris? His forgery skills were rare. They'll struggle to replace him. Maybe they asked him whether he'd seen us and didn't accept his denials. The garrotte might've been their way of trying to make him talk, and afterwards they killed him.'

'If he talked, then they may already know we're heading to Victoria Falls and Zambia.'

'That's a chance we must take. The direct route to Botswana, which would be the logical route for us to take, sounds too risky.'

They walked back to the hotel in silence, keeping an eye out that no one followed. It was a relief to get back to the relative security of their hotel room. Like Harare, Bulawayo was now also getting too hot for them. With luck, tomorrow night they'd be on the train to Victoria Falls.

CHAPTER 45

25th August 2009

LUNCH had come and gone. Ian looked at his watch. 'It's time to get down to the station and buy tickets for tonight's train.'

'Is it safe for us to go out in daylight?' said Sarah.

'No, we'd be too conspicuous together. Stay here, I'll be back soon.'

'Do you think I should go? A black person would be less noticeable.'

'If I go by taxi, there'll be less chance of me being seen. Besides, I know this city better than you do. Don't worry, I won't be too long.'

'OK, but be careful.'

Sarah liked it when Ian took the lead, but she worried he was naïve about the situation in the country. Much had changed from when he last lived in Bulawayo.

Ian stood in the short queue at the station ticket office. He studied the faces of the surrounding people and imagined they all watched him. Being a fugitive sharpened all his senses, and he was ready for anything. If anyone hunted for them, the airport and the railway station were two obvious places to check. Sarah, back at the hotel, waited for him. A mixed-race couple walking the streets in broad daylight would have been too easy to spot.

Booking a train ticket to Victoria Falls was no problem. The trains weren't busy, so it was just a matter of rolling up on the day and buying a ticket for the overnight journey. At twelve dollars per bunk and four dollars per roll of bedding, a total cost of fifty-six US dollars was cheap for such a trip. The Africans in front of Ian in the short queue all bought economy class tickets. That meant they would sit on benches all night. The queue moved fast, and Ian soon reached the reservations window.

'May I have four first-class tickets to Victoria Falls tonight please?' said Ian.

'What are the names of the travelling passengers, Sir?'

'The names are Ian and Sarah Jones.'

'And the other two tickets?'

'We want to be alone.'

The clerk lowered his head and looked up at Ian over his reading glasses and asked, 'You're travelling with your wife, Sir?'

'Yes,' said Ian, wondering at the question.

'Ah! You have a new wife then, Sir?' The clerk smiled and wrote out four tickets. 'Don't forget to bring your own food and drink, Sir. There's no dining car on this train. Departure time is half past seven. Please don't be late. Enjoy your trip, Sir.'

Ian left the ticket office and walked along the quiet, broad, shaded platform. There were no commuter trains in Bulawayo, and most long-distance trains arrived in the morning and departed in the evening. Late morning and afternoon were quiet. On sunny days, the station had a warm and sleepy atmosphere, but the open platforms with their broad roofs helped cool the breeze on even the hottest of days. Rhodesia Railways extended platforms one and two to seven hundred and six metres in the late 1950s, and they were then the second longest in the world. Ian walked the five roofed platforms many times as a boy, either travelling with his parents or seeing off friends. He dreamed of travel and faraway places, and he'd often cycled here on a dreary Saturday afternoon to catch the mood. His blood still tingled with the memory of the train journeys he'd made. Ironic that his dreams of faraway places brought him right back to where he started out. Tonight, the platforms would be full of noisy and excited travellers, and the thrill of it all would return.

Back in the present, Ian looked at his watch. Time was short, and he needed to hurry back to the hotel to pick up Sarah. Taxis were unreliable, and they might end up having to walk to the station with their backpacks.

Ian left the railway station and walked past the tall railway administration building on his left. He turned right into Railway Avenue and walked past the row of small shops where the wizened old witch doctors sat cross-legged on the pavement. In front of them they laid out their odd assortment of twigs, ointments and body parts of dead creatures. 'Do you want to know your future, Sah?' one of them called out.

'If I don't hurry, My Friend, I know what my future holds.' The old witch doctor laughed and gave him a wave. Ian lengthened his stride as he had about a dozen city blocks to walk back to the hotel. On the way he passed the old power station, small businesses, old houses and blocks of flats. Eight blocks down Thirteenth Avenue, Ian turned left into Josiah Tongogara Road and walked the three blocks to the Rainbow Hotel. It was the Hotel Victoria in the fifties and sixties and then the Southern Sun in the seventies.

Sarah waited for Ian in their room, packed and ready to go. 'That took you a long time.'

'I had to walk back. There're no taxis at the station in the afternoon.'

'Did you get the tickets?'

'Yes, I did. I'll have a quick shower.'

'Should I call a taxi while you're getting ready?'

'If it takes as long as the last one to arrive, it may be quicker to walk.'

'Is it safe for us to walk?'

'Yes, the evening rush hour will be over, and it'll be quiet.'

'And it'll be dusk, so we won't attract too much attention.'

'OK, I'll be ready in five minutes.' Ian had a quick shower, brushed his teeth and packed. It was time to leave. They both dressed in jeans, T-shirts, windcheaters and baseball caps. Ian found that walking with Sarah made the return trip to the station seem so much shorter. At a small supermarket they bought biscuits, potato chips, sandwiches and drinking water.

At a quarter to seven there was still no sign of the train, but before much longer, it rumbled into platform four. Passengers, and their friends or relatives, there to wave them off, gathered around their respective carriages. The long train comprised a few passenger coaches and many goods wagons destined for the Hwange Colliery.

'We have a four-berth compartment,' said Ian, 'so we'll have plenty of room.' Most of the passengers crowded around the cheap economy class carriages with their basic bench seating. The second-class sleepers looked full, but the single first-class carriage seemed almost empty. Their tickets had the carriage number and compartment letter written on them.

'Our false names should help if your friends in the COU carry out checks on who's travelling. But I paid cash, so there's no trail to follow.'

'The hotel had our real names. If they are checking up on us, it shouldn't be difficult for them to discover we stayed there.'

'Did you notice the steam engine Sarah?' said Ian, changing the subject. 'Isn't it beautiful?'

'Yes, I saw it, but what's the big deal?'

'People travel the world to ride in steam trains. They go back to a romantic era of travel.'

'You mean the colonial era you whites hanker after; the grand old days of empire.'

'It's more than that Sarah. Diesel is soulless. Don't you like the smell of the steam locomotive? Even the whistle is more romantic than the diesel's horn. Before you can claim you've enjoyed the experience of train travel, you need to have had soot in your eye. And the beautiful sound that puts you to sleep. You know the sound: CHOOGA chooga, CHOOGA chooga, CHOOGA chooga, CHOO CHOOOOOOO?'

'Are you OK?' said Sarah with an amused smile. 'I've never been on a steam train. Every train I travelled on had a diesel engine.'

'Well, let me tell you, you're in for a real treat.'

'We'll see.'

'Air travel has also lost much of its romance. People used to dress up, and the women would all be wearing their sexiest perfume and lipstick. Apart from businessmen on short flights, today's air travellers don't dress for the occasion.'

'That's true,' said Sarah, thinking back to her trip to Egypt.

'Come! Let's inspect the engine.'

'What's there to see?'

'It's a beautiful piece of engineering, the smell and the noise.'

'If we must, but it's just a machine. If you're that interested, I'll ask my mother to show you her sewing machine.'

'It's not quite the same thing, Sarah, but if it operates on steam, I would like to see it.'

The huge locomotive stood like an angry, restless beast. The engine driver sitting high in the window looked small and inadequate for the job of controlling this monster.

'Isn't it fantastic, Sarah? Listen to the hissing steam escaping from the boiler. Can you smell the coal burning in the firebox?'

'Can we go to the compartment now?'

Sarah missed out on some of the simple pleasures of life, and it pleased Ian to introduce her to something she'd not experienced.

The compartment had two upper bunks and two lower bunks that doubled as bench seats during the day. 'That's my bunk,' said Sarah, pointing to the upper bunk on the side nearer the guard's van.

Ian selected the lower bunk with his back to the engine. 'If you get up in the middle of the night, don't forget that you're in the upper bunk. It'll be black in here without the lights.'

'It's dark in here already even with the lights.'

The wood panelling was a rich chestnut brown, and the seats a bottle green leatherette. Between the two windows, a fold-down stainless-steel wash basin, concealed a broken mirror behind it. This was one of the old carriages built in Britain in 1952. With all the charm of its era, it was much cosier than the newer Formica lined carriages used on the other lines in Zimbabwe.

'I prefer this carriage to the one we had coming down from Harare,' said Sarah, 'and not just because it's a four-birth compartment.'

'No, I expect the old Rhodesia Railways emblem on the windows makes you feel more secure.'

'I doubt that's the reason, but this carriage looks and feels warmer than the last one we had.'

'The first time my father visited the falls, the carriages were even older than this one. They dated back to around 1930 and had open balconies at each end, with gates so you could cross over to the next carriage. He was standing on one of those balconies when the train crossed the Victoria Falls Bridge.'

'Ooh! That would have been nice.'

'Yes, but they retired those old carriages in the late fifties. I first saw the falls after lunch on a hot, sunny day. With the high humidity, the scene was lush and tropical. I walked onto the bridge, and the next minute the falls came into view. It felt as if I'd entered paradise. Anyone who sees the falls for the first time would find it a humbling experience.'

'The way you speak makes it sound so exciting.'

'Let me tell you, Sarah, you're in for an unforgettable couple of days.'

The guard took everyone by surprise when he blew his whistle and waved the green flag at half past seven, the scheduled departure time. The steam locomotive lurched forward with a jolt that raced through the train like falling dominoes. It took Sarah by surprise and threw her onto the bench seat under her bunk. 'I forgot to warn you Sarah, steam trains can be a little jerky when they release the brakes.'

'Oh! Thanks. You could have told me earlier.'

Slowly the train eased forward. The sudden departure caught out a few passengers. African men and women raced down the platform and threw their bundled possessions through open doors and windows onto the train before jumping into the carriages. The National Railways of Zimbabwe seldom left on time.

The train rumbled out of the station at a pedestrian pace. After two kilometres, the brakes squealed, and the train stopped. Everyone stared out the windows, into the darkness, but the reason for the halt was not clear. Shouted voices somewhere along the track did nothing to explain the delay. After a few minutes another big jolt preceded smaller jolts as the couplings took up the strain and the train gathered pace.

The compartment was stuffy, and Ian opened the window next to his bunk. He and Sarah dressed warmly, wearing their sweaters under their windcheaters against the chill of the air in the pitch-black night. They saw the occasional lights of isolated properties through the open window. In the dull lighting of the compartment, Sarah looked at her image reflected in the closed window next to her. The light flickered a few times, reminding them they should keep their torch handy. It was an essential item on this train.

Ian and Sarah were both hungry and had eaten their sandwiches by the time the conductor came around to inspect their tickets. 'We need bedding for two please,' said Ian.

'Yes, Sir, the bedding attendant will come soon.' Minutes later, the attendant arrived with their two bedding rolls. The made-up bed rolls comprised clean, crisp white sheets, a fat pillow and two thick blankets on a canvas-based under-blanket. With practised ease the attendant unrolled them in no time at all.

The compartment light was too poor to read by, and the beds were inviting. An early night looked attractive. The water in the compartments wash basin was a trickle that soon stopped. Ian and Sarah used bottled water to brush their teeth. Before turning in, Ian visited the toilet at the end of the carriage. In his absence Sarah changed into her long T-shirt nightdress and wriggled into her made-up bed. It was like sliding into a sleeping bag.

Ian returned and locked the compartment door behind him. 'Sarah, when I came back from the toilet just now, I saw two African men standing in the passage outside the next compartment. They look like the two who came to my hotel room the morning I met you. They're in casual clothes, but I'm sure it's them.'

'Don't all blacks look the same to you whites? How would they know we'd be on this train?'

'Perhaps they've been following us. This carriage isn't full, so they might have bought tickets at the last moment.'

'OK, we'd better be alert, but I doubt it would be them.'

'Don't forget Sarah, I was born here and can recognise different African faces. The exception was that time I mistook you for Desmond Tutu.' Ian enjoyed his little joke, and it even amused Sarah.

'Are you going to close the window?' said Sarah, 'the air is cold.'

'In a minute,' said Ian, peering out the window as the train squealed to yet another halt. Loud voices and shouting accompanied each stop as passengers threw their bundled possessions off or onto the train. Around ten o'clock Ian slid into his made-up bed but then realised he'd not closed the window. He felt lazy, so he'd wait another few minutes before closing it.

Ian loved sleeping on the train. On most trips the rhythmic sounds of the steam locomotive and the carriage bogey wheels on the rails would make him drowsy, and he would soon be asleep. But on this occasion, he kept thinking about the two African men in the passage. Every little stop woke him; the squeal of the brakes, the voices carried on the night air, the hiss of the steam locomotive, and the jolt and jerking of the train as it moved off again. The cosy bed contrasted to the cold night air coming in through the open window.

Around midnight, Ian told himself for the umpteenth time he should get up and close the window. But he was drowsy, and with the mesmeric clickety-clack of the carriage's bogie wheels on the steel tracks, Ian again drifted off to sleep. In his slumber the train whistle blew. Somewhere in the glorious state halfway between drowsiness and sleep, Ian heard the haunting whistle of the locomotive, and then something else—a scraping sound. He thought he was dreaming, but wide awake now, he heard it again. A scraping sound at the window. The compartment was pitch-black, darker than the night sky. Ian was alert, straining his ears to pick up every sound—the scraping noise again. The hairs on the back of his neck stood erect. A cold chill ran down his spine, like a drop of iced water running down his back. He eased himself out of the cocoon-like bedding and laid on top of it, listening for the sound. It felt cold now with the window wide open. There, the sound again; something at the window. Still lying on his back, Ian drew his knees up to his chest, moving his legs well away from the window. He waited, listening, hardly daring to breathe. Could it be a monkey or baboon trying to enter the compartment, emboldened in their search for food? In certain areas, tourist hotels advised guests to keep their windows closed when they left their rooms. But would a monkey or baboon board a moving train at night?

Ian's heart jumped when a vague shape suddenly filled the window. Just then the locomotive's whistle blew its long blast. With no time to think, Ian shot out his legs with explosive force and hit the solid object. The sound of the train's whistle and a loud clatter on the floor drowned out a muted scream. The intruder disappeared as the train rattled through the night.

Sarah woke. 'What happened?'

'Something tried to climb through the window, and I pushed it out with my legs.'

'What did you drop on the floor? I heard something fall.'

Ian turned the compartment light on, and Sarah switched on the torch and played the beam on the floor. She saw it first. 'Hey that looks like a handgun.'

'What! You mean—'

'It's a Glock 26 handgun. Same as we had at the COU. That must have been one of their operatives you kicked off the train.'

'He must have come from the next compartment. I told you those guys in the passage looked familiar.'

'Let's check next door,' said Sarah. 'Come with me. If someone asks who's there when I knock on the door, just give a deep grunt. If they open the door, get back into our compartment fast and close the door behind you. When I tap on the wall, come in as quick as possible to help me.'

'What are you going to do?'

'I'll shoot them and shove them through the window before they bleed all over the compartment. That's why I need your help. A dead body can be heavy.'

'Don't be mad, it's too risky.'

'There's no going back now. Those guys aren't playing. It's obvious they're onto us, and now you're a killer on the run, we have to get rid of any witnesses.'

'I didn't know it was a person climbing through the window.'

'Tell that to the judge. Do you think they'll believe you?'

'But innocent people may be next door.'

'Innocent people don't climb through windows into the next-door compartment. Believe me, no one next door is innocent.'

Sarah removed the magazine from the Glock, checked the chambered round and replaced it. She opened the door and went to the neighbouring compartment. She looked at Ian to make sure he was ready. Sarah used the nose of the Glock to tap on the door. No response. She tapped again. No response. 'Get back into our compartment,' she whispered. 'Remember, two taps and you come in fast.' After Ian retreated, Sarah turned the compartment handle and swung the door open. Empty; there was no sign anyone occupied the compartment.

'They've gone,' said Sarah. 'They never work alone. Maybe they saw their man fall and made a run for it. We must be on high alert now. What's the time?'

'One o'clock.'

'If the train is on time, we'll reach Dete in about three quarters of an hour. If we're running on schedule, the next station should be Malindi. Let's watch who gets on or off the train.'

Ian and Sarah dressed and put everything into their backpacks before switching off the lights. 'We should get off the train a stop or two before Victoria Falls,' said Sarah.

'Yes, if our intruder's partners have raised the alarm, the police may wait for us there. When we—' There was a sudden squeal as the engine driver applied the brakes, and the wheels of the train slid on the steel tracks. Sarah and Ian peered through the windows. The train had stopped in the middle of nowhere. There was no station or siding, and no movement outside the train. A minute or two later, the train moved off again, yet another inexplicable stop on the train's journey. Sarah and Ian breathed once more. 'Perhaps it was an elephant or some other animal on the line,' said Ian.

At half past one the train rolled into Malindi. 'Wow! We're only twenty minutes late,' said Ian, jumping up to peer out the window. 'At this rate, we should reach Dete by two o'clock.' The train stopped for a minute or two before it moved off again, making a slow approach to the next stop. 'Five minutes past two. We're coming into Dete now.'

A dog came around the corner of the station entrance, a German shepherd on a leash. 'Look,' said Sarah, 'police; lots of them.' Ian and Sarah peered out onto the dull lit platform. Five policemen dressed in their winter greatcoats stood there, and two of them had dogs.

'Quick,' said Ian, 'let's go.' They grabbed their backpacks, slammed their compartment door shut and ran to the end of the passage and swung open the carriage door on the side away from the platform. They jumped off the steps before the train stopped, but they were much higher off the ground than Ian expected. He stumbled and fell on the gravel beside the railway track. Sarah's COU training came in handy, and she alighted without difficulty. Ian leapt up, and they raced across the adjacent track and into the bushes. The train shielded their escape from the eyes on the platform. They walked as fast as the darkness would allow, getting as far away as possible from the station. 'I wonder if anyone saw us leave the train,' said Ian, panting from the sudden exertion.

The police entered the first-class carriage from both ends and ran down the corridor, checking the toilets and each compartment. 'They've gone,' a policeman shouted. 'They may have got off at Kennedy or Malindi.' Curious passengers took an interest in the proceedings. 'Did anyone see a murungu leave the train in the last hour?' the policeman called out. If anyone had seen anything, they were not saying. The police weren't popular in any part of Zimbabwe.

Ian and Sarah put as much distance as possible between them and the station. They ran alongside the railway line, which gave them a sense of direction in the darkness. 'If we keep going at this rate,' joked Ian, gasping for breath, 'we'll beat the train to Hwange.' The train stood at the station, way behind them. It reminded Ian of the annual foot race against the *Puffing Billy* steam locomotive, in Melbourne's Dandenong Hills. He wished he was back there now.

For ages, nothing happened. The train was stationary for at least half an hour. Ian and Sarah moved as fast as possible, half running and half walking, in the near pitch blackness beside the railway track. Ian struggled to catch his breath. Damn! His desk job and long walks did not keep him as fit as he'd hoped. Sarah settled into a nice rhythm. Then they heard it, the barking of the police dogs in the distance. They crossed back over the railway line and kept going, but the barking got louder. 'They're catching up with us,' said Ian. The police didn't have backpacks to carry. It was dark, and Ian and Sarah couldn't see where they were going, and progress was slow. If they used their torch, they risked being seen. Where was the moon when you needed it? The barking got louder still, and they saw the flickering of powerful torches in the distance.

At last the train moved. Ian looked around and saw the locomotive's headlight coming their way. 'We'll hide in the bushes before we get caught in the light.' They ran on, but the train was closing fast. 'Quick, let's get into those bushes.' They raced down the slope away from the track. Ian slipped on loose stones and slid down the rest of the slope, grazing his right forearm and left hand. He cursed the darkness. They crouched down in the bushes and dry grass and waited for the train to pass. But they were still too close to the railway track, and for a moment the ark of a dazzling flood of light blinded them. Although only a matter of seconds, the beam seemed to rest on them too long, and then, bit by bit, it eased away in front of them.

'What's that on the railway line in front of the train,' said Sarah, pointing down the track to tawny shapes caught in the locomotive's headlight.

'It looks like buck crossing the track. No, hang on, they're lions,' said Ian, ducking lower into the bushes. 'Yes, they're lions, just one hundred metres away. If we had run any farther, we would have run straight into them.' The lions grudgingly moved to one side when the huge locomotive lumbered up to them, much in the same way they moved aside for elephants approaching a water hole.

'We can't stay here,' said Sarah, 'the police will catch us.' The barking was closer now. A sudden loud and raspy roar followed by several asthmatic sounding coughs stilled their thoughts.

'That's a male lion calling,' said Ian, 'and it sounds close.' The terrifying sound seemed to rattle the surrounding bushes. Ian knew the sound could carry up to eight kilometres. He also knew it was hard to tell the distance from a lion's roar, but to him it sounded nearby.

As his eyes got used to the dark, Ian noticed the shape of a large tree about twenty metres from the railway track. 'Let's get down to that big tree. We can hide behind it, and it will give us protection from this cold wind. Here in the bushes we are exposed on all sides.' They were cautious as they made their way to the tree. If any danger lurked, they wouldn't see it in the darkness. The lion continued calling, but as they got used to the fearsome sound, it seemed more distant.

Ian and Sarah dumped their backpacks down and sat on the ground with their backs against the trunk. They made sure it was between them and the point where the lions had crossed the railway line. 'Listen!' said Ian.

They sat in silence for a while listening.

'I can't hear anything,' said Sarah.

'Well, that's it. It's all quiet. There's no more barking. I wonder if the police have stopped following us.'

'The lion's roars might've made them turn back.'

'Do you have your handgun ready?'

'Yes, but a Glock 26 won't stop a lion.'

'The noise may frighten them.'

'I hope you're not expecting me to protect you against the lions. You're the man. You should protect me.'

'There aren't any low branches on this tree to climb.'

They sat listening for any sounds that might alert them to danger. The male lion continued to call in the distance. At last, all was quiet.

'I never imagined,' said Sarah, 'anyone could climb through the window of a compartment while a train was moving. At most sidings there're no platforms, and the windows are high off the ground. But it would be possible to climb through a compartment window from the platform at a large station.'

'You know, something similar happened years ago. On Christmas Eve in 1971, a man bashed, raped and strangled a young American trainee nurse, on the Victoria Falls to Bulawayo train. They found her body in her compartment when the train pulled into Bulawayo station at half past seven in the morning. The compartment was locked on the inside, so the police concluded the killer climbed through the window from the next compartment and gone back the same way. The court found a twenty-year-old man guilty of her murder. He was the first white man hanged after Rhodesia's UDI.'

'How do you know all this?'

'My dad told me about it when he spoke of the old days. A lot of the stuff he talked about happened before your time. You never knew Zimbabwe when the whites ran it. All you can go on is what Mugabe and ZANU-PF tell you, so you think the whites are terrible racists. It was a happy place. Although there was little mixing, blacks and whites coexisted, more so than in South Africa.'

'But there was little mixing.'

'It's normal for people to mix with their own kind, isn't it? People in the same socio-economic group stick together. There was no apartheid. It was more a question of *birds of a feather flock together*.'

'You've seen how different Jemma and I are. I don't see us as *birds of a feather*.'

'Yes, but you are sisters, so you're close. How many educated blacks remain in Zimbabwe? A lot returned from overseas when ZANU came to power. But after experiencing Mugabe and ZANU-PF, many of them have left. And look what happened to your family.' After this, Sarah was silent. Ian cursed himself for again bringing up her father's murder. Either way, he regarded it as a small if cruel victory. He never conceded that she'd won an argument, but he couldn't compete with her endurance. Somehow, she always had the last word in their debates, but this time she was quiet. Perhaps she was digesting his comments?

It was their current predicament on Sarah's mind. They were in danger from both the wild animals in the bush and the security services. Why was she a fugitive? Was it, as Uncle Charles suggested, because of her father, or because they suspected her of having avenged her father's murder? Perhaps, because she'd worked for the COU, they thought she knew too much? She and Ian may also now be wanted for the murder of the COU operative Ian kicked off the train.

Sarah thought it ironic she'd grown up believing the whites were the enemy. Now, her salvation might depend on this murungu with whom she'd little in common.

After several minutes, Sarah said, 'You said I was in for a real treat. Was this it?' Ian opened his mouth to respond but then closed it again. No matter what he said, Sarah would somehow have the last word.

Ian broke the silence. 'I admit it was not the best train travel experience I've had. But it's a shame you didn't have an uninterrupted journey so you could appreciate how wonderful steam trains are.'

'Pff, I'm over train travel.'

'Don't you think it's romantic, travelling with your "husband" on a steam train to one of the seven natural wonders of the world?'

Sarah gave Ian a disparaging look. 'Well, it would be more romantic than walking through lion country on a cold night. But you're right about one thing.'

'Oh yes! What's that?'

'It looks like I will be in for an unforgettable couple of days.'

CHAPTER 46

26th August 2009

THE insistent ringing of the cell phone on his bedside table woke Captain John. 'Elijah, do you know the time? Five o'clock in the morning.' John got up and walked out onto his front veranda. 'What's the problem?'

'Sorry to disturb you, Sir.' Elijah's voice was breathless. 'Samson has disappeared and Sarah Kagonye and the murungu have escaped.'

'What do you mean Samson has disappeared? How can he disappear?'

'He climbed from our compartment window into their compartment and then I never saw him again. Something must have gone wrong, so I phoned the police and reported him missing from the train. They met the train at Dete and searched it, but there was no sign of him anywhere.'

'What about Kagonye and her companion?'

'They have also disappeared. The police think they left the train at Dete. They put their police dogs onto their scent and followed for a while in the National Park, but lions were in the area, so they called off the search.'

'When Samson climbed into their compartment what was the plan?'

'He'd unlock their compartment door for me to help him. If they resisted, we'd push them off the train when it moved fast.'

'So where is Samson now?'

'Kagonye and the murungu may have taken him with them, Sah.'

'No, Elijah, I don't think so. Might they have pushed him from the train?'

'Yes, Sah.'

'Get the police to search the line for him.'

'Yes, Sah.'

'Get to Victoria Falls and keep a watch out for Kagonye and her companion. I will fly up and meet you.'

'Yes, Sah.'

'If they don't resist arrest, we can bring them back to Harare to interrogate them. If they resist, finish them on the spot. You can feed them to the crocodiles. Don't forget, no bullet holes. It must appear to be an accident.'

'Yes, Sah, but why don't we just kill them when we find them?'

'We must question them, Elijah. If we take them back to Harare, we'll have plenty of time to get information from them; information about the MFF for example. But remember, Kagonye is our main prize. Get her at all costs. The murungu is a bonus, but Kagonye must not escape.'

'Yes, Sah.'

John put down the phone. Damn! Losing Samson was the last thing he needed. He was already under fire for losing his teams A3 and A4. He wouldn't mention anything to the boss. What he didn't know wouldn't hurt him.

It was pointless going back to bed. He wouldn't sleep. A cup of tea is what he needed. Then he'd go to the office and find the quickest way to Victoria Falls. A direct flight to Victoria Falls would be better than Livingstone on the Zambian side. Although he held a permit to carry a gun, the Zambian customs and immigration might prove to be an obstacle. He'd take Akashinga with him. He lacked brains, but sometimes that was an advantage, and he could be useful if it came to a showdown. Two other operatives would drive to Victoria Falls to help search for Kagonye and Sanders, and when they found them, they'd bring them back to Harare in the car.

* * *

Huddled under a huge baobab tree with a chilly swirling wind, was not the way Ian planned to spend the night. He'd relished the thought of a cosy railway compartment on the train to Victoria Falls. The August night breeze buffeted them with cold blustery gusts. At one thousand and ninety metres above sea level, even summer, late night breezes can be chilly, but this was early spring.

It was hard to get comfortable and sleep, sitting backed up against the tree. Ian, stiff with aching bones, found it an effort to get to his feet. Cold and hungry was not part of the plan for his long-awaited visit to Victoria Falls. On foot and over one hundred and seventy kilometres to go, Ian was not happy.

At about four in the morning a lion roared in the distance, but it seemed to move away as the roars became a husky far off sound. That was small comfort in lion country.

Ian couldn't see much in the black, moonless night. Too dark even for predators, he fancied. At least they'd escaped detection. The cold wind deadened their senses. They shivered so much they wouldn't have heard an elephant approaching. But then, despite their size, elephants can move silently through the bush, so perhaps the chilly night wouldn't have made any difference. Ian was unaware that lions are more active on moonless nights. Their night vision was eight times better than man. The reason Ian and Sarah remained undetected was more than likely the swirling, cold wind which either removed their scent or dispersed it, making it hard for the lions to tell from which direction it came.

Ian looked at Sarah. How had she fared? He'd considered cuddling up close to her to keep them both warm, but he'd never laid a finger on her, so that didn't seem an option. She looked rested, but then, she was twelve years younger than him and as tough as anyone he'd ever met. Sarah might even have considered it a pleasant August evening. She'd been awake for the past half hour, but he'd been awake for most of the night.

At ten minutes to six, the first light of dawn crept up on the surrounding darkness. Sunrise would be in half an hour. Neither spoke a word until Ian broke the silence.

'Sleep well?'

'Yes, I did thanks; how about you?'

'Don't ask. Were you cold?'

'Yes, freezing, but we'll warm up as soon as we get going.'

'We should wait here until it gets warmer. We don't want to bump into those lions again. Once, I saw a tourist leave his car to take a photo of lions resting under a tree. Nothing happened, but when we told the game rangers at Robins Camp that evening, they said lions were hungry at night and first thing in the morning. That's when they'd be most dangerous.'

'Great! So that means we stay in this cold spot till mid-morning.'

'The sun will be up soon; in fact, here it comes, right on cue.'

Ah, the beautiful sun! At first, it warmed their faces, and then bit by bit the warmth spread through the rest of their bodies like a slow defrosting.

'The early morning sun is like standing in a warm shower with the water flowing over you,' said Ian.

Sarah agreed. She remembered the early days before her family had hot running water at home. If they didn't want to wash themselves in cold water, they needed to boil it over an open fire.

'The sun makes you feel so alive,' said Ian. 'Everything depends on it for energy, and sunrise and sunsets are so beautiful. Early morning, the best time of day. The whole world awakens. Listen to the birds.'

'Um, nice if you are on holiday I suppose.' Sarah had mixed feelings about sunrise as it always reminded her of her sister leaving home before dawn. Prior to working for Ian, Jemma had to start work at a quarter to seven. That meant getting up at five, having breakfast, and taking tea to her parents and Sarah in bed. She would then get ready, wait in a long queue at the bus stop, and walk from the bus station to the other side of town where she worked.

Sunsets represented the end of the working day, and both sisters could enjoy the radiant beauty on their way home. For Sarah, the early evening, when the sun had lost its sting, was the best time of day.

'The sun is the source of life. Nothing would survive without it. No animals or plants.' Ian was getting effusive after the cold and miserable night. 'Thank goodness it didn't rain.'

'It doesn't rain in August. The clear sky made it cold last night, and even worse with the breeze.'

'Aren't you more cheerful on a sunny morning?'

'In Zimbabwe, most mornings are sunny.'

'That's why Africans are so cheerful, Sarah.'

'Perhaps, but bad things can still happen on sunny mornings.'

'Yes, being a lion's breakfast would be one of them.'

By ten o'clock, Ian and Sarah were ready to move. They put their light coats into their backpacks, and Ian put on his golf cap and sunscreen. Sarah declined the sunscreen but put on her sunglasses and produced a broad brimmed, floppy, straw sun hat that looked elegant enough for the races. Warmed up and energised, they set off on their walk.

'Let's follow the railway line,' said Ian, 'but keep an eye out for those lions. Take care to check under the trees. They love resting in the shade.'

The first hour was easy going and the sun a welcome companion. By half past eleven, it was getting warm. The going was harder, and Ian put on his sunglasses. Little conversation passed between them as they focussed on not tripping over the railway sleepers. They kept an eye out for any potential danger, animal or human. By noon, it was hot on the exposed railway track, with no opportunity for shade.

How could Sarah look so cool? She was much fitter than him. 'This damn sun is relentless,' said Ian at last, looking hot and bothered.

'If you're hot, perhaps we should walk down in the bush where there's more shade.'

'No, that would slow us down and mask the view of the surrounding countryside. Who knows what's down there? We're right on the edge of the Hwange National Park here.'

'Yes, but walking on this raised rail track also makes us more visible to whatever or whoever is down in the bush.'

Ian did not respond. He mopped his face and brow with his hanky. His hair was soaking wet, and rivulets of perspiration ran down his face and neck, and his shirt showed large wet sweat patches on his chest, back and armpits. He'd not spent this much energy in years. Now, he hated the sun. It was intense and burned his skin even through his shirt. Ian worried about sunburn and put a hanky under his hat to protect his ears and the back of his neck. The jeans he wore were hot but protected his legs from the sun. Ian rolled down his sleeves and put more sunscreen on his face, ears and neck. His efforts to avoid sunburn amused Sarah.

'You look like David Livingstone, so it's appropriate you're on your way to discover the Victoria Falls.'

'Better this than risk sunburn and skin cancer. Sunburn is uncomfortable. Your skin is tight and sore for two days and then peels for a week.'

'You said you loved the sun?'

'No, I hate it. I love the sun on a cold morning, but now it's relentless. Everything fades and deteriorates in the sun. The plants get dry and scorched. And all the water holes evaporate, and animals die of thirst.' Ian's voice cracked in his parched throat.

'Focus on something else,' said Sarah. 'The Borrow Street Baths for example.'

'That's easy to say,'

'You're funny. One minute you love the sun and the next you hate it. If we spend another night in the bush, you may love it again tomorrow.'

'I won't if I'm sunburnt. A cold breeze feels icy on sunburnt skin.'

'Isn't it amazing, we're just the right distance from the sun to love it sometimes and then hate it at other times?' Sarah also perspired now, but she didn't complain and seemed to enjoy the walk. Did she put on a brave face for his benefit? She was always so damn competitive. But despite his discomfort, he now focused on something else. Sarah's comment about the Borrow Street Baths made him wonder what Jemma might have told her about their weekend in Bulawayo.

The conditions exposed Ian's lack of fitness, and his shoes rubbed against his heels and the balls of his feet. Blisters were a concern, but if they could make it to Hwange by the next evening, they might get a lift to Victoria Falls. While Ian struggled, Sarah took it all in her stride.

Sometimes, Ian stumbled over a sleeper, but walking on the track was easier than walking in the bush. One train passed heading towards Bulawayo and they hid in the bushes until it was out of sight. There was little sign of life. They surprised the occasional buck that bounded away in alarm and were thankful they saw nothing of danger to them. Ian glanced at his watch, half past two already. It was hard to judge the distance they'd covered. The blistering sun bore down on them, but they walked without stopping on the seemingly endless track. Even their banter dried up in their parched throats. They were intent on covering as much distance as possible during the daylight hours.

CHAPTER 47

26th August 2009

IAN's thoughts drifted back to the railway compartment he and Sarah shared. It needed significant maintenance. The rolling stock and the railway line were in a state of disrepair. Economic sanctions and a shortage of foreign currency were at the root of the problem. Most of the lighting in their compartment did not work, and the leatherette bench seats were torn with holes. The temperamental washbasin ran out of water. The bedding was the saving grace. It was comfortable and cosy.

Ian always loved sleeping on steam trains, but this time the pleasure was too brief. Diesel was imported and in short supply, but coal was plentiful. To the delight of many long-distance train travellers, steam locomotives returned to service in 2004. Ian hoped to relive the experience, but luck was against them.

The heat and the sun were relentless. Ian glanced at his watch, half past three already. 'We can walk for another hour at the most, so we had better keep an eye out for suitable shelter. We don't want to spend another night with that wind blowing around us.'

For the next half an hour they scoured their surroundings as they walked, but there was just thick bush with few opportunities for shelter. 'If we climbed a tree, we may be safe from lions,' Sarah suggested.

'Perhaps safe from lions but not leopards, and it would be cold in a tree. Anyway, lions can climb trees, and I read somewhere they can jump as high as three-and-a-half metres, so we would have to find a big tree.'

'Better cold than eaten.'

Ian and Sarah debated the pros and cons of lions, leopards and the cold wind at night. They were unaware sensitive noses had already picked up their scent. Worse still, several pairs of eyes watched them, and hungry mouths salivated. The pride was on its way to a water hole when they spotted the two humans walking through their territory. In the rainy season water was everywhere, and the game that provided the bulk of their diet was dispersed. But now in August, conditions were dust dry. Most days, the pride would wait at a water hole for dinner to arrive. But this pride had tasted human flesh before and knew it made a tasty treat. Man-eaters love the saltiness of human blood, and the pride picked up their trail.

Ian and Sarah were tiring, and their pace slackened. The thick bush thinned out. 'The trees are smaller here,' said Ian. 'I wonder if we should go back to that last big tree we saw. It wasn't ideal, but it's better than spending the night in the open veld.'

'Hah! You agree with me then?' said Sarah. 'Let's see what's over that rise, and if it's not promising we can go back.'

They took a few minutes to reach the top of the undulating open grassland, and all the time the danger behind them got closer.

Then, there it was, a bungalow with a broad open veranda, just two hundred metres ahead. There were no sheds and no vehicles. 'Who could live there?' said Ian.

'It looks deserted,' said Sarah. 'But we'd better be careful until we're sure.'

As they approached the house, they noticed there were no curtains. They looked through the windows and saw it was empty bar one or two pieces of furniture. Ian tried the door handle. 'It's open. Imagine leaving an empty house open like this. Welcome to the Hotel Paradiso my lady.'

'Anyone could come in here,' said Sarah.

'Anyone just did. Let's investigate.'

The front door led into an open-plan lounge, dining room and a kitchen with a door to the backyard. To the left, a short passageway led to a laundry, bathroom and toilet, looking onto the back of the property. Opposite the bathroom, a bedroom faced the front of the house. A large, second bedroom at the end of the passage, had views to the front and back. The sides of the house were windowless. All the windows were barred, and a long front veranda ran the length of the house. The house faced south, so there would be no direct light at sunrise or sunset. Perhaps it kept the house cooler in summer, but it looked dark and foreboding in the late afternoon. Two large bolts secured the front door: one near the top and the other near the bottom.

'Nothing here except the dining room table and sideboard,' said Ian. 'No food or drink and no electricity. Whoever was here has gone, but why would they leave the table and sideboard? Imagine living out here in the middle of nowhere.'

A quick look around outside proved fruitless. Yellow grass and a few scattered acacia thorn trees were all there was to see. The rise of the land at the front of the house hid from view the thick bushland they passed earlier in the afternoon. They went back inside, and Ian bolted the front door, oblivious to the yellow and amber eyes watching from the top of the rise.

'The cold-water taps work,' said Ian, 'but the water looks brown and murky. It must come from the rainwater tank in the backyard. If you want a shower, Sarah, you'd better hurry before the sun goes down and it gets cold. Someone was kind enough to leave a little soap in the shower. If you brush your teeth, don't swallow the water. I'll check the water tank before you get into the shower. Who knows how long it's been stagnant in there?'

Ian unlocked the back door and walked out to the rainwater tank. He climbed the steel ladder built onto the wooden platform on which the tank stood. There was no cover, and Ian stood on his toes to peer into the tank. 'Yeah, it's not too bad,' he shouted to Sarah, who watched from the kitchen window. 'There're two drowned birds in there, so don't drink the water, but a shower should be OK.'

Ian started down the ladder when Sarah shouted, 'Look out!' Ian turned to see her pointing to the bottom of the ladder. He glanced down and saw a large lioness waiting patiently for her dinner to descend. Ian jumped back onto the platform. He looked at the lioness, and she stared back at him with penetrating, unblinking eyes. A shiver ran down his spine.

'Get your gun,' Ian shouted. Sarah's head disappeared from the window. He again looked down at the beast as she sat on the ground, seeming to assess the situation. Ian remembered the height lions could jump; three-and-a-half metres. Was the platform that high? He doubted it. The lion crouched as if to leap. Then it appeared to change its mind and sat up before walking a few steps back from the platform and crouching again. Oh no! It will try a running leap. Ian's heart almost stopped when two loud bangs rang out. The lioness jumped up and ran around the corner of the house. Ian jumped from the platform and raced to the kitchen door. Thank heaven for Sarah and her loud handgun. She'd fired two shots into the air, and that did the trick.

After they had brushed their teeth and showered, using their dirty clothing as towels, they felt much fresher. Feeling safe for the first time since leaving the train, their thoughts turned to food. 'We saw nothing outside,' said Ian, 'but we didn't look too hard. Perhaps we should search farther from the house. There might be an old vegetable patch or *marula* tree.'

'What, with that lion hanging around here?'

'It should be OK; you scared it off with your shots.'

'No!' said Sarah, 'lions are persistent, and it's getting dusk. I have two peanut bars in my backpack.'

'Why didn't you say so earlier? We could have eaten them for lunch and had the energy to go faster.'

'If we'd eaten them for lunch, we wouldn't have them now. And we wouldn't have gone past this house even if we'd reached it an hour earlier.'

'Yeah, I suppose so. You don't by any chance have a thermos of hot tea or a bottle of water in your backpack, do you?'

'Sure, I do; sparkling or tap water?' It wasn't too funny, but they both laughed.

'They could have left us a bed,' said Ian looking around the empty house. 'All we have is the parquet floor.'

'Well, it's better than last night. At least we're sheltered from the wind.'

'I estimated it would take us two days to make Hwange, but judging from today, it might be three. We didn't make halfway today. While we're still inside the park, we can't walk more than about six hours a day, from about half past ten to half past four. Even that's optimistic.'

'Tomorrow, we must try to find food. We won't get far if we're starving,' said Sarah. 'I'm sorry I dragged you into all this.'

'No, Sarah, it's OK. There's nowhere else I'd rather be.' They laughed because they both knew it was a lie. But Ian's lie contained a grain of truth. No food or drink, cold nights, lost in the National Park with just the railway line to guide them, surrounded by dangerous animals and hunted by the authorities; what a rich experience for his novel.

'We'll go to bed with the birds tonight. Half past six and dark already, and it's getting cold. It'll be a long night. Why don't you tell me a story Sarah?'

'I don't know any stories.'

'OK I'll tell you one first and then you can think about a story you can tell me. Do you believe people can change into animals?'

'No, I don't.'

'The story starts in Tanganyika before the Second World War. There was a witch doctor who was headman of his village. The villagers accused him of corruption and the tribal chief replaced him. Soon after, lions attacked villagers in the area, and rumours spread that the killings wouldn't stop until the tribal chief reinstated the witch doctor. The villagers thought the man-eaters were human beings who could change into lions, and the witch doctor controlled them. The terrified villagers gave gifts to the witch doctor as insurance against attack.'

'Is this a true story?' asked Sarah.

'Uh-huh. For thirteen years they terrorised a large area and had killed and eaten hundreds of villagers. Soon after the War, a game ranger from the Tanganyika Game Department set out to shoot the lions. It took two years to kill the twenty man-eaters. At about the time he shot the last man-eater, the tribal chief agreed to reinstate the witch doctor as village headman. The villagers believed it was the reason the attacks stopped.'

'That's a good story,' said Sarah, nodding. 'Some people still believe such things happen.'

'Isn't it strange how such similar beliefs occur all round the world? In Europe they believed in werewolves. The same thing applies to reincarnation. Do you believe in that, Sarah?'

'Yes, I do.'

'I do too. I can't accept humans go through all their learning, experience and emotions, to end up as nothing, but it's a controversial topic.'

'If it's true,' said Sarah, 'how would you like to return? Some Africans think newborn babies are their ancestors who have been reborn. You could come back as a girl.'

'Ouch! There're fleas here,' said Ian slapping his thigh. 'Some people believe you can return as a lower form of creature if you have lived a bad life. I would rather return as a lion than a flea.'

'But fleas have a shorter lifespan. If you came back as a flea, then you might return sooner as a human.' Ian couldn't argue with that logic.

They dressed as warmly as possible with the limited clothing they carried, and they used their shoes as pillows. Despite the cold parquet floor and no blanket or any other form of cover, they were soon both fast asleep, the telling of Sarah's story forgotten. It had been an exhausting day, and Ian had not slept since their hasty departure from the train. He dreamt of the apartment back in Harare and the noisy kid next door who kicked a soccer ball against the wall every afternoon between four and five.

* * *

There were seats available on the flight from Harare, and Captain John and Akashinga arrived at Victoria Falls in the mid-afternoon. Elijah was waiting to greet them. Samson's disappearance and the unfamiliar surroundings agitated him.

'Slow down, Elijah, stop talking so fast,' said John. 'I can't concentrate on what you're saying if you chatter like a monkey.'

'I'm sorry, Sah, but there's no sign of Samson. The police searched the line but didn't find him. Maybe wild animals ate him.'

'Yes, perhaps that's what's happened.'

'There are many Ndebele in Victoria Falls, Sah. I can smell them, and it puts me off eating.'

'Oh good, Elijah, that will save me a lot of money then.'

'No, I was joking, Sah, I can still eat.'

'Let's forget about the Ndebele for now and concentrate on finding the Kagonye woman and her companion. Have you seen or heard anything?'

'No, Sah, but if they got off the train at Dete, it may be two days before they arrive.'

'OK,' said John. 'Check into your lodgings while I check into my hotel. Meet me at the front of my hotel at half past two.'

The Kingdom Hotel was close to the border post with Zambia. John was sure Sarah and Ian would pass that way. He'd booked a room for himself at the hotel and looked for cheaper lodgings for the others, settling on a backpacker hostel, not too far from the Kingdom. Cost was part of the reason that John separated his accommodation from that of his men. But he also realised it would give him more freedom if he did not have them hanging around him.

'Welcome to The Kingdom Hotel, Sir,' said the pretty receptionist. John had a roving eye, and he made a mental note to consider her for attention later. A hotel porter carried his bag up to his room and showed him how the air-conditioning system worked. The porter stood there, shuffling from one foot to the other, waiting for a tip. John always made sure he got his money's worth for every dollar he spent. A US dollar went a long way in Zimbabwe, but no, the porter had seen no one that fitted Ian or Sarah's description.

The room was large with a huge king size bed and a brilliant peacock blue and orange carpet and a railed balcony. A view of golden yellow grass and wide canopied mopane trees with light green, yellow and red leaves gave the room an outdoor feel.

John hung up his two sports jackets and three pairs of slacks in the cupboard and laid out his toiletries in the bathroom. He was fastidious about placing his silver-backed hairbrush and comb side by side, next to his safety razor, shaving brush, shaving cream and a bottle of eau de cologne. He laid them in a neat row and put his toothbrush and toothpaste in a tumbler. Before he knew it, it was time to meet his men.

They were already there, waiting for him at the hotel's front entrance. Akashinga and Elijah were pleased with their lodgings, and John wondered if he'd misjudged their needs. Perhaps something cheaper would have done. The rest of the afternoon they spent sightseeing and getting their bearings. Victoria Falls was not a large area, and it did not take them long to become familiar with the town and its immediate surrounds.

'It's difficult to talk to people here, Sir,' said Elijah. 'Many are Ndebele, and if we ask questions, they might warn Kagonye and the murungu. Also, they might not give us correct information.'

'I'm sure that Kagonye and the murungu have guessed we'll be waiting here for them, Elijah, so don't worry about that.'

In the early evening, John dismissed his men for the rest of the day. 'I will call you if I need you. In the meantime, get in touch with the hotels and see if any guests fit the descriptions of Kagonye and her friend. The others should arrive in the car by late tomorrow. They can keep an eye on the border post while we search the area.'

John returned to his hotel room, trimmed his moustache and took great care in shaving. Army discipline died hard. After a shower, he brushed his teeth and patted on eau de cologne. Next, he selected what he'd wear for the evening. He settled on a lightweight pair of navy-blue trousers and matching socks and a light blue long sleeve shirt. A pair of stylish, tan, crocodile skin shoes and belt set off his clothes well. His gold watch, and gold rings on the ring fingers of both hands, were the finishing touch. John slipped on his lightweight, mid-brown, checked sports jacket and admired himself in the mirror. 'Yes!' The result pleased him.

Sitting at a table in the outdoor bar, John soon made eye-contact with a shapely young African woman perched on a high stool at the bar counter. Her smile showed a brilliant flash of white teeth. She wore a short red dress decorated with gold edgings, and her mid-length hair fell in loose curls around her face. John accosted a waiter and ordered another Scotch on the rocks for himself and a drink for the young lady at the bar. He watched as the waiter spoke to her to get her order. She did not look in John's direction, but when the bartender gave her the drink, she turned and looked at him and smiled. John raised his glass in a salute, and the young woman slipped off the high bar stool and walked across to his table carrying her glass. 'Thank you for the drink.'

'It's my pleasure, won't you join me?' said John, standing up and pulling back a chair for her. It's as easy as that, he thought; like plucking a ripe plum from a small tree. He had no trouble attracting women. John was good-looking, well dressed and smelt of money. He was well off by Zimbabwean standards.

'Are you on business or pleasure?' the young woman asked.

'I planned to be here on business,' John replied, 'but now I'm thinking perhaps it'll be pleasure. I was planning a nice dinner and early to bed. Not alone, of course.'

The young woman smiled. 'What business are you in, if I may ask?'

'I'm a hunter.'

'What do you hunt?'

'Mainly men, but tonight it might be women.'

'And what's your weapon of choice?' said the young woman fixing her gaze on her empty glass.

'I'm sure you've already guessed what that is,' said John, 'waving to attract the waiter's attention.'

* * *

The energetic sex back in his room had tested John's endurance to the limit. He had the crushing realisation he'd spent far too much time behind his desk. John admired the young woman's attractive features. After all the action, she still somehow looked fresh and inviting. She was young and full of energy, but his exertions had drained him. 'How would you like to join me on one of my hunts?' he said.

'It sounds like fun,' she said, leaning closer to him. 'What does it involve?'

'I don't know yet, but we should stay in touch, and I'll call you on your cell phone when I've sighted my quarry. Often hunts need a lure to attract the target. Are you willing to be a lure?'

'Is your target a man this time?'

'Yes, a murungu, but he's travelling with a black woman. I don't know for sure if I'll need your services, but I need to know you're available if I do.'

'I'm available. You can count on me.'

'Good, now how about desert?'

'As I told you, I'm available.'

'What's your name?'

'Suzette.'

'Ah, that's the name of one of my favourite deserts.'

CHAPTER 48

27th August 2009

As dawn broke, Ian and Sarah stirred. Ian felt chilled. A jumper and light jacket didn't keep out the August night chill, even indoors. He itched all over his body. 'Ouch! Fleas are attacking me.' Ian leapt to his feet. 'Fleas invade empty houses. They're everywhere.' He rushed into the shower to wash away as many as possible. Red spots covered him. The shower was like the icy waters of a mountain stream, but preferable to a blanket of fleas to greet the day. Ian did not risk more fleas by using his dirty clothing as a towel as he'd done the previous evening. By now they might also be infested. He used his hands to sweep away as much water as possible off his arms, legs and torso. Then he tried to jump himself dry by hopping on the spot and shaking himself like a dog. The drying process was cold and slow, but the jumping and shaking warmed him up a little. Ian beat his clothes on the hand basin to rid them of remaining fleas, but he knew he might not eradicate them all.

Now it was Sarah's turn. A short time later, she emerged from the bathroom looking cool and fresh. She'd not suffered to the same extent as Ian, who sat cross-legged on the dining room table to keep away from the fleas. Both their backpacks were on the kitchen counter.

'Do you imagine fleas are afraid of heights?' said Sarah, laughing. 'Did you have a dream last night?'

'Yes, I dreamt of the neighbours' kid thumping our wall with his soccer ball.'

'After that story you told me, I dreamt lions attacked us. Villagers in remote areas are helpless against man-eating lions. Why did the authorities not act sooner?'

'Perhaps they took time to recognise the seriousness of the problem, and then the war intervened. But you are right. It should have been dealt with quicker. The lions killed hundreds, and it was the greatest incidence of man-eating in the whole of Africa.'

'Let's get some fresh air,' said Sarah, unbolting the front door. She stood in the doorway and took in a deep breath. Ian moved to join her when she took a quick step back and slammed home both bolts.

'What's the matter?'

Sarah tried to speak, but no words came out. At last she said, 'A lion, lying on the front veranda.'

Ian laughed. 'You're a good actress Sarah. You should be on the stage.'

'No! It's true. The lion was lying on the veranda, right next to me.'

Ian laughed. Was she teasing him after last night's episode? He was about to voice his doubts when the words caught in his throat. The tip of a tail passed the window.

In the few moments it took Sarah to gasp out her story, the huge lioness yawned, got up and walked to the door with slow lazy steps. She stood on her hind legs with her full weight behind her front paws against the door. From inside it sounded like a dull thud. Ian and Sarah held their breath as the old wooden door creaked and groaned under the weight of the lioness. The door flexed, and the two bolts looked under strain, and Ian noticed the screws on the top bolt protrude. Would they hold?

Again, and again, the lioness rose on her hind legs and thumped her front paws against the door, and each time it appeared the hinges might give way or the door splinter. It wouldn't have withstood the weight of a male lion. Males were almost twice as heavy as the females. The dull thuds on the door reminded Ian of something—the noisy kid next door in his dream. The hairs on his neck stood up as he realised the lioness must have tested the door during the night.

'Thank God for the burglar bars on the windows. Where's your gun Sarah?' Ian looked around and noticed with relief that Sarah already had it in her hand.

'If the door breaks, a handgun won't be much use against a full-grown lion.'

'The noise might frighten it away again.'

Suddenly, the dull thuds stopped. All was quiet. 'Let's see where she's gone,' said Ian. 'Don't go too near the windows. If she charges us, she might break through those old bars.' They edged towards the front room windows, nothing there. Next, they crept into the first bedroom. There she was, lying on the front veranda, below the window. The lioness appeared relaxed and in no hurry to go anywhere. 'I'm surprised she came back after yesterday evening.'

'Look,' said Sarah. Several lions sat like posted sentries, fifty metres away.

'We're not leaving until they go, so now's a good time for your story.'

Sarah told Ian the story of her childhood and memories of growing up in a poor but happy home, drawing it out into a long, engrossing tale.

Ian looked at his watch, one o'clock already, lunchtime. Hunger pains gnawed at his stomach. 'Let's check on the lions.' One silent step at a time they approached each window, but there was no sign of them. 'They've gone by the looks of it.'

'What about the side of the house? They might rest in the shade.'

'OK, I tell you what; keep an eye on the front left, and I'll check around the corner on the right. Then we'll do the reverse. Warn me if you see anything.'

'Here, take the Glock, just in case.'

'I'll be quiet. They might not hear me. Their hearing isn't much better than ours.'

Sarah stood in the doorway while Ian crept along the veranda with his weight on the outer edges of his shoes. His father taught him the old army trick to walk silently, and it seemed to work well now. As Ian peered around the corner of the house, a shiver ran down his spine. Nothing there. They must have gone.

'Ian,' shouted Sarah, in a sharp voice.

His heart jumped and hammered in his chest. Ian leapt back and made for the door faster than he'd ever moved. In his haste he bowled over Sarah, who'd been standing in the doorway, and they both sprawled across the floor. Ian jumped to his feet and slammed the door and shot both bolts home. 'Did you see the lions? Where are they?'

'No, I didn't see them. Did you?'

'Then why did you shout my name?' Sarah hadn't called him by his first name before, and it had added to his sense of urgency.

'A truck is coming.'

'What! Is that all?' Then they both burst out laughing. They laughed and laughed until the tears rolled down their cheeks and their sides ached. Ian had survived the biggest fright of his life. 'Lucky I have a strong heart.'

'I got a big fright too. When you raced in so fast, I thought the lions chased you, and you ran for your life.' The two of them burst out laughing again, and even when they recovered a measure of control, they couldn't stop chuckling and giggling.

The truck door slammed, and it brought them back to the present. A tall, strong looking African man approached the house. It surprised him when the front door opened and out stepped two smiling faces, looking pleased to see him. Ian and Sarah, both still amused by their big scare, found it difficult to keep a straight face.

'What are you doing here?' the African asked in a pleasant tone. 'They told me the house was empty. I'm here to pick up the furniture.'

'Ah yes,' said Ian, 'the table and the sideboard. Is it your furniture?'

'No, it belongs to the Parks and Wildlife department. They asked me to pick it up and take it to their new house. But why are you here?'

'We were hiking and got lost. The railway line helped us to avoid getting even more lost. When we saw this house, it was already getting late, so we came in here.'

'If you walked along the dirt track, the main road is not far, maybe twenty kilometres. On the main road you can get a lift, but on the railway line there's nothing. Did you get off the train?'

'The walk along the railway line was more interesting,' said Ian, ignoring the question.

'Haw! It might be more interesting but also more dangerous and much slower. This part of the railway line goes through the national park. There are lions here, and poachers.'

'Humans aren't a natural food for lions,' said Ian, trying to justify their apparent stupidity.

'Lions aren't fussy. They'll even eat rats. Last month, two railwaymen working on the line near here disappeared. No one knows what happened to them, but they say the lions must have got them. They'd eat you for sure. Where are you going? If you're heading for Hwange, I can give you a lift.'

'Thank you,' said Ian, much relieved. 'That will be great.'

'Now as you are here, you can help me load the furniture.'

'Sure. How would you manage if we'd not been here?'

'Ndebele are strong. I would do it on my own, but you are here, so I can use you.'

After struggling to get the heavy mahogany furniture onto the truck, they were ready to leave. Ian and Sarah picked up their backpacks and jumped into the cab. The truck bumped and bounced along the rough dirt track and, with no seat belts to secure them, threw the occupants from side to side. 'My name is Aaron,' said the African driver. Ian introduced himself and Sarah. Aaron said, 'does the woman not speak?'

'Yes,' said Sarah, irritated by the chauvinistic tone of the comment, 'I speak.'

'Ah! You're a Shona. A white man and a Shona woman walking along the railway line through the national park. That is strange. Maybe you are running from someone? But don't worry. In this area, we don't like the government. You can be safe with me.'

'How far is Dete?' said Ian, changing the subject.

'Dete by road from here is forty or fifty kilometres, but by railway it's only twenty. Why do you go to Hwange?'

'We want to go to Victoria Falls.'

'I'm going there tomorrow. If you stay here tonight, I can take you.'

'Where can we stay in Hwange?'

'Better, you stay in my village. Hwange is a small place. People can see you. I'll take you to my village first, and my wives will look after you while I deliver the furniture. I'll be about two hours.'

Ian and Sarah exchanged glances. Could they trust this man they'd just met? What choice did they have? What if he reported their presence to the police? Aaron did not wait for their acceptance. He'd already decided for them. They bounced along the rough dirt road with its deep ruts made by tyre tracks in the last rains and hardened like concrete by the African sun. The old truck shook and vibrated, sounding more like a tractor than a truck. It took half an hour to reach the main road where they turned left towards Hwange. The tarred road was smooth and in good condition, but the old truck shook and rattled as if it hadn't noticed the change in surface. After ten minutes on the main road, Aaron turned right onto a dirt road. A quarter of an hour later, they arrived at a cluster of about eight huts on a grassy knoll with views in all directions.

A tall, dignified looking woman came to meet the truck. 'This is my first wife, Awande.' Everyone you see here is part of my family. I have two wives and six children, and my brother also lives here with his wife and two children. They are away at present, so you can sleep in their hut. All the children, and Aaron's second wife, Fikile, came running to greet Aaron and stare at the visitors. Guests, unrelated to the family, were rare. Aaron left Ian and Sarah in the care of his wives when he drove off to deliver the furniture. The wives fussed around them and made them comfortable, and Ian and Sarah relaxed. They put their rucksacks into the hut Awande showed them.

Two hours later, when the shadows were lengthening, Aaron returned. The wives prepared food for the evening meal. Aaron brought with him a quantity of the cheap, maize based, opaque Chibuku beer. With its thick sediment, they needed to shake the container before each mouthful. That's why the Africans called it *shake-shake*. Ian didn't like it when he'd tried it as a youngster, but now he was famished. They said Chibuku was the beer you could eat. Despite its milky white appearance and strong yeast flavour, it now seemed like one of the best beers he'd tasted. Sarah gulped it down with no trouble and clearly was no stranger to the brew.

Soon, a real party atmosphere developed in the little village. The fire crackled and spat, and the warmth was a wonderful contrast to their previous two chilly nights. Drinking Chibuku on an empty stomach is never a good idea, and it was a relief for Ian when the wives arrived with plates of sadza and gravy and strips of meat for cooking over the open fire. Sadza was the thick savoury dish of cooked, ground maize meal, looking like thick semolina. Ian never cared for it, but now with his hunger, it seemed like a dish fit for a king. It was the staple food of Africans, and many whites enjoyed it at a *braaivleis*.

Ian enjoyed the night. It was like talking to old friends. Sarah and the wives got on well despite their differing backgrounds. She spoke fair Ndebele, and that helped build the jovial atmosphere. Ian had forgotten much of the Ndebele he picked up as a child on the family farm, but he still knew a little *kitchen kaffir*. This was a mix of essential African and English words, and it marked him as a white of local origin. But both of Aaron's wives and most of the children spoke English. Communication was not a problem. The children ran around laughing and enjoying the novelty of the strangers in their midst.

It was late when the women and children went to bed, and Sarah withdrew, leaving Ian and Aaron to men's talk. 'Aaron, you have a good family, lovely wives and nice children. You must be proud of them.'

'Yes, I am proud of them. But you have a fine woman too.'

'She's not my woman. We are just travelling together. She already has a man.'

'We Africans know these things. If she's not your woman now, she will be soon. I can tell she wants to be your woman, but perhaps loyalty is preventing her. I am thinking you like her too. Where is her man?'

'Ah! It's a question only the authorities can answer. He left for work one morning about six months ago, and neither she nor his family have heard from him since then. They're all worried. His employer said he might have gone to South Africa, but in that case, why didn't he tell her or his family of his intentions? And if he got to South Africa why didn't he make contact?'

'Perhaps he is dead. Many Zimbabweans have gone to South Africa, but it's a dangerous journey, and people have died. Crocodiles and lions have taken many of them. I have heard of this often. Your woman understands he is dead and has accepted this, so now she is free for you.'

Ian ignored Aaron's comment and took a swig of Chibuku and stared into the fire. 'Do animals from the park come here?'

'Not too much. They stay on the other side of the railway line. Once, long ago, an elephant came. Now, we see only buck sometimes.'

'What time do we leave for Victoria Falls tomorrow?'

'In Africa we leave when we leave. No hurry, I don't have a boss to worry me. Today is Tuesday, so tomorrow we can leave at Wednesday o'clock or Thursday o'clock or even Friday o'clock.' They both laughed at Aaron's little joke.

'It's good. My Chibuku needs rest,' said Ian, adding to Aaron's joke.

After saying goodnight to Aaron, Ian walked back to the hut. Without windows, the lack of fresh air contributed to the musty odour—the smell of Africa—that Ian recognised from his childhood. The servants' quarters always smelt like that, and he found it cosy and comforting. Ian curled up on the reed mat on the floor with the two blankets Awande gave him. He was comfortable enough, but competing thoughts crowded his mind, and he found it difficult to sleep. It was a long time since he'd enjoyed such a sociable and happy evening with friends. Barbecues at his parents' house in Melbourne were fun, but he'd done little socialising apart from his visits to Johannesburg. His work absorbed him. Aaron's family made him feel they were amongst old friends.

What would his father have thought if he could have seen him that evening sitting around the fire with his new friends? And what he would think if he could see him now, lying on the floor of a *rondavel* in a little African village in the bush, with Sarah breathing deeply in her sleep next to him? Ian almost laughed out loud. The thought amused him. Fancy old Aaron trying to be the matchmaker! Sarah was an attractive woman, but she belonged to another. Was Aaron right in thinking she'd accepted Thomas was dead? She never acted as if she believed it. And they came from such different worlds. No, he couldn't imagine them being together. And what would his father say? He'd have a heart attack. Ian didn't believe, deep down, his father was a racist. He always treated the servants well, and he showed them respect, but he was a colonialist at heart. He always said the blacks needed the guiding hand of the whites. Ian knew his father would find it difficult to accept any intimate association with a black. In his view, it would be wrong.

CHAPTER 49

28th August 2009

THE small doorway to the hut framed the first light of dawn. Sarah stirred, woken by the movement at the door. Fikile brought hot, sweet tea for them. 'Wow!' said Ian, 'room service. I could get used to this.' He sat up and groaned. His throbbing head reminded him of the previous night's Chibuku. His mouth was dry, and his lips stuck to his teeth. The welcome tea did much to relieve his morning-after mouth, but his head still hurt, and his stomach was uneasy. Sarah seemed even brighter than usual. 'Didn't someone say, "a man's got to know his limitations"?'

Ian relished the breakfast of sweet oatmeal porridge with fresh goat's milk, toast with jam and more tea. It made him feel so much better. After breakfast the children were ready to walk to school. There were excited goodbyes. The boys shook hands, and the girls curtsied. Aaron's oldest daughter, the twelve-year-old Bongile, shyly shook Ian's hand and curtsied and then shook Sarah's hand. Without warning, she gave Sarah a light kiss on the cheek before running off giggling with the other children.

At noon, Ian and Sarah said goodbye to Awande and Fikile. There were many thanks, good wishes and promises to return one day. Ian was sorry to be leaving so soon after meeting them. He would have liked to know Aaron and his family better.

Aaron turned the key in the ignition. The engine of the old truck cranked and started, coughed and died. Aaron pulled the choke and tried again. This time the engine roared and raced before he eased the choke home. He grated the gear stick into first, and off they trundled. The old truck bumped, rattled and squeaked along the dirt track as it bounced over rocks and potholes. A quarter of an hour later they reached the main road and turned for Victoria Falls.

Soon an African store came into view, and Aaron stopped to buy cigarettes. 'It's best you stay in the truck,' he said to Sarah. 'The police may have been making enquiries about a white man and a black woman travelling together.' Ian walked into the store with Aaron. The friendly storekeeper greeted them in the dark, cool interior. Two African men leaning on the counter, barely glanced up when they entered. It looked like they were there for a social lunchtime chat, rather than to buy anything.

Full shelves catered for the day-to-day needs of the local rural population—blankets, pots and pans, tin plates and mugs, maize meal, salt, sugar, cooking oil, matches, candles, sweets and biscuits. Paraffin lamps hung from low beams, and tins of paraffin sat on the floor, and hoes for tilling the soil rested in one corner of the store.

Ian bought cool drinks and packets of potato chips and returned to the truck. Aaron bought a packet of cigarettes and offered one to the storekeeper. While they smoked, they chatted. When Aaron returned to the truck, he said, 'My friend says there has been no unusual police activity in the area.'

Starting the truck and coaxing it into gear seemed to be a skill Aaron still needed to master. The cogs grated whenever Aaron depressed the clutch and tried to change gear. Perhaps this was a rare instance where the workman could blame his tools. The truck was already old but getting older fast with Aaron's driving. Within the hour they passed Hwange, visible in the distance from the main road high above the town. 'We'll be at the falls by three o'clock,' said Aaron. 'What will you do? Where will you stay?'

'We haven't booked a hotel, but we'd like to stay for a day or two and then cross into Zambia.'

'You will stand out at the Victoria Falls Hotel. A smaller hotel or one farther from the centre may be better for you. The Ilala Lodge is a small hotel close to the falls, and you'd soon know if anybody over there concerned you. Or, the Elephant Hills Hotel might be safer for you. It's about four kilometres from the falls, and it's a bigger hotel, so you would be less noticeable there. The hotels are not full these days. There are too few visitors.'

Aaron looked in the wing mirror and frowned. 'Is anything wrong?' said Ian.

'A black Mercedes car has been following us almost all the way from the Hwange turnoff.' Ian looked in the wing mirror and saw the black car about a hundred metres behind them. 'It's kept that distance behind us the whole time,' said Aaron. 'It would be faster than this truck, but they don't seem to want to pass.'

'Go slower and we'll see what they do.'

But when Aaron slowed down so did the black car. 'It still won't pass.'

'Let's stop for ten minutes for a cool drink, and we can see what they do then.'

Aaron pulled over into a lay-by, and they watched the black Mercedes with its tinted windows drive past. Ian passed the cool drinks around and tore open a packet of potato chips. 'Do you reckon they may be CIO, Sarah?'

'Black Mercedes are often government cars, so they might be CIO.'

'What about your lot?'

'No, we didn't have luxury cars. We always kept a low profile.' They sat in silence watching the minutes tick by on the old truck's clock. Soon it was time to go. Aaron started the engine and grated the gear lever into first. The old truck rattled and shuddered in the low gears. One kilometre down the road, Sarah said, 'There they are.' The black Mercedes stood parked on the side of the road with four African men leaning against it, smoking cigarettes. All wore dark suits, white shirts and dark ties, with aviator sunglasses perched on their noses. 'Yes, they could be CIO,' said Sarah.

When their truck passed the black Mercedes, the four men climbed back into the car and resumed following them. 'We can't outrun them in this old truck,' said Ian.

'No,' said Aaron, 'but I'll try.' But when he sped up, the black Mercedes kept pace. When he slowed, the black Mercedes slowed. 'Uh-oh!' said Aaron, 'roadblock ahead.' Two policemen stood at the roadblock waving them down to stop. They came to a halt, and the black Mercedes pulled up about ten metres behind them. A policeman came to Aaron's window and said, 'Wait here,' and then moved on to the black Mercedes.

After a few minutes the black Mercedes sped past, and the policeman came back. 'Who were those men, Officer?' said Aaron. 'They followed us from the Hwange turnoff and wouldn't overtake our old truck. They look suspicious.'

'That's what they said about you,' said the policeman. Then switching from English to Ndebele, he said, 'Is this woman your wife?'

'No, she's my brother's wife,' said Aaron in English. 'She's been visiting my village and now I'm taking her home.'

'Village women don't dress like that.'

'No,' said Aaron in Ndebele, 'she is one of those empty-headed city women who spend all their time on their appearance. I tell my brother to swap her for a hard-working village woman, but he won't listen. He's as empty-headed as her.'

'And who's the murungu?' asked the policeman.

'He's my boss' brother, here from South Africa to visit the falls.'

'I must search their bags.'

Aaron got out and opened the back of the truck for the policeman to search Ian and Sarah's backpacks.

Ian remembered Sarah's handgun. 'Oh no, are they going to find your Glock?'

'No, I've got it tucked into the back of my jeans under my windcheater. I knew we might have to pass through roadblocks.'

'Phew! It's a good thing you remembered. I'd forgotten all about the roadblocks.'

'What about your passports?'

'They're in my jacket pocket.'

'Yes, mine too.'

'Where are the immigration stamps?'

'They're right in the bottom compartment under my backpack. They often forget to search there.'

'Hell! Let's hope so.'

'The inks are in my makeup bag with my nail varnish. He might not notice them.'

They waited with fingers crossed. The minutes dragged. 'They're taking a long time,' said Ian.

The policeman returned with Aaron to the front of the truck. 'OK, you can go.' Aaron and Ian exchanged glances. They waved goodbye to the policeman, and the three of them all breathed a sigh of relief as the roadblock disappeared into the distance.

'What did he say?' said Ian.

'It was strange. He searched everything and then said African women should stick to red nail varnish.'

Ian and Sarah burst out laughing. Sarah's ruse worked.

'Oh, and thanks for your comment about *the empty-headed city women*,' said Sarah in mock indignation. 'And you think I should be swapped, do you?'

Aaron smiled. 'How else could I explain why you dressed so well?' His face told them he'd enjoyed that little joke with the policeman. 'And don't worry; your white friend would never swap you.'

Twenty kilometres farther on, the black Mercedes raced down the road towards them. 'Here they come again,' said Aaron. The Mercedes sped by. 'It looks like they're patrolling this road.'

'I wonder why they told the policeman we looked suspicious?' said Ian.

'I expect it's because they guessed we didn't want them following us,' said Sarah.

'Would the CIO be looking for us?'

'No, my lot never shared anything.'

'Close now,' said Aaron, relaxing after the tense drive. 'When the river is high, the spray from the falls rises three hundred metres into the air, and you can see it from fifty kilometres away. It looks like the smoke from a bushfire. That's why they call it Mosi oa Tunya, the smoke that thunders.'

'When is it at its peak?' asked Ian.

'The river is too high in March and April. From July the water gets less, and it will be low from September to January.'

'And when is it at its lowest?'

'In November and early December, it's too low.'

The heat in the cab became oppressive even with the windows open. 'It's getting hot in here,' said Ian.

'I think the engine is overheating,' said Aaron. 'It's even hotter and more humid in the Zambezi Valley. In winter it can be twenty-five degrees centigrade high in daytime and six degrees low at night.'

* * *

With no further roadblocks and no sign of the black Mercedes, they'd been lucky. Aaron took Ian and Sarah for a drive around the town to help them get their bearings. Warthogs, monkeys and baboons roamed in the town centre. He drove them past the picturesque railway station and the grand old Victoria Falls Hotel. 'It's a good hotel, but you'd be noticed there.' He turned the truck into Zambezi Drive and parked near Livingstone Statue, to let them view the falls near Cataract Island.

'I think the Elephant Hills Resort would be OK,' said Ian. 'It's far enough out of the town centre and big enough for us not to stand out.'

In September 1977, a rocket fired from Zambia hit the hotel's thatched roof, and the whole place went up in flames. It used to be a boutique hotel known as the Elephant Hills Country Club and Casino. Now it was on a far larger scale and a popular venue for business conferences. The first hint of the change was the large thatched front entrance to the grounds with guards on duty at a wheeled boom gate.

'Be careful, there're few tourists these days, so people will notice you.'

Ian and Sarah thanked Aaron for his hospitality and promised to keep in touch. 'Aaron, you have a lovely family. I would like you to take this to help towards Bongile's school fees,' said Ian, handing Aaron two hundred U.S. dollars. Aaron had told Ian the night before that once the girls completed primary school, they would have to leave. The school fees were too high, so Bongile would finish school this year.

'Now you force me to send Bongile to high school. I will use this opportunity for her and try to keep her in school until the sixth form. Thank you, my friend.'

'*Hamba kahle*—go well,' said Aaron.

'*Sahle kahle*—stay well,' said Ian.

With those words they parted. Ian and Sarah passed the stone columns at the hotel entrance and mounted the wide front steps to the circular hotel lobby. Dry stone walls and traditional African motifs decorated the lobby area. A friendly female receptionist greeted them and gave them a top floor room facing the golf course. 'Our guests like that view the best,' she said. 'Enjoy your stay.'

They booked in under their false married names. Ian thought it too risky to use their real names. He would also pay in U.S. dollars, as he dared not use his credit card when he suspected the authorities might check the hotels in their search for them.

'What a lovely big room!' said Sarah. 'And the beautiful views of the golf course and the river.' Though not as glamourous as the room she had at the Peninsula Hotel in Sharm el-Sheikh, the setting was every bit as romantic. 'After the last three nights, it's wonderful to be in civilisation. I'm booking the first bath.'

'Yes, go ahead,' said Ian, 'I'll enjoy the views from the balcony. If I see any wildlife, I'll come and tell you.'

'You can shout it through the door, thanks.'

Sarah emerged from the bathroom, and now it was Ian's turn. Ah! What luxury. After roughing it for the past few days, soaking in a deep, hot bath was heaven. Although it was just their fourth day since the comparative comfort of Bulawayo, it seemed much longer. Ian relaxed in the bath and washed his hair. It made all the difference. He trimmed the moustache he'd grown since leaving Harare, but his beard remained too short to trim. After combing his hair and brushing his teeth, he felt rejuvenated. He put on his cleanest shirt and freshest pair of slacks, collected his dirty clothes for the laundry and stepped out into the bedroom. He stopped at the sight of Sarah.

'Wow!' She looked radiant in a bright yellow, belted dress and mid-heeled light brown sandals. Again, he saw how attractive she was. She didn't appear as if she'd spent three nights roughing it. 'Wow! Ian said again. Was that dress in your backpack?' Before he could stop himself, he blurted out, 'You look wonderful!' Ian felt a little sheepish and annoyed with himself after his comment. Up till now he'd played it cool. Sarah didn't need to have her self-esteem boosted as she already had more than enough. The way she spoke and reacted to him made that clear.

'Thank you, I ironed it while I waited for you. And you don't look too bad.'

'Let's have a drink in the Game View Bar downstairs,' said Ian. 'I could do with a cold beer or two before dinner. We'll leave if we don't like the looks of anyone down there.'

'Yes, that would be nice thank you.'

Five o'clock; the warm air lingered before the cool of the evening. A dozen people occupied the bar lounge, but Sarah judged them to be regular tourists. Like us, she thought, before the irony of that struck her. Tourists entered Zimbabwe to visit the falls, but she and Ian came to the falls to exit Zimbabwe. The first sips of the cold Zambezi beers trickled down their throats.

Sarah attracted admiring glances from other guests, and to his surprise, Ian realised he was proud to be her escort. Much changed in his way of thinking in the short time he'd been in Zimbabwe. Aaron and his matchmaking triggered something deep inside him that made him a little uneasy. A sudden possessiveness, like the flow of an incoming tide, flooded Ian's mind. It was an uncomfortable, if not a frightening feeling. To see Sarah as a tolerated nuisance made it a lot easier for him.

They drank Zambezi beers while watching warthogs and antelope on the golf course. They watched the beautiful African sunset and then made their way to the restaurant for dinner. Ian pulled out the dining chair for Sarah and helped her select from the menu. Crocodile tail steak was a first for them. In the quiet restaurant, the polite and helpful waiters hovered in the background.

After the tasty meal, Ian said, 'Crocodile tastes like chicken, don't you think?'

'I thought it tasted more like snake,' said Sarah, with a mischievous grin.

Ian laughed, 'Yes, I've heard snake also tastes like chicken.'

A third Zambezi beer, and Sarah was becoming giggly. How had she managed all that Chibuku? Three beers were also enough for him.

'We can have a drink on our balcony,' said Ian.

'Mmhm, let's do that.'

Ian did not miss the tone in Sarah's voice, and it added to the sexual tension in the air. He sensed it and wondered if she noticed it too. He blamed Aaron for the sudden change in his attitude towards her. Sarah couldn't have overheard his chat with Aaron. Had one of Aaron's wives said something to her? There was much merriment and laughter between the three women as they conversed in Ndebele. Ian couldn't follow the chatter, but it crossed his mind they might have been sharing a private joke.

Back in their room they settled for tea on the balcony and gazed at the millions of stars in the Milky Way. The setting stirred Ian's acute consciousness of Sarah's proximity. The hairs on the back of his hand, beside hers on the balcony rail, stood up, and his arm tingled. She seemed like an electric current, drawing every atom of his being towards her. They'd shared the super king-size bed for over six months, but that was a practical necessity for sheltering her. Their single physical contact was when he bowled her over in the doorway of the isolated bungalow. But tonight, was different. Old Aaron's words seemed to have opened a flood of feelings and awareness in Ian. He'd always considered her attractive, but now she seemed so bloody beautiful. What was happening to him? Was he going mad? It must have been those beers.

Had Sarah detected the change in his manner? She seemed warmer and softer this evening. He knew he was more attentive, and he'd dropped his feigned indifference to her. When their eyes met, she held his gaze for a moment longer than usual.

Chatting with Sarah was always easy, but tonight, Ian searched his mind for what to say. His mouth was dry, and his tongue seemed too large. The beautiful night sky helped mask awkward silences. They both seemed lost in their own thoughts as they admired the stars. What was she thinking? The sky was clear, and by the minute the countless stars seemed to increase as their eyes got used to the dark. It was many years since he'd spent any time observing the Milky Way. Ian didn't think he'd ever seen it in Melbourne. But now, his mind raced, and his palms were clammy. It seemed like a first date, and for Ian, a long-forgotten nervousness replaced the earlier sexual tension. Sarah often made it clear she was not available, and now the shadow of Thomas grew by the minute.

Ian glanced at Sarah. 'We'd better turn in if we want to go to the falls early before it gets too busy.' She smiled, but her face told him nothing, no flicker of disappointment or surprise. Had she imagined something might happen that evening? Earlier on, walking back to their room, he sensed she might welcome a move from him. The evening air hung heavy with the prospect of romance. What did her *Mmhm, let's do that* mean? Perhaps he'd misread her. Now she was inscrutable. Ian cursed himself for his cowardice. The moment had passed.

Sarah soon fell asleep. On most nights, Ian slept well, but tonight he found it difficult to switch off his thoughts. His newfound interest in Sarah made things more complex. He'd planned to help her leave the country and then return to Harare and complete his novel. Now he'd an increased concern for her welfare. Before leaving the country, Sarah wanted to view the falls from the Zimbabwean side which had the best views, but was she being foolish? Ian knew the risk in hanging around the area longer than necessary. Why take that chance? Maybe in the morning he'd try to convince her to abandon the idea. The quicker she left Zimbabwe the better, but he knew it was next to impossible to convince Sarah to change her mind about anything.

The thoughts went around in his head. What should he do? The book was unfinished, and he'd not visited much of the country. But now, he didn't want to part from Sarah. If the COU or police caught her, what would happen to her? If they caught him, what would happen to him? How did everything get so complicated? The incident on the train might be a big problem for him if he remained in Zimbabwe. Also, the trumped-up murder charge remained, and his supposed involvement with the MFF that Chief Inspector Chamisa mentioned. Was anyone still looking for them? It wasn't even three days since they abandoned the train. He couldn't imagine the authorities giving up the chase so soon. Ian was sure someone would lie in wait for them at Victoria Falls.

Chapter 50

29th August 2009

Ian and Sarah were ready to go by five in the morning. They planned an early start and view the falls before the other tourists arrived. The entrance gate to the falls opened at six, and Ian talked Sarah into making it a quick visit. They allowed an hour to walk from the hotel to the falls. It was dark, not yet daylight. There were warnings of elephant and buffalo in the hours of darkness, but they'd walked through the Hwange National Park which was a much greater risk. Ian carried his camera and money, but the rest of their valuables remained locked in the mini safe back at the hotel.

Windcheaters protected Ian and Sarah from the nip in the early morning breeze. The cold made it a comfortable walk, and they kept up a good pace. The air was still fresh and bracing when they arrived at the entrance to the Rainforest Walk a few minutes before opening time. Ian paid the entrance fee, and they passed through the gate and took the left path towards the Livingstone Statue. The first turn to the right took them along the path that ran parallel to the falls.

In the early morning light, the path they followed took them past exotic tropical plants and a dense growth of waterboom and red milk-wood trees. Other vegetation included wild date palms, fig trees such as the Cape fig, and strangling creepers and lianas—the woody vines that hung down from above in tortured twists. Ferns and a variety of small herbaceous plants covered the ground. Other small plants and long grass formed a border on the edge of the gorge into which the raging waters plunged. For a large part of the year the spray from the falls kept the area soaking wet.

Ian and Sarah stuck to the main path, bypassing the lookout points close to the edge of the gorge. They walked on to Danger Point, which lay opposite the Rainbow Falls and the Knife Edge in Zambia.

The water flow, though not at its peak, created a deafening roar that limited any attempt at conversation. Ian and Sarah stood side by side watching the spectacle in silence, overawed by its magnificence. The grandeur of the vision was humbling as the unforgettable sight burned into their memories. Nature gave a breathtaking display of power and beauty as the water tumbled one hundred and eight metres into the gorge. No film or photograph could ever do it justice.

Sarah found it hard to believe she'd waited so long to view the mighty scene. Ian knew of whites who'd lived all their lives in Bulawayo without once visiting the falls. The railway and a good road served the area, but some never made the four-hundred-and-forty-kilometre trip. Perhaps they thought they'd see it someday, but someday often never comes, and time runs out. Others came from across the globe to view it. Close by, the Hwange National Park boasted all the big game of the Kruger National Park in South Africa, and far less traffic. This small area held all the wonders of Africa, and if that didn't attract those local whites, what could?

Apart from their shirts under their windcheaters, Ian and Sarah's clothes got soaked from the spray of the falls, but their baseball caps did a fair job of keeping their hair dry. Ian tried to keep his digital camera out of the spray. He would whip it out from inside his windcheater, snap a photo of Sarah standing in front of the falls, shove it back into his pocket and hope for the best. It wasn't the best place to check the quality of the photos. They walked on to the view of the Victoria Falls Bridge where photography was easier. The massive gorge dwarfed the bridge, making it look fragile and precarious.

'Let's head back to those lookout points we passed earlier,' said Ian.

'Will you get decent photos there?'

'Some views have less spray, but it would be impossible during the high-water season.'

First, they made their way to Horseshoe Falls View with its light spray, where Ian could keep his camera dry. Then they moved on to the next lookout point. Sarah laughed at Ian's attempts to take photos.

'Come on, Sarah, stand beside the Livingstone Island sign.' The spray was heavier here. Sarah stood with the falls in the background and smiled. Ian raised the camera to look through the viewfinder when a loud voice interrupted.

'Miss Kagonye, Mr Sanders, what a pleasant surprise to meet you here.'

Ian spun around to face a big African man with a moustache. Neither he nor Sarah noticed him approaching. He was one of the two men who had searched Ian's hotel room on his first morning in Harare. Now, standing in front of him, the large man seemed bigger than Ian remembered. In his hand he held a thick walking stick with a brass handle.

'So, you found the room maid Mr Sanders,' said the man with a thin smile.

'I thought I recognised you and your partner on the train,' said Ian. 'When did you realise we'd left Harare?'

'When you suddenly left your apartment, we guessed you'd head to Bulawayo on your way to South Africa or Botswana.'

'How did you discover I was in the apartment?' said Sarah.

'We asked your caretaker to report anything unusual to us. But the silly woman went to the police who bungled your arrest. She told them Mr Sanders' maid didn't recognise her when she walked past the apartment. It made her suspicious. If she'd reported back to us, we may have saved ourselves all this trouble.'

'How did you pick up our trail?' said Ian.

'We lost track of you for a short time, but it didn't take us long to trace you to the Bulawayo Rainbow Hotel. Thanks to you, we found out how loyal the forger was.'

'If you knew we were at the Rainbow Hotel, why didn't you pick us up then?'

'When you booked train tickets for the falls, we thought it might be easier to deal with you on the train.'

'You mean it would have been easier to get rid of us on the train.'

'Yes, just like you got rid of my partner Samson. Now you must come back to Harare to answer for your crimes.'

'And let's not forget your murder of Morris Ndlovu,' said Ian.

'I remember you from Sharm el-Sheikh,' said Sarah. 'Are you with the COU?' 'Can you tell me where Thomas Chimedza is?'

'Thomas is at our mine.'

Sarah gasped. 'Thomas is still alive? What mine? Where is it?'

The man smiled. 'You misunderstand Miss Kagonye. When Thomas helped us dump heavy sacks into a mineshaft, he lost his balance.'

'I don't believe it. If it was an accident, why didn't Jedson tell me or Thomas' family about it, and why didn't they recover his body? Someone must have pushed him.'

'No matter, he was a traitor like your father and deserved to die.'

'My father and Thomas weren't traitors.'

'Thomas squealed like a pig on his way to the bottom. No one will ever find him. Even if the fall didn't kill him, he would have drowned or starved. Captain John said a dog should die like a dog.'

'But why kill him?'

'He snooped around the office and listened in on Captain John's phone calls.'

'Why have you been following us? Why does the COU want me?'

'You've been naughty Miss Kagonye. You never told us you had a relationship with Thomas.'

'How did you find out?'

'After Thomas fell into the mine, we had to cover ourselves, so Captain John sent me to his house to enquire why he hadn't come to work that day. Thomas hadn't told his parents about his work. His mother said he hadn't come home the previous evening, and he'd not been in touch with you, his fiancée.'

'But why is the COU after me?'

'Thomas Chimedza knew too much. What did he tell you?'

'He didn't tell me anything. What did he know?'

'We should ask you that question, Ms Kagonye. He was your fiancé.'

'We're leaving Zimbabwe today,' said Ian, lamely. 'We can't go back to Harare.'

'And you, Mr Sanders, were foolish to involve yourself in our country's affairs. Now we must assume you also know too much.'

'So what happens now?' said Ian, his voice croaking.

'Captain John is eager to talk to Miss Kagonye. Our instructions are to take you both back to Harare or finish it here if you resist.'

Ian looked past the big African, looking for an escape route.

'Don't be a hero Mr Sanders. Even if you got away, your girlfriend here won't, and she's the one we really want.'

The thunderous noise of the falls forced them to shout to each other. This early in the morning, there was nobody to help or witness what was happening.

The big man took a step forward, and Ian stepped back. Another step forward and another step back. Ian tried to stay out of the big man's reach, but at the end of the path on the edge of the gorge, he could retreat no further. Sarah stood behind him. There was no escape. As quick as a flash the big man lifted his walking stick and swung the brass handle at Ian like the head of an axe. Sarah caught Ian by his shoulders and pulled him back hard. The heavy brass handle whistled past Ian's face and within an inch of his right knee, embedding itself in the soft earth beside the path. Ian leapt forward and grabbed the brass handle and pulled the walking stick with all his might. But the big African was strong, and Ian couldn't wrench it from his grasp. He needed to use all his strength to avoid losing his own grip on the handle.

The two men strained to keep their hold on the walking stick, being careful not to slip on the wet path. They both placed their right foot forward, leaning back with all their weight. As they struggled, bit by bit, they rotated in their desperate bid to keep their balance and their hold on the walking stick. Ian couldn't match the strength of the big man, so Sarah put her arms around Ian's waist to add her weight to his efforts. Inch by inch they circled, and neither man gained any advantage.

Slowly, they turned through almost one hundred and eighty degrees when Ian saw an opportunity. He heaved the walking stick with all his strength, and as the big African responded, Ian let go of the stick and fell back onto Sarah in a heap on the path. The big African flew backwards, trying to keep his balance; one, two, three, four steps before he fell and slid on the wet grass. He tried to stop his slide, but there was nowhere to get a hold. The big man slipped towards the sheer edge of the gorge. Desperately, he clawed at the ground searching for something to grab. In a frantic last effort, he seized long clumps of grass and hung on, but his legs dangled in mid-air.

The walking stick lay on the ground where the big African had fallen. Sarah picked it up and moved towards the edge. The man's eyes widened in terror as he struggled to keep his hold. The whites of his eyes against his black skin intensified the panic in his face. Sarah raised the stick. 'Now my friend, let's hear who else squeals like a pig on his way to the bottom.'

'No Sarah!' Ian shouted. 'We're not like them. Give me the stick.'

To his amazement, Sarah meekly handed him the walking stick. 'Here!' shouted Ian, holding out the walking stick to the desperate man. 'Grab the stick.' The big African tried to reach for the walking stick with his left hand. As he did so, his whole weight transferred to the clump of grass in his right hand, and the roots pulled free. Ian and Sarah stood mesmerised as the face of the man fell away from them, deep into the gorge. The thunderous roar of the raging water drowned out any sound. He seemed to fall in silent slow motion with his eyes fixed on the end of the walking stick Ian held out.

Ian and Sarah stood frozen, staring into the gorge where the man had fallen. There was no hope of recovering his body. By the time anyone missed him and worked out what may have happened, the crocodiles would have had their fill. The four-and-a-half-metre monsters lurked in the gorges below the falls, waiting for the cascade to deliver drowned creatures to them.

'Let's forget the sightseeing and get going,' said Ian, quietened by the experience. 'There may also be others here looking for us. This guy got lucky, in a way. We don't want any of the others getting lucky, do we?'

They were both pensive walking out of the rainforest. Sarah spoke first. 'I'm glad I didn't knock him off the edge of the gorge. Thank you for stopping me. No matter how much someone deserves to die if you kill them it stays with you all your life. It's not like in war when you are shooting at anonymous figures. Today was close and personal. I'm pleased he fell, but I'm glad I didn't cause it.'

'Yes, even the death of an evil person is sobering. It was pitch-black when I kicked that man off the train. I never saw his eyes, and I didn't know it was a human being climbing through the window. Today was different, and I felt sorry for him when he fell, even though he was a monster.'

'I can't believe I was one of them.'

'Yes, but you didn't know everything they did.'

'No, but I had an idea, and though I only did translations, Thomas warned me that down the line I would have to become active and follow orders. While I was in the COU, someone else always did the dirty work, and it didn't affect me. Thomas worried about it, but I was in denial. Now, it makes me sick to think of it.'

'It's time for you to move on, Sarah.'

'Yes, but what of those poor people Thomas and I helped the COU to trace? I realise now that everything we did was feeding The Leopard.'

Ian and Sarah walked the rest of the way back to the hotel in silence, each with their own thoughts. By the time they'd covered the four kilometres back to the hotel, their clothes had dried in the warm morning sunshine. They almost missed breakfast, and the waiters had cleared the tables. After bacon and eggs and several cups of tea they felt ready for the border post and collected their backpacks. They missed the shuttle bus, so it meant another walk for them. Half past nine in the morning, and this time the walk was much warmer and far less comfortable. They'd scheduled their check out for the day after next but said nothing to the hotel about leaving early. It was best if the hotel staff believed they were still there. It would give them plenty of time to get well away from the area before their pursuers worked out they'd gone.

Sarah would cross the border first. Together, they would attract attention if the authorities alerted the border post to be on the lookout for them. Once she'd pass through, Sarah would call Ian on his cell phone, and he'd follow. Both would use their false passports. In Zambia, they'd use the stamps and ink that Morris gave them to copy the exit and entry stamps into their genuine passports.

They timed their border crossing for mid-morning. Ian hoped it would be busy by then and they might be subject to less scrutiny. He held his breath as Sarah said goodbye and entered the Zimbabwean border post. Customs and immigration, nerve-racking at the best of times, was downright scary when going through as fugitives on false passports. His stomach knotted. How long before Sarah phoned? In the meantime, he would look for a decent toilet nearby.

Ian found a place under a shady tree to wait for Sarah's call. Moments later, a serious looking Sarah emerged from the building. Oh no! What happened? No one escorted her, but she didn't look happy. Sarah caught sight of Ian waiting in the shade, and she hurried across to him. 'I can't go through the border, Jedson's in there, watching everyone who goes up to the counter. If the whole COU is here, they must be desperate to catch us. Let's get out of here fast before we're spotted.'

'Do you think he might have seen you?'

'No, I don't think so.'

It was too dangerous to stay in the small, town centre, so Ian and Sarah headed back to the hotel. This, their fourth long walk, and their backpacks feeling heavier in the day's heat. They returned to their room and put the backpacks away. Ian suggested a plan. 'Let's have lunch and then we'll go to the boathouse and see if we can hire a boat to cross the river. Take everything we wouldn't want customs and immigration to find. Tomorrow, I'll try to go through the border post. I've never met Jedson, so he may not recognise me with this beard and moustache.' Ian had not shaved since their sudden departure from Harare. Even the photo Morris took for his false passport was now out of date. The big African at Livingstone Island View recognised Ian, but then maybe it was because he'd been there with Sarah.

Ian and Sarah made their way down to the restaurant for a light lunch. The night before, they'd enjoyed a relaxing evening, but this day was turning into a test of endurance. They'd walked at least sixteen kilometres, and the struggle at Livingstone Island View sapped Ian's energy. Ian was weary, but they needed to cross the river that afternoon. He allowed himself one Zambezi beer with his lunch. They would have far preferred to spend the afternoon relaxing by the hotel pool, but that wasn't an option as they couldn't risk another encounter with the COU. If Jedson was in Victoria Falls, how many others looked for them? And what about Captain John; was he here too? It wouldn't be long before the COU realised one of their operatives was missing. That would reinvigorate the search for them.

Chapter 51

29th August 2009

Captain John yawned. He'd not slept well after drinking too much in the casino and getting to bed late. It was a total waste of time, trying to pick up the young croupier. John liked his women young, but maybe she was too young. She didn't seem at all impressed by his worldliness. She was gauche; the sort who'd be impressed by a rapper or a member of a boy band.

'Akashinga, where is Elijah?' said Captain John, in a harsh voice.

Akashinga jumped at the loud voice close to his ear. He'd been leaning against a pillar at the entrance to the Kingdom Hotel and hadn't seen his boss approach. 'I don't know, Sah. We split up to search for the Kagonye woman. I searched in the town, and he went to look in the Rain Forest.'

'Now it's almost noon. I wanted you two here by half past eleven to debrief. We'll start without him. What did the hotels say? Did you find out anything?'

'No, we found out nothing, Sah. The big hotels wouldn't tell us about their guests, and the other hotels had seen no one that looked like them.'

'Give me a list of the hotels that wouldn't tell you about their guests. I will speak to them myself. Did you go to the hotels, or did you phone them?'

'Some we phoned and others we visited, Sah.'

John looked at Akashinga and thought it wasn't surprising that the hotels refused to give him information about their guests. He looked like a thug. This job required finesse. Elijah looked more presentable, but a lot depended on how he'd approached the hotels. Did he give a plausible reason for enquiring about the couple? Perhaps this job called for John's personal attention. 'Akashinga, go back and visit the small hotels and backpackers' hostels. No phone calls this time. Visit each one, and I'll check the big hotels. The other two can take turns watching the border post.' The previous day's search for the fugitives yielded no result, but John was sure they'd not slipped through his net. It was a simple matter of waiting for them to arrive.

Soon it would be lunchtime, and Elijah had not appeared. John knew something must have gone wrong. Perhaps Kagonye and Sanders were already in the area. He set out in the car to visit all the major hotels to enquire about them.

'Excuse me, my sister and her husband are staying here, and I am due to meet them. Can you please tell me if they have arrived already? Their surname is Sanders.'

'Sorry, Sir, we have no one by that name booked in here.'

'That's strange. She's married to a murungu. Here are photos of them. Have you seen them by any chance?'

'No, I'm sorry, Sir, we have seen no one like that.'

* * *

The mid-afternoon sun was hot on their backs as Ian and Sarah walked to the boathouse. On the map it didn't look too far from their hotel, but the walk was longer than Ian expected. Sarah carried her backpack, but Ian left his at the hotel. 'I'll pass through the border post as soon as I can tomorrow morning and meet you at the David Livingstone Safari Lodge. I've booked us in for three nights. Now let's see if we can hire a boat.'

The African man at the boathouse hesitated when Ian explained that he wanted to hire a boat but did not want a tour guide. 'Without a guide it costs more. A tour costs one hundred and forty dollars. Without a guide it's one hundred and ninety dollars for two hours.'

'Why is it more without a guide?'

'I am not supposed to rent out boats without a guide. Fifty dollars is my risk money. And you also must deposit five hundred dollars in case you damage the boat or don't bring it back. I can take a credit card.'

'This is getting expensive.'

'If you don't have the five-hundred-dollar deposit, give me two hundred dollars cash, and I'll give you one hundred dollars when you return the boat.'

'Is that a special offer because you like me?'

The African laughed out loud. 'No, one hundred dollars is my risk money.'

'OK, two hundred dollars then.'

'That's three hundred and ninety dollars in total.'

'That includes the hundred-and-fifty-dollar risk money, right? With all this money left behind, the boat will be lighter, and we'll be travelling higher in the water.'

'With crocodiles in the river, it's better to be high in the water,' said the African attendant laughing. He reminded Ian that he would be in big trouble with his boss if Ian did not return the boat in good condition. 'You must be back by half past five.'

Ian had studied the map and planned to paddle upriver past Kalunda Island on his right. They would then round the west end of Siloka Island and head downriver towards the Zambian bank. 'Once we have passed Siloka Island, it should be an easy run down to the David Livingstone Safari Lodge.'

The afternoon felt hot and humid. 'Isn't it supposed to be winter?' said Ian. Rivulets of sweat ran down his face and the back of his neck. The bright afternoon sun bounced off the water, dazzling them with its glare. They entered the river with the bow of the canoe facing upstream. The flow of the river was less strong close to the bank. Ian and Sarah worked hard to make headway. The breeze on the water made it cooler than the riverbank. On their right, they passed Kalunda Island, which lay between them and the much larger Siloka Island. When, at last, they'd passed the islands, they turned the bow of the canoe towards the Zambian bank and held it at thirty to forty degrees against the current. Paddling just hard enough to hold their position in the river, the canoe moved across towards the other bank. This was the *upstream ferry* technique used by kayakers and canoeists to allow the river flow to do most of the work in the crossing. As soon as they reached a point between Canary and Siloka islands, they leant into a turn and swung the bow of the canoe downriver towards the Zambian bank.

Ian prided himself on covering all contingencies, but he'd not considered the size of Siloka Island. It took more time to round the island than he'd expected. The hippos entertained them with their loud bellows and splashing. A lone bull elephant stood half submerged near one island, less than fifty metres away. Ian was happy to see no sign of crocodiles, but was it safe to be crossing the Zambezi in a canoe? Crocodiles pulled people out of boats on the Congo River. And on the Daintree River in Queensland, the huge saltwater crocodiles could leap right out of the water to snatch their food. To put on a show for visitors, the river cruise operators encouraged the behaviour. It seemed the Zambezi crocodiles hadn't yet learnt that little trick. The sound of birdlife was everywhere. A small flock of four or five birds flew by fast, skimming the surface of the water. Soon the sun was low in the sky, dancing on the water in hypnotic zigzags of red and gold. If they were not short of time, it would have been an idyllic paddle in the cooling early evening breezes. But they needed to move on as fast as possible.

Sarah was sitting in front of Ian and was paddling with strong even strokes. It surprised him how well she took to the task. 'You're good at this.'

'We learnt to canoe as part of our training in the COU.'

'I doubt they ever thought their training would be used against them.'

The lowering sun painted a romantic scene on the river. It looked so tranquil. 'I wish we could stop and enjoy the sunset,' said Ian.

'Perhaps, we can enjoy it tomorrow.'

When they started out, the river reflected the blue of the sky. As the sun lowered, the blue of the river deepened. Then, the yellow sun rested on the horizon, washing everything in a soft golden hue. When the sun dipped behind the dark silhouette of the trees along the riverbank, the sky turned a deep red and grey. The river reflected a palette of purple and rust. The beauty and tranquillity of the scene belied the horrors that lay below the surface, waiting for the unwary.

Ian and Sarah drew up to the grassy bank at the Lodge and pulled the canoe out of the water. 'It looks nice,' said Sarah. 'I bet they don't get too many guests arriving by canoe.' As they made their way to the hotel check-in, they looked like tourists returning from a trip on the river and didn't attract too many stares from curious guests.

A polite, young, female receptionist welcomed Ian and Sarah to the hotel. 'You have a first-floor room with river views on the western wing Mr Sanders. Enjoy your stay.'

It was getting dark, and Ian was keen to get back to Zimbabwe. After checking in, he and Sarah returned to the canoe. It was heavy on land, and they struggled to get it back in the water. 'Take care, Sarah. I'll see you tomorrow morning. Here's three hundred bucks, in case I'm delayed.'

'Be careful on your way back, Ian. Sleep tight and thank you.' He liked her using his name. It was only the second time she'd done so, and it gave him a warm feeling. His plan was to go with the river flow to the east end of Siloka Island. There, he would turn sharp right and paddle across to the boat-hire jetty on the Zimbabwe side.

* * *

At each hotel, John checked with reception and the concierge desk. It took much longer than he expected, and the answers were the same wherever he enquired. The Elephant Hills Hotel was his last call before returning to his own hotel for dinner with Suzette.

The receptionist looked at the photos. 'I'm not sure. The woman looks like Mrs Jones. Mr Jones is a murungu, but he looks different to the photo. He has a beard and moustache. It could be him, but I'm not sure.'

'I'd like to give them a surprise. Could you tell me their room number?'

'Wait, I will ring their room and check if they are there. I saw them go out this afternoon, and I haven't seen them return. I think Mrs Jones may have gone because I saw her carrying her backpack when they left.'

'Don't tell them I'm here. Say you are checking to make sure everything's OK. Ask them if there's anything they need before they retire for the night.'

The receptionist rang Ian and Sarah's room, but no one answered.

'OK,' said John. 'If it's them, I'll come for my sister and her husband in the morning. Could you please call me on my cell phone when they return? Don't tell them I was here. I want to surprise them. When are they due to check out?'

'They're booked in until day after tomorrow, Sir.'

'All right, thank you for your help. Let me write my phone number for you.'

Outside the hotel John called Akashinga on his cell phone, but there was no reply. After several attempts he gave up trying. That damned fool Akashinga. Why isn't he answering his phone? The idiot must be drunk or chasing after women. John tried calling the others but again got no response. He slammed his fist on the car roof. 'Bloody hell!' he shouted. 'Where is everyone?' While I'm hard at work, those bastards are making a holiday out of this trip.

Chapter 52

29th August 2009

THE canoe sliced through the water. Practice made a world of difference. Ian struggled with it on the trip over, battling to keep the nose pointed straight ahead. Earlier it veered to one side and then the other, but now it moved smooth and straight. It was a two-man canoe, and Ian found it harder to handle than the kayak he'd used on his Fiji trip, five years earlier. On the first crossing, Sarah helped paddle, but now he returned alone. The sun, low on the horizon when they reached the Zambian side, had now sunk beyond the trees. When he rounded the end of Siloka Island, Ian couldn't see the Zimbabwe riverbank, but the flow of the river gave him a sense of direction.

Ian found the return trip in the gloom a little confusing, and he had to concentrate. He needed to keep Siloka Island on the right, but on a moonless night, the islands all looked similar in appearance and size. They seemed to blend into each other. The map showed the big islands, but several smaller ones loomed.

Perhaps he should have waited until dawn before going back. But the canoe rental people might have raised the alarm, and he didn't want the police or search and rescue looking for him. On the return trip, he seemed to have paddled for much longer than when he'd crossed with Sarah. How much farther? Ian's frustration got the better of him and he shouted. 'Dammit! How many damn islands are there?'

Unaccustomed to paddling, Ian's arms tired from the effort, but the smaller islands proved to be a blessing. Eddies that formed downstream from them gave him the chance to rest, and Ian would need all his strength to make it to the boat-hire jetty. The *upstream ferry technique* proved more difficult in the darkness, and soon, Ian needed to paddle against the river flow.

Ah, at last! Was that the Zimbabwe riverbank ahead or one of the large islands? Ian wasn't sure. At first, he planned to return by the same route they'd used earlier. But he gave up the idea when he realised he would have to paddle against the river flow for almost the whole length of Siloka Island. Now, it was well past half past five. The trip had taken longer than he'd expected. The boat-hire attendant wouldn't be happy. Ian hoped it wouldn't affect the return of the one-hundred-dollar deposit. The profusion of islands and a return in darkness via an unfamiliar route confounded him. Ian paddled upstream for a time. If he'd already passed the jetty, he'd have to turn around and paddle down river again. But if the jetty was farther upstream, and he turned too soon, he'd face another exhausting paddle upriver.

Ian's arms ached. Fatigue set in, and the morning's excitement had drained him. Suddenly, a loud thud, and the canoe shuddered and spun. For a moment it disoriented him. Ian's mind raced. Which way to the riverbank now? What happened? Perhaps the canoe hit a sunken log or a sandbank? Did the flow of the river turn the canoe? Then, just when he recovered his bearings, the front of the canoe rose out of the water, and the canoe capsized.

The shock bewildered Ian. Everything seemed to move at snails' pace. He imagined he saw the bank ahead, but the pull of the river moved him downstream. He tried to swim towards the bank, but his clothes and the *veldskoens* on his feet weighed him down, and his arms turned to jelly.

But then, his predicament hit him like a hammer blow. Oh God! It can't end like this. Please don't let it end like this. A hippo might have capsized the canoe. The beasts are active at night. Each year, they supposedly kill more people in Africa than any other animal. What could be worse?

Anxiety turned to fear, then dread. Oh no! Crocodiles are worse than hippos. At least hippos kill quickly. Crocodiles drag you under and drown you. The river's swarming with them, and they're nocturnal.

Ian remembered the old warning signs posted all along the riverbank in Zambia; Bathing is Suicidal. Something brushed past him. Bloody hell! I don't want to be dragged under and drowned. Please, God, help me.

Ian also imagined the river taking him downstream and over the falls, one hundred and eight metres into the gorge. No one would ever find him. His parents would have no idea what happened to him. Ian prayed in his predicament. Please, God, let me reach the bank.

With all his strength Ian struck out towards the bank. The pull of the river, less noticeable now with only ten metres to go! He made painfully slow progress. Now, only five metres! All the while the chill of fear churned and twisted inside him. He imagined a grip on his leg, jaws pulling him back. His splashing might seem like a fish or animal in distress, a magnet for crocodiles. Only two metres to go! Ian prayed he wouldn't get caught a metre from the bank, the most dangerous part of a river crossing. Oh no! Something grabbed his trouser leg, and he kicked out in panic. Oh, thank God! Only a sunken tree that snagged him, but now he was bleeding and frantic. Seconds seemed like minutes. The nearer he got to the bank, the slower his progress seemed as his muscles turned to jelly.

Close now. A few more strokes would do it. A heavy thud on his back pushed him under the surface. Ian swallowed water. His heart raced. He'd reached the limit of his endurance. Just when he thought he'd reached safety, a crocodile caught him and pulled him back. There was no pain, but that would come soon enough when the crocodile started its deadly roll. Ian looked around and his heart jumped. The monstrous beast towered over him. Wait! It's not a crocodile. It's the canoe. The flow of the river had slammed the canoe into his back. The pull he experienced was the pull of the river which seemed to grow stronger as his arms weakened. Ian reached for the nearby riverbank.

His heart hammered against his chest wall, and he wanted to vomit. It felt like he'd swallowed a jack hammer.

At last, Ian reached the bank, but it stood about thirty centimetres above the water. Too high! Somehow, he found the strength to pull himself up on his arms. He'd not managed that at the swimming pool in years. But when he tried to bring his legs up onto the bank, his feet kept slipping in the mud, back into the water. In his mind he pictured a crocodile bursting from the water like a missile from a submarine. The water's edge was where they often caught their unsuspecting victims. Using only his arms, Ian dragged his body out of the water and collapsed into the mud on the bank.

For a moment he lay there gasping and coughing up water. Then he remembered crocodiles follow their prey onto land. Ian leapt up and ran, stumbling, away from the river. Only then he realised he'd arrived back at the boat-hire jetty. No one remained at the boathouse. The boatman must have gone home. He was lucky to be alive. Thank God! His most pressing thoughts seemed almost irrelevant. What about the canoe? Ah, there it stayed, bumping up against the jetty and pinned by the river flow. Ian walked out onto the jetty and pulled the canoe towards the bank. Then with great effort, and jellied muscles forgotten, he pulled it up out of the water onto dry land. The paddles had disappeared. Tomorrow he'd pay for them. How much would it cost?

Ian looked back at the river. Were any eyes watching him? He shuddered and set out for the hotel. A brisk cool breeze followed the warm day. With soaking wet clothes, the breeze added wind chill, and now Ian shivered. What would he say at the hotel about his appearance? Perhaps he should suffer the discomfort and wait until his clothes dried? No, it would take too long. He'd say he slipped on the edge of the riverbank.

* * *

After Ian paddled into the darkness in the canoe, Sarah walked back into the hotel to find her room. It was nice, very nice, but she wished Ian was there. That was crazy. Why would she want the arrogant and impatient murungu with her? Last night at the Elephant Hills Hotel he'd been different. She was better on her own, but somehow, she'd become accustomed to him hanging around her. Sarah showered to wash off the day's grime. The David Livingstone Safari Lodge was luxurious, and once again Sarah realised, she missed Ian's company. She also worried about him crossing the dangerous river on his own at night.

There'd not been time for her to absorb the news of Thomas that the big African gave them at the falls. It surprised her to find her feelings were more one of relief than sadness. She'd spent seven months coming to terms with the probability of Thomas' death. All that time, she'd mourned him, and now with the news of his violent end, she hated the COU and Captain John. They murdered both her father and Thomas. What did Jedson know about it? She found it hard to imagine he'd taken part in any moves against her or Thomas. He'd been their team leader and mentor and seemed to like them. But it shocked her to see him at the border post. In her heart of hearts, she knew Thomas would never return, and now with his death confirmed, she found it a release.

Sarah headed down to the bar and ordered a beer. She blamed Ian for giving her a taste for the brew. Somehow the ice-cold trickle down her throat comforted her and made her feel more secure. Perhaps it reminded her of Ian. Tomorrow morning, he would be here. Please let him get through this safely, she prayed. The emotional stress of the day and the single beer played with her mind. Sarah felt a sudden need for his support. It was madness. She was a lot tougher than him; not stronger, but tougher. He's the one who needed her support, not the reverse. Perhaps it was mutual. Perhaps they needed each other. She shook her head to clear the conflicting thoughts.

A well-dressed African man approached Sarah to enquire if he could buy her a drink. He persisted until she made it clear he took a big risk.

'If my boyfriend finds out you've been pestering me, I won't be able to save you,' she said. The man faded into the background. At dinner, an American tourist tried to join her at her table. 'My boyfriend doesn't like me talking to strange men. The last one he found me talking to should be out of hospital soon.' The American got the hint. Sarah was more than capable of carrying out those threats for herself, but it amused her to delegate the task to Ian.

After dinner, Sarah returned to her room and went to bed. She prayed for Thomas' soul and dozed off thinking of Ian's arrival in the morning. After a short while she woke again. Despite an exhausting day, she found it hard to sleep. She worried whether Ian would get through the border post the next morning. What would happen to him if the COU or the police caught him? What would she do? The money Ian gave her wouldn't last too long. Sarah realised she relied too much on Ian. She'd not considered what she'd do if something went wrong and he didn't show. Here she was in Zambia with no valid stamp in her passport. How would she get into Botswana? In the early hours, Sarah at last drifted off to sleep.

* * *

Captain John made it back to the Kingdom Hotel in time for dinner with Suzette. 'There's a change of plans for this evening. Tonight, the hunt begins. Here are photos of the couple I'm hunting. Are you ready for action?'

'Yes, I told you I'm available.'

'All right, after dinner, go to the Elephant Hills Hotel, and see if they've returned from their afternoon outing. If they are both there, phone me, and I'll come to the hotel with my men as soon as I can find them.'

'That will be easy,' said Suzette. 'What have they done?'

'Never mind what they've done. Just do what I tell you. The hotel receptionist said the woman might've gone. If the man is alone, keep him there until tomorrow morning, and I'll come and get him.'

'How can I keep him in the hotel until tomorrow morning?'

'Use your imagination. Use any means necessary. I'll pay you well for it.'

'How can I get to meet him?'

'Go straight to his room. Tell him you've heard he might need company. I'm sure you'll be most persuasive. Here's his room number. I watched the receptionist dial it.'

'What if he doesn't want my company?'

'Phone me and let me know, and I'll come as soon as I can. If I don't hear from you, I'll assume you're keeping him company, and then I'll see you in the morning. The receptionist said he has a beard and moustache, so he may look different to the photo.'

John excelled at using other people to do his dirty work. Tired from lack of sleep and too much alcohol, he was irritable. Suzette kept him up late the first two nights, but she was young and could handle it. Then last night, it was the casino. Now, his eye was on the receptionist at his hotel. She was back on duty tonight. Perhaps she could keep him amused until Suzette called. The receptionist was a fresh challenge. Suzette was old news.

'When does your shift end?' said John, with a smile.

'Ten o'clock.' said the receptionist, looking coy. 'Why do you ask?'

John loved that shy look. The shy ones were often the hottest.

'Maybe I could buy you a drink?'

'I don't know, maybe.'

She played hard to get, but John loved the chase. Resistance was there to be overcome, and he found her hesitation irresistible. 'I'll meet you here at ten then,' he said, satisfied that his strategy would draw her into his net. She smiled but said nothing. John took it to be a *yes*.

* * *

Back at the Elephant Hills Hotel, the young female receptionist didn't comment on Ian's bedraggled appearance when he returned. But she noticed that Sarah was not with him and enquired about her. 'She got a lift back to Bulawayo with friends, so I'm leaving tomorrow morning instead of day after tomorrow.'

'Yes, Sir. An African gentleman was here earlier this evening, looking for you and your wife.'

'Can you describe him?'

'Yes, Sir, he said he was your wife's brother. He was not as tall as you. He had a moustache and dressed well.'

'Oh yes, did he leave a message?'

'No, Sir, he wanted me to phone him when you returned. Here's his cell phone number.'

'Thank you. Don't worry about calling him. I'll phone him now.' It was a lie, but Ian couldn't imagine anyone he'd want to see who fitted the receptionist's description. 'Can I fix up my bill now please?' said Ian. 'I want an early start in the morning. I haven't used the minibar.'

The receptionist worked through the checkout procedure with measured efficiency. 'Would there be anything else I can help you with, Sir? Would you like dinner or room service?'

Ian declined the offer. After an exhausting and traumatic day, he didn't want to eat or drink. He needed sleep.

When he returned to his room, Ian packed his things ready for a quick getaway. The stranger who'd made enquiries about them fitted Sarah's description of Jedson, but it might have been someone else from state security or the police. It was time to leave.

For a short while, Ian sat on the balcony and stared at the stars in the moonless night sky. A shiver ran through him when he thought of the river crossing. It was an ordeal, negotiating those islands at night. He pictured Sarah across the river in the David Livingstone Safari Lodge. What would she do now? She'd no family outside Zimbabwe and no work references. She'd abandoned her post at the hotel with no notice or explanation.

Ian's own plans were also in a mess. He'd intended to visit the Eastern Highlands to see Nyanga, Vumba and the Chimanimani mountain range. He'd also hoped to travel to the Lowveld to visit the Great Zimbabwe Ruins, the large, fort-like, stone structure with five-metre-high walls. Its origins were unknown, but the Shona claimed their ancestors built it. Ian planned to visit the Kariba Dam and the nearby national parks, but now his Zimbabwe odyssey was coming to a premature end. His first-hand view and the local colour for his book would be a little thin. A return to full-time consultancy was the last thing he wanted, but he'd worry about that tomorrow. His immediate concern was getting out of the country and over to Zambia.

There was a knock on the door. It was late. Who could it be? Ian was wary. He opened the door a crack and put his foot against it. A young woman, with a head of loose curls hanging round her face, stood there. She looked familiar. No, it can't be. 'Hazel, is that you?'

'Ian, what are you doing here?'

'They said you were dead.' Ian opened the door for Hazel to enter.

'I would have been if I hadn't left Harare. A man looked for me at the Monomotapa Hotel, and then the next night someone strangled a girl named Hazel in Harare Gardens. I had to leave in a hurry. I'm sorry I didn't have the chance to say goodbye.'

'But why was that man after you?'

'He wanted to know which girl befriended the white man. It seems he got the wrong Hazel.'

'How did you know I was here?'

'I didn't. A man named Captain John is looking for a Mr and Mrs Jones.'

'Yes, that's the name I'm using.'

'He showed me photos of the people he looked for and gave me this room number.'

'He said if you were alone, I should keep you here until morning. The photo didn't look like you, so I didn't realise it was you he wanted.'

'It must have been my passport photo. Those photos never show a good likeness.'

'After I left Harare, I came here and changed my name to Suzette, and I also changed my hairstyle. With so many tourists in Victoria Falls, business is good. Three nights ago, I met Captain John in a bar at the Kingdom Hotel.'

'Yes, and?'

'He's planning to come here with his men in the morning, but he's not an early riser, so if you leave early, you'll miss him.'

'What about you? Won't you be in big trouble?'

'I'll say I kept you company, but you weren't the person he wanted.'

'I'll leave early. The border post opens at six, and I should be through by eight, so after that you can phone him and give him your report.'

'OK, I'll phone him as late as possible.'

'Now that's settled, let's see what's in the minibar. Tell him I drugged you; it'll be the truth,' Ian joked.

They stayed up late chatting and catching up on each other's news.

'Hazel, what would you have done if it had not been me you found here? Would you have handed the person over to Captain John? He's a bad man.'

'Ian, not all bad men are black. Sometimes they are white. But before I handed him over to Captain John, I'd have tried to find out about him. Then, I would have had to decide. The captain may be bad, but I didn't know that.'

'You're a good person, Hazel.'

'I heard your black girlfriend had left.'

'She's not my girlfriend. I just helped her to get out of the country.'

'But you shared a room with her. If you like, I can be your next black girlfriend.'

'Thank you, Hazel, but all I need for the moment is to cross the border into Zambia.'

'I would stop seeing other men, and I'd do everything to make you happy.'

'I'm sure you would, Hazel, and I'll keep it in mind.'

'Here; this is my cell phone number. You can call if you want me and I'll come.'

Several drinks later, Hazel lay down on the bed and fell asleep within a few minutes. Although exhausted, Ian only dozed. After a restless night, he didn't feel too good, and he made a mental note to never touch another drop of alcohol again. He hadn't had enough sleep, but at five o'clock he got up, had a quick shower and dressed. Ian kissed Hazel on the cheek, 'After eight o'clock it should be OK to phone Captain John with your news. In the meantime, get more sleep.'

Ian picked up his backpack and hurried downstairs to the hotel foyer. At the reception desk he paid for the drinks taken from the minibar. There were no messages or further news of the African man who'd enquired after him and Sarah last night. 'Please don't wake the young lady in my room. She needs to rest.' The receptionist smiled and invited him to come again. Ian was well on his way to the town centre by five thirty.

CHAPTER 53

30th August 2009

IAN planned to go back to the boathouse to collect his deposit and pay for the lost paddles, but he thought better of it. Time was short. The deposit would cover the cost of new paddles, and it was unsafe for him to hang about the area. He strode out and kept up a good pace. Although walking along the road was risky with the authorities on the lookout for him, he'd no choice. Alone, the four-kilometre walk seemed much longer than when he'd done it with Sarah. The quicker he got into the town centre and lost himself among the buildings and tourists, the better. Ian covered the distance in good time, and the town's low skyline soon came into view.

A dry tongue and a thumping headache made the walk more arduous. Ian was paying for last night. He and Hazel chatted past midnight, and though he only drank a few beers, they'd affected him.

It was past six o'clock. Ian was eager to get to Zambia as soon as possible, and he lengthened his stride as he neared the border post. A few blacks stood around, waiting in the patient African manner. The border post was not open. 'What's going on Ian asked.' No one knew. An African man said, 'It might be closed for sickness or for security reasons.' Ian didn't find the comment reassuring, and the obvious lack of tourists also worried him. What was he to do now?

Ian had not eaten since lunch the previous day, and now he was hungry. He returned to the town centre, and at a small café, he ordered eggs and bacon. Focused on getting through the border, he barely tasted the food he ate. He planned to wait near the border post and join the first tourist group crossing over the Victoria Falls Bridge into Zambia.

After breakfast, Ian walked back to the border post, but it was still not open. The group of patient Africans had grown. Ian considered phoning Hazel to tell her to delay her call to Captain John, but he dismissed the idea. She already took a big risk on his behalf. Ian walked to the nearby Victoria Falls Hotel for a cup of coffee and to see the historic hotel one last time. The waiters looked smart in their dark brown trousers and loose-fitting, kaftan-style white shirts with three quarter length sleeves and maroon sashes around their waists. Gone were the white gloves, starched white suits with shiny brass buttons, and maroon fezzes from the old days. Ian ignored the Hotel Guests Only sign and walked through the gardens to the spectacular view of the Victoria Falls Bridge from the back of the hotel. As a child, he'd stayed in this beautiful hotel with his parents.

It was getting late, and Ian walked back to the border post to see what was happening.

* * *

John woke with a start. It was eight o'clock, and the sun streamed into his room, making it warm despite the early hour. The flirty receptionist was a disappointment. She ordered the most expensive cocktail on the bar menu, but he fancied the price would be worth it. After two cocktails she was giggly. In John's experience that was the sign his quarry was ready to go back to his room. John was sure he was onto a good thing, but then her boyfriend showed up to take her home. That bastard probably got the service for which he'd so generously paid. Ah well, he needed a good sleep. The two nights with Suzette exhausted him. And the late night in the casino didn't help. It pained him to acknowledge it, but he felt his age.

It was time to move. John rolled out of bed and looked in the mirror. There were bags under his eyes. Was he really getting that old, or was it the late nights and good living? Last night, he'd slept well, but he didn't feel rested. After the shower, he felt better. The phone rang while he was still drying himself.

'He's not the one you wanted.'

'What?'

'He's not the one. He was a different person.'

'I'll be the judge of that. Is he still there?'

'He left while I was sleeping. He's taken all his things and checked out.'

'You idiot, you should have kept him there until I came to get him.' John slammed down the phone. Now, he had to rush to the border post, or he might miss Ian Sanders altogether. If Sarah Kagonye wasn't with the murungu where the hell was she? Despite his hunger and thirst, John skipped breakfast. He'd grab something on the way.

John cursed Suzette for letting Ian get away. That fool. You can't rely on anyone to do anything properly these days. That idiot Akashinga still didn't respond to the messages he'd left for him, and neither did the others. John raced down to the border post, and to his relief, he found it closed. At least the murungu can't have crossed the border unless… unless he drove to Kazungula. John found the phone number and called the Kazungula border post to warn them to keep a sharp lookout for Ian Sanders.

When that fool Akashinga shows up, I'll skin him alive. Where is Elijah? Something serious must have happened to him. Elijah was the team's best operative. At least, he possessed a brain and was reliable. He wouldn't disappear without good reason. And that fool woman, Suzette, needn't expect any payment. She was a total failure.

John was reluctant to report Elijah's disappearance to the police. He didn't want to give the boss in Harare any more excuses to criticise him and threaten his position in the COU. No, he'd keep quiet, for now at least.

The customs and immigration officers at the border post didn't dare question John's authority. They assumed he'd taken command while their regular boss was away. His manner intimidated them, and they viewed him with unease as they watched him standing against the wall by the entrance. Their boss, the senior officer in charge at the border post, was on a visit to Bulawayo. He'd said nothing about someone coming in and taking over in his absence. The boss was due back later in the morning. They'd let him deal with the imposing stranger. In the meantime, John pressured a reluctant junior officer at the border post to go to the nearby café and buy him tea and muffins.

* * *

When Ian returned to the border post, he found it open but quiet. The queue of Africans had gone. Perhaps it would get busier later in the morning. But soon a noisy group of about ten tourists arrived. Ian could blend in with the English, American and German accents he heard amongst the excited tourists. This was the opportunity he'd been waiting for, and he attached himself to the back of the group.

A large, loud American standing in front of Ian turned to him. 'Have you travelled much in Zimbabwe, or are you only visiting the falls?'

'Just the falls,' said Ian, in a low voice he hoped wouldn't draw attention to him and would discourage further questions. Before long, he stood in front of the immigration officer at the counter. 'How did you enjoy your visit to Zimbabwe Mr Jones?'

'It was most enjoyable thank you.' The officer stamped his passport and handed it back to him. Ian breathed a little easier now, and soon he would be across the border into Zambia and meet up with Sarah.

As he turned to leave, a man standing to one side came up to him and said, 'May I see your passport please?'

'Why, what's wrong?'

'Just routine, Sir, please come into my office.'

Ian's mouth was suddenly dry. Is there a problem?

The man dressed in a mid-grey suit, black leather shoes and an open neck white shirt. He sported a neat moustache and had the look and bearing of a military officer. Ian's disquiet crept through him like a slow-moving lava flow.

'Please be seated,' the man said, pointing to a chair. He was polite, and his smile, amiable. 'Is it Mister Jones, or should I call you Mister Sanders?'

The question slammed Ian in the guts—a dreadful hollow sensation, as if he'd received a heavy blow. He opened his mouth to speak, but his brain had stalled, and he didn't know what to say. His voice crackled under the strain. 'Who are you?'

The man put his right foot on the desktop and twirled a pencil between his forefingers and thumbs. 'You can call me Captain John. We've had you and Miss Kagonye under surveillance since you left Harare.'

'Oh!' said Ian, feigning surprise.

'We hoped to deal with you and Miss Kagonye with as little fuss as possible, but somehow you always wriggle out of our traps. I must congratulate you on your resilience. The two of you are like cockroaches, hard to eradicate.'

Ian did not comment.

The man sat forward putting his elbows on the desk. 'One of my men is missing here at Victoria Falls. Do you know what happened to him?'

'No,' Ian blurted out.

'Well, no matter, I'll take you back to Harare. A lot of questions need answering. And where, may I ask, is Miss Kagonye?'

The blood drained from Ian's face. He somehow doubted he would make it back to Harare. 'Friends drove her back to Bulawayo.'

'Ah yes, it would have been her friends in the MFF–the Mthwakazi Freedom Front.'

'I think you are aware,' said Ian, regaining a little of his courage, 'neither of us is associated with the MFF.'

'You deny delivering two cartons of MFF flyers to your contacts in Bulawayo?'

'I thought the cartons contained photocopying paper.'

'So, you admit delivering them then?'

'I delivered two cartons, but I didn't know they contained MFF flyers.'

'We will get much information out of you back in Harare, Mister Sanders. Do you understand how serious it would be for you to not cooperate with the authorities?'

'Yes, I do.'

'Good. Then I'll ask you again. Where is Miss Kagonye?'

The veins in Ian's temples throbbed. 'As I said—'

Loud shouting at the front desk interrupted their discussion. A man dressed in a white uniform with epaulettes, shiny brass buttons and badges on his short sleeves stormed into the office. 'What's going on here? What are you doing in my office? Get your foot off my desk.' The officer glared at Captain John.

'The man I'm interviewing is a fugitive. This office was the only private place to interview him.'

'No one can use my office without my permission. By what authority do you presume to take it upon yourself?'

'I've the highest authority to apprehend this man. His name is Ian Sanders, and he is wanted by the authorities in Harare.'

'I'm in charge of this border post, and I have the highest authority here. What highest authority do you have? You say you have the highest authority, but you work alone, do you? Show me your identification.'

'My name is Captain John, and my men are in the field. Our unit is top secret, so we don't carry ID.'

The explanation did not impress the officer. 'Show me some proof of your authority. You have fifteen minutes. Now get out of my office. And you,' he said, pointing to Ian, 'stay where you are.'

John rose from the chair, his face dark with anger. At the office door he turned and said, 'Today is Sunday, it may not be easy to get quick proof of my authority.'

'A quarter of an hour,' said the uniformed officer, that's all you'll get. He threw his peaked cap onto the desk with a theatrical flourish and walked around it and sat on his chair. 'Show me your passport.'

Ian handed him his false passport with the Zimbabwe exit stamp.

The officer looked through it. 'You're already clear for exit Mr Jones. That man had no authority to hold you once we cleared you for exit. What's in your backpack?'

'Clothes and personal effects,' said Ian, relieved that he'd given his genuine passport and laptop to Sarah to hold.

'If I search your backpack, will I find anything incriminating?'

'No, there's nothing.'

'OK, you can go.'

Ian couldn't believe his luck. Captain John had offended the senior officer at the border post. Ian thanked the officer and left, trying not to make his haste too obvious.

John was in a rage. He'd deal with that fool at the border post later, but now, he needed to call the boss to verify his status. He couldn't take Ian Sanders into custody until he proved his bona fides to that idiot commander of the border post.

The phone rang on the other end of the line, and an unfamiliar male voice answered.

'This is Captain John; I need to talk to the boss. Tell him it's urgent.'

'It's Sunday morning. The boss doesn't take work calls on Sundays.'

'I need to speak to him now. It's a serious matter.'

'Wait, I'll see if he'll take your call.'

John paced in circles in the shade of the large tree outside the border post. Damn him! The fool is taking his time to find the boss. John stopped only long enough to curse all the fools he dealt with in his work.

'Hello, the boss is busy and can't take your call.'

John almost choked. 'Did you tell him what I said?'

'Yes, I did.'

'Listen you fool. It's most urgent. I don't care if he's screwing his secretary or what he's doing. I need to talk to him now.'

The phone went dead.

Blast them! The fools act as if the world stops on weekends. John worried he might have overstepped the mark. If the fool on the other end of the line accurately relayed his comments, he might end up in serious trouble. Perhaps he'd better phone back and in a calmer tone explain why it was so important he speaks to the boss. He'd never met the boss, and it amused him to imagine him as a fat little pig or a scrawny bespectacled runt, the gopher for an anonymous committee. Such people have too much power.

Ian saw John walking around in circles under the tree, talking on his cell phone. It was the same tree under which he'd stood the day before, waiting for Sarah to pass through the border post. He hoped John was engrossed in his phone call and wouldn't notice him. Ian turned away and hurried to a taxi waiting beside the building. He half expected a shout from John at any moment. 'Can you take me to the Zambian border post?' Ian asked the taxi driver.

'Yes, but we must wait until the taxi is full.'

'What is the fare?'

'Five dollars to the border post.'

'I'm in a big hurry. Will you take me now if I give you fifty dollars? That's more than double what you'll earn from a full taxi.'

'OK, it's a deal.'

Ian jumped in with his backpack on his lap. 'Hurry now. Go!'

As John redialled the number, he saw Ian getting into the taxi. He raced towards it, losing one of his expensive slip-on shoes. He'd almost reached the taxi when it sped off, leaving a trail of dust. Damn and blast! Blast that fool at the end of the phone and that fool boss of his. Blast them all. And blast that fool commander of the border post. John almost always got his own way. Before now, he'd never needed to prove his identity or verify his authority. People always deferred to his imposing manner and did as he instructed. It never occurred to him that a little, jumped-up, egotistical border post commander would question his authority.

Instead of trying to reach his superior again, John dialled a different number. He slipped his shoe back on as he waited for an answer to his call. 'Hello,' said the tired sounding voice at the other end.

'Akashinga,' John shouted, 'where the hell are you? I phoned you several times and got no reply. Come to the border post, now.'

'Yes, Sah.'

Akashinga arrived a quarter of an hour later looking hot and sweaty. He'd run all the way from his hotel room where he'd been trying to catch up on much needed sleep. The taxi which had taken Ian to the Zambian border post was back, but John got no useful information from the driver. 'Akashinga, get to Zambia and find where Ian Sanders is staying. Remember, he might call himself Jones.'

'My passport is in the hotel, Sah.'

'You fool, Akashinga, coming to the border unprepared for hot pursuit. You're an idiot. I don't know why I keep you. I would've sent Elijah if he wasn't missing. But now I must rely on you. Where are the other two?'

'I don't know, Sah.'

Nor could John have followed Ian. His passport was also back in his hotel room in the safe, and he cursed himself for his oversight. In his hurry to get to the border post he'd forgotten to take it with him. This time he included Suzette in the list of people he cursed. It was her fault he had to rush to the border post. Someone would pay for the shambles. 'Get your passport and whatever else you need and get across into Zambia. I want you to check all the hotels in the area. Also check the Livingstone hotels.'

'Yes, Sah.'

'Call me when you've found them, and we'll decide what to do then.' John was getting desperate. He'd lost Samson off the train, and Elijah seemed to have vanished. The two other operatives still did not answer their phones. Now, only he and Akashinga remained on the operation. If he was lucky, Akashinga would find Sanders and Kagonye and finish them. Now, John wanted them dead. He no longer thought of returning them to Harare and risk them slipping through his fingers again.

Ian had seen John running after the taxi, and he was thankful no other taxis waited at the rank for Captain John to give chase. It was a short drive but a long walk to the Zambian border post. The COU's excessive secrecy had proved to be both its strength and its weakness. The senior officer at the border post might have given more credence to John's claims if he'd known of the COU's existence. As it was, he might have thought John was just another crank making wild claims about his mission and authority.

At the busy Zambian border post, Ian waited in the queue for his turn. He recognised others from the tourist group to which he'd attached himself earlier. He'd not expected to find them still there. It seemed to Ian, the Zimbabwe border post delayed him for ages, but it was only about twenty minutes. The queue moved fast now, but for Ian every minute dragged. His concern was that Captain John and the police would arrive at any moment to take him back to Zimbabwe. Did the Zambian and Zimbabwean authorities cooperate? Would the Zambians hand him back, or would they detain him in Zambia? Neither was a pleasant prospect. At last it was Ian's turn. The immigration officer took Ian's passport and flicked through the pages two or three times. Ian worried that something was amiss. But then the officer found a blank page and stamped it and handed the passport back to Ian. 'Enjoy your stay in Zambia Mr Jones.'

'Thank you, I shall.' The tension drained out of Ian. Good old Morris; his work had passed scrutiny. The customs officer waved Ian through without looking at his backpack.

Ian stepped out of the building and walked straight up to a taxi. When the taxi turned onto the road towards Livingstone, he relaxed. The air smelled sweeter, and he felt he was on his way and could breathe a little easier now. Ian turned to look back at the Zambian border post. No vehicle followed them.

CHAPTER 54

30th August – 1st September 2009

THE Zambian side of the river looked different from Zimbabwe. For a short distance of about three kilometres, the main road to Livingstone sticks close to the Zambezi River. Hotels and other developments had gone up along the river since Ian's last visit. In between the road and the river were areas of large, shady trees and bare, hard earth. Along this stretch, once stood the signs that so impressed Ian as a boy—Bathing Is Suicidal. It was a lovely spot for walks along the riverbank.

The David Livingstone Safari Lodge was a short drive from the border post. The taxi turned off the main road a little before the Livingstone CBD and headed towards the river. Now late morning, the taxi pulled up at the hotel. Ian checked in the previous evening when he dropped Sarah off, so he walked straight to the room and knocked. Sarah opened the door and squealed in delight to see him. She threw her arms around him and gave him a big hug, but then, embarrassed, she backed away. Her relief at seeing him might have been a little too obvious. Even though they'd lived together for six months, a formality remained in their relationship, and she wouldn't take the lead in changing that.

Ian's own sense of relief after the morning's tension gave him an appetite. He and Sarah enjoyed a Mosi beer and an open burger and chips on the hotel veranda. The name Mosi came from Mosi-oa-Tunya, the smoke that thunders, the Zambian name for the Victoria Falls.

After lunch, Ian shaved off his beard and moustache before he and Sarah set to work on their genuine passports, copying the fresh entries in his false passport. It took much longer than they expected, but their forged entries needed to be perfect. The stamps and ink that Morris gave them did the trick, and their genuine passports now looked as if they'd passed through the border posts that morning. 'Good old Morris,' said Ian. 'It would be impossible to tell we stamped them ourselves.' Ian and Sarah Jones were now Ian Sanders and Sarah Kagonye once more.

'So, what happened after you dropped me off last night?' Sarah asked. Ian gave Sarah a detailed account of his traumatic crossing, and it horrified her. 'Goodness, you might have drowned, or a crocodile could have attacked you.'

'Yes, but it ended well,' said Ian, playing down the episode. He didn't tell her about the terror he experienced, and he also "forgot" to mention the late-night visitor to his room. But nothing happened; there was nothing to tell. Ian noticed how Sarah always became quiet when he mentioned Hazel, and it would raise needless suspicions if he mentioned her now. What was the point of that?

'Any problem at the border post this morning?'

'Well, I met Captain John. That caused a delay.' Ian related all the details of the drama at the border post. But he didn't tell her the thing he feared most—the prospect of not seeing her again. More than his concern of arrest in Zimbabwe was the fear she wouldn't know what happened to him. She might then have disappeared out of his life forever.

For Ian it was a traumatic day, and the emotional strain exhausted him. After dinner, they were both glad for an early night.

* * *

The crisp early morning air soon warmed. Breakfast overlooking the Zambezi was relaxing. Ian and Sarah spent the morning chatting and watching the flow of the river. Argument and debate were absent as they both enjoyed the peaceful scene. After lunch, the infinity pool proved too tempting to ignore. 'How about a swim?' said Ian. They changed into their costumes and walked down to the pool. On their way through the hotel lobby, Ian booked them onto the sunset cruise the hotel ran from their private jetty. At the pool when Sarah took off her robe, memories of Jemma flooded Ian's mind. Sarah wore the yellow and black, one-piece costume she'd lent Jemma for the Bulawayo trip. 'That's a striking swimming costume you're wearing, Sarah,' he said, with a small sense of nostalgia. His weekend with Jemma was like a dream, and it didn't seem real. It was so improbable, yet he knew it was true. Now, it felt like he was reliving the Bulawayo experience, here in Zambia. But it was Jemma who wore that costume a fortnight ago. Dressed in it, they looked more alike than ever.

Ian and Sarah swam in the cool water of the pool in the beautiful surroundings on the edge of the Zambezi River. Unlike Jemma, Sarah was a good swimmer and kept up with Ian as he swam a few laps.

All too soon they returned to their room to change for the sunset cruise. In the later part of the afternoon the burning sun lost its sting. They wore baseball caps and sunglasses and sat under the shade of an awning on the boat. The tranquil river scenery slid by, giving them a real sense of peace. The trees that hung over the water's edge were a paradise for birds and fish. Crocodiles lazed on the sandbanks, and hippos announced their presence with loud grunts and splashes. A herd of elephants stood knee deep in the water, enjoying the cool. The yellow sun slipped into a brilliant orange ball and then crept into a glowing red. The rays on the water sparkled in a silvery gold, and as the sun sank lower, the river turned to a burnished copper.

Ian and Sarah sipped on their beers while they watched nature's spectacular light show. The sky and water took on a gentle mauve tint as the sun dipped behind the trees. The lifebuoy on the wall caught Ian's eye. It wouldn't be of much use if the boat sank but could be helpful if someone fell overboard. Falling into the crocodile-infested river would be a dreadful prospect. Ian shuddered. He knew the feeling only too well.

A gentle breeze sprang up on the water, making Sarah's bare arms chilly. As the temperature dropped, she sat closer to Ian on the bench seat. She leant in against his chest, and he put his right arm around her shoulder to give her warmth. They looked like a romantic young couple on holiday.

'This time tomorrow,' said Ian, 'we'll be in Botswana.' They regretted having to leave this idyllic spot so soon, but they knew they should put as many kilometres as they could between them and Captain John. They did not know his reach, but it was not worth taking any chances. After dinner, Ian and Sarah tumbled into bed and soon fell sound asleep. Neither of them had the courage to extend their brief intimacy past the end of the sunset cruise.

* * *

Tuesday morning, and the hotel buzzed with activity. A large tour group prepared to leave, and the hotel readied for new arrivals. Ian and Sarah enjoyed a leisurely breakfast, and they walked out to the pool and boat jetty for one last look. It was time to move on from the scenic oasis as they hoped to be at the Kazungula ferry by mid-morning. The hotel called a taxi for them, and they said goodbye to the friendly staff.

Ian and Sarah walked to the boot of the taxi to stow their backpacks. But the driver said the boot was full and they should take their backpacks inside the taxi with them. He picked up Ian's backpack and put it on the floor of the front passenger seat. As he reached for Sarah's backpack, she said, 'Hold on, I need to put on my top. I feel a little chilly.' Sarah picked up her backpack and walked back into the hotel lobby and through to the ladies' toilet. A few minutes later, she emerged wearing an unbuttoned, orange, cotton blouse over her white T-shirt.

Sarah dumped her backpack next to Ian's on the floor of the front passenger seat and hopped into the back of the sky-blue taxi. She slid across the rear seat and sat behind the taxi driver. Ian followed and sat beside her.

The driver confirmed with Ian that they wanted to go to Kazungula, and then he drove out of the hotel grounds. Ian asked him to take them for a quick spin around the town before they set off for Kazungula. As they drove through the CBD, Ian asked questions about various buildings and construction sites. Many of the driver's brief responses appeared to be wrong. He was a poor tour guide. When Ian asked to see the railway station, the driver found it difficult to find even though they'd driven past it on the way into the CBD. The driver did not seem familiar with the area, and when he asked if they'd seen enough, Ian was glad to say they had.

As they drove towards Kazungula, Ian fancied the taxi driver watched him in the rear-view mirror. He couldn't be sure because he couldn't see the driver's eyes through the dark sunglasses he wore. A baseball cap, pulled down low in front of his eyes, obscured the driver's face. He looked straight ahead when he answered Ian's questions, even when the taxi stood still. At first, it was reassuring the driver focused on the road. Ian studied him from the back of the taxi, noting his thickset frame and muscular arms.

Ian focused on the taxi driver as his suspicions grew. The more he studied him the more concerned he became. It was getting hot, but the taxi's air conditioning didn't work. The windows were open, but the air was humid. Ian noticed the rivulets of sweat running down the man's face. The driver took his cap off and placed it on the front seat next to him, turning his head a little to the left as he did so. A shock of recognition ran through Ian's mind. He'd seen that face before now. The driver was balding, with a thick neck and a heavy looking profile. Ian rocked back in his seat.

'Sarah, let me give you a hug.'

She smiled in puzzlement. It was a strange request at that moment, but then whites could be strange in their ways. Sarah let Ian put his arms around her and pull her close. Ian pressed his face against her left cheek to shield his face from the driver's view. He whispered in her ear. 'Remember the first night you arrived at the apartment?' She looked at him, waiting for his romantic reminiscence. 'This is the man who attacked me.' Ian sat back in his seat, and Sarah looked at him, placing her right hand at the front of her neck as she did so. Ian nodded imperceptibly. Did she understand what he'd said? She must have, but Sarah sat without saying a word, and Ian's sense of apprehension grew. Yesterday's feeling of peace and wellbeing faded fast.

About five kilometres past Simonga village, the driver turned left off the main road onto a dirt track leading to the river. It didn't look like a proper road at all. 'Where are we going?' said Ian.

'I must drop off parcel in boot.'

Surely, no one lived down there. Ian's sweaty palms betrayed his taut nerves as they drove along the bumpy dirt road stirring up the dust. The sun and shade flickered through the tall trees like a strobe light, and it added to Ian's sense of dread. What made it worse was he'd wound down and relaxed since leaving Zimbabwe. He thought they were safe, and he never expected their pursuers would follow them over the border. When would it end? How would it end? Ian looked across at Sarah, but she did not seem in the least bit concerned, appearing relaxed and admiring the passing vegetation. Perhaps she misunderstood what he told her. This man tried to garrotte him the night she arrived at the apartment. Where was her handgun? Their backpacks lay on the floor of the front passenger seat. How would she get the gun if she needed it?

Large trees and tall grass overgrew the area. An ideal spot to finish them. At the edge of the river they entered a clearing. It was hard, bare earth about ten metres in diameter and looked like a weekend fishing spot. Here the bank sloped into the river and was ideal for launching a fishing boat. The driver stopped the taxi and pulled on the handbrake. 'What's this place?' said Ian, sitting forward in his seat. 'There's nothing here.'

The man did not reply. He got out of the taxi and wrenched open Sarah's door. In his left hand he held a handgun. With it, he indicated for Sarah to exit the taxi. 'Get out! Hurry! You too,' he said, pointing the gun at Ian. Ian jumped out of the taxi and tried to open the front passenger door to get Sarah's backpack. Damn! Locked! That's done it.

'You have a Glock 26,' said Sarah, 'are you with the COU? What's your name? Who's your boss?'

'My name is Akashinga. My boss is Captain John.'

Akashinga walked down to the water's edge, beckoning with the handgun for Ian and Sarah to follow. About three metres from the water, he made them halt.

'Before you kill us,' said Sarah, 'can you please tell me what happened to Thomas Chimedza?'

'Thomas fell into the mine. He helped us throw sacks in the big hole. They were too heavy. Two people must hold them and swing them back and forwards. Samson let go too soon, and the sack pull Thomas towards the edge. I try to catch him, but too late. It was a bad accident.' Sarah almost believed Akashinga, but then he burst out laughing.

'And where is this Samson?' said Sarah.

'He fell off the train when you come to Victoria Falls.'

'What happened to Thomas' cell phone?'

'My phone's battery was too flat, so I borrow his. I give it to Captain John.'

'Who then used it to lure me with a false SMS from Thomas.' said Sarah. Akashinga shrugged. 'And what about Jedson Ziyambi?' said Sarah. 'I saw him at the border post at Victoria Falls.'

'Silly woman, Jedson, Captain John and The Leopard are all same person. His real name is John Ziyambi, and he tells us to get rid of Thomas.'

'How did you get hold of the taxi?' said Ian.

'Once I found where you stay, I bribe man at taxi company to tell me when Mr Sanders order a taxi. They let me come for a ride.'

'Then where's the taxi driver?'

Akashinga frowned. 'Now we must finish business.' With the toe of his right shoe he splashed the surface. 'The water is good. Nice day for swimming.'

'Are you going swimming?' said Sarah with a look of mock surprise.

'No, it's a nice swim for you. Now take off clothes.'

'Why must we take off our clothes?' said Ian.

'They are too bright. With no clothes, no one see you.'

Sarah slipped off her orange blouse and dropped it onto the ground. Ian couldn't understand her meek compliance with Akashinga's orders. Was she resigned to her fate? His mind raced. They stood halfway between the taxi and the river. Could he get back to the taxi, jump into the back seat, lean over the front passenger seat, grab Sarah's backpack, find her handgun and shoot Akashinga? No, it was impossible. In that time, the burly assassin would shoot Sarah, and he'd be next.

'You both take off everything. Hurry,' said Akashinga, moving his aim from one to the other.

As Ian slowly took off his T-shirt, he saw Sarah undo her belt and move her hands around to the back of her jeans to drop them. A flash of movement, and a silvery spray of water drenched Ian and Sarah. Ian recoiled at the loud bang as a bullet hissed into the mud, centimetres from his feet. A second spray of water arched high in the air and fell with a heavy thud on the ground in front of them. Akashinga shouted something. The sound of firing; five shots: bang, bang, bang, bang, bang. Ian ducked. Sarah stood her ground with her Glock in her hand, smoke coming from the barrel. Ian looked up in time to see a huge crocodile backing into the river with Akashinga's right foot caught in its mouth. In a second, all that remained was Akashinga's handgun lying in the mud on the edge of the river. 'Did you get him, Sarah?'

'I shot at the crocodile. I should have aimed at Akashinga, but I suppose it's human nature to save a man from a beast.'

'How did you get your gun? I thought it was in your backpack.'

'I tucked into the back of my jeans. When I heard Akashinga speak back at the hotel, I knew he was a Shona. It's unusual for a Shona taxi driver to be working in Livingstone.'

'Aren't there any Shona's here?'

'Yes, but better safe than sorry, don't you think? My COU training would be a waste if I didn't keep one step ahead.'

'So that's why you went back into the hotel with your backpack and put on your orange blouse over your T-shirt?'

'Yes, to be on the safe side.'

'If I'd known you had the gun, I wouldn't have worried so much.'

'You worry too much. Did you think I would let anything stop us now?'

'Well, we'd better get moving before anything else happens.'

'We can't take the handguns through customs and immigration,' said Sarah.

Ian plucked Akashinga's handgun out of the mud and hurled it far into the river where it disappeared with a small splash. Sarah weighed her handgun in the palm of her right hand, but then she hesitated. 'What if others are coming after us?'

'No, you were right when you said we can't take a handgun into Botswana.'

Sarah sighed and swung her right arm back and threw the second handgun even farther than the first. It too disappeared with a small splash.

'Let's get out of here pronto,' said Ian, turning towards the taxi. 'Damn! We have a puncture.'

The front left tyre was flat, making it impossible to drive on it. 'I hope the spare's got air,' said Ian, turning the key in the boot. He gasped and took a quick step back. In the boot lay a body partially wrapped in a blue, painter's drop sheet. Ian and Sarah stood in stunned silence for a few moments. 'This must be the real taxi driver,' said Ian, 'before Akashinga got to him.'

'What should we do now?'

'First, we must change the flat tyre, but I don't think we should go to the border in this taxi. The hotel will know they called it for us, and the police will think we're responsible for the missing driver. Let's go back to Livingstone and park the taxi in a quiet spot where it won't attract too much attention. Then we can catch a bus to the border.'

Sarah stood, contemplating the body in the boot. 'It looks like he was shot in the head. When they find the body, they'll still think we did it.'

'Unless,' said Ian, 'we put the body in the river.'

Ian took the dead man under the armpits and Sarah took his legs. They struggled with the weight, carrying the body to the river's edge so as not to leave any drag marks. 'We wouldn't want any signs of what happened here,' said Sarah, struggling for breath after carrying the great weight. 'He wasn't small, was he?'

'It's true what they say about dead weights; they seem heavier.' They got the body into the water's edge and pushed it half floating, half sinking into the river. As the flow caught it, the body began a slow, macabre roll before vanishing downstream.

'With luck, the crocodiles will take care of the evidence,' said Sarah.

Ian rinsed out the traces of blood from the painter's drop sheet, being careful not to get too close to the water's edge and any lurking crocodile. They found cloths in the boot and wiped the drop sheet at the points where they had held it; folding it and wiping it as they went. Afterwards, they placed the neatly folded drop sheet under a bush for a "lucky" fisherman or passer-by to find and take away.

Luck was on their side. There was air in the spare tyre. After a struggle with the over-tight wheel nuts, Ian changed the flat. They took their time to wipe the rims of the flat and spare tyres, the boot, door handles and any other surface they may have touched. They didn't want to leave any incriminating fingerprints. 'OK,' said Ian. 'Do you know how to drive, Sarah?'

'Yes, we had to learn to drive in the COU.'

'I can't drive. A white taxi driver would look suspicious.'

Ian and Sarah drove back to Livingstone in silence, both lost in their own thoughts. Sarah drove the taxi wearing her sunglasses and her baseball cap pulled well down in front of her face. Ian again saw that Sarah was a person of action. She didn't mull over things. She did what was necessary and calmly cleaned up afterwards. Her training kicked in and she took charge of the situation. He'd met no one like her, man or woman. The COU's loss was Ian's gain. Why would anybody want to cross her?

They parked the taxi in a side street on the edge of the Livingstone CBD, taking care to wipe the steering wheel, gear stick and door handles. Ian and Sarah hoped no one saw them leave it there. They walked into the CBD and asked directions to the bus station. Several minibuses waited at the main market, and it was easy enough to find one heading to Kazungula. The bus was cheap, crowded and noisy, but it was a short trip of about sixty kilometres, and they were at the border in an hour and a half.

Ian and Sarah were on foot and had no trouble getting on the ferry. It took an age for the trucks to offload and load onto the pontoon. The Zambian border post was quick, but there was a traffic jam at the ferry, and it was an hour before they were under way. 'Goodbye Zambia, and not a moment too soon,' said Ian.

The crossing took less than ten minutes. They leant against the railing of the pontoon and watched the peaceful river roll past them. In the distance, hippos splashed in the water. The warm, late morning breeze blew off the river. Halfway across, they passed the pontoon going the other way, also laden with trucks.

Passing through the Botswana border post with their genuine passports was no trouble at all. They would worry about their next move later. Of one thing they were sure—neither of them could return to Zimbabwe in the foreseeable future.

Chapter 55

1st – 6th September 2009

KAZUNGULA was the point where Zambia, Zimbabwe and Botswana met. Ian and Sarah were keen to move on as soon as possible because anyone who hunted them would look there first. They found a taxi to take them to Kasane, from where they could catch a bus for the South. Tired, they didn't want to travel far. A taxi driver suggested their best plan may be to stay in Kasane overnight or make their way to Nata which was only a four-hour drive. Most buses for the South left early in the morning, and no seats were available on the next scheduled bus. An African man standing nearby overheard their conversation. 'Where are you going my friends?'

'If possible, we'd like to get to Nata this afternoon,' said Ian.

'If you pay me fifty dollars, I will take you in my truck.'

The taxi driver laughed. 'Fifteen dollars is the most you should pay.'

'OK, twenty-five dollars then,' said the truck driver.

Ian and Sarah hauled themselves up into the cab, high off the ground. They'd have a good view of the countryside and any game. 'You can't see much when it's hot in the daytime,' said the truck driver. 'If you're heading south, I can take you all the way to Francistown for fifty dollars.'

Ian and Sarah agreed they needed a break from being on the move. The truck driver had a tourist brochure in the cab of his truck. Ian flicked through and found the number for Nata Lodge and booked two nights in a thatched chalet. 'Thatch may appeal to you whites,' said Sarah, 'but I've lived under thatch much of my life. For me it's not a novelty. Corrugated iron roofs have less bugs falling down onto you.'

'A top-class lodge would be fumigated,' said Ian.

The truck driver enjoyed the banter. 'Me, I prefer asbestos roof. No fires.'

'Asbestos is bad,' said Ian. 'It can affect your lungs.'

'We Africans are used to it.'

The drive was long and hot though it was still early September. Ian couldn't imagine doing it in mid-summer. The dry countryside raced past, reminding him of the drives to their family farm so long ago. The driver was right; apart from a lone elephant, they saw few animals and little sign of human habitation. There'd been almost no rain since the end of March, and the grass looked yellow and dust dry. The trees in the forest reserves retained their green leaves, but much of the trip was through open scrub. Parts looked like desert country, and then other areas were thick with long, yellow grass.

At half past five, the truck driver dropped Ian and Sarah at Nata Lodge. Ian paid the driver the twenty-five-dollar fare and thanked him for the ride. The truck rumbled into the distance as they surveyed the lodge. There was an impressive central building under thatch and a sparkling swimming pool. Thatched chalets dotted the area. The central building burnt down one year earlier and was rebuilt. It looked and smelt brand new. 'You are one of our first guests in the new lodge,' said the receptionist. 'Normally, you wouldn't get a room unless you booked well in advance.'

The free-standing chalet was on stilts and angled to its neighbours to give the greatest privacy. Twin beds pushed together formed a double bed. The light-coloured timber walls and red timber furniture gave the chalet a warm, cosy look. Ian and Sarah hurried to freshen up after their long drive. They didn't want to miss sundown as it was the most beautiful part of any day in sub-Saharan Africa. The St Louis Export beer slid down nice and cold, chilling their cores. The velvety sky was perfect for the barbeque meal served at the outdoor tables in front of the thatched reception area.

After dinner, they returned to their chalet for an early night. Ian was first in the outdoor shower. The moon hung overhead like a lantern in the sky, making it a romantic setting, but he was too tired to appreciate it. The pounding spray of the shower did little to revive him. Ian stood under it, letting it soak him in a watery massage he was too weary to end. The warm and embracing spray was in sharp contrast to the cool night air.

Ian felt a touch on his shoulder and turned to see Sarah, naked, joining him under the shower. Neither of them spoke as they soaped each other's back. Sarah was beautiful, every inch of her. Just like Jemma, a perfect body and a lovely face. They stood under the shower, luxuriating in the spray's warm sting on their bodies, reluctant to turn off the taps. They dried themselves and each other's back. Still, neither spoke a word. Exhausted, and too tired to bother putting anything on, they slipped naked into bed. In a moment they were asleep.

Dawn painted the sky, and Ian stirred. Sarah looked fast asleep as he eased out of bed and padded to the bathroom. Ian slipped on his jeans and stepped out onto the veranda of the chalet. The early morning air was fresh, and it promised to be a fine cloudless day. Looking up, he noticed how big the sky looked, a big blue African sky that seemed to engulf the earth like a blanket might engulf a campfire. The yellow of the grass accentuated the endless blue of the sky. These were the colours of Africa.

The rainy season ended months ago. The green of the trees remained, looking like oases in the desert, but the unrelenting dry that followed the rainy season soon swept away any traces of green from the grass. Marula and monkey-thorn trees and mokolane palms were predominant in the area.

How odd he'd not noticed the big blue sky before now; not even yesterday. But yesterday, his only thoughts were of reaching safety. Prior to that, ever since he'd returned to Africa, he'd either been in the city or travelling through the country where the bush crowded up against the road. And on the drive to Bulawayo, he was preoccupied with Jemma and the roadblocks. Ian felt a great weight lifted off his shoulders, and he'd been able to rise at his leisure and enjoy his surroundings. He didn't have to look over his shoulder the whole time as he breathed in the fresh air. How quiet and empty this place was, beautiful in its desolation with that big, blue African sky.

Ian's thoughts were up there in the blue yonder. The past few days had been stressful, and he noticed the effects of it. He jumped with the sudden tap on his shoulder. 'Come back to bed. It's only six o'clock.' said Sarah. 'You've got all day to admire the sky.'

'We went to bed at nine, and we've already had nine hours sleep.'

'I didn't say you had to sleep.'

Sarah pulled off her nightshirt and lay down naked, propped up on her right elbow, looking expectantly at Ian. She lay on his side of the bed, an unmistakable invitation. Ian unzipped his jeans and dropped them to the floor. He stepped out of them and joined Sarah on the bed. She put her arms around his neck and kissed him full on the mouth. Their tongues explored each other with their deep kisses. Ian dreamed of this moment, but he couldn't remember when that dream started and never imagined it would ever come true. Dreams are cheap, even cheaper than talk. Mostly she'd been a pain in the arse, aloof and superior, but now he'd have her. Aaron seemed to have flicked a switch in Ian when they sat around the campfire drinking Chibuku and talking late into the night. Ian fancied Sarah before that night, but her stated unavailability and contrariness held him at bay.

Suddenly, Ian stopped and pulled back. 'There's something I should tell you.'

Sarah smiled and put her left hand on his chest. 'You mean about Jemma?'

'You know about that?'

'Yes, she told me all about your Bulawayo weekend when she came back to work.'

'You never said anything.'

'Neither did you.'

'It wasn't my prerogative to say anything, so I left it to Jemma. When I saw no sign you two discussed it, I thought maybe she hadn't told you. It wasn't my place to break her confidence, but now, I had to tell you.'

'You're a good man, Ian, and you've shown great respect for both of us. That's why we love you.'

'So it's not a problem then?'

'It's not at all a problem because I love my sister, and I wanted you to have her. You're the first man she's been with since her husband died.'

They kissed again, and their bodies entwined and seemed to melt into each other. The subservient and gentle Jemma took control of their lovemaking, but the feisty Sarah submitted to Ian. To her surprise, she wanted him to be dominant. Her feelings for him blossomed at the Elephant Hills Hotel when he'd been such a gentleman. She first realised her need for him when he'd paddled back across the Zambezi after dropping her off at the David Livingstone Resort. Now she knew she longed for him and wouldn't let him go if he would have her.

Ian and Sarah made slow and sensual love. Surrendering herself to him did not prevent her from taking part in the action. She moved her hips in that rhythmic African fashion and drove him crazy as they came together again and again.

They sweated from their exertions and felt drained. 'We shouldn't miss breakfast,' said Sarah. Ian looked at the clock, almost half past eight. They'd made love for over two hours. They hurried, laughing, to their private outdoor shower. It was beautiful and refreshing. Afterwards, they dried themselves and each other on the sunny side of the shower where the morning rays warmed their skin. How wonderful life can be.

Ian had booked two nights at the Nata Lodge, but it was not enough. Neither Ian nor Sarah wanted the romantic holiday to end so soon. After breakfast, they walked to the reception desk to extend their stay by another two nights. 'Oh!' said the receptionist, 'We're booked out, but let me check.'

'While she's checking,' said Ian, 'I'll see what the story is with the tours.'

'OK, I'll wait here.'

'Are you on your honeymoon dear?' Sarah turned to see a smiling, elderly white woman with twinkling eyes and tightly waved white hair.

'Well—'

'It's easy to see when a couple are in love, and I thought you and that handsome man of yours might be on your honeymoon.'

'Mavis, let the young woman be. I'm sorry, Miss,' said the large, balding man turning to Sarah, 'my wife has these damn fool romantic notions and then asks personal questions.'

'Oh, that's all right,'

'Please excuse him my dear. I'm afraid he's grumpy this morning.'

'Come on, Mavis, we'll be late again if we don't hurry.'

When the elderly couple walked away, the hotel manager stepped forward and spoke to the receptionist. 'We can't turn out the first honeymoon couple to book in since our reopening. Give them two extra nights. There's always a last-minute cancellation.'

'Actually, we're…' Sarah was about to explain that she and Ian weren't on their honeymoon, but then she changed her mind.

'Yes Madam,' said the receptionist, 'we can extend your booking for a further two nights.'

Sarah caught up with Ian who was looking at the tour options.

'It's OK, we've got another two nights.'

'Didn't they say the lodge was full?'

'Yes, but I talked them into letting us stay,' said Sarah, turning her face away to hide her smile.

'Well done. I'm impressed. Now we can go on this tour to the Nata Bird Sanctuary this afternoon.'

Half past three and it was time for the visit to the bird sanctuary. Ian and Sarah made their way to the hotel lobby where five others were waiting for the tour. The guide warned them to bring jackets and hats as the tour would be three hours in an open vehicle, and the evenings got cool. The featureless vista emphasised the distant horizon, and the silvery-grey salt pan shimmered in the heat haze. Huge light grey dust devils (willy-willies) made their way across the empty landscape. The sky on the horizon was a pale lavender shade that became bluer and bluer higher up, ending in a breathtaking deep blue overhead. The salt pan stretched from horizon to horizon. *Big sky* was a fitting description for this place.

'There are one hundred and sixty-five species of birds in this sanctuary,' said Ian. 'Most of them are waterbirds.'

'Well, they're in hiding then,' said Sarah. 'Where are they?'

'Probably, it's not the season for them.'

The Sua Pan in the Nata Sanctuary was flat to the horizon and made a spectacular sight. It was part of the Makgadikgadi Salt Pans, the largest area of salt pans in the world.

'This sanctuary is the largest of the three flamingo breeding areas in Africa,' said Ian. 'Did you know that?'

'So, you also read the tourist brochure,' said an amused Sarah.

The edge of the pan was a sea of dry yellow grass, broken by a few small islands of green palm trees. The raised viewing platform gave shelter from the sun. It was the only man-made structure in sight, and it brought home the area's isolation. The tour party watched in awed silence as the brilliant orange and red sunset turned the salt pan a shade of purple.

'This place is so desolate,' said Ian, 'you can hear the silence.'

The quiet isolation of the salt pan had a subduing effect on the tour party, and no one spoke on the return trip to the hotel.

When they got back to their room, to their surprise, Ian and Sarah found a bottle of champagne waiting for them.

'What does the card say?' Ian asked.

'The hotel management and staff wish us well in our future life together. We're their first honeymoon couple since the fire.'

'Did you tell them we were on our honeymoon?'

'Well, not exactly, but I didn't deny it.'

'You must have said something.'

'No, it was the little old lady's fault.'

'What little old lady?'

'She's a guest here. While I was waiting at the reception desk this morning, she came up and asked me if we were on our honeymoon. Before I could answer, her husband arrived and whisked her away. The hotel manager must have overheard us.'

'Perhaps, we should tell the manager it was a mistake.'

'No, we can't do that. The only reason we got the two extra nights is because they think we're their first honeymoon couple since they reopened.'

'Aha! So you never talked them into letting us stay on longer?'

'Yes, I talked them into it by not saying anything about us not being married.'

It was the familiar logic Sarah used against him in their debates. Ian thought it wise to let the matter drop.

The blue pool sparkled in the sun, but because of the low night-time temperatures the water was cold. Ian and Sarah's dip was brief, and they settled for drinks by the pool. In her striking yellow and black one-piece costume, Sarah drew the gaze of many other hotel guests. It wasn't only Ian who appreciated her appearance by the pool.

All too soon, they said goodbye to Nata Lodge. They planned to make their way to Gaborone, and this time they would travel in the air-conditioned comfort of a tourist bus.

The road from Kazungula to Nata ran south-east, close to the border with Zimbabwe. Too close for Ian's liking. From Nata to Francistown the road continued south east for another two-and-a-half hours. Francistown once again brought them close to the border. Did Jedson's reach stretch this far?

'What's the matter?' said Sarah. 'You seem jumpy.'

'That business with Akashinga has put me on guard. That's all.'

'Don't worry about the COU. Jedson has limited resources down here.'

Ian relaxed as the road to Gaborone took them away from Francistown and the border.

The eight-hour bus trip from Nata exhausted Ian and Sarah. Tired and dirty from their six hundred and twenty-five-kilometre bus ride, they needed a comfortable hotel room to rest up from their journey. The bus driver suggested the Gaborone Sun would be a good choice and dropped them off at the hotel entrance. They booked into a lovely room for their first night in the city, but they were too tired to appreciate it or to worry about what tomorrow might bring.

* * *

Ian and Sarah hadn't eaten the night before, and they were hungry. After a hearty, cooked breakfast, they walked out to the swimming pool. They selected two pool loungers under the shade of an umbrella and lay back admiring the clear blue sky. No one else was around, and they relished the freedom of having nothing urgent to do. It was their first good opportunity to discuss the past few days, and they pondered on the implications of what had happened.

'I don't understand. All that fuss to find me. I know nothing. Thomas never told me anything.'

'Surely he said something to you about his work? Any comment he made, no matter how insignificant it might seem, could be relevant.'

'The main thing he questioned was why they sent us to Sharm el-Sheik in Egypt. He thought they may have set us up to take the fall if something went wrong. But Jedson didn't give us any details or the reasons for the operation, and he sent us home the day after Zambian President Mwanawasa had his stroke. That's what made Thomas suspicious.'

'He questioned why they sent the two of you home at such short notice?'

'Yes. We never saw our own president, and we didn't know another COU team was there.'

'Did he suspect foul play with Mwanawasa's stroke?'

'I don't know, but the whole trip seemed strange. I told him to drop the matter as it would bring him trouble, but I don't think he took my advice.'

'Sarah, think hard. Did Thomas ever speak about his work or the COU?'

Sarah considered Ian's question for a time. 'Thomas said our team would, in time, take an active role in the dirty work, assassinations and stuff like that. Our team designation was LA4, and he said Jedson once told him it stood for language and assassination four. I thought it was a joke, and I never took it seriously.'

Ian drained his cup of coffee. 'Do you remember in the Rainforest at Victoria Falls, the COU man said even if I got away, you wouldn't? He said you were the one they wanted.'

'Yes.'

'And then, he said, by my association with you, they would have to assume I also knew too much.'

'Yes.'

'So, everything hinges on what Thomas may have said to you. One thing that stands out is this question of assassination.'

'What do you mean?' said Sarah, sitting up in her pool lounger.

'I expect the COU had a lot more going on than Mwanawasa and Sharm el-Sheikh.'

'Yes, they were always busy.'

'Could the COU be behind the mysterious deaths of all those politicians and party members? If they were, and it became known, it could embarrass the government.'

'I can't imagine the COU did all that.'

'Well, not all, but maybe some. The point is, no one has heard of the COU or knows who runs it. Even your Uncle Charles had never heard of it, and he said it might be a criminal organisation. What a perfect way for the guilty party or parties to keep their hands clean. There's no proof of any crimes and no evidence of who's responsible.'

'But why so desperate to find me?'

'If the COU had its cover blown, it would be hard for them to continue with their covert operations. As an insider, people would listen to you if you exposed them. If I made such claims, they'd say I was just another disgruntled white man trying to besmirch the regime. Now you've got out of Zimbabwe, I wonder if the mysterious deaths of political figures will stop, for a time at least.'

Ian and Sarah lay back in their pool loungers, admiring the surrounding trees and the big blue sky, deep in their own thoughts about their discussion.

The morning paper lay on a low table beside Ian. He picked it up and glanced through it while Sarah used her straw hat to cover her face to shield it from the reflected sun. One article caught Ian's eye, and the blood drained from his face. Tourists found the battered body of a young woman on a golf course at Victoria Falls. Locals identified her as Suzette, a prostitute who'd been working in the area for about six months.

Sarah hadn't seen the look on Ian's face, but from under her straw hat she said, 'I hate Jedson. He had Thomas killed and then pretended concern for me. If I'd agreed to meet him, I would have been next. I wish he were dead.'

'Yes, he deserves to die.'

They were silent for a long time.

'What do you plan to do now?' said Sarah, furrowing her brow.

'If I returned to Australia, what would you do?'

'I don't know.'

'I thought as much. It looks like I must stick around for a while and try to keep you out of trouble.'

'You, sticking around, will be trouble enough,' said Sarah, under her breath.

'What's that? I didn't catch what you said.'

'Oh nothing,' said Sarah. Her broad-brimmed straw hat hid her smile.

Chapter 56

September 2009

The phone rang, and Captain John picked up the receiver. He disliked receiving phone calls at work, other than calls from his operatives.

'So, Captain,' the voice said. 'The woman and her companion escaped over the border.'

Before John could answer, the voice continued. 'You can call that operation a dismal failure.'

'No, Sir, we'll find them and bring them back.'

'No, Captain.'

'Well then, we can kill them where we find them.'

'Captain, you'll do no such thing. Haven't you done enough damage already?'

'But, Sir, they must be in Botswana or Zambia, and it shouldn't be too difficult to locate them.'

'Or, Captain, they might be in any of our neighbouring countries. No, leave it alone. Why stir up a hornets' nest?'

'But they may go to the media.'

'We'll worry about that if or when it happens.'

'But, Sir, surely—'

'Forget it, Captain. All COU operations are suspended with immediate effect, and I'd recommend you keep a low profile for now.'

'But, Sir, I'm rebuilding my teams. To stop now would—'

'That's enough, Captain, the decision is final. We might reactivate operations at some point, but right now your activities are attracting way too much attention.'

'But what will I do?'

'You'll get your orders in the next few days.'

The phone went dead. John slammed down the receiver. 'The stupid bastards!' he shouted. 'The stupid, cowardly bastards! One little hiccup and they go running for cover.' His mind was in turmoil. Suspending the COU would have major consequences for him. John made a lot of money through the COU and lived a lifestyle befitting a government bigwig. He was glad now he'd resisted the temptation to boast about his possessions to the boss or to his own staff. In Africa, a show of wealth often attracted unwanted attention. If his superior knew how lucrative the COU was, he might give it to one of his own relatives. That's how things worked in Africa.

John planned to have his office refurbished. All those wasted hours spent pouring over the drawings. John had considered buying the property to become his own landlord, but now that was another dream in the dust.

He'd say nothing to his men until he received his new orders. A decaying venture was a depressing prospect. People would mope around the office looking gloomy and worrying about their future. If possible, he would keep his team together. Damn! He'd scheduled interviews later in the day with new candidates for the COU. Oh well, he'd go ahead with the interviews and keep them on file for future reference.

Operations suspended, for how long? What would he do in the meantime? John hated the prospect of returning to the military and a mundane job. The money was poor, and payment, irregular and uncertain. Everyone knew soldiers and government employees often waited months for their pay. He'd become used to being his own boss.

As John saw it, Sarah Kagonye caused all his problems. She must have guessed his plans for her. Why else would she be so elusive? If he ever laid his hands on her, she would regret it. That damned Thomas got what was due, but she'd keep.

John was about to call for Akashinga, but then remembered he'd not returned from his assignment in Zambia. His task was to kill Sarah Kagonye and her companion, but it looked like the fool once again failed in his mission. What happened to him? John missed him. Who could he vent his frustrations on now? Akashinga took all his abuse without responding or sulking. Although he'd not been too bright, he always tried to do his best to please John. He was loyal, a good friend and colleague, and hard to replace. John felt the pressure behind his eyes just before they moistened and shone with suppressed tears. Deep down, John knew his tears for Akashinga were really tears for his own shattered dreams. Damn that Sarah Kagonye! Damn that Ian Sanders!

The crystal glass sat empty on the bookshelf behind John's desk. He reached for it but changed his mind. Instead, he would join his remaining three operatives for a glass of Chibuku in the open plan office. John closed his office windows and pulled down the venetian blinds. One window looked onto the open space that Sarah once overlooked from her office window. The high window behind his desk looked onto the empty, narrow back yard. John locked his desk drawers and the cabinet below his desk, and he checked to make sure he'd locked the filing cabinets.

He looked around his large tidy office, the mark of a military background. He was proud of the way he kept it. John locked his office door and walked into the open plan office. His men all stood dressed in their hats and coats.

'Where are you lot going?' John enquired.

'We're going home, Sir. It's home time.'

'Oh! I thought I'd join you for a drink.'

'My father's expecting to meet me in town, Sir. Maybe we can have a drink tomorrow?'

The two others also made their excuses and left. John fancied he could already smell the foul stench of decay. Oh well, there's always the wife and kids. He'd go home and have a drink and a chat with the wife. It was ages since he'd done that, and now he looked forward to it. He locked the front door of the building, got into his car and waved good night to the security guard on the gate.

John turned into his driveway. The house was in darkness. Damn! He'd forgotten his wife and kids were on a visit to her mother that evening. She'd suggested he should buy dinner for himself on the way home. She planned to stay over at her mother's house and return the next day. John put his head in his hands. His men, his wife, his children; where were they when he needed them?

The dog sat there, wagging his tail, tongue hanging out and looking at John as if to say, well, what are we having for dinner tonight? John took out a crystal glass from the display cabinet. He crossed to the drinks cabinet and stared at his collection of single malts. Somehow, he wasn't in the mood tonight. The dog stood beside him and surveyed the bottles with him but saw nothing to its liking.

'Out of the way stupid dog!' John shouted.

The dog jumped up, ran a few paces, turned and sat down again, looking at John as if to say, my goodness, we are in a bad mood tonight.

Chapter 57

November 2009

Ten days after arriving in Gaborone, Ian and Sarah rented a small furnished apartment in a nice part of the city and applied for permanent residency in Botswana. Sarah applied as a refugee and Ian as a freelance writer and author. Uncle Charles acted as a character reference for Sarah over the phone and explained the situation to the immigration authorities. He offered to travel to Botswana to support her application. But Ian would need to return to Johannesburg to apply. Until then he would stay in Botswana as an Australian tourist.

'If Uncle Charles comes here to support your application, he may tell them I'm a wanted man in Zimbabwe. That way he could get rid of me and save your family from my evil influence.'

Sarah laughed. 'No, I doubt that. No one will come between us now.'

'Botswana is a nice peaceful country. I wouldn't mind settling here. What do you say, Sarah?'

'Wherever you are, is where I want to be, but yes, I also like Botswana.'

'This apartment is no bigger than the one in Harare.'

'For now, it'll be fine.'

'The book hasn't progressed in the last few weeks. Claiming to be a self-supporting writer makes me feel like a fraud,' said Ian, staring into his cup of tea.

Sarah stood behind Ian with a hand on his shoulder. 'Writing was the last thing to worry about when we were running for our lives. We've been so busy trying to sort out things you've had no chance to progress.'

'Yes, writing the novel seems so trivial now.'

Sarah put her arms around Ian's neck and kissed him on the cheek. 'Well, my darling, why don't you write our story? Wouldn't that make a good novel?'

'Doesn't it seem a little far-fetched?'

'No, truth is often stranger than fiction. Change the names of people and places. Voila! There's your book.'

'Hmm, yes, that might work.'

'Yes, and I'll help you write it.'

'And be the joint author.'

'No, you don't have to add my name.'

'No, I insist. And I'll dedicate it to you because you're the story.'

'If I'm to be the joint author, dedicate it to Jemma and Thomas. They're also a big part of the story. Oh! And I have news,' said Sarah, with the broadest grin.

'Yes,' said Ian, drawing out the word, wondering what was coming.

'Remember when we made love at Nata Lodge?'

'How could I forget?'

'You never used a condom.'

'We've never used a condom.'

'Yes, and now I'm pregnant.' Ian's jaw dropped. 'Are you angry?'

'No, it's wonderful news,' said Ian, hugging Sarah. 'But I never gave it a thought. I assumed a modern, sophisticated girl like you would take care of that side of things.'

'Why would I be on the pill? How was I to know you'd take advantage of me the first chance you got?'

'As I recall, it was the reverse.'

'And you realise you're adding to Africa's overpopulation problem?'

'Yes, and it's been a pleasure.' Ian was happy to contribute to the problem. It was the seal on their relationship.

Ian and Sarah went out for a celebratory dinner and a bottle of champagne at Caravela, the well-known Portuguese restaurant in Gaborone. They sat outside and listened to the band play, and afterwards drove home and made love—without a condom. 'In case you've got it wrong,' said Ian.

Ian and Sarah made good progress with the novel over the next few weeks, working every day from early morning to sunset. They worked hard and loved hard. 'You're a slave-driver,' said Sarah.

'Do you mean in the office or in the bedroom?'

'Both, but I'm not complaining about either. I'm just making the point.'

Sarah was intelligent and educated, but Ian never imagined what a great help she'd be. With minor adjustments, their writing styles complemented each other well. Ian loved working with Sarah, and with her input, his confidence in the book grew.

Ian sat editing chapters in the book and reflected on the story. He realised they'd completed an important phase in a journey, their journey. Ian recognised he'd changed, become a better person. The cost of his earlier ambition was a narrow and shallow life, but now he'd put the safety and interests of Sarah beyond his own, and it was the same with Jemma. His relationship with the sisters gave him no choice. His journey plucked him from a quiet home life in Melbourne, given him a shake, and dumped him down in Botswana. There'd been risks and dangers along the way, but somehow, he'd come through unscathed.

The women on Ian's journey were most significant. Louise in Melbourne helped him become a better lover. Ruth Bernstein was a memorable experience with the promise of more. Both were older women looking for fun, making it easy for Ian to enjoy the experience and grow as a man.

Thoughts of Jemma brought Ian pangs of guilt. It was not common for local-born whites to engage in sex with a black person. It was social suicide to cross that line. What would his parents and friends say? They'd grown up in a time when colonial views prevailed. Ian liked

Jemma a lot, but his feelings for her were confused. She was intelligent but not educated. She was his servant, and he'd taken advantage of her. Ian did not plan for an ongoing relationship with Jemma, and it pricked his conscience whenever he thought about it.

Then there was Sarah. They were in love, but they'd both grown up with racial prejudice. Sarah went through her own transition after her father's death. Her chance meeting with Ian spurred her on that path though at first, she'd resisted it. Ian often felt she wasn't grateful for the refuge he'd given her. He was unaware of the turmoil in her mind created by the events that challenged her lifelong beliefs. Sarah interpreted Ian's lack of appreciation of what she was going through as a sign of arrogance. They'd both been unsure whether the other's racist views were steadfast or just a tool to provoke argument. It was ironic their banter and debate drew them ever closer. Neither would yield until their mutual realisation that there was merit in both points of view. The cauldron of their debate brought them together, and their journey was one of personal growth.

'Darling,' said Sarah, plonking herself down in Ian's lap as he sat at the dining table in front of his laptop computer, 'I've been thinking.'

Uh oh, Ian recognised the look on her face. What was she planning now?

'If Botswana lets us stay, can we rent a nice big house with say… five bedrooms and a big garden?'

'Why rent a house with five bedrooms?'

'Well, apart from us, there's my mama and Jemma.' Ian had long since worked out that Sarah referred to her mother as *my mama* when she was trying to get him to agree to something. 'Life in Zimbabwe is difficult. Wouldn't it be nice if they came to live with us?'

'The immigration department would never agree to it,' said Ian.

'Yes, they would. I've spoken to them and they're supportive of family reunion. We'll have an even stronger case when our baby is born, and it might help your application too.'

Ian frowned. 'Sarah, you know what happened between Jemma and me in Bulawayo. How would it work, her living in our house? Wouldn't it create problems between us?'

'No, Silly, remember it was me that wanted you to make love to Jemma. When you took her to Bulawayo, I told her she'd have to make the first move because you never would. Jemma's been in love with you for longer than I have and has as much claim to you. I love my sister and I want her to be happy too.'

'It wouldn't work. It would seem like I was cheating on you, or Jemma, or both of you.'

'Our cultures are different, but you'd soon get used to it. Have you ever visited a chinchilla farm?'

'No, I haven't, why?'

'Each female chinchilla wears a big wide collar, so she can't get through the small hole that leads into her pen. The male doesn't have a collar, and he can use a corridor to visit as many females as he likes. It would work like that for us.'

'Your mama is not included, is she?'

Sarah laughed. 'Of course not, Silly. But maybe if I asked her—'

'No, I was only joking.'

'So was I, Silly. But if you're good, you can take off one of our collars and have both Jemma and me together. She and I make a great team.' They both laughed, but Ian wasn't sure why he had.

'Hmm, I've done a few things, but never that. But how would you react if I slept with your sister as often as I slept with you?'

'I'd love you more than ever. Jemma would be like a second wife to you; she'd be thrilled. I'm happy now, but I'd be even happier if Jemma were here.'

'Sarah, despite all your education and sophistication, you're still an African at heart, aren't you?'

'Yes, is that a criticism?'

'No, just an observation, that's all. And I don't love you any the less for it. Would Jemma agree to such an arrangement?'

'Yes, she'd love the idea. We agreed long ago to share you.'

'What! When? The cheek of it! How did you know I'd want either of you?'

'It started as a joke. Remember when you agreed to take Jemma to Bulawayo? That's when we decided. You may have thought you were being discreet, but we both noticed you ogling us when we wore our nightshirts, and we knew then we had you.'

'But you weren't just wearing your nightshirts; you were flaunting yourselves in front of me.'

'You didn't object.'

'Hmm, two women, it would seem like being married to a Gemini.'

'How about four women?'

'Four?' said Ian, his voice cracking. 'Why four?'

'Well, Jemma and I are both Geminis.'

* * *

After two months in Botswana, Ian and Sarah found a four-bedroom house with a granny flat. A high wall around the large front garden gave privacy. A shaded gazebo stood beside a braai on one side of the front garden and would be an ideal spot for Ian to write.

At the rear of the building was a beautiful, secluded, tiled courtyard with a large, inviting, swimming pool. The courtyard separated the granny flat from the main house. 'The granny flat will be perfect for mama,' said Sarah.

'Would mama cope with the swimming pool?' Ian asked. 'What if she fell in the pool?'

'Oh yes, she can swim.'

'It's a lovely big courtyard, but a little bare.'

'Don't worry. Mama will see to that.'

'That tree over-hanging the courtyard wall will give shade from the hot afternoon sun. That's the spot for the pool loungers.'

'And I love the back veranda facing the courtyard.'

'OK, Sarah, if you're happy, we'll take it.'

Ian signed the lease and he and Sarah spent the next two weeks buying furniture and getting the house ready. Sarah was now a permanent resident of Botswana and hoped her mother and sister would arrive soon. But first, Ian's parents were visiting for a week, on the way to Europe for a long-planned holiday.

A colleague in a writers' group recommended Ian's novel to a literary agent in London, and things were moving fast. But even if a publisher accepted the book, it might be quite a while before it appeared in the book shops. In the meantime, the outline of a second novel was taking shape. That would keep him busy while waiting to hear from the publisher.

* * *

Ian's parents were due. 'Come on,' said Sarah, waiting at the front door with the car keys, 'we don't want to be late for your parents.'

The airport was ten kilometres north of the city of Gaborone. The South African Airways evening flight from Johannesburg was due at a quarter to six.

Sarah had made an extra effort with her appearance and so had Ian. Both had worked hard getting the house in order. 'Will they like the house?' asked Sarah.

'Yes, I'm sure they will. Who wouldn't?'

'It's a pity my mama and Jemma aren't here to meet them.'

'Uh-huh,' said Ian, not sounding too enthused.

His response struck a chord with Sarah. 'Tell me,' she said, shifting in her car seat to face Ian, 'what did your parents say when you told them about me?'

'Mum is dying to meet you and so is Dad, though he doesn't show his emotions.'

'What did they say when you told them I was black?'

Ian frowned. 'It was a while ago. I don't remember now. I'm not sure I mentioned it.'

'What! You mean they don't know?'

'It won't make any difference. Mum will love you straight away. I'm sure she will. And Dad will get used to it soon enough.'

'Ian, that's not fair. It's not fair on your parents, and it's not fair on me.'

'I didn't deliberately hide it from them, but it never crossed my mind.'

'Your father will have a heart attack. We've had months to get used to each other as an interracial couple. Do you expect your father to accept it at a moment's notice?'

'Well, we'll soon find out if he's a racist, won't we?' said Ian, laughing.

'Ian, it's not funny.'

'What you've got to understand, Sarah, is that I don't see you as black. If I were describing you, I'd say you were beautiful, intelligent and sophisticated. The last thing I'd think of is that you're black.'

'Do you think of Jemma as black?'

'Yes, I do.'

'Why is that?'

'Perhaps, it's a language issue. Her English restricts our communication. With you, it's easy because you're educated. Even if Jemma is intelligent, the way she speaks marks her as uneducated.'

'Is that so? What if you were talking with Jemma, my mama, Uncle Charles and Mrs Chamisa? Have you considered that to them you might seem uneducated because you don't speak Shona? And you would continue to appear uneducated until you were fluent in the language.'

'Well, I'd better learn then.'

'If you haven't told your parents I'm black… Oh no! Now, I'm really nervous.'

'What's the matter?' said Ian, looking at Sarah.

'You haven't yet told them I'm pregnant, have you?'

'No, it'll be a nice surprise for them when they're here.'

'A nice shock you mean. I'm not showing, so wait until they get used to me.'

'No, I want to tell them; I'm proud you're carrying my baby.'

'You'll be giving all of us heart attacks if you're not careful.'

Keen to change the subject, Ian said, 'Jemma and I have little in common, other than the Bulawayo trip.' Ian turned into the airport car park entrance. 'I have feelings for her, but I can't converse with her in the way I can with you, so it would just be sex between us. Are you sure you wouldn't be jealous about that?'

'How could I be jealous of my sister when she's the one who brought us together? She made me see all the positive things about you. And besides, if I weren't available, I'm sure you'd make do with her. You can't just drop her now I'm available.'

'If she had more schooling and spoke better English, it might be different. Communication is essential for a proper relationship.'

'Yes, but you don't want a clone of me, do you? Isn't variety the spice of life? You could go to her when you're tired of my arguing and come back when your conversation comes to a halt. Most men could only dream of that.'

'Well, yes—'

'Besides, it's what's in one's heart that's important. Not the way one speaks.'

'Yes, but it would be better if Jemma could join in our discussions on a higher level.'

'I've thought about that. I've always told Jemma that one day I'd like to pay for her education. Wouldn't it be good if she at least completed a high school education? And it would make a big difference if she also had elocution lessons. Then you might stop seeing her as black. Could we afford that?'

'Yes, I'm sure we can; why not?'

'And while Jemma is studying, I'd help mama with the housework and help look after the babies.'

'Babies, what babies? You're not having twins, are you?'

'Oh! Didn't I tell you? You and Jemma have more in common than you think. She's missed her periods since your Bulawayo trip.'

'Ha-ha, very funny.'

'No, I'm serious.'

'You said Jemma couldn't have children.'

'No, I said the doctors said she couldn't have children.'

'You're kidding, right?'

'Come hurry, we mustn't be late for your parents. Let's get into the international arrival hall before they come out.'

Ian and Sarah hurried through the crowd up to the barrier outside the customs and immigration area. The first passengers from the Johannesburg flight were coming through the exit.

'Be serious now, Sarah. You're joking about Jemma, aren't you?'

'You'd better not tell your father you've made two black women pregnant within weeks of each other. He'll think Africa's loosened your screws, and then he really will have a heart attack.'

'Stop messing about, Sarah. I know it's not true.'

Sarah smiled. 'Isn't it?' She struggled to keep a straight face. She opened her mouth to say something. 'Well—'

'Ian,' a woman's voice called out. It was Norma, Ian's mother.

She came rushing across and hugged him. Greg Sanders followed, pushing a luggage trolley. He shook Ian's hand. 'Hello Son. Good to see you. Now, when are we meeting this new girl of yours? Your mother can talk about little else.'

Norma noticed Sarah standing close by watching them and listening to their conversation. 'Ian, does this woman want something?'

Ian swallowed hard, 'Mum, Dad, I'd like you to meet...'

Epilogue

November 2014

FIVE years on, Ruth and Solly Bernstein still had no idea who leaked information about their activities. They took extra care when talking in front of the servants and their relationship with Manfred and Ivana Schwartz changed. Manfred didn't seem to be a likely culprit though he did a lot of work for the Zimbabwe government. Might those contracts be payment for information?

Ivana was also on the radar, but the Bernsteins seldom saw her. Any information she had would come from Manfred or Nelson in the Harare office. They thought it improbable that Frida, an Ndebele, would pass information to her. The problem was how to warn Manfred, without offending him, that Ivana shouldn't be privy to confidential information. 'It's for her own safety,' said Ruth. 'The less she knows the better. The Zimbabwean authorities keep an eye on all of us. There's always the risk the police could detain one of us when we visit Zimbabwe.' Manfred appreciated the sense in that, but from then on, the Bernsteins only gave him select information.

Captain John heard nothing more about his angry phone call to the boss' home on the Sunday morning Ian Sanders crossed into Zambia. Perhaps the person who took the call did not relay his provocative comments. Nor did the officer in charge of the Victoria Falls border post hear from John or anyone else about his decision to let Ian Sanders go. John decided it was best to let things lie. If he reported the events at the border post, the boss would twist everything around to make it end up looking like his fault.

John lost his entire team A1 on the Victoria Falls operation. He'd planned to build a new team from scratch, but events overtook him. John raged against the COU's suspended operations, but what to do about it? A promotion to the rank of major and a desk job at army HQ did little to quell his anger.

Sarah got word her former workplace was now a night club and bar, but there was no news of Captain John or Jedson Ziyambi.

In May 2010, Levy Mwanawasa's wife spoke on a BBC - Network Africa programme. She said, the Zambian government did not thoroughly investigate the death of her husband. Maureen Mwanawasa said they ought to look into what happened thirty minutes before he collapsed with the stroke that led to his death. She also said his history of ill health did not eliminate the possibility of foul play; and that a sick person can also be killed. Many took her comments to suggest Robert Mugabe's involvement. Levy Mwanawasa planned to challenge Mugabe's legitimacy at the summit meeting of the African Union but suffered a stroke only hours before the opening session. Many Zambians and Zimbabweans felt the timing was suspicious.

Emmerson Mnangagwa was one of the most senior ministers in the Mugabe government. In October 2014 he was in a motor accident in Herbert Chitepo Avenue, close to the US Embassy in Harare. An approaching Kombi minibus veered across the road and rammed the car he was driving. The accident badly damaged his car but did not injure him. There'd been rumours he would challenge the vice-president, Joice Mujuru, for her position. Just seven weeks later he attained his goal. When Mugabe announced the change, he also revealed there had been an attempt that morning to poison Mnangagwa. Someone sprinkled an unnamed powder, possibly cyanide, on his desk. His secretary disturbed the powder when she opened his office in the morning, and there were claims she'd breathed it in and was critically ill in hospital.

Mnangagwa hoped to take the presidency when Mugabe left the post, but there was the small matter of Mugabe's wife, Grace. Some reports claimed she'd also expressed a wish to succeed her husband.

* * *

'What about those attempts to kill Mnangagwa?' said Ian.

'More like attempts to discredit Joice Mujuru, if you ask me,' said Sarah.

'Yes, I agree. These things happen when there's internal conflict in ZANU-PF.'

'So, what you're saying is…'

'Well Sarah, consider the situation now. Grace Mugabe talked her husband into getting rid of Joice Mujuru. Now there're two new vice-presidents, one of whom is a serious contender for the presidency. They're all jostling for position, and I'm curious what will happen this time. Who'll get the blame if one of them comes to a sticky end?'

'Are you suggesting the suspicious deaths might start all over again?'

'I've wondered about it. When you got out of Zimbabwe, the suspicious deaths stopped, but now that the politics is hotting up again, your friend Jedson Ziyambi might be back in business.'

'Hmm, perhaps. I often think about what Jedson did. He hasn't paid for his crimes, and I sometimes dream if it weren't for you and the children, I'd go back and make him pay.'

'Jemma will be back with the kids soon,' Esther called from the front door. 'I'll bring the tea out now.'

It was an afternoon ritual in the gazebo. Ian would close his laptop and clear the table of any notes or papers. The whole family would gather round the table for tea. Esther would bring it from the kitchen on a large wooden tray, Sarah would pour, and Jemma would make sure the children behaved. Sam Junior was a month older than his 'twin sister,' Kemi. The hospital said it was not common, but twins have occasionally been born weeks apart. It seemed not to have occurred to anyone that the children might have different mothers. 'More proof,' said Ian, 'of how similar you two look.' After school each day, the two children competed to relate the exciting events of that morning.

Jemma studied English and Mathematics for her advanced level (A Level) school certificate, and she dreamed of the day when she could stop studying and help Ian and Sarah with the books. Her elocution was little improved, and this was most noticeable when she was excited or angry. But the way she spoke didn't seem so important to Ian anymore, and it helped distinguish who was calling him from the other end of the house. Despite his best efforts, Jemma still called him *sir*, though somehow, the way she said it no longer made her sound like a servant.

Ian was content with his life. He was halfway through his fifth novel and hoped it would emulate the success of the first four. The royalties had helped pay the mortgage for the house they now owned. Ian looked at his happy family and marvelled at his circumstances. He grew up in a society where racial prejudice was the norm, and he never would have imagined he'd be the head of such a family. Yet here he was, happier than he'd ever been. The children did not marvel at their circumstances. To them, their family was normal.

* * *

Ian and Sarah relaxed on the loungers by the pool at the end of a warm Gaborone day. Jemma carried out a tray of drinks and handed a lemon lime and bitters to Sarah. As she gave Ian a beer, she nuzzled his neck and kissed him on the ear. Ian looked up and patted her on the backside. Sarah smiled as she recalled Ian's protests that living with the two of them would never work. It worked a treat. Jemma sat down on a lounger on the other side of him and sipped her drink. 'Ah, this is the life,' said Ian, as he took his first sip of beer while admiring the blue sky, edged with gold in the setting sun. Esther was in the kitchen preparing the evening meal, and the children were playing in the lounge.

'Soon, I will have completed my *A level* school-leaving exams,' said Jemma, 'and I can help you and Sarah with the books.'

'That will be nice,' said Ian, 'but I hope it will be enough to keep you occupied.'

'Oh yes, with that and the new baby I'll be busy.'

'You're pregnant? How, when?'

'Do you want us to explain it to you?' said Sarah, with one of her trademark mischievous smiles. 'Well, when a man—'

'I mean, Jemma, aren't you on the pill?'

'Maybe I missed one,' said Jemma. 'I'm sorry.'

'There's no need to be sorry. We must celebrate. Isn't that a wonderful surprise, Sarah?'

'Yes.'

'You don't seem surprised.'

'Do you imagine I didn't know? A sister always knows.'

'But Jemma, how could you forget to take the pill?'

'It's easy,' said Sarah. 'I've also forgotten now and then.'

'What, when?'

'The last time was a week ago.'

'You forgot to take it?'

'Uh-huh,' said Sarah, with a smile.

'No, I don't believe you.'

'Remember the last time you didn't believe me?'

'We'll have another set of "twins" then,' said Jemma.

'Yes, five years between the pairs is a good gap,' said Sarah.

'Have you told your mother?'

'No, we wanted to tell you first,' said Jemma. 'We'll tell mama tonight.'

'Let's go out for a celebration dinner tomorrow.' said Ian.

'We can go out for a nice dinner,' said Jemma, 'but I'm sure mama would like to celebrate at home with one of her special dinners.'

Ian beamed with the news of his growing family. 'Even here in Botswana, some would say I'm a kaffir lover. They don't openly express it, but it's in their eyes.'

'Don't make me laugh,' said Sarah, sipping on her drink. 'You're a white racist, and you always will be. Your father is the same.'

'Ha-ha, yes, I'm a white racist who loves two black women.'

'What about mama,' said Jemma, 'that makes it three black women?'

'Yes, I love your mama too.'

'Anyone who says you're a kaffir lover is wrong,' said Sarah. 'You don't love us because we're black; you love us despite us being black.'

'And,' said Jemma, 'we don't love you because you're white; we love you even though you're white.'

'You know,' said Sarah, 'how you say, although I'm black, you don't see me as a black because I'm educated and because of the way I speak?'

'Yes.'

'Well, even though you're a white racist, we don't see you as a white racist because you are intelligent, kind and caring.'

'But you still label me a white racist.'

'What does it matter,' said Jemma, 'as long as we love you and you're our very own white racist?'

'And my parents couldn't be any prouder of their grandchildren, and they love you two and your mama.'

'Yes, your father came around once he got over the shock of meeting me,' said Sarah. 'I'll never forget that moment; it was priceless. He looked at me and his eyes went wide, and his mouth dropped open. I'd swear it was a whole minute he didn't know what to say or do. I could see his mouth moving, but nothing came out. When your mother saw his reaction, she burst out laughing and hugged me and kissed me on the cheek. Then you and I were also laughing. Finally, your father shook my hand and said, "Pleased to meet you my dear." After that, he seemed to accept it.'

'I told you he wasn't a racist. Australia must have mellowed him. He didn't react at all when he met Jemma and your mama. He took it all in his stride.'

'I expect by then he wouldn't have put anything past you,' said Sarah with a twinkle in her eye. 'But we all have Jemma to thank for our family situation. She always felt you had promise, and she saw the possibility of the arrangement we now have. She was the one who first fell in love with you and somehow, against my better judgement, I got dragged into it.'

'They said it would take a generation after black rule to wipe out racist views,' said Ian.

'It will take longer in Zimbabwe. Probably, it will take at least a generation after all the old pre-independence leaders have died out.'

'I'm sure you're right, Sarah, but take us for example. We both had our own racist views when we first met less than six years ago and look how things have changed.'

'We were at opposite ends of the pole then, but now we've met in the middle.'

'Yes, it goes to show what a fantastic pair of tits and a great arse can do.'

The sisters set upon Ian with their cushions, squealing with laughter and tumbling onto his lounger in one of their frequent mock fights.

'Dinner's ready,' shouted Esther. 'Come and get it. Hurry up, the children are hungry.'

Glossary

List of frequently used words and terms, and people and organisations relevant to Zimbabwe.

Abel Muzorewa *Prime Minister of Zimbabwe Rhodesia: 1st June – 11th December 1979*

Bakkie *Ute or pick-up*

Baas *African pronunciation of Boss*

Braai or Braaivleis *Barbecue*

Chibuku *African beer brewed from sorghum, maize or millet. Due to its heavy sediment content it is also known as shake-shake*

CIO *Central Intelligence Organisation*

COU *Covert Operations Unit*

GFC *Global Financial Crisis*

Henry Kissinger *National Security Advisor and later US Secretary of State for presidents Richard Nixon and Gerald Ford*

Gukurahundi *Shona word meaning 'the early rain which washes away the chaff before the spring rains'*

Ian Smith *Prime Minister of Rhodesia: 13th April 1964 – 1st June 1979 Leader of Opposition in Zimbabwe: 18th April 1980 – May 1987*

Jambanja *Shona word for state-sponsored lawlessness – white farm invasions*

John Vorster *Prime Minister of South Africa from 1966 to 1978 State President of South Africa from 1978 to 1979*

Joshua Nkomo Founder and *leader of ZAPU and Vice President of Zimbabwe: 1987–1999*

Knobkerrie *African carved wooden club with a knob at the end*

Kraal *Small African village or cluster of huts*

Levy Mwanawasa *President of Zambia: 2nd January 2002 – 19th August 2008*

Lobola *Bride price, traditionally paid in cattle to the bride's family*

Madala *Zulu word for old man*

Marula *Tree which bears fruit like lychee*

Mealies *Maize plants or corn on the cob*

MDC *Movement for Democratic Change*

Morgan Tsvangirai *Leader of the MDC opposition in Zimbabwe*

Mthwakazi *Area including Matabeleland and eastern edge of Midlands, ruled by King Lobengula before white settlement*

Murambatsvina *Shona word meaning 'drive out the rubbish'*

Murungu *Shona word meaning white person of European origin, or urban-youth slang for blacks with money or power*

Panga *Machete approximately forty to forty-five centimetres long*

Robert Mugabe *Prime Minister of Zimbabwe from 4th March 1980, and President from 22nd December 1987*

Rondavel *Round African pole and dagga hut with a thatched roof*

SADC *Southern African Development Community*

Thabo Mbeki *South African President: 14th June 1999 – 24th September 2008*

UDI *Unilateral Declaration of Independence*

Varungu *Plural of Murungu*

Veldskoens *Suede bush shoes; usually grey or brown*

Wits *University of the Witwatersrand in Johannesburg*

ZANLA *Zimbabwe African National Liberation Army – ZANU's military wing*

ZANU *Zimbabwe African National Union*

ZANU-PF *Zimbabwe African National Union - Patriotic Front –the merger of ZANU and ZAPU in December 1987*

ZAPU *Zimbabwe African People's Union*

ZIPRA *Zimbabwe People's Revolutionary Army – ZAPU's military wing*

Map of Zimbabwe

Showing towns, roads, railway lines and national parks.

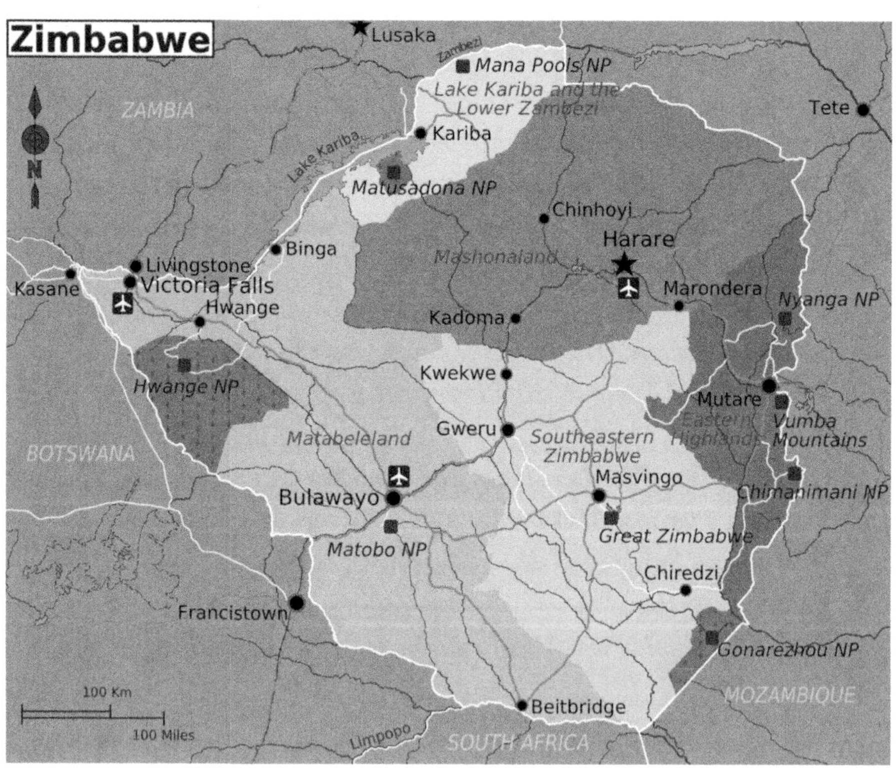

AUTHOR'S NOTE

THE story is set in the period from mid-2008 to late 2009 when Robert Mugabe ruled Zimbabwe.

The Covert Operations Unit (COU) is a fictitious organisation, but it sits comfortably with the factual Central Intelligence Organisation (CIO) and other shadowy branches of the security services. Similarly, The Matabeleland Freedom Front (MFF) is fictitious, but groups with similar goals exist.

In June 2013, the media reported the government was building the Robert Mugabe National School of Intelligence, about eleven kilometres from Harare, near the National Defence College. The aim of the school was to counter the supposed growing threat from Western powers with their regime-change agendas'.

The estimated cost was twenty-two million US dollars. Many people thought the expenditure, at a time of economic crisis, showed how the government placed its own survival ahead of the interests of the Zimbabwean people. The country's infrastructure was in a state of decay. Health, education, water and roads cried out for funding. Zimbabwe's well-known abuse of human rights led to fears the School of Intelligence would add fuel to the fire.

In November 2017, pressure from the military forced Mugabe's resignation. But that's another story.

L. T. Kay
Find out more at my website https://ltkay.com

About the Author

Bulawayo was my home town. That's where I grew up and got my first job.

Anyone who has lived in Africa, even for a short time, will confirm you can never really leave it. No matter how far you travel, like the grass seeds that stick to your socks, Africa goes with you.

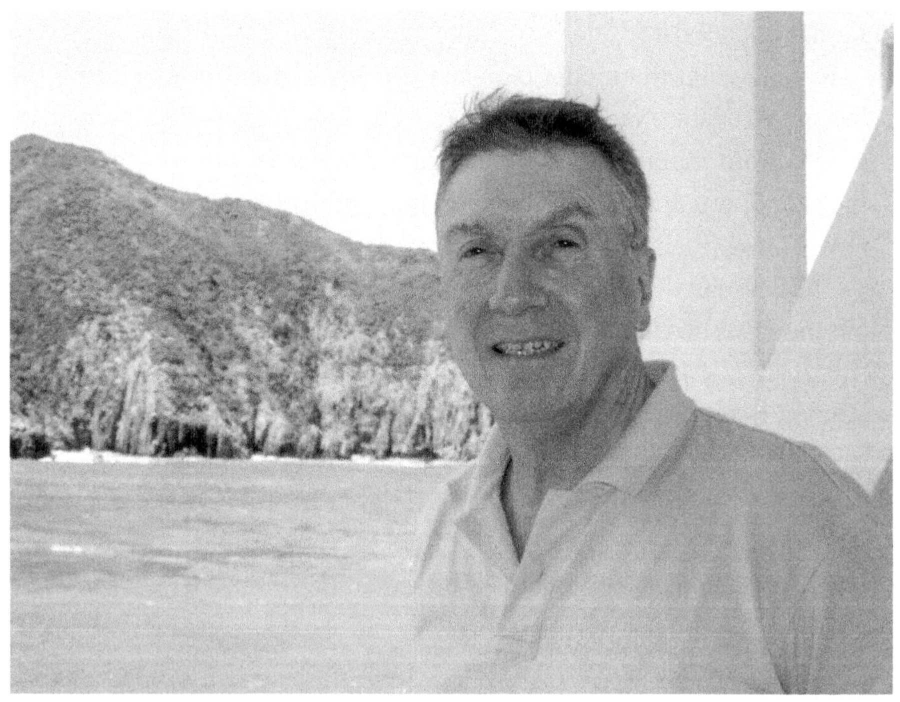

I lived and worked in Zimbabwe/Rhodesia and South Africa for over thirty years, alternating between Bulawayo, Salisbury (Harare) and Johannesburg.

The Bush War got serious while I was living in Hong Kong, and on my return to Rhodesia, I was called up for military service in the army.

Professional qualifications in accounting and marketing helped me secure senior management positions with companies in diverse fields, including engineering, textiles, clothing and cosmetics manufacture, and service industries.

Today, I live in Melbourne with my wife Maggie and write fiction set in Southern Africa, principally Zimbabwe. Since the turn of the century that country has led a dark, surreal existence that keeps many people shaking their heads in disbelief. It would be funny if it wasn't so sad.

L. T. Kay

Find out more at my website https://ltkay.com

Other Books by the Author

The Leopard Series is a trilogy of novels set in the troubled years of Robert Mugabe's dictatorship in Zimbabwe. The first two books in the series are published and the third is a work in progress. *Feeding The Leopard* is book 1 in the series.

The Bulawayo Boys' Club – Book 2 in The Leopard Series
When there's nothing to lose, a person can afford to play fast and loose. But what if someone raises the stakes?

Alan Drake, formerly with the Australian Special Forces, drifts aimlessly, chasing the good life in Melbourne. For him, that means bars and clubbing.

When his wealthy controlling father, George, sends him on a mission to Zimbabwe, Alan has no idea what's in store for him. He regards the venture as a crazy plan and doesn't take the task seriously. Alan has no interest in the country, and he's never even heard of Mthwakazi, let alone the sinister figure known as The Leopard.

Zimbabwe is a land of shortages, and Bulawayo lacks the bright lights that so appeal to Alan. He can't wait to get back home. He soon discovers the city can generate more than enough adrenalin to keep his blood racing, but not in the way he might have hoped.

The mission takes Alan into the national parks where he sees the plight of the wildlife and the hardship endured by the nearby rural population. It leads him into an unintended war with an unknown foe. How can he fight a faceless enemy? People are relying on him. Has he left it too late to leave?

Alan soon realises someone wants him dead. And to make matters worse, the people he's come to help are now also on a death list. The ambitious project has become a fight for survival, with unexpected consequences. His father never warned him of the dangers of the mission.

How could his simple role in the venture lead to this?

Can he extricate himself and his colleagues from the mess he's created?

What can he salvage from the fiasco?

Can Alan resist Africa's many temptations?

L. T. Kay

Find out more at my website https://ltkay.com

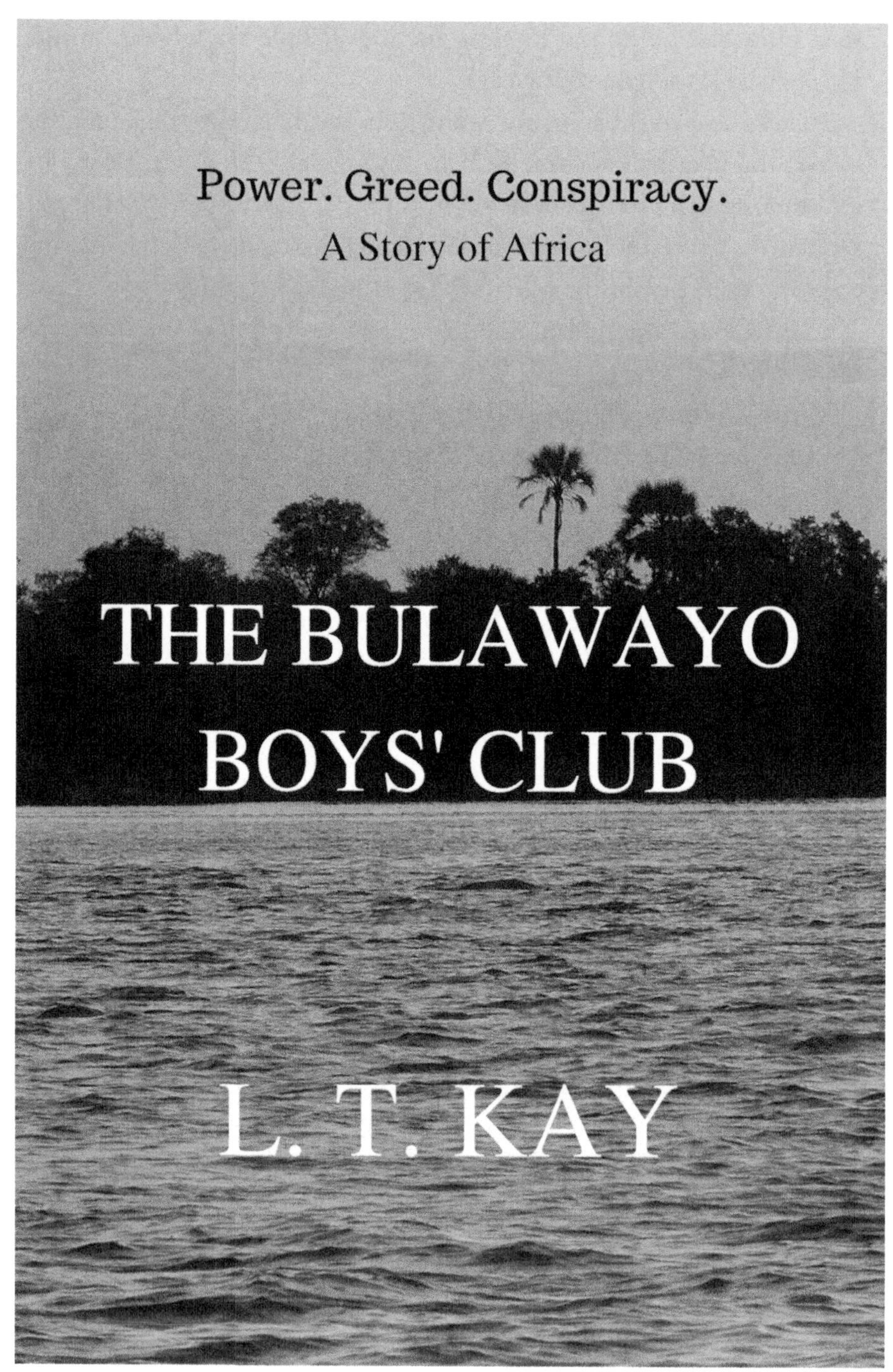
Power. Greed. Conspiracy.
A Story of Africa
THE BULAWAYO
BOYS' CLUB
L. T. KAY

Printed in Great Britain
by Amazon

79924555R00263